By Anne Perry

FEATURING WILLIAM MONK

The Face of a Stranger
A Dangerous Mourning
Defend and Betray
A Sudden, Fearful Death
The Sins of the Wolf
Cain His Brother
Weighed in the Balance
The Silent Cry
A Breach of Promise
The Twisted Root

Slaves of Obsession
Funeral in Blue
Death of a Stranger
The Shifting Tide
Dark Assassin
Execution Dock
Acceptable Loss
A Sunless Sea
Blind Justice

FEATURING CHARLOTTE AND THOMAS PITT

The Cater Street Hangman
Callander Square
Paragon Walk
Resurrection Row
Bluegate Fields
Rutland Place
Death in the Devil's Acre
Cardington Crescent
Silence in Hanover Close
Bethlehem Road
Farriers' Lane
Hyde Park Headsman
Traitors Gate

Pentecost Alley
Ashworth Hall
Brunswick Gardens
Bedford Square
Half Moon Street
The Whitechapel Conspiracy
Southampton Row
Seven Dials
Long Spoon Lane
Buckingham Palace Gardens
Treason at Lisson Grove
Dorchester Terrace
Midnight at Marble Arch

BLIND JUSTICE

ANNE PERRY

BLIND JUSTICE

A William Monk Novel

BALLANTINE BOOKS • NEW YORK

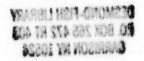
Blind Justice is a work of fiction. Names, characters, places, and incidents are the products of the author's imagination or are used fictitiously. Any resemblance to actual events, locales, or persons, living or dead, is entirely coincidental.

Published in the United States by Ballantine Books, an imprint of
The Random House Publishing Group, a division of Random House, Inc., New York.

BALLANTINE and the HOUSE colophon are registered trademarks of
Random House, Inc.

LIBRARY OF CONGRESS CATALOGING-IN-PUBLICATION DATA
Perry, Anne.
Blind Justice : a William Monk novel / Anne Perry.
p. cm
ISBN 978-0-345-53670-9
eBook ISBN 978-0-345-53671-6
1. Monk, William (Fictitious character)—Fiction. 2. Private investigators—
England—London—Fiction. 3. Mystery fiction. I. Title.
PR6066.E693B53 2013
823'.914—dc23
2013022771

Printed in the United States of America

First Edition

2 4 6 8 9 7 5 3 1

Book design by Karin Batten

To Susanna Porter

BLIND JUSTICE

Hᴇsᴛᴇʀ ʟᴇᴛ ᴛʜᴇ ʜᴀɴsᴏᴍ cab pass, then crossed Portpool Lane and went in through the door to the clinic for sick and injured prostitutes.

Ruby saw her and her scarred face lit up with welcome.

"Is Miss Raleigh in?" Hester asked.

Ruby's shoulders slumped. "Yes, ma'am, but she don't look right. I thought as she were 'andmade for the job, like, but this mornin' you'd'a thought she'd got left at the altar. All weepin' an' can't believe it, like."

Hester was stunned. When she had hired Josephine a few weeks earlier, the girl had said she was not courting and had no intention of giving up nursing in any imaginable future.

"Where is she? Do you know?" she asked.

"We got someone in all beat up, blood everywhere. She'll be seein' to 'er," Ruby replied. "That were 'alf an hour ago, mind."

"Thank you." Hester went through the far door and along the passageway, asking after Josephine each time she encountered someone.

In the old pantry where they kept medical supplies she finally found her, moving between the shelves, counting and sorting. She was a pretty girl, perhaps too much character in her face to be conventionally beautiful. Now her cheeks were stained with tears, her eyes were blank, and her lips were pressed so tight the muscles were visible along her jaw and in her neck. It was clear that she did not even hear Hester come in.

Hester closed the door to give them complete privacy before she spoke. As always, she was direct. Medicine, she had found, was not an art that allowed for much roundabout conversation.

"What's wrong?" she asked gently.

Startled, Josephine swung round to face Hester. She was blinking rapidly as the uncontrolled tears slid down her face.

"I'm sorry. I'll . . . I'll be all right in a moment." She was clearly ashamed at being caught giving way to her distress, whatever it was.

Hester put her hand ever so gently on Josephine's arm. "Something must be very wrong for you to be so upset by it. You've seen terrible wounds and nursed the dying. Something that hurts you so much isn't going to be dealt with in a few minutes. Tell me what it is."

Josephine shook her head. "You can't help with this," she answered, her voice choking in her throat. "I . . . I need to work. Really . . ."

Hester did not loosen her grip.

"There's nothing that anyone can do," Josephine repeated, still attempting to pull away.

Hester hesitated. Would it be intrusive if she insisted? She liked this young woman on a deep, instinctive level; she reminded Hester of herself, years ago. And Hester knew exactly the pain and loneliness one felt when starting out in the profession. She had felt the overwhelming sense of helplessness that comes when witnessing the realities of physical agony and death, the moment when things go beyond anyone's reach and all you can do is watch. All that, on top of the ordinary heartache of life and youth—it had been a difficult burden to bear when she was younger. Even now, at times.

"Tell me anyway," she said gently.

Josephine hesitated, and then straightened herself with an effort. She swallowed hard and fished for a handkerchief to blow her nose.

Hester waited, leaving the door closed. No one else could come in without a key.

"My mother died a long time ago," Josephine began. "My father and I have become very close." She took a deep breath and tried to keep her voice level, almost emotionless, as if she were recounting figures in a calculation, something with no personal weight. "He has been going to a Nonconformist church for just over a year now. He found many friends among the congregation. He said there was a degree of warmth in it that appealed to him more than the ritual of the Church of England, which he found . . . cold." She swallowed hard again.

Hester did not interrupt. So far there was nothing odd, let alone disastrous, in what Josephine was saying. She hadn't known Josephine long, but the girl did not strike her as the type to care exactly which religion her father followed, as long as it was broadly Christian, so that couldn't be the cause of her distress.

Josephine took another shaky breath. "He told me that they do a great deal of good work, both here in England and abroad. They need money to provide food, medicines, clothes, and so on, for those in desperate circumstances." She searched Hester's face for understanding.

"It sounds a very Christian thing to do." Hester filled in the silence. Then a thought occurred to her. "Oh dear—did your father discover that was not what they were using the money for?"

Josephine looked startled. "Oh no! No, it wasn't that. They just . . . they wanted so much! They pressured him for more and more. He is not a wealthy man, but he always speaks well, dresses well . . . if you know what I mean? Perhaps they thought he was wealthier than he is . . ."

Hester began to understand where this might lead.

Josephine was watching her intently now. Her voice wavered. "They kept on asking him, and he was embarrassed to decline. It isn't easy to say you can't afford any more, especially when they tell you people are starving, and you know that you can eat whenever you wish, even if it is a modest meal."

Hester looked at the pain in the young woman's face, in her eyes, at the clenched hands gripping the handkerchief. She seemed frightened, embarrassed, and racked with sadness.

"They pressed him into giving them much more than he could afford?" Hester asked quietly.

Josephine nodded, her jaw clenched hard to help her control the emotion that welled up inside her.

"Is the debt serious?" Hester continued.

Josephine nodded again, the hopelessness clear in her face. She looked down, as if to avoid the condemnation she obviously expected to see in Hester's eyes.

Hester was overwhelmed by a sudden, wrenching memory of her own father, as she had seen him before she left for the Crimea, a dozen years ago, when this young woman was but a child. He had been so proud of her, seeing her off on a noble enterprise. She could smell the salt on the wind again, hear the gulls crying and the creak of ropes as the ship rose and fell, straining against its moorings.

That was the last time she had ever seen him. The reasons for his falling into debt had been different than Mr. Raleigh's reasons, even if they had also been tied to his compassion and sense of honor; but the pain his debt caused his family was the same. He too had been pressured and then cheated. The shame of it had caused him to take his own life. Hester had been away in the Crimea, nursing men she did not even know, and her family had faced that grief without her. Her mother had been almost unable to bear it and died shortly after the news of her second son's death in the Crimea reached her.

Hester had arrived home in England to face her one remaining brother's bereavement and his fury that she had not been there when she was so badly needed, that she had spent her time and her pity on strangers instead.

They were still distant, no more between them than the occasional exchange of Christmas cards, the odd stiff letter in formal language now and then.

Hester understood sorrow, guilt, helplessness, and the lethal burden of debt more intimately than Josephine Raleigh could have imagined.

She realized that Josephine was gazing at her now, confused. She felt foolish for drifting off into her own memories.

"I'm sorry," she said gently. "I was thinking of someone I loved . . . someone who also suffered, in a similar way. I wasn't able to help him because I was in the Crimea with the army. I didn't come home until it was too late. How deep is your father's debt?"

"Very," Josephine said quietly. "Much more than he can pay. I've given him everything I have, but it's far too late. And I can't earn enough to—" She stopped. There was no point in explaining what was so obvious.

Hester's mind raced, searching for something to say that might help; her painful memories still churned, the hopelessness, the despair of being too late to help, and the ache she still felt to turn back time and do everything differently. When she spoke her voice was husky. "I imagine these people ask every member of the congregation whom they think might have anything to give to donate?"

Josephine gulped. "Yes . . . I . . . I think so."

Footsteps sounded in the passage outside, hesitated, then went on.

"Well. Maybe there is something dishonest about the whole thing," Hester said thoughtfully. "To pressure people that way isn't . . . right . . . even if it's not illegal. Maybe there was a reason. I don't know. I will ask my husband. He is a police officer. There might be something we can do."

Josephine's face filled with distress. "Oh no! Please don't . . . my father would be mortified! The shame would be—" She gulped again and all but choked. "It would make him look as if he were . . . reluctant to have given charity to those in far more need than any of us. It would be—"

"Josephine!" Hester said quickly, feeling the heat wash up her face. "Of course I wouldn't reveal his name or his circumstances to anyone. I have no intention of being so clumsy. I am aware that would humiliate him."

Josephine shook her head. "You don't understand—"

"Yes I do," Hester replied. She took a minute to weigh her next words before continuing. "The man I was thinking of a minute ago was my own father. I think the shame of what happened to him was what killed him. So I do understand. I shall look into this as far as I can, without mentioning any names, I promise you."

Josephine was still uncertain. "If he finds out, he will think I've betrayed him."

"He won't know anything of it," Hester promised again. "Don't you think he would want to prevent others from suffering in the same way? And for that matter, I would be surprised if he is the only one of the congregation in this position. Wouldn't you?"

"I . . . I suppose so. But how will you do it?"

"I don't know yet. Perhaps I will have no clear idea until I try," Hester admitted. "But if people are being forced into this position, it must be stopped."

Josephine gave a very slight smile. "Thank you."

Hester smiled back at her. "Where is this church, and what is the name of the man who leads it?"

"Abel Taft is his name. The church is on the corner of Wilmington Square and Yardley Street," Josephine replied, frowning. "But you live on the south side of the river, miles away! How will you explain going to a church up there?"

Hester smiled more widely. "Their reputation for true and active Christianity, of course!" she replied sarcastically.

Josephine laughed in spite of herself, and tears of gratitude filled her eyes. She shook herself abruptly, straightened her shoulders, and smoothed the skirt of the gray dress. "I have work to do," she said more steadily. "I'm all behind myself."

THERE WERE TIMES, ESPECIALLY in the winter, when William Monk found his duties as commander of the Thames River Police to be more arduous than usual. The knife-edge of ice on the wind across the open water could cut through almost anything, except oilskins. It whipped the flesh raw on exposed cheeks and froze the heavy cloth of trouser legs when the rain or the river water dampened them.

But this late spring evening was balmy, and over the shining water arched a pale blue, almost cloudless sky. The breeze was welcome, the tide was high, and there were no naked banks exposed, which meant there was no dank smell of mud. Pleasure boats passed by with colored banners waving, laughter drifting toward the shore where a hurdy-gurdy played a popular song from the current music-hall shows. All the warm hope of summer lay ahead. It was a perfect time to be finishing a patrol on the river and thinking of going home.

Monk had always managed a boat easily. It was one of the skills from his forgotten past, although his memory of how he acquired the ability had been obliterated by an injury in a carriage crash, just before he had first met Hester, nine years ago, in 1856. It always fascinated him that the mind could erase all sorts of things that the body seemed to recall.

With ease he brought the police boat to the bottom of the dock steps, shipped the oars, and stepped out with the mooring rope in his hand. He tied it loosely so that later on the receding water would not strain it and walked up the steps to make his final report at the station.

He spoke briefly with Orme, his second in command, made a last check of everything else, and half an hour later he was back on the water again—this time as passenger in a ferry as it approached the dock at Princes Stairs, on the south bank at Rotherhithe.

He paid the fare and walked up the hill toward his home on Paradise Place, the panorama of the Pool of London behind him, black masts and cross spars against the fading sky, water still as polished silk.

He found Hester in the kitchen, stirring something on the stove, and Scuff, the onetime mudlark they had adopted—or, more accurately who had adopted them—sitting hopefully at the table, waiting for supper. He had been more or less resident for nearly two years now and was beginning to take them rather more for granted, as if finally he had accepted that this was his home, that they would not suddenly change their minds and turn him out back onto the dockside.

He had grown considerably since they had taken him in. There was a lot of difference between a half-starved boy of eleven—Scuff's own estimate of his age, though they couldn't confirm it—and a boy of thirteen, who eats at every possible opportunity, mealtimes or not. He was several inches taller and was beginning to appear less angular; he no longer looked as if a sharp twist would break his bones.

He was also beginning to acquire a rather self-conscious dignity. Instead of unabashed pleasure, he now welcomed Monk with a grin, but remained seated, far too grown up to give away his emotions.

Smiling to himself, Monk acknowledged Scuff equally casually and went over to Hester to give a much warmer and completely spontaneous greeting. They spoke of the day and its events. Scuff reported on his time at school, an experience that was only slowly becoming familiar to him. It had not been easy; he had always been able to count, and he knew the value of money to the farthing. As a child of the docks and the streets around them, he was skeptical, brave, and very able to take care of himself. It was impossible to lose him on the dockside. But learning about other countries remained, to him, a pointless exercise, even though he knew them by name and knew the products they shipped to the Port of London because he had seen them unloaded. He knew what these goods looked like, how they smelled, how large or how heavy they were. However, reading and writing about them, and even spelling their names correctly, was another matter entirely.

Later in the evening, after Scuff had gone to bed and they were in the sitting room, Hester told Monk about Josephine Raleigh's father and the problem he faced.

"I'm sorry," Monk said quietly. He looked at her troubled face and could see her pity for the man, and perhaps for young Josephine as well. It was terrible that a church would do this to someone, abuse their faith so. "I wish it were a crime," he added. "But even if it were, it wouldn't have any connection with the river, and that's all I have power to deal with. Do you want me to speak to Runcorn, and see if there's anything he can suggest?" Superintendent Runcorn had once been Monk's colleague, long ago, then his superior, and then his enemy. Now finally they had understood and overcome their differences and were allies.

Hester looked suddenly crushed, as if his words had struck an additional blow.

Monk did not understand it. Surely she could not have believed there was a way for him to intervene?

"Hester . . . I sympathize. It's a vile thing to do, but the law offers no way of addressing it."

She looked at him for a moment, and then rose to her feet wearily. "I know." There was defeat in her voice and an overwhelming misery. She turned to walk away, hesitated a second, then went on, going out of the sitting room back toward the kitchen, her shoulders square but her head bowed a little.

Monk was confused. She had, in a way, closed a door between them. But what had she imagined he might do? He started to rise to go after her, realized he had no idea what to say, and sat down again. He thought of all the years he had known her and the battles they had fought together against fear, injustice, disease, grief . . . and then memory washed over him, not like a tide so much as a breaking wave, battering and submerging him. Hester's own father had committed suicide because of a debt he could not honor. She spoke of it so seldom he had allowed himself to forget.

He stood up quickly; he was still not sure what he would say, but it was imperative he find something. How could he have been so stupid, so clumsy as to forget?

He found her in the kitchen, standing by the stove with a saucepan in her hand, but her attention somewhere in the middle distance. She was not moving, and her eyes were filled with tears.

There was no honest excuse to give, but even if there were, it would only make things worse.

"I'm sorry," he said quietly. "I forgot."

She shook her head. "It doesn't matter."

"Yes, it does."

She turned and looked at him at last. "No, it doesn't. I'd rather you didn't think of him that way anyhow. But I know how Josephine feels, exactly as if it were me all over again. Except that I wasn't there when I should have been. Maybe I could have done something if I had been there."

Monk knew there was nothing she could've done, but he also knew she would not believe him if he said so; she would think he was lying automatically to comfort her, although that was something neither of them had ever really done. They had always faced the truth together, however bitter; gently, perhaps slowly—but they had never lied.

"I'll see if I can find out anything about the people involved." He said it knowing it was a rash offer, and probably of no use, except to prove that he cared about what troubled her.

She smiled at him, and he saw that she knew exactly what he was doing, and why. However, she was still grateful that he understood and had not evaded helping her.

"I'm going to church on Sunday," she replied, straightening up a little and replacing a saucepan on its rack. "It's time Scuff learned something about religion. It's part of our job as . . . as parents"—she chose the word deliberately, as if testing it—"to teach him. What he decides to believe is up to him. But I don't think I'll go to the Church of England. I'll find a Nonconformist one."

"Do you want me to come with you?" Monk asked uncertainly.

That was one of the gaps from his amnesia he had never attempted to fill. He knew what he believed about many things, good and evil. Perhaps even more importantly, he understood that an entire lifetime was insufficient to answer all the questions that each new situation raised. It was clear to him that humility was not just a virtue, it was a necessity; but he had not bothered to consider a formal religion. He did not really want to now, but he would if she wished him to.

A glance at her face answered that.

"No, thank you!" she said vehemently, as if for him to come were the last thing she wished. Then she smiled. "But thank you all the same."

Scuff amazed himself at how easily he had become used to living in Monk's house in Paradise Place. Occasionally he dreamed he was still back on the docks, sleeping wherever he could find a sheltered place out of the wind or rain and avoid being trodden on or tripped over. He was even used to being warm enough almost all of the time, and clean!

He was still always hungry; but now he ate at regular times, as well as in between, when he could, and he didn't have to find the food himself, either buy it or steal it. He had become used to the fact that no one would steal it from him.

It was not that he was an orphan, but after his father died his mother had been unable to support her children alone. The new man she had taken in was happy enough with the girls, but he was not willing to house another man's son, so for the survival of the rest, who were not much more than babies, Scuff had left to look after himself.

He had met Monk when Monk was new to the dockside area and pitifully ignorant of its ways. For the price of an occasional sandwich and a hot cup of tea, Scuff had taken care of him and taught him a few things.

Then together they had taken part in some very unpleasant adventures. After one, when Scuff had come far too close to being killed, he had spent a few nights in Monk's home. Those few nights had stretched into a few more, and then a few more. Gradually, a step at a time, he had even become used to Hester. He was far too grown up to need a mother, but now and then he didn't mind pretending that wasn't the case. Actually, he was not sure if being a mother was even what Hester wanted. She seemed rather more to be a really good friend—but one with considerable authority, of course. He would not have told her so, but he was more in awe of her than he was of Monk himself. She never backed off from anyone. Scuff knew, even if she didn't, that she needed him to keep an eye out for her.

He should have been more suspicious when she suddenly decided to take him to buy a new suit, a proper one with jacket and trousers that matched, and two white shirts. It was quite true that the clothes he had were rather short. He had grown a lot lately. It must have been all that food, and having to go to bed early. But even so, they would have done a few more months.

Perhaps he should have had a clue when, the same day, she bought herself a new hat. It had flowers on it, and it made her look pretty. He told her so, and then felt awkward. Perhaps it had been too personal a thing to say. But she looked pleased. Maybe she was.

Understanding came like a flash of lightning on Saturday evening.

"Tomorrow morning I am going to church," she told him, facing him squarely and not even blinking. "I would like you to come with me, if you don't mind."

He stood motionless, as if rooted to the kitchen floor. Then he turned to Monk, who was sitting at the table reading the newspaper. Monk raised his eyes and smiled.

"You coming?" Scuff asked nervously. What did it mean? They had never taken him to church before. What would happen there? Some kind of ceremony?

"I can't," Monk replied. "I have to go to the station at Wapping. But I'll be back for Sunday dinner. You'll be all right. You might find it quite interesting. Do as Hester tells you, and if she doesn't say anything, copy her."

Scuff felt panic well up inside him.

"You don't have to do anything at all," Hester assured him. "Just come with me, so I don't have to go by myself."

He let go his breath—a sigh of relief. He could do that. "Yeah, all right," he conceded.

They set out on Sunday morning, first across the river, then on an omnibus for what seemed like a considerable distance. Scuff wondered why they were going so far, when he could see they were passing churches much closer. They were rather obvious buildings; apart from having towers that you could see from a quarter of a mile away at least, a lot of them had bells ringing, just to make certain you couldn't miss them. A couple of times he drew in his breath to point this out to Hester, who was sitting very upright beside him and staring forward. She did not seem like her usual self at all, so he changed his mind and did not ask.

But he did ask a number of the other questions that rose in his mind.

"Does God live only in churches?" he said very quietly to her. He did not want the other people in the omnibus to hear him. They probably all knew the answer and would think he sounded stupid.

She looked a little surprised and instantly he wished he had said nothing. If he paid attention, he would probably have learned the answer anyway.

"No," she replied. "God is everywhere. I think it's just that we give him more thought inside churches. Like learning at school. You can learn to read and write anywhere, but school makes it easier to concentrate."

"Do we have a teacher at church too?" That seemed a reasonable question.

"Yes. He's called a minister."

"I see." That was a bit worrying. "Is he going to make me answer questions at the end?"

"No. No, I won't let him do that." She sounded very sure.

He relaxed a little. "Why do we have to go?"

"We don't have to. I would like to."

"Oh." He sat in silence for almost half a mile.

"Will he tell us about heaven?" he asked finally.

"I expect so," Hester answered. Now she was looking at him, smiling.

He felt encouraged. "Where is heaven?"

"I don't know," she said honestly. "I don't think anybody truly does."

That troubled him. "Then how are we going to get there?"

She looked awkward. "You know, that's something we'd all like to know, and I have no idea. Perhaps if we go to church often enough and really pay attention, we will figure it out eventually."

"Do you want to go there? To heaven, I mean?"

"Yes. I think everybody does. It's just that too many of us don't desire it enough to do the things that are necessary to get there."

"Why not? That seems silly," he pointed out.

"We don't think about it, or believe in it, hard enough," she answered. "Sometimes we decide it's too hard to get there to be worth the trouble, or that we won't make it anyway, no matter what we do."

He thought about it for several minutes while the omnibus went up a slight incline, slowing as it did so. The horses must have struggled a bit.

"Well, if you're not going to heaven, then I don't think I want to either," he said at last.

She blinked suddenly, as if she were going to cry, only he knew she wouldn't because Hester never cried. Then she put her hand on his arm for a moment. He could feel the warmth of it, even through the sleeve of his new jacket.

"I think we should both try to get there," she told him. "In fact, all three of us should."

He thought about that and made a note of several other questions he wanted to ask. He would save them for another time—he felt like he had bothered her enough for now. So they rode in silence until the omnibus pulled up at their stop. They walked about fifty yards along the pavement to what looked like a meetinghouse. It was not really a proper church, the kind he had expected with the tower and the bell, but Hester seemed quite sure, so he went in beside her through the large open doors.

Inside there were rows of seats, all very hard, with the sort of backs that made you sit up straight, even if you didn't want to. There were crowds of people there already. All the women he could see had hats on: big ones, small ones, ones with flowers, ones with ribbons, pale colors, dark colors, but nothing particularly bright, no reds or pinks or yellows. All the men wore dark suits. It must be some kind of uniform, like at school.

They had been there only a few moments when a handsome man came forward, smiling. He had fair, wavy hair touched with silver at the sides. He held his hand out, looking for an instant beyond Hester. Then, realizing there was no man with her, he withdrew his hand and bowed very slightly instead.

"How do you do, ma'am? My name is Abel Taft. May I welcome you to our congregation?"

"Thank you," Hester said warmly. "I am Mrs. Monk." She turned to introduce Scuff, and his heart almost stopped beating. Who was she going to say he was? An urchin she and Monk had picked up from the dockside, who knew no other name but Scuff? Would they make him leave?

Taft turned to meet Scuff's eyes.

Scuff was paralyzed, his mouth as dry as dust.

Hester smiled, her head a little to one side. "My son, William," she said, with only the barest hesitation.

Scuff found himself smiling so widely his face hurt.

"How do you do, William?" Taft said formally.

"How do you do?" Scuff's voice came out scratchily. "Sir," he added for good measure.

Taft was still smiling too, as if his smile were almost fixed on his face. Scuff had seen expressions like that before, on the riverbank, when people were trying to sell you something.

"I hope you will feel uplifted by our service, Mrs. Monk," Taft said warmly. "And please feel free to ask any questions you care to. I shall hope to see you often and perhaps get to know you a little better. You will find the entire congregation friendly. We have some very fine people here."

"I am sure," Hester agreed. "I have already heard so from others."

"Indeed?" Taft had started to move away but stopped, his attention suddenly renewed. "May I ask whom?"

Hester lowered her eyes. "I think it might embarrass them if I were to say," she replied modestly. "But it was most sincere, I assure you. I know, at least, that you do a great deal of truly Christian work for those who are not nearly as fortunate as we are."

"Indeed we do," he said eagerly. "I am delighted to see that you are interested. I shall look forward to telling you more after the service."

She looked up at him very directly. "Thank you."

Scuff regarded her with confusion. He had never seen her behave like this before. Of course, lots of women looked at men like that—but not Hester! What was wrong with her? He did not like the change in her. She had been perfect just as she was.

Hester led him toward a couple of seats near the back of the hall, and they took the rather squashed places as other people moved along a bit to make room. There were certainly far more people present than he had imagined would want to be here. What was going to happen that was worth all this jostling and shoving, not to mention dressing up and wasting a perfectly good Sunday morning? The sun was shining outside, and hardly anybody had to go to work!

He started to pay attention when the service began. Mr. Taft was in charge, telling everybody when to stand, when to sing, and saying prayers on everyone else's behalf. All they had to do was add "Amen" at the end. He seemed to be full of enthusiasm, as if it were all rather exciting. He waved his arms about a bit, and his face was alight. It was a bit like it was his birthday party and all of them his guests. Scuff had seen a party once for a rich boy whose parents had hired a pleasure boat. There were colored ribbons everywhere and a band playing music. It had stopped at one of the docks and Scuff had crept close enough to watch.

There was music here in this church as well, a big organ playing, and everybody sang. They seemed to know the words. Even Hester did not have to do more than glance at the hymnbook that she held open so he could see it as well. But he had never heard the tune before and got lost very quickly.

Hester gave him a little nudge now and then, or put her hand gently on his arm, to warn him they were about to stand up or sit down again. He noticed that she looked around rather a lot. He thought she was watching to see what they were doing, so she could copy them. Then he realized she knew what to do; she just seemed to be interested, almost as if she were looking for someone in particular.

When it was finished and Scuff assumed they were free to go home again, Hester started speaking to the people around them. That was a bit of a blow, but there was nothing he could do except wait patiently. On the way home he would ask her what it was all for. Why did God want what seemed to be such a pointless exercise? Was the real reason something else altogether, like maybe to keep them all from going out and getting drunk, or to make sure they didn't just lie around in bed all day? He used to know people who did that.

Hester was talking to Mrs. Taft, who was a very pretty lady, in a fair-haired, soft-blue-eyed sort of way. Scuff had seen a little china statue of a lady like that and been told not to touch it because he might break it.

"It is a marvelous work," Hester was saying enthusiastically.

Scuff tried to listen. If she cared about all this, there had to be a reason, and he should pay attention too.

"Indeed it is," Mrs. Taft agreed with a sweet smile. "And we find so much support, it is most heartening. You would be amazed how much even the poorest people manage to give. Surely God will bless them for it. They will have joy in heaven." She looked as if she really meant it. Her eyes were shining, and there was a faint flush of pink in her cheeks. She wore a lovely hat decked with flowers in all sorts of colors. Scuff knew they weren't real, but they almost looked it. Hester would look prettier than this woman in a hat like that, but it probably cost more than a week of dinners for all of them.

"Do you not worry about them though?" Hester asked anxiously.

Mrs. Taft looked puzzled.

"What will happen to them, between here and heaven, I mean," Hester added in explanation.

"God will take care of them," Mrs. Taft replied with gentle reproof.

Hester bit her lip. Scuff had seen that expression before. He knew she wanted to say something but had decided against it.

They were joined by two girls, a few years older than Scuff and looking a lot like grown-ups already, proper ladies' shapes, their hair in ringlets, and straw hats with ribbons on their heads. They were introduced as Mrs. Taft's daughters, Jane and Amelia. The conversation continued about generous donations to the wonderful work the church was doing for the unfortunate, especially in some distant and unnamed part of the world.

Scuff was extremely bored and his attention wandered again, this time toward some of the other members of the congregation. A lot of the women were older than Hester and rather fat. Those closest to him creaked a little when they moved, like the timbers of a ship on the tide. They looked unhappy. He supposed they might be late for luncheon and resented being kept in pointless conversations. He sympathized with them. He was hungry too—and tired of this. One of them caught his eye, and he smiled at her tentatively. She smiled back at him, then her husband glared at her and she stopped instantly.

Why was Hester still here? She didn't know these people, and she certainly wasn't talking to God, or listening to him. Yet she still looked very interested.

She looked even more interested when she was introduced to a good-looking man with thick, dark hair and a rather prominent nose. His name was apparently Robertson Drew, and he spoke to Hester in a condescending manner. His glance took in her costume and her new hat, and then her reticule and the fact that her boots were a little worn at the toes.

Scuff disliked him immediately.

"How do you do, Mrs. Monk?" Drew said with a smile that barely showed his teeth. "Welcome to our congregation. I hope you will join us regularly. And this is your son?" He looked momentarily at Scuff and then back to Hester. "Perhaps your husband will be able to be with us in future?"

Scuff thought the likelihood of that was about the same as the chances of finding a gold sovereign in the drain.

"I shall do all I can to persuade him," Hester said smoothly. "Please tell me more about your charitable work, Mr. Drew. I confess it was report of that which brought me here. I live some distance away, but it seems to me most pastors speak a great deal about charity, but practice very little."

"Ah! How perceptive you are, Mrs. Monk," Drew agreed fervently. Suddenly he was all interest. He put out his hand as if to take Hester by the arm. Scuff was ready to kick his shins hard if he actually touched her, but he took his hand away again at the last minute and started to speak intently about all that the church had done for the needy.

Hester listened as if she were spellbound. Even to Scuff, who knew that it couldn't be entirely real, it looked as if she genuinely cared.

Then Scuff realized that she was not precisely pretending. She was asking questions. She *wanted* to know but not for the reasons he had first assumed. A tingle of excitement ran through him. They were not here to sing hymns and repeat prayers—she was investigating something!

Now he began to listen closely, even though he did not yet understand what she was looking to find out.

Drew noticed his attention with pleasure, and he began to direct his speech to both of them.

They escaped at last outside into the sunlight, walking rapidly toward the nearest main street where they could catch an omnibus to the river and then the ferry home. Scuff challenged Hester almost at once. "Ye're detecting, aren't yer?"

She hesitated, then gave up and smiled. "I'm trying to. Thank you for helping me."

"I didn't do nothing."

"Anything," she corrected him automatically.

"I still didn't. What did any of 'em do, 'side from being about as straight as a pig's tail?"

"Was that your impression?" she said curiously. "What makes you think that?"

"I seen that look on an opulent receiver's face, one who's trying to sell yer gold when 'e knows it's pinchbeck," he replied.

"That's very unkind, Scuff—and probably true," she said, trying to keep the amusement out of her face and failing. An opulent receiver was the slang term for a receiver of stolen goods who specialized in expensive and hard-to-sell things.

"Now what are we going ter do?" he asked, taking it for granted that he was part of the plan.

She walked several yards without answering.

He kept pace with her. His legs were long enough now. He was almost the same height as her, and in a year or two he would definitely be taller. He wondered what that would feel like. He was still wondering when she answered.

"I shall weigh up all I know, which I admit is not a lot, and then I shall go and see Squeaky Robinson, at the clinic."

"Why?" He knew Squeaky Robinson a little. He used to be a brothel keeper, until Sir Oliver Rathbone had tricked him out of the buildings he owned and used. Now those buildings were the clinic Hester ran for street women. Squeaky had had nowhere else to go and no means of earning his living. Protesting indignantly all the way, he had accepted their offer to earn his lodgings by keeping the accounts of the new establishment—which he did remarkably well. He certainly knew about money, and he understood that his survival depended on being honest to the farthing.

"Because if they really have been dishonest, Squeaky Robinson is the one person who might catch them," she replied.

"How will 'e know?"

"I'm not certain yet," she said reasonably. "But because they are a charity, they must account for their money. It won't be easy to catch them out if they are doing something dishonest with it, but it's worth trying."

"Why?" he asked. "I mean, why are we doing it?"

"Because they have ruined the father of someone I like," she told him. "Someone who seems quite a lot like me when I was younger. And I suppose because a long time ago, someone did that to my father too, and I wasn't there to help him."

He looked at her face and saw the sadness and the guilt in it. He knew this was not the time to ask anything more.

"Righto," he replied. "I'll 'elp."

"Thank you. Now let's hurry up and get the next omnibus home to lunch."

HESTER WENT TO THE clinic in Portpool Lane on Monday morning as usual, and, as usual, attended first to the urgent medical matters, then the household ones. Lastly she went into Squeaky Robinson's office to inquire about the state of the finances.

Squeaky was a scrawny, cadaverous man of uncertain years, somewhere between fifty and sixty. He greeted her with his usual dour expression. "Could always use more money," he answered her question. "But we aren't desperate . . . not right today."

"Good." She dismissed the subject as dealt with. She pulled out the chair opposite his desk and sat down. "Squeaky, I need your advice, possibly your help."

He squinted at her suspiciously. "There ain't nothing to spare," he said immediately.

"I don't want money," she replied, keeping her patience with difficulty. "I think there might be some fraud going on in a local church . . . at least, I hope there is."

His straggly eyebrows shot up. "You what?"

"Fraud," she replied, realizing she had not phrased it in the clearest way. "I suspect and hope it is fraud. I want to find out, and then I want to do something about it." She explained what she knew of the victim, mentioning no names, and the little she had discovered on her own visit to the church.

"Leave it alone," Squeaky said, almost before she had finished.

That was always his first reaction, so, as usual, she ignored it. She went on to describe Abel Taft and Robertson Drew, all the time watching Squeaky's face crease up with greater and greater distaste. Finally, she mentioned that the victim she was concerned about was Josephine Raleigh's father. She had kept that piece of information until last intentionally, knowing it would have the most effect. She knew Squeaky could be trusted to keep his mouth shut about it.

Squeaky glared at her balefully, quite aware that he had been manipulated. He liked Josephine, and Hester knew it.

"I don't know what you think I'm going to do!" he said indignantly. "I ain't going to church. It's against my beliefs."

"I think this particular church goes against my beliefs too," Hester agreed. "Can't you find a way to take a bit of a look at their accounting?"

"Their books in't going to have 'cheat' written across them," he pointed out.

"If they did, then I wouldn't need you," she returned. "I'm quite good at reading words; it's figures I find rather more difficult, especially when it's all in accounting ledgers and looks perfectly honest. It will need someone cleverer than they are to catch them."

He grunted. He would never admit that he was flattered by her trust, but he was. "I'll try to take a look at it," he said grudgingly. "If I can get a hold of the books somehow, that is. Can't promise it'll do any good."

She gave him a warm smile. "Thank you. You shouldn't find it difficult to gain access to the books. After all, it is a charity. You'll think of a way. I would dearly like to see Mr. Raleigh get some of his money back. And I dislike admitting it, but I would also very much like to see Abel Taft somewhat curtailed in his actions. They are rather despicable."

Squeaky looked at her steadily for a couple of long seconds, then he smiled back, showing his crooked, snaggled teeth.

She knew in that moment that if Abel Taft could be caught, Squeaky would do it.

A FEW DAYS LATER, HESTER sat in Squeaky Robinson's office. Papers were spread out across the desk, covering it completely. Squeaky had a fresh cravat around his neck, perfectly tied, and he looked remarkably satisfied with himself.

"It's all very clever," he said, his fingers touching the top sheet. "But I got 'em! It's all there, if you know where to look. 'Brothers of the Poor,' indeed!" He assumed an expression of profound disgust. "Very bad. Thieving from the rich is one thing, but gulling the poor like this, an' in the name of religion, that's low."

"You're quite sure?" Hester knew the necessity of being exact in court. She still felt a touch of ice when she remembered past times, one in particular, when she had been so certain of a man's crime that she had not been sufficiently diligent in the proof, and Oliver Rathbone had caught her out on the witness stand. The result had been humiliating, and disastrous. Her carelessness—even hubris—had lost the case and the man had gone free. They had got him in the end, but not before other lives had been lost, very nearly including Scuff's.

"Of course I'm sure!" Squeaky replied, his ragged eyebrows raised so high they nearly disappeared into his hair. "Suddenly you don't trust me?"

Hester kept her temper well under control. "I've made enough mistakes in taking things for granted before. I won't let it happen again," she replied.

He knew immediately what she was referring to. He let his breath out in a sigh. "Right. Yeah, I'm sure. But it don't matter anyway, since the police and the lawyers are the ones adding it all up. You just give 'em these. If they look careful, it'll prove there's bin thieving."

"I will," she said, starting to put the papers together. "Thank you."

He snatched them from her and shuffled them into a pack, almost as easily as if they had been cards.

"You're very welcome." He glared at her, then all of a sudden he smiled, like a wolf. "You go get 'em. Hang 'em as high as their own church tower."

"It's not a hanging offense," she corrected him.

"Well, it should be," he said flatly. "On second thoughts, a good stiff ten years in the Coldbath Fields'd be worse. I'll be happy with that. You just take it to the police!"

OLIVER RATHBONE SAT IN the judge's seat, slightly above the body of the room at London's central criminal court known as the Old Bailey. This was possibly the crowning point in his career, to be presiding in such a place. He had been arguably the most brilliant barrister in England, and recently, after a string of notable cases, he had been offered this elevation to the bench. He had been surprised by how much it meant to him. It was recognition not only of his intellect but also of his ethical standards and his personal, human judgment.

This promotion had come at a time when other parts of his life were far less happy. His wife of only a few years had accused him of arrogance, selfishness, and of placing his own professional ambition above loyalty or honor, specifically loyalty to his family. He had tried and failed to explain to her that with Arthur Ballinger's case he had had no choice but to adhere to the law. She could not afford to believe him.

The grief of that was still burning slowly inside him, unreachable by reason or by any of the success that had followed since.

Now he watched as the jurors filed back into their seats ready to deliver their verdict. They had been out only two hours, a far shorter time than he had expected. The charge of fraud and the evidence had been extensive and complicated, as it usually was in fraud cases. Robbery was simple: one act. Even violence was usually limited in time and place. The hidden duplicity of fraud required numerous papers to be read, figures to be added and traced to one source or another, and inaccuracies found that could not in any way be ascribed to honest human error.

His conduct of the trial had been a balancing act of some dexterity.

Rathbone looked over at Bertrand Allan, the prosecutor. He looked nervous. He was a tall man, a little stooped, with a shock of brown hair beginning to go gray. He appeared at a glance to be quite relaxed, but his hands were hidden from sight, and his shoulders were so rigid the cloth of his jacket was pulled a little crooked. His junior beside him was drumming his fingers silently against the top of the table.

The lawyer for the defense was anxious. His eyes went one way then the other, but never to Rathbone.

Up in the dock the accused man was white-faced, at last in the grip of real fear. All the way through until this final day he had seemed confident. He swayed a little, as if the tension were too much for him. Rathbone had seen it too many times for it to stir more than an instant's pity.

The foreman of the jury stood to deliver the verdict when asked.

"Guilty," he said clearly, looking at no one.

There was a sigh of relief around the room. Rathbone felt his muscles relax. He believed very strongly that this was the correct conclusion. Any other would have evidenced a failure to grasp the weight and importance of the evidence. It would not be appropriate to smile. Whatever he felt, he must appear impartial.

He thanked the jury and pronounced on the convicted man a sentence of imprisonment close to the maximum the law allowed. The crime had been far-reaching and callous. He could see from the expressions in the gallery, and from the nods and murmurs of approval, that the public was also satisfied.

An hour later, still only midafternoon, Rathbone was sitting in his chambers reading papers on a case coming up in a day or two. There was a sharp rap on the door, and as soon as he answered it opened and a stocky man with thick, prematurely gray hair came in.

Rathbone knew him immediately; his reputation was impressive. It was Mr. Justice Ingram York, a man far senior to Rathbone though he was only ten or twelve years older. He had been elevated to the bench early in his career and had presided over some of the most famous cases in the last two decades.

He nodded slightly, standing just in front of the door, having closed it as he came in. He was expensively dressed. His cravat alone probably cost more than many people's entire wardrobes. His features were good, as he must have been aware, except that his mouth was a little ungenerous; but now he was smiling with a degree of satisfaction.

Rathbone rose to his feet as a matter of courtesy, and out of respect for York's seniority.

"Well done, Rathbone," York said quietly. "Very complicated case. I was concerned that the weight of evidence would confuse the jury, but you sorted it out for them with great lucidity. You put that duplicitous devil away for a good many years and possibly set an example for a few others to follow."

"Thank you," Rathbone said with both pleasure and surprise. He had not expected a man of York's eminence to call by to express his satisfaction.

York smiled. "Wondered if you'd care to come to dinner tomorrow evening? Asked Allan and his wife as well. He made a very good showing, I thought. He's a sound man."

"Thank you, I'd be delighted," Rathbone said. It was only after York had given him the time and address, then excused himself and left, that Rathbone sat back and wondered if York was aware that Rathbone's wife, Margaret, was no longer with him. The invitation was a signal honor, and Rathbone admitted to himself how pleased he was to receive it. It was a kind of acceptance he had not expected so soon. Now he was uncertain if he was going to be embarrassed to arrive alone.

It took only a moment's reflection to settle the question as to whether there was an alternative. It was months since he had spoken to Margaret personally. Such communication as they had had was entirely through third parties, usually her mother.

Looking back now, he could see that possibly there had been something lacking in their relationship, an understanding deeper than the exchanges of pleasant conversation, even the physical tenderness they had shared in the beginning. Had they ever really understood each other? He had thought so. He had seen a gentleness in her, a rare and very lovely dignity. He still remembered how her mother had unintentionally humiliated her when she was still single, trying to persuade Rathbone, as an eligible bachelor, of Margaret's virtues. It had made her desperately ashamed, and yet she had tried to put him at ease and allow him to escape without seeming rude.

Instead he had found himself actually wanting to dance with her, even to get to know her better. Her intelligence and honor set her above and apart from the other young women at that particular function. He could not recall now what the event had been; all he remembered was Margaret.

But that was over. Surely the gossip among the legal community would have reached York's ears? He would be perfectly aware that Margaret had not accompanied Rathbone anywhere in more than a year. It was hardly unnoticeable.

What about Lady York? Would she find her dinner table less than balanced because of it? Perhaps she would have invited some other woman? How embarrassing.

Of course he had expected all this. It was part of the sense of loss. With Margaret he had believed himself happy and at the beginning of a whole new time of peace in his life. He felt a completeness he had never possessed before. Now alone, his feelings of failure were acute. Being alone now was nothing like the occasionally rather pleasant solitude he had known well before his marriage. Back then he had been in

love with Hester, and he had hesitated to make any decisive move, uncertain if he really wished his comfort disrupted.

How absurd that seemed, looking back, even cowardly. Hester had
never used that word to him, but he could not help wondering if she
had thought it.

Should he have said anything to York about his single status?
Hardly. It would have been inappropriate, even faintly ridiculous.

He would go, and perhaps enjoy himself. He had done well with
this very difficult trial. It was a celebration, and he had earned his place
in it.

RATHBONE DRESSED IMMACULATELY, AS always. Elegance came to him
quite naturally. He arrived at the Yorks' magnificent house exactly at
the time the invitation had mentioned. He was used to precision and he
imagined York might be also. The door opened before he had time to
pull the bell rope, as if the footman had been watching for him, as indeed he might.

Rathbone thanked him, gave him his hat, and was escorted across
the tessellated marble floor to the double doors of the withdrawing
room. The footman opened them and announced him quietly.

"Sir Oliver Rathbone, sir, ma'am." He waited as Rathbone went in
then closed the doors behind him without sound.

The withdrawing room was very large, more than twenty feet long
and at least as wide. The floor was luxuriously carpeted; the curtains on
the four high windows were of a rich wine color, dark as burgundy, and
in spite of the summer evening they were drawn closed. That part of
the room faced the street, Rathbone realized; it was a quiet street but
perhaps too open to passersby for comfort.

The furniture echoed the same warm colors, and the chandeliers
were reflected in polished wooden surfaces and the glass-fronted cabi-
nets against the farthest wall. The mantelpiece was a superb piece of
carving, simple in architecture but elaborate in decoration. It was the
centerpiece around which all else was ordered.

York himself was standing beside it. He was clearly comfortable, his suit expertly cut to hide his expanding waistline, a cigar in his hand. He was very much master of the situation. But it was York's wife Rathbone looked at, with interest, then with surprise. The latter feeling sent a jolt running through him, almost of warning, a reminder to himself that he was no judge of character where women were concerned.

He had expected someone rather ordinary, assuming York had married for financial, social, and dynastic reasons, probably with affection but certainly not out of the kind of passion that overrode reason. Everything he knew about the man, and his very considerable reputation, spoke of a person who never acted rashly. As a lawyer he had taken wise cases, never crusading ones. His political views were discreet. His two sons appeared to be cut from the same cloth: solid, intelligent, but without fire.

Beata York did not in any way fit with that conception. She was older than Margaret—at least in her late forties—but she had a far more turbulent face. Her gray eyes were wide and burning with intelligence. Her hair was surprisingly fair, gold so pale as to be almost silver. At first Rathbone thought that she was truly beautiful, then thought the impression must be due to her gown; she was exquisitely dressed in some soft color that was neither gray nor cream. Then she smiled at him and moved forward to greet him, and he knew he had been right to begin with: she was beautiful.

"Good evening, Sir Oliver." Her voice was low, even a little husky. "I was so glad you were able to come. It would seem incomplete to celebrate without you." If she had expected his wife, there was no hint of it in her expression.

"Thank you for having me," he answered, meeting her gaze. "It would be a poor celebration alone. And I believe the verdict was absolutely right; he was a man much in need of being removed from society and prevented from doing further damage."

"I'm told it was a very complicated case," she went on. "How on earth do you remember all the details? Do you take a great many notes?

When I write in a hurry I can never read it afterward." She gave a little grimace of self-mockery, and then laughed lightly.

"Neither can I," he agreed. "I write only a word or two, and hope to remember the rest. I don't have to make the decisions, thank goodness, only see that the game is fair."

"Is fair always the same as right, do you think?" she asked with sudden grave interest.

He was caught off guard. It was far more profound a question than he had expected. It demanded an honest answer, not a trivial one. "Perhaps it is my duty to make it so," he said quietly.

She smiled at him, meeting his eyes, and turned to greet Bertrand Allan and his wife. They had just arrived and were talking to York closer to the door into the hall.

Introductions were made and Rathbone found himself with Mrs. Allan. She was a woman of very ordinary features, a little too thin, but agreeable enough.

"Congratulations, Sir Oliver," she said courteously. "My husband says that it was an unusually difficult case that he did not expect to win so convincingly. It must take great skill to disentangle all the threads of evidence and summarize them so the jury understands their meaning and weight."

"Thank you," he accepted. "Your husband presented his arguments very clearly, which made it a great deal easier for all of us."

She smiled her acknowledgment. "I dare say you will be pleased to have a change to something a little less complicated for your next case. Or do you enjoy the challenge?" She did not look truly curious, just mildly interested.

He had no idea how to answer. He wished he could go back and speak to Beata York instead, but the moment with her was one that could not be caught again.

"I accept the challenge, as I have to. I have no control over the cases I am given, though," he replied. "Perhaps that is just as well."

Dinner was announced and they went into the dining room. This too was exquisite. A long table was set with silver and crystal, which sparkled in the lights. Swaths of pale flowers twined down the center of the table: pear blossom, late narcissus, white hyacinth, every petal perfect. They sent up the faintest of delicate perfumes, a few dark green leaves stark against the white linen.

The carpet was dark blue, the curtains ivory and blue. The walls were ivory with a delicate gold beading at the edges of the panels. Over the mantel was a huge painting of a seascape after the Dutch School, its cool colors complemented by the classic pallor of the walls. On either end of the mantel shelf crystal candlesticks held perfect white candles, unlit, waiting. The house said much about York. It was expensive, of high quality without open ostentation, and made up in the best possible taste. Was that York himself, or Beata? There was an intellectual quality to the décor rather than true warmth, and Rathbone could not equate that with the glimpse of humor he thought he had seen in Beata. But perhaps he had imagined it.

Each of them was shown to his or her place, York at the head of the table, Beata at the foot. Mrs. Allan sat next to Rathbone and Allan himself opposite Rathbone. The table had been set with as much balance as possible, so as not to make Rathbone's lack of a companion any more obvious than it was already.

The first course was a light vegetable consommé, followed by grilled white fish, and then roast duck with a rich red-wine sauce. The servants came and went with only the occasional murmur, everyone trained to perfection.

York was a gracious host. He spoke to both Rathbone and Allan about the case, complimenting them obliquely by saying how important it was.

"I think fraud is a crime often dealt with far too lightly," he said, looking from one to the other of them. "Because there is no open violence people think of it as less serious. And I quite see how that can be." He took a delicate mouthful of the baked fish on his plate, and continued when he had swallowed it. No one interrupted him. "When there is no blood, no bruised or bleeding victim, we feel safer. They can walk away. How serious can it be?"

Rathbone drew in breath to reply, and then let it out again without speaking. He knew York wished to answer the question himself. He glanced across at Beata and saw the amusement in her eyes. The next moment it had vanished, and he was not sure if he had imagined it because it was a reflection of his own feeling.

Allan was nodding, and his wife smiled with satisfaction at the praise he was receiving. It was appropriate that she, too, say nothing.

But York didn't speak; he was looking at Rathbone. Having watched his face during his remarks, Rathbone was certain he expected more than mere acknowledgment. He wanted a commitment to the same view. He was searching for allies, or perhaps supporters would be more accurate.

"That is the perception of those who are not the victims," Rathbone said in the silence. "Fraud is just as much a crime of robbery as that done in the street with a knife to the ribs. The physical fear is not the same, but people perhaps forget or discount the sense of shock and betrayal that still occurs in the victims. Those are wounds as well, and I am not sure if the pain of them is so quickly healed. There may be very large amounts of money involved in fraud cases, as much as one's home is worth. And more than that, there can be a sense of shame in the victims, as if somehow they were foolish not to have seen it earlier, gullible because they did not suspect. They have been made a fool of by the perpetrator. That feeling isn't present in a street robbery, when someone threatens you with physical harm and you have little choice but to comply."

York nodded, his face smooth with satisfaction. "Exactly. It is quiet, but it is a deadly sin. Just because the wounds are not easily visible does not mean you cannot bleed to death from them. You have put it very well. With your permission, I would like to use your words when I next address the Law Society."

It was a question, in a roundabout way, but not one to which no was a possible answer. It would be professional self-injury of a remarkably clumsy kind to refuse, as York was perfectly aware.

Rathbone forced himself to smile. "Of course," he agreed. "I think you had exactly the same thought yourself, sir." He lowered his eyes to his plate, but not before he'd stolen a glance at Beata.

Her brows were slightly puckered, her generous mouth pulled a little tight. She knew exactly what her husband had just done, and she did not approve of it. Or was that merely what Rathbone wanted to believe? He must stop thinking about her! He needed to clear his mind and pay total attention to the conversation, or he would make more stupid errors and lose the game. And it was a contested game, a match of wits; he should make no mistake about that. Success was the prize, visible success as seen and understood by others.

He was suddenly aware Margaret had accused him of seeking exactly that: professional fame and success before love and loyalty to family.

Was he like that? Was that the reason he was sitting here in this beautiful house with Ingram York? Was he like Bertrand Allan, who was clearly an ambitious lawyer looking for the next opportunity to climb another step?

Allan was talking eagerly to York again. Rathbone watched him, watched the flicker of his eyes and the moments of hesitation and tried to remember himself ten years ago. Had he been as easy to read? Or was it only that, having been through it himself, he could now understand Allan? Maybe then York, by token, could read both of them with ease.

He turned to Mary Allan, discreetly searching her face. She was watching her husband with admiration in her eyes. Was that emotional or intellectual? Did she understand the nuances as Allan commented on other cases and his views of certain judgments and York agreed with him? Was any of it completely honest? Possibly Allan was expressing what he believed, but he definitely selected to please.

What would happen if Allan's loyalties were ever torn, as Rathbone's had been? Would Mary Allan be so certain of her husband then? Perhaps they had been married longer. No one had mentioned children, but then one did not at a professional dinner party. What would

Margaret have done had she and Rathbone had children? He would never know.

They were still talking about fraud. Recent large cases were being mentioned, and how the defenses and prosecutions had been handled. Allan was saying, with the wisdom of hindsight, what he would have done.

Rathbone looked at Beata. She had been looking at him. She lowered her eyes quickly, hiding the gleam of interest. For an instant he was certain that had it been appropriate she would have asked him what he thought and if he read Allan as easily as she did. It was almost as if they had spoken, though no words had been uttered.

"There'll be more, of course," York said grimly. "And God knows how many we don't find; that is the worst thought."

"Maybe this verdict will put off a few," Allan said hopefully.

"And the severity of the sentence also," Mary Allan agreed with a sideways glance at Rathbone.

"I'm afraid it isn't the severity of punishment that is most effective," Rathbone replied. "It's the certainty."

She looked surprised. "Surely no one would be willing to face ten or fifteen years in prison, no matter how much money was involved?" she said with open disbelief. "In some of the prisons we have they might not even survive it! What use is money then?"

"It doesn't matter what the sentence is, if they are not caught," he explained. "And they all think they will be the one to get away with it. But if you know you will be caught, then even one year is too much."

"We need a rather better police force for that," York pointed out with a bleak smile.

Rathbone's instinct was to defend the police, but he bit the words back. Instead it was Beata who spoke.

"There is no point in catching people who commit fraud if they can't be successfully prosecuted," she observed. "As Sir Oliver says, it is the certainty that stops people, not the weight of the punishment. Surely no one commits a crime if they know they will have to pay for it."

Mary Allan turned to her. "I don't see your meaning," she said, her brow furrowed. "If the police find sufficient proof then is that not all we need?"

Beata looked at her husband with a slight warning in her expression, then at Mary Allan. "With the right prosecution and the right judge, yes of course it is." She lifted her wineglass so the others noticed it. "Let us drink to success."

"To success," they echoed obediently.

The subject changed to other matters. Beata asked if anyone else had been to the theater lately.

Bertrand Allan surprised Rathbone by saying that he had been to the music hall a short while ago, in order to see Mr. John "Jolly" Nash perform. Catching sight of York's raised eyebrows he hastened to explain that he had done so because he had heard that Nash was a favorite of the Prince of Wales, who particularly, it was said, enjoyed his rendition of "Rackety Jack."

"Really?" Beata responded with interest. "I hadn't heard." Mary Allan looked blank.

Rathbone glanced at Beata, who instantly concealed a smile. He looked away.

"I believe Mr. Nash is somewhat . . ." Beata hesitated, looking for the right word.

"It was for gentlemen only," Allan assured her.

"Then uncensored it would be, I imagine, to the prince's taste," Beata observed. "How entertaining."

Rathbone was happy to watch and listen. He went to the theater very seldom these days. He realized with a sudden dismay that he and Margaret had gone on only a few occasions and had rarely cared for the same work. How often had he pretended to agree with her when he had not? Her opinions had seemed predictable to him; they provoked no new questions in his mind, stirred no questions he had not considered before, stirring no new depth of emotion.

It had not occurred to him until now to wonder how often she had feigned an interest in something he had chosen, probably hiding her boredom more skillfully, and perhaps more kindly, than he had done.

The subject had moved to another play now, something a little more decorous. Beata was guiding the conversation into more comfortable areas.

"Did you like it?" Rathbone asked her a trifle abruptly, and then felt ashamed of his clumsiness. He wanted to add something to make it seem less demanding but did not know what.

She seemed amused, far more so than Allan, who had been about to speak and was now at a loss.

York looked from one to the other of them, his expression unreadable.

Beata gave an elegant little shrug. "You have caught me out, Sir Oliver. I'm not certain that I did. People are talking about it, but I fear it is more for the performance than any content of the drama itself. I would have found it more interesting if it had concluded less satisfactorily. An awkward ending would have given one something to think about."

"People don't like confused endings," Mary Allan pointed out.

"A thing should be either a comedy, in which case the ending is happy, or else a tragedy, when it is not," Allan agreed, supporting his wife.

York was amused. He watched them with undisguised satisfaction.

Beata turned her wineglass gently, watching the light glow through it. Rathbone noticed that she had beautiful hands.

"Surely life is both, even farce at times?" she asked. "A little ambiguity, even confusion, allows you to come to some of your own conclusions. I rather enjoy having to complete the thoughts myself. If the answer is easy, the question hardly seems worth asking."

"It's a play—entertainment," Mary Allan frowned. "We want to enjoy ourselves, perhaps laugh a little. There are times when I find tragedies moving, but I admit it is not very often. And I prefer the ones I know, such as *Hamlet*. At least I am prepared to see everyone dead at the end." She said it with a slight, rueful gesture, robbing the remark of any offense.

Beata accepted it without demur. "There is so much in *Hamlet* one may see it dozens of times and never grow tired of it. Of course, that needs to be over several years!"

Rathbone laughed in spite of himself, and reluctantly Allan joined in.

"Did it make you think?" York asked, looking pointedly at Rathbone.

"It certainly made me wonder how on earth an actor can remember all those lines and have energy and attention left to pour emotion into them as well, while still managing not to fall over the furniture," he answered.

"Training," York said drily. "They only recite the words; they don't have to invent them. And a wise stage manager keeps the furniture to a minimum."

"Perhaps that explains why judges are allowed to remain seated," Rathbone suggested, then wished he had not.

Mary Allan looked at him as if he were totally eccentric, York pulled a slight face, and Bertrand Allan was confused. Only Beata half hid a smile.

"I hear that the police are investigating the possibility of fraud in one of the local London churches," York remarked, changing the subject.

"Really! I wonder if that will come to trial." Allan looked at York, slightly turning his back toward Rathbone.

"Not certain if they can raise enough evidence to make a charge." York smiled, taking another piece of Stilton. He ate it with relish before replying. "I am very relieved that I am extremely unlikely to get the case. It is always messy prosecuting a churchman." He looked across at Rathbone with a gleam of amusement. "After your success with this one, perhaps you'll get it."

Rathbone was caught out, uncertain as to whether it was a compliment or a joke at his expense. Had he appeared to be too pleased with himself? A case of fraud against a church would not be easy at all.

Intentionally he deflected the barb. "You are quite right; anything to do with religion, money, and the possibility of fraud will make headlines. People will follow the case for all kinds of reasons, good and bad. It will be the topic of heated debates, and no matter what the verdict, it will infuriate as many people as it pleases." He smiled very slightly. "For that reason alone, I imagine they will be very careful as to whom they give it. I have been fortunate so far, but my experience is very slight." He turned to Allan. "If you appear in this one, would you prefer prosecution or defense?"

"I don't think I would be likely to get a choice," Allan replied. "But I do agree with you that it will be very high profile—if it actually comes to trial at all, that is."

"Who could a church defraud?" Mary Allan asked of no one in particular. "They are not doing any business. Do they handle so much money that fraud would even be worth their while? Surely not."

"We will see, if it comes to trial," York answered her.

She looked concerned. "Do you think it will?"

York considered for a few moments, aware that they were all watching him and waiting. He gave a small smile. "I'm not a betting man, but if I were, I would say about evens." He looked at Rathbone, then at Allan.

Rathbone raised his eyebrows. "If you were a betting man, what would be your odds on getting a conviction?"

York blinked. "Ten to one against, I should think."

"What a good thing you are not a betting man," Beata murmured. "The temptation would be enormous."

York opened his mouth to retort sharply, and, realizing that she was not even looking at him, closed it again with irritation.

Rathbone saw the smile on Beata's face, sad, wry, and completely inward, not intended to communicate with anyone else. He wondered what the conversation between her and York would be when the guests were gone and they were alone—or even if there would be any.

Mary Allan gazed around the room. "I think this is so charming," she remarked, as if everyone had been speaking of décor the moment before. "The colors are so restful, and yet have such dignity."

"Thank you," York replied, acknowledging the compliment without even glancing at Beata. Rathbone assumed he must've chosen the colors himself.

"I think if I were to do it again, I would choose something warmer," Beata said deliberately.

York raised his eyebrows. "Warmer? How can blue be warmer, unless you go into purple, which I would dislike intensely. I cannot imagine living with purple curtains."

She did not retreat. "I was thinking of yellow," she replied. "I have always thought I would like yellow one day, like sunlight on the walls."

Rathbone thought how pleasant that would be. He found himself smiling.

"A yellow room?" Mary Allan said, unimpressed.

"What would you do for curtains?" York asked. "I refuse to live in the middle of a glass bowl like a goldfish!"

"Perhaps the color of whisky?" Rathbone suggested.

Beata flashed him a sudden smile then looked down the moment before York turned to stare at her.

"It sounds very . . ." Mary Allan started, and then gave up.

"Like scrambled eggs on burned toast," York responded.

Allan laughed nervously.

"Afternoon sunlight, and a good glass of single malt," Rathbone said with a smile, meeting York's eyes and challenging him to be rude enough to argue.

RATHBONE TURNED OVER THE conversation again on the ride home. He took a hansom because he no longer kept a carriage of his own. He could easily afford it, but without Margaret to use it, it was an unnecessary luxury.

Was there really going to be a major fraud case brought against a church, or was York simply playing a game with Allan and Rathbone to see whose ambition was greater? He considered that quite a serious possibility. He had sensed a detachment in York, as if other people's feelings were of amusement to him, but of no concern. He found it disconcerting. The man was clever, but he could not like him.

Beata York was a different matter altogether. There was a grace in her that he found quite beautiful. Even sitting here in the hansom jolting over the cobble in the flickering light of street lamps, if he closed his eyes he could see her face again quite clearly in his mind's eye. He imagined the curve of her cheek, the quick humor in her eyes, and then the loneliness he had seen in that single smile, when she disagreed with York but could do no more than hint at it because of the restrictions of company. Was it different when they were alone? Was the distance between them less disguised?

The church case he mentioned would be very difficult indeed to handle. People's religious feelings ran deep and were often completely irrational. It would take considerable skill to disentangle the law of the land from what might be perceived to be God's law. The trouble was everybody had a different picture of God. Opposing views were not considered interesting, but rather all too often were felt to be blasphemous, and as such to be punished. Some religions even considered it the duty of their followers to undertake the delivering of such punishment themselves.

And who were the victims of such a theft? That was a whole other complicated area.

If it came to trial, did Rathbone want that case? It would be an honor to be given it, wouldn't it? Or would he get it simply because he was too new on the bench to have the power and the connections to pass it off to someone else?

But it would be interesting, a challenge to his skill, and if he succeeded he might build up a reputation for dealing with complicated and sensitive issues. Dangerous, perhaps. The risk of failure always carried a price, but the rewards were correspondingly high. He had no one to consider but himself. Why not? Perhaps something with high stakes to play for, whether he won or lost, was what he needed.

He sat back in the hansom and watched the dark houses slip by him. Occasionally he saw chinks of light and imagined families sitting together, perhaps talking over the day. Where there were no lights they might already be in bed. He passed little other traffic and what there was moved briskly. Everyone had somewhere to go.

Yes, he would like the case, if he were given it. He would not look for excuses to pass it on.

A FEW WEEKS LATER, INTO the real warmth of the summer, Rathbone stood in the doorway of his drawing room and gazed at the immaculate beauty of the garden. Beyond the shade of the poplars the sun was hot. The first roses were in full bloom. The house next door had a rambler that had spread up into the lower branches of the trees, and its clusters of white blossoms gleamed in the sun.

His eyes took in the beauty of it, but it was curiously meaningless to him. His instinct to turn and say "Isn't that lovely?" was so strong he had to remind himself there was nobody in the house to say it to. It was far too personal a thing to say to a servant. A maid would think it inappropriate and perhaps even be alarmed at the familiarity of it. A butler or footman would be embarrassed. To any of them it would betray his loneliness, and one did not do that. Servants knew perfectly well that masters or mistresses were flawed, made mistakes. No one was more aware of that than a lady's maid or a valet. They knew of physical weaknesses and many emotional ones as well. But it was all unspoken.

He had lived alone quite happily before his marriage. In fact, long ago, when he had been in love with Hester and considering asking her to marry him, it has been the loss of his privacy, the thought of always having someone else in the house that had stopped him.

Could he have made her happy? Probably not the same way Monk did. He had not Monk's fierce, brave, erratic passion. That was what Hester needed, to match her own.

But would Rathbone have tried, if he had had the courage to risk the hurt as well as the happiness? Now he would never know.

Should he have behaved differently with Margaret? He had been so certain of her, of them, in the beginning; it seemed incredible now how that had changed. Was he deluding himself? He remembered it all so clearly with a sharpness that was like the edge of a knife on the skin. She was not beautiful, but she had had a grace that was worth far more to him. That was an inner quality. Too often beauty masked the lack of anything deeper. How long could one remain fascinated by the glow of lovely skin or the perfect curve of a cheek or a neck if there were no courage or passion beneath it, no laughter or imagination, above all, no tenderness?

He had seen those things in Margaret, or he thought he had. Was it his fault that they had not survived her father's disgrace and Rathbone's failure to save him? It was unclear to him what else he could or should have done to try and fix them.

It was, after all, Margaret who had insisted Rathbone defend Arthur Ballinger. He had seemed the obvious choice then. He had been the most brilliant lawyer in London. That was not an affectation, simply the truth. And both of them had been certain that Ballinger was innocent.

The unraveling evidence had shown Rathbone his error, but Margaret had never accepted it. Even now, after Ballinger's death, she refused. She still blamed Rathbone. He could see her face in his mind's eye, ash pale, twisted with fury and a pain she could not bear. She had accused him of putting ambition before loyalty, love of himself before love of his family. She believed he had sacrificed her father on the altar of his own pride.

Nothing he said could persuade her that he had had no choice. Ballinger had been guilty, and whatever Rathbone had wanted, he could not prove anything else. God knew he had tried! To begin with, the evidence had been slight and could have been used to argue several different conclusions. Then, one by one, other events had driven the case to the final tragedy. Rathbone would never forget the horror of that, but nothing he could say or do mitigated his guilt in Margaret's eyes. She knew Ballinger only as her father, the man who had loved her and protected her all her life. She could not see him as a blackmailer, a criminal.

Rathbone was only the man she had married and loved briefly. She had begged for his help, assumed his loyalty, and could not forgive his failure. In her eyes, there were but two possibilities: either her father was not as she had believed or her husband was not. It was all her life, all the memories, the fabric of who she was compared with a short marriage to a man she had cared for but perhaps never been passionately in love with. Looking back, Rathbone thought there had never been a real conflict in her mind. Of course she had chosen her father.

After his terrible death she had no longer wanted to be under the same roof as Rathbone. Her grief, her rage had been overwhelming. She had taken the few belongings that were hers and gone back to comfort her mother in her new widowhood and social disgrace.

At first Rathbone had believed that she would return within a few weeks, but time had gone on, and it was now more than a year since she had left. Several times he had attempted to bridge the gulf between them. He had thought she would realize that she was being unfair, blaming him for Ballinger's death. She would accept that there was never anything he could have done to save him.

But every attempt at reconciliation had only driven the wedge deeper between them. Now he began to question whether they had ever loved each other at all, or if it had been more a matter of wanting to love, wanting not to be alone, and therefore seeing the good, building on it, slowly sharing more of the small pleasures of their daily lives.

When tragedy had come the fabric had proved too weak.

Should he have loved her more? Or should he have waited for a searing passion, a love that governed his whole life, before he married?

That was ridiculous. How many people even felt such a thing? Perhaps it was no more than a fever that passed anyway. Infatuation is not love. Love needs trust and balance. It needs both sharing and also the ability to be at peace in silence. Perhaps it needs a common faith in certain values, in honor and compassion, and the courage to go forward in the face of pain. It has to contain mercy, and gratitude for the joys of life, on both sides.

It must not demand perfection. What would perfection know or understand of the frailties of a vulnerable person, the failures of someone brave enough to try what is difficult?

Margaret had been immature.

Rathbone had been immature also. He should have been gentler with her. Certainly he should have been wise enough not to undertake Ballinger's defense alone. But if he had taken assistance she would have blamed him for not having thrown his whole weight behind it. She would have said his backing away from the case in any regard would make the court assume he thought Ballinger guilty from the start.

He had still not told her the whole story about the dreadful legacy her father had deliberately left to him, his final vengeance. She would still blame Rathbone, and hate him the more for it. It would mend nothing.

Was it a gentleness in him that stilled his tongue? Disillusion is one of the bitterest pains anyone can face. Some people cannot bear it; they break under the weight. Margaret was one of those. Maybe he still had some lingering tenderness toward her, a need to protect her from the truth if she did not have to know it.

Or was he simply too bruised and too weary inside to face another series of quarrels and rejections? Not that it mattered. There was no need to tell her.

He had never had to face the worst of disillusion himself, not one that came anywhere near hers. His own father was the best man he had ever known. Even standing here on the edge of the empty summer garden, watching the birds and the few butterflies sitting on the silent, brilliant flowers, he smiled thinking of Henry Rathbone. Of course, his father was fallible, and he himself would be the first to admit it. He was a mathematician and inventor, a man whose mind was brilliant, yet when others spoke of him it was his kindness they spoke of first.

He could remember his mother only as a slim figure from his childhood, someone warm and safe who made him laugh, comforted his early pains and fears, and who told him he could accomplish anything, if he tried hard enough. She believed in him totally.

She had died when he was twelve and away at boarding school. She had said he could do anything; he had thought then if he had been at home surely he could have saved her. He remembered the sharp, twist-ing pain of loss and the disbelief in his boyish mind, and then the guilt. He should have been there. Why had she not told him, not trusted him? What was wrong with him not to have seen it himself? She must have been ill for a long time before. It wasn't sudden.

All that had gone through his thoughts. Only later, several years after, did he realize she was protecting him. He was twelve, thinking himself almost a man, but she knew what a child he was. Had he been there, he would've wanted to save her, and he would've failed—and that would've hurt him deeply. She had known that.

There was only the echo of those memories left now, a gentleness in the mind when he thought of her and the things she had cared for, when he imagined her presence. She had never lived to see him pass the bar examinations, see his mounting success, his triumph in battles for justice that had seemed impossible. Had she ever imagined he would be knighted by the Queen, would be Sir Oliver? And now he was a judge. She would have been so proud!

Margaret likely had none of those emotions when she thought of her father. To lose someone you love because he dies from illness is a sweet ache. To lose everything good you believed of him is a pain that stains all he left behind. It poisons the very air of memory.

Ballinger had had his revenge on Rathbone, from beyond the grave. He had bequeathed him the obscene photographs at the heart of the case. They were hidden away now, locked in a safe so well concealed he doubted anyone else would ever find it. He had used one of the photos once. He loathed doing it, and he had sworn he never would again.

Maybe he should have destroyed them when they were first deliv-ered to him after Ballinger's death. He knew how they had come about, why Ballinger had created them, and how he had first used them and why. It was what had happened later that was the terrible wrong.

Was all power like that? You use it for good, then for less good, then finally simply because you can. Surely he was strong enough to resist that kind of temptation? He was not like Arthur Ballinger. He would not even look at them again, and perhaps one day soon he would smash the glass photographic plates to pieces. The paper prints he could burn.

He heard a noise of wings and looked up at a flight of birds across the soft blue of the sky. It must be after six o'clock. The breeze was stirring the poplars, shimmering the top leaves. It would be a long, delicate evening, too good to waste in pointless remembering.

He made the decision easily. He would go out to Primrose Hill and have supper with his father. He had a really good Belgian pâté, one of Henry's favorites. He would take it, and the plum pie that his cook had made with rich, flaky pastry. Maybe he should take half a pint of cream as well, in case Henry didn't happen to have any.

Henry Rathbone had been sitting in the garden reading one of the German philosophers he was so fond of. He had finally fallen asleep with the book upside down on his lap.

Oliver walked silently over the grass and stopped just short of where his shadow would fall across his father and, in all likelihood, wake him up. He stood still for a few moments then turned and went back to fetch another chair. He sat down a few yards away and allowed the peace to settle over him. He was comfortable enough to go to sleep, but instead he chose to bask in the pleasure of it.

There was no sound but the birds and the faintest wind occasionally stirring the leaves of the elms. The quiet settled into his bones as heat does, easing out the hurts.

When Henry woke up he would be delighted to find Oliver here. They would talk of all manner of things, funny and sad, interesting, new, or odd. They always did. Perhaps Henry would have some new jokes. Oliver had a limerick he knew would amuse him. Henry liked dry humor, the more absurd the better. Oliver wanted to talk about what disturbed him most at the moment: the complex moral issues surrounding the idea of loyalty. Henry would advise him without making it personal or emotional, without laying blame. Oliver would speak without having to worry about every word being judged, or misunderstood.

He looked across at Henry now, still sound asleep. He was well into his seventies. His hair was very gray, his face was getting a little gaunt, but his mind was as strong as ever, except that he repeated himself now and then.

Oliver never told him so. He received every remark with interest, as if he had not heard it before. Usually he hadn't.

But even as he saw the shadows lengthening in the garden and the color deepening in the light to the west, he knew that he would not always be able to come here and find Henry. One day it would be the last.

This was the most important relationship in his life. Maybe it always would be. If Margaret had loved her father like this, how could he blame her for her inability to cope with the loss? The destruction of everything she had believed she had—the smearing of it, the shattering of the beauty and the safety of that relationship, the pieces laid bare for strangers to tread on—was terrible, perhaps more than anyone could bear. In a way it was worse than if she herself had been the one sitting in the prosecution box.

How was he going to deal with Henry dying, when it happened? It would be a new loneliness, such as he had never experienced in his life.

How childish of a man his age to think of such a thing. The great gift of a marvelous father had been given him, and here he was wondering how he would deal with losing it at some time in the future.

But what faith did he have to nourish him with hope? What did he really believe in? The law. The morality of the Church, more or less, but what about the passion and the faith of it? He did not know the answer to that. Perhaps he should! With the disillusion in her father, and all that she had believed of him, Margaret was alone as Oliver never would be, robbed of the past as well as the present. How had he not seen that before?

Monk was not alone. As long as Hester was alive he never would be. And if there were a time after that, then the memory of her would sustain him and drive him to be all that he could, all that she had believed of him, even as he would hurt from missing her.

Henry moved a little and the book slipped out of his grasp. Its fall to the ground woke him up. He reached for it and saw Oliver sitting a few feet away. For an instant he was startled; then his face broke into a smile of pleasure.

"Didn't hear you," he apologized. "Have you been here long? How about a cup of tea? Can you stay for that?" He climbed slowly to his feet, took a moment to adjust his balance, and waited.

Oliver rose also. "I had intended to stay all evening," he replied. "I've brought some pâté and a plum pie, hoping you'd provide the rest."

"Excellent." Henry started to walk back to the house, going in at the garden door. "Plenty of crusty bread and butter and a little French cheese. I'm not sure about any cream for the pie . . ."

"I brought some." Oliver followed him in through the door and closed it behind him, turning the key, just in case they forgot later.

"Tea and fruitcake now?" Henry offered. "Or some Madeira cake, if you prefer? I've got a nice new little seascape I must show you." He picked up an art folder of heavy cardboard and unfastened the ties. He laid it flat on the table and lifted the cover. "It's only amateur, but it's really very pleasing. Found it in an antique shop the other day."

The painting was small, as he had said, but the colors were beautiful. The artist had used the paper in true watercolor style, allowing it to show through and give the whole picture light. The wind-whipped sea seemed almost luminous.

Oliver wanted to ask Henry his opinion about Ballinger's photographs, and if he should destroy them. Or if perhaps the information they held was too valuable to be allowed to disappear. Once obliterated, their power could never be used for evil or for good. There was also the question of whether one should destroy evidence of a crime, which the photographs most certainly were. It was hard to find the words to sort through the tangled situation.

"It's quite lovely," he said instead, looking at the little painting. "I think he could well become professional, don't you?"

Henry smiled. "Actually it's a 'she,' so I doubt it. But I'm delighted you like it. I'll have it framed, I think. Now, what kind of cake would you like with tea?"

"Fruitcake, thank you," Oliver replied, knowing it was also Henry's favorite.

Henry looked up and caught Oliver's troubled face. "What is it?"

"Ballinger's photographs," Oliver replied. "I . . . I'm still undecided whether I should destroy them or not."

Henry thought for a few minutes before speaking.

Oliver waited.

"I presume you have weighed the arguments on either side, and reached no conclusion," he said finally.

"I'm not sure that it's quite that simple," Oliver answered frankly. "To destroy them would be irrevocable. I suppose I'm reluctant to do that. What if a situation arises where, with them, I could right a great wrong, but I had thrown that opportunity away because I was too cowardly to deal with the responsibility of keeping them? I would have to face the fact that I destroyed a precious means of helping make a difference. Ballinger himself first used them to save countless lives after all."

There was no joy in Henry's face, no light of agreement.

"To begin with, yes," he said. "But I think it's more important to remember where he ended up."

"Are you saying I should destroy them?" Oliver asked.

Henry regarded him slightly critically. "No, I'm not. It is too big a decision for you to allow anyone else to make for you. You are dealing with an immense power. Be very careful." He took a deep breath and let it out in a sigh. "Whatever you do there is a terrible risk. That is no doubt what Ballinger intended." He smiled bleakly; then his face lifted with gentleness. "I'm sorry."

3

The summer weather was beautiful. Rathbone stood by the window in his chambers and watched the traffic pass below him. The sun glinted on harnesses and the shining coats of the horses as a brougham went by, coachman sitting upright. In the carriage two ladies held colored parasols, the frilled edges fluttering in the breeze.

There was a brief knock on the door. As he turned to respond, the door opened and his clerk came in, his face somber.

"Yes, Patmore?" Rathbone said, curious. Usually Patmore would begin to speak as soon as he had closed the door. Obviously this was a matter of some gravity.

"There is a new case added to your docket, Sir Oliver," he said quietly, then cleared his throat. "I think you might like some warning before it actually comes to court."

Rathbone was intrigued already. "Scandal?" he asked. "Something we need to handle delicately?" He was used to such things.

"Yes, sir, but not in the usual way," Patmore replied. "It's . . . it's really very nasty."

"Things usually are if they find their way to the Old Bailey," Rathbone observed a little drily. "Murder?"

"No, sir. As far as I know, nobody was physically harmed. It's all quite literally about money."

Rathbone almost lost interest immediately. Greed was one of the most boring motives for breaking the law. "Then why do you think I ought to be warned before I consider it more seriously?" he asked.

"You might wish to find a way to pass it on to someone else, sir," Patmore replied, explaining it as if to someone slow of understanding. "I think it will get very ugly, and whatever the verdict, it will offend people we would prefer not to."

Rathbone's attention was fully engaged now. He recalled the conversation at Ingram York's dinner table. "What on earth is so sensational in a case of greed?" He said carefully, not wanting to assume the case was anything too extraordinary. "We see them every day."

"Not when the accused is a churchman and the victim is apparently his flock, sir."

Patmore had a sense of irony that had not escaped Rathbone, but he was still far from used to it.

"I see." Rathbone exhaled slowly.

"It will be unpleasant and require a great deal of tact," Patmore continued. "I rather fancy you have been handed it because everyone else would prefer to watch from the sidelines, preferably far enough away for flying mud not to attach itself to them."

"If anyone can counsel you to curb your opinions, Patmore, you might consider it seriously, for your own survival—but please never do it for mine. I should miss your frankness. Now tell me more specifically what the accusation is against this churchman."

Patmore inclined his head, by way of accepting what he took to be a compliment, as indeed it was. "Mr. Abel Taft has been accused of defrauding his congregation out of several thousands of pounds, sir," he answered. "In fact, the amount named would be sufficient to buy a row of quite respectable houses. Half a street of them."

"Several thousands?" Rathbone said in disbelief. "How on earth could he swindle his congregation out of so much without their knowledge? And where on earth is his church that his parishioners had that much to give?" He was quite certain now that this was the case that York had mentioned.

"That is rather the issue, sir," Patmore remarked. "It has been given, allegedly, by ordinary men and women, out of their savings, in the belief that it was going to the starving and the homeless."

"And it was not?" Rathbone felt his anger rising.

"Allegedly not, sir. Rather more than stated was going to a very nice savings account, not to mention a high standard of living for Mr. Taft himself, and of course his young and very appealing family."

"I begin to see what you mean about the possibility of this getting ugly," Rathbone conceded. "We had better ensure that the evidence is more than good and that both lawyers know what they are doing. Mr. Taft is represented, isn't he?"

"Oh, yes, sir. By Mr. Blair Gavinton. Having him appear in your court will be quite an experience for you."

"I don't like the way you say that, Patmore."

"I could say it a lot worse, sir, I promise you."

"Exactly what is wrong with Mr. Gavinton?"

"Greasy, sir. There's just something about him, but the minute you put your finger on it, it slips away."

"Indeed. And what do you know about Mr. Abel Taft? I've never heard of him."

"Does very well, sir," Patmore replied, all expression very carefully ironed out of his voice. "I've taken the liberty of looking him up. He has a nice house, very handsome wife, two young daughters just about the right age to be looking for husbands. Dresses very well, does Mr. Taft, at least so I hear. Dines even better. Belongs to some good clubs too. I wouldn't care to pay his tailor's bill."

"Interesting," Rathbone conceded. "Do you know who is prosecuting this case?"

"No, sir, not yet. But I have made discreet inquiries. He'll have to be very good indeed to catch Mr. Gavinton out."

"We must assume the police have concrete evidence, or they would not be wasting everyone's time or risking looking incompetent."

Patmore inclined his head very slightly. "Precisely, sir. I shall keep you informed. I believe we have three weeks yet before the trial begins. Rather depends on the Warburton case, and how long that takes."

"Not three weeks, please heaven!" Rathbone exclaimed.

"Indeed not, sir."

Rathbone gave him a wry look, and Patmore withdrew, his expression unreadable.

After the door had closed Rathbone stood still for quite some time. This *had* to be the case York had been referring to. He had said it would require considerable legal skill to keep it under control and make it clear enough for justice to be truly served. Was there a reason York had brought it up in the first place? Had he wanted the church exonerated? Or did he consider this to be a sect richly deserving a setback?

Rathbone wondered who would be prosecuting. It certainly would have been decided already. There would be a great deal of paperwork to go through, many witnesses. Presumably the victim was the entire body of the congregation, or at the least, all those who had contributed. There would be bookkeepers and accountants as witnesses of bank records and whatever financial proof of donation the various parishioners had kept—if any.

The more Rathbone thought about it, the more he agreed with Patmore that presiding over such a trial was an unenviable task. His task was to see justice prevail, but in order to do that he would have to make certain that the jury understood exactly what had happened. One could very easily become exhausted with detail, confused by the sheer weight of facts and numbers, and fall back on the faith that a churchman couldn't possibly be guilty of such a crime.

Was there any way Rathbone could control the testimony without denying due process of law to either side?

The defense would fight hard. A man's freedom and his reputation were in the balance. It was not quite his life, but it was his way of life that was at stake.

Would the prosecutor try equally hard? He had less to gain, or lose.

What about the religious loyalties of either of the lawyers? Would that matter? Would anyone be angry that the name of religion in general was being blackened in the public eye?

Rathbone would have to be very careful not to overstep the boundaries of his discretion if his own prejudices were attacked.

He thought of the cases he had defended in his long career. Some of the criminals had been accused of appalling acts; some of tragic ones, painfully understandable. In certain cases he had thought that in the same circumstances, he might have made the same judgments and ended up in the same disastrous position.

He had always cared a little too much, and he had not always been right in his judgment. One of the worst villains he had ever defended was Jericho Phillips, a fearful man accused of blackmail, child pornography, and murder. He winced as he recalled it now, standing in this old wood-paneled chamber with its rows of leather-bound books and its rich rugs on the floor.

It was in Newgate Prison that he had first met Phillips, alive and well, his vulpine face full of satisfaction, all but certain that he would escape the rope. The last time he had seen him had been months later, after the acquittal, and after Monk had hunted him down again. It was as the Thames tide receded, leaving the hideous iron cage of Execution Dock naked above the water. Inside it had been the drowned corpse of Jericho Phillips, his mouth stretched wide in his final scream.

Should Rathbone have defended him? There was no serious doubt in his mind about that. He had thought Phillips guilty, but he had also thought other men guilty in the past and been proven wrong.

If someone harms a stranger, then it is usually the fault of the thief and the misfortune of the victim. But if the victim and the perpetrator know each other, both of them need to be considered carefully in order to find justice. Extortion, bullying, and consistent cruelty are so often practiced that sometimes there is no course of action short of violence—a reaction born out of desperation, because the so-called criminal was terrified, exhausted, and at wits' end. It did not justify murder, but it raised complicated questions of self-defense, where no answer was fair to all.

Many cases had come to him through Monk, and of course through Hester. Some of those from the time when she was a nurse for private patients had tested him to what he had believed were his limits, showing him tragedies with no simple or just answer. Nature and society between them created Gordian knots impossible to unravel.

The case of Phillips, which had seemed at the beginning a simple matter of serving the law, had become so entangled in violence and in Rathbone's own conflicted emotions that even the death of Phillips had been only a brief respite before the continuation of the crimes connected to his life.

It had ended in the destruction of Arthur Ballinger, and of Rathbone's marriage. Even that was not as simple as it appeared. For a while Ballinger had seemed to Rathbone an irredeemable man. Then, in that final encounter, he had told Rathbone not only what had happened, but why; he had explained his slow descent from idealism, step by step downward to the conscienceless brutality that marked his character at the end of his life.

It all made a case of a clergyman embezzling money seem cut-and-dried—the evidence would be complex, full of detail that would need to be explained with great clarity—but essentially, it was a matter of simple greed. He certainly would not attempt to pass the case off to anyone else.

HESTER WAS ALSO LOOKING forward to the trial of Abel Taft. She had worked extraordinarily hard to bring it about. It was extra-good news to her that it was Oliver Rathbone who had been appointed to try the case.

"What a good thing I didn't say anything to him. I had thought about it, a few weeks ago," she said as she and Monk walked under the trees in Southwark Park, a mere stone's throw from their own house. "I suppose that could have compromised him so he wouldn't have been allowed to hear the case, couldn't it?"

"Possibly," he agreed, smiling in the evening sun. Below them in the distance the light was mirror-bright on the water, making the ships stand out almost black. "Is that why you didn't tell him? In case he was chosen to hear it?"

"Not really," she admitted. "I rather thought he wouldn't approve."

"When on earth has that ever stopped you?" he asked incredulously, turning to look at her with amusement and a sudden surge of affection.

"Since he was placed in a position to be able to stop me," she said frankly.

How very practical. How like her—a mixture of the wildly idealistic and the totally pragmatic. He put his arm around her and walked a little closer.

"Of course," he agreed.

APPROXIMATELY TWO WEEKS LATER the trial of Abel Taft began. It was a hot, almost windless day in mid-July, and the courtroom of the Old Bailey was uncomfortably warm. Even though the public gallery was not full, the atmosphere seemed airless.

The proceedings began as usual. The court had been called to order, the jurors were sworn in. As always the gravity of it gave Rathbone a sudden sharpening of his awareness of exactly who he was, and—more importantly—what his responsibilities were toward the people in this old, beautiful, and frightening chamber. Lives had been ripped apart here; dreams shattered, guilt and tragedy exposed, and, please God, justice done.

He should never forget that sometimes it could be the opposite. Lies had covered truth, oppression had crushed freedom, and violence beyond the walls had reached inside and silenced protest.

He looked at the participants today. As he already knew, Blair Gavinton represented the accused. He was slender, graying a little. Everything about him was smooth, immaculately tailored. He smiled easily, as if he believed it were charming. To Rathbone, he seemed to have too many teeth. He was sitting very calmly today. The expression suggested that he knew something that the rest of them did not.

On the other side of the room Dillon Warne represented the prosecution. He was a good height, perhaps an inch or two taller than Gavinton, and his hair was dark. He had an elegance that did not look as if he had struggled to attain it. Indeed he gave one the feeling that he was not even aware that he had a certain grace. Rathbone was always surprised to notice that when Warne walked he did so with a slight limp. He had never mentioned, in the few times he and Rathbone had spoken, what had occurred to cause it, nor did he ever say whether it gave him any pain.

He was sitting pensively, no indication in his face as to what he might be thinking.

The dock where the accused sat between two jailers was raised above the rest of the room, and entered separately, from a stairway apart from the main court. The accused could see and hear all the proceedings, but was removed in a sense.

Abel Taft sat there now, a calm, handsome man with magnificent hair. He looked patient rather than afraid. He might almost have been preparing for the room to come to order so he could begin his sermon. Was he a superb actor, or was he really so very confident that he wouldn't be found guilty?

Warne rose to his feet and began to address the court as to the nature of his case against the accused, and what he intended to prove. Rathbone looked at Taft's wife sitting in the gallery behind Gavinton. Mrs. Taft was a pretty woman, but today she looked as if she kept her composure only with considerable difficulty. Her husband might not be afraid, but she most certainly was. Another woman, rather older, sat next to her, leaning a little toward her as if to offer comfort.

Once, Blair Gavinton turned round and gave Mrs. Taft a reassuring glance. Rathbone could not see his face, but he could well imagine his expression. Hers softened into a hesitant smile, and Gavinton looked toward the front again, and listened to Warne, who now called his first witness.

Mr. Knight was a very ordinary young man, rather overweight, and at that moment extremely nervous.

Warne tried to set him at ease. Obviously he would have done all he could to prepare him, because if Warne himself did not know the testimony he could hardly present it to the court.

"If you would give us the facts and figures as clearly and briefly as you can, please," Warne requested.

Knight swallowed, wiped his brow with a rather small handkerchief, then swallowed again.

"Begin at the beginning," Warne prompted.

Gavinton smiled, looking down at the papers in front of him. It was a simple gesture, and yet to Rathbone it conveyed a certain smugness, as if Gavinton were awaiting his opportunity to destroy the young man.

Knight must have felt the same because when he began his voice was a squeak. First he listed sums of money, reading from a ledger that had been produced in evidence and of which the jurors had copies.

It was all very tedious, and Rathbone had only to look at the jurors' faces to see that they were already bored. The figures had no meaning to them at all.

Mr. Knight himself must have realized it. He hurried up until he was practically gibbering.

Warne heard him out as if he were interested. Finally he held up his hand.

"Thank you, Mr. Knight. I think this is sufficient for us to have the idea that these sums of money, added together, amount to a very considerable total. You have mentioned dates, but possibly in all the figures, we missed them, or we've forgotten. Will you give us the total sum for the year ended last 31 December?"

"Yes, sir. Two thousand, four hundred and twenty-seven pounds, fifteen shillings and sixpence."

"Is that typical of a year? How does it compare, for example, to the year before?"

"It increases slightly every year, sir, by about a hundred pounds, or maybe a hundred and fifty."

"So always sufficient to purchase several very agreeable houses?"

"Yes, sir."

"And is this year set to reach a similar amount?"

"If it continues like this, more, sir."

"And is it made up of similar random amounts?"

"Yes, sir."

Gavinton stood up wearily. "My lord, the defense will stipulate to the amounts mentioned being the sums donated by the parishioners to the charitable endeavors of Mr. Taft's Church. I think it is something to be proud of, not a cause for shame."

"Thank you, Mr. Gavinton," Rathbone said drily. "I imagine Mr. Warne is establishing the amount, and its source, in order to pursue exactly where it ended up, not to question your skill in assessing it." He turned to Warne. "Please come to your point, before we are so numbed by these figures we forget that they represent the life savings of many people."

A flicker of annoyance crossed Gavinton's face, but he sat down again.

Warne inclined his head in acknowledgment. "My lord." He turned to Knight. "Those sums must represent pennies and shillings collected over every week of the year, to have reached such an amount."

"Yes, sir," Knight agreed.

Gavinton rose again. "My lord, this is pointless. We agree that many people gave generously. It is a waste of the court's time, and these gentlemen's indulgence." He waved to indicate the jury, who all looked bored and impatient.

"Mr. Warne, is there some point you wish to make?" Rathbone asked. "So far you have not shown us anything a simple statement of account would not have done."

Warne smiled bleakly. "My point, my lord, is that these individual figures show a pattern." He turned to Knight, who was looking more and more wretched, as if Gavinton's objections were his fault. "Mr. Knight, what conclusion did you draw from these figures, sir?"

Knight swallowed yet again. "That these people had given money to Mr. Taft every week, sir. The amounts are random, often including odd pennies, as if they had turned out their pockets and given all they had. And because the number of donations every week corresponded pretty clearly with the number of adults attending the service, it seems as if they all gave . . . sir."

"Thank you," Warne said with a bow. "Your witness, Mr. Gavinton."

Gavinton rose to his feet. The satisfaction still gleamed in his face. "Mr. Knight, do you go to church, sir?"

"Yes."

"And do you give an offering?"

"I do."

"And does it compare roughly to any of the amounts you found in these records?"

"Yes, sir. I give what I can."

Gavinton smiled. "I imagine everyone in your congregation does. And in every other congregation in London, indeed in England." He looked a little wearily at Warne. "I don't understand your point. And forgive me, Mr. Knight, I haven't any idea what you think you are testifying to! Other than the perfectly obvious fact that Mr. Taft has a more generous flock, and perhaps a larger one, than most congregations of rather more orthodox faith!"

Knight leaned forward in the witness stand, his plump hands gripping the railing. "You could if you understood figures, sir," he said distinctly. "These people are giving all they can, pennies and ha'pennies, whatever they have left at the end of the week. All of them—every week."

"All you are saying is that they are noble and generous," Gavinton pointed out with a faint smirk. "And possibly that Mr. Taft is a better preacher than most. Thank you, Mr. Knight!" The smirk was wider.

"No!" Knight said loudly as Gavinton walked away from him. "It shows that they believed with all their hearts that Mr. Taft was going to do something with it that they cared about, so much so they were willing to go cold and hungry," he said angrily.

"Willing to make do with less, you mean?" Gavinton suggested. "Did he ask anyone to go into debt? To fall short on their own commitments?"

Warne rose to his feet. "We shall show that that is exactly what he did."

"If he did, that is not a crime," Gavinton shot back. "He could ask, but he couldn't force anyone to do anything against their will. You are wasting the court's time and bringing a righteous man's name into disrepute by making those frankly absurd charges."

"Gentlemen!" Rathbone demanded their attention. "It is you who are wasting our time. We are here to provide evidence and test it on exactly these matters. Please continue to do so, with facts, however tedious they may be to unravel. Mr. Gavinton, have you anything more to ask Mr. Knight?"

"I don't think Mr. Knight can tell me anything at all," Gavinton said ungraciously.

Warne raised his eyebrows. "I don't think anyone can," he responded.

There was a titter of amusement from the gallery, and one juror laughed outright.

Gavinton was far from amused.

Rathbone kept his face straight with something of an effort. "Have you anything to ask or redirect, Mr. Warne?"

"Thank you, my lord," Warne said. "Mr. Knight, you deduce from these figures that a number of people, almost the same number every week, gave random amounts to Mr. Taft's Church. The numbers vary from a few pence to many pounds, in fact whatever they could possibly manage. Is that correct?"

"Yes, sir."

"And in what way is that a crime?" His voice was very light, curious, no more.

"It's not, sir," Knight replied. "So long as Mr. Taft used the money for exactly what it was given for."

"Ah . . ." Warne breathed out slowly. "That is rather a big condition, is it not? If . . . it was used for that purpose, all of it, and that purpose alone."

For the first time there was attention in the gallery. People moved, exchanged glances. Journalists were busy scribbling on their pads.

In the jury box more notes were made. Suddenly faces were grave, showing sharp interest. Several of them looked up at Taft with the beginnings of doubt and even dislike.

In her seat in the gallery, behind Gavinton, Mrs. Taft was clearly anxious.

THE TRIAL WENT ON like that for three days. The facts and figures were boring even to the jurors, who were paying as much attention as they could manage. Many wrote things down, but there was far too much detail for anyone to record, and even then it would have meant little. It was the conclusions that mattered. Rathbone had thought at first that the detail would have affected them. There were no crushing boulders, only endless grains of sand, and the sheer volume of their assumed and monstrous weight. The figures all tallied at first glance, but time-consuming evidence showed again and again that they did so only through sleight of hand, duplicity, and shifting of the boundaries and the terms of reference.

Gradually the jury's reaction of boredom and confusion changed to one of pure suspicion that they were being deliberately duped. They resented it, as if they had been patronized by someone who thought them too stupid to fathom a trick when they saw one, or too easily distracted to follow a trail of slow and well-concealed theft.

As Mr. Knight had said at the beginning, as much as you might deplore it, taking the last penny a man had to give, or even beyond that, sending him into debt, was not a crime. But when he had given it in trust for a specific and limited purpose, and it had been used for something else, then it assuredly was—and keeping it for oneself was fraud, pure and simple.

On Thursday, the fourth day of the trial, Warne presented Mr. Bicknor, the elderly father of a young man named Cuthbert Bicknor, who had apparently given to Taft a great deal more money than he had the right to dispose of. As a result of his mismanagement, he had lost his job and after that his health had suffered, and he was now confined to his bed with pneumonia.

Warne treated him as gently as he could.

"Mr. Bicknor, could you please tell the court of the change in your son after he joined Mr. Taft's Church?"

Bicknor looked wretched. The whole situation obviously embarrassed him acutely. He hated being here, stared at by so many people and obliged to recount his family's shame.

"He became totally absorbed in it," he said so quietly Rathbone had to ask him to speak a little more loudly.

"I'm sorry," Bicknor said, jerking his head up to stare at Warne. "He seemed to be able to think and talk of nothing else. He stopped going out to the theater or the music hall, or out to dinner with friends."

"Did Mr. Taft's Church teach against such things?" Warne asked gently.

Bicknor shook his head. "No—Cuthbert said he shouldn't spend the money on such things, not when there were people cold and hungry in other places. It is unchristian to indulge ourselves, he said. He stopped even buying himself new shoes."

Warne looked puzzled. "And did you not admire him for that, Mr.

Bicknor? It sounds a most generous and truly Christlike attitude. Perhaps if more of us thought like that, the world would be a better place."

There was a murmur of approval from the gallery, and some discomfort in the jury box. Several of the jurors looked intently at the woodwork, avoiding anyone's eyes.

Rathbone wondered if Warne was really thinking about what he was saying. He seemed to be playing into Gavinton's hands.

"If the whole world was like that, yes," Bicknor replied, clearly distressed. He looked as if Warne's question was unexpected. "But it isn't, is it? My son's going around with shoes that have holes in them, and a shirt with a frayed collar that's already been turned once. Look at Mr. Taft. He's got brand-new boots with a shine you could see your face in. And I've seen him myself in three different pairs. And I'll wager he doesn't have his wife turn his shirt collars so the frayed edges don't show. He has a nice carriage and a matched pair of horses to pull it, while my son walks to save the omnibus fare."

Warne nodded slowly. "Then Mr. Taft is a hypocrite. He does not himself do what he expects of others. But that is not a crime, Mr. Bicknor. Certainly it is contemptible, and repugnant to any decent man, but I'm afraid we find such people not only in the Church but in all walks of life." He looked unhappy as he said it, his dark face rueful.

"We don't give them our money!" Bicknor retorted angrily, his frustration at his inability to convey the injustice of the situation ringing in his voice. "He's a cheat! He lied to us . . . in the name of God!" His cheeks were flushed and he was trembling, grasping the rail of the witness box with hands whose knuckles shone white.

Warne smiled, his lips drawn tight. "If Mr. Taft has asked for money in order to give it to the poor, and then taken it for his own use, then it is a crime, Mr. Bicknor, and we shall prove it so. It is particularly despicable if he has taken it from those who have little enough in the first place. Thank you for your testimony. Please remain there in case my learned friend has anything to ask you."

As Warne returned to his seat, his limp a little more noticeable, Gavinton stood up. He walked across the open space of the floor as if he were entering an arena, a gladiator swaggering out to battle. He looked up at Bicknor, a lumbering man by comparison, who now was regarding him with apprehension.

"Mr. Bicknor, you are naturally very protective of your son. It sounds as if he is an unusually vulnerable young man, desperate to have the approval of Mr. Taft. Do you know why this is?"

"No I don't," Bicknor replied a little sharply. "The man's a charlatan. Mind, my son didn't see that. He thinks a man in the pulpit, preaching the word of God, has to be honest. We brought him up to respect the Church, and any man of the cloth. Maybe that was our mistake."

"No," Gavinton shook his head. "It is right to respect the Church, and those who represent it. But it seems your son's emotions were far more radical than simple respect would dictate. Did you teach him to give all he possessed, more than he could possibly afford, to anyone who asked for it?"

"Of course not!" Bicknor was angry. Rathbone could see his self-control, which Warne had guarded so carefully, already beginning to slip out of his grasp. One should not underestimate Gavinton.

Gavinton smiled, flashing his teeth again. "I'm sure you didn't, Mr. Bicknor. I imagine you are a great deal more careful with your money. You give what is safely within your means?" He made it sound somehow mean-spirited.

"Yes." Bicknor could give no other answer.

"A pity you did not teach your son to do the same," Gavinton shook his head. "Without offense, might I suggest it was your duty to have done that, not Mr. Taft's?" He ignored Bicknor's scarlet face and his hunched, shaking body. "How was Mr. Taft to know that your son was in financial difficulty? He has hundreds of parishioners. He cannot possibly be aware of the affairs of all of them. Why is it that you expect him to be? How many sons do you have, Mr. Bicknor? Correct me if I am mistaken, but is it not just the one?"

"Yes . . . but I don't ask him for money to support me!" Bicknor said with a rising note of desperation. "I don't bleed him dry and then make him feel ashamed if he can't give me even more. I don't use Christ's name to get him to do things I want him to."

"Is that what your son told you happened? Or possibly it is simply what you assume, knowing that Mr. Taft is a man of God?" He raised his eyebrows. "I take it that you were not there while this was happening, or you would have intervened, would you not?"

"'Course I weren't there at the church." Bicknor's control was slipping even further out of his grasp.

Rathbone could see from Warne's face that he longed to help him, but there were absolutely no grounds for him to object. There was nothing Rathbone could do either, whatever he felt personally. Gavinton was very possibly testing the emotional value of the testimony, but that was his job. And there was always the possibility, remote as it seemed, that he was correct. Young Bicknor might be a naïve young man who had misunderstood what was said to him. His father might be blaming Taft for faults in his son that he himself should have checked.

"Mr. Bicknor," Gavinton continued, "is it not possible that your son sought out Mr. Taft, and became so dependent upon his good opinion, because he wished to overcome some doubt or fear within himself? Possibly it was even God's forgiveness he sought, for some sin that burdened him heavily?"

"How dare you?" Bicknor burst out, rage and humiliation thickening his voice. He banged his closed fist on the railing. "First he was robbed blind, deceived by lies and canting ways, and now you accuse him of some terrible sin! He's never done anything worse than dodge school a few times when he was younger. You—you're disgusting!"

Rathbone leaned forward a little. "Mr. Bicknor, Mr. Gavinton is only putting to you a possible reason as to why your son might have been coerced so easily into giving more money than he could afford. There is nothing dishonorable in seeking to pay your debts to God by giving generously to those less fortunate." He drew in a breath. "And we all have debts to God—the honest among us acknowledge it."

Bicknor looked at Rathbone in silent misery. He wanted to argue, but he dared not. Rathbone represented the majesty of the law, which

Bicknor had respected all his life. The answers were in his head, but he was afraid to give them.

"Thank you, my lord," Gavinton said, instantly turning Rathbone's remarks to his own advantage.

Rathbone had a sudden flash of empathy for Bicknor. The result was not what he intended. He must be more careful.

"Do not thank me yet," he snapped. "It is one of the skills of those who cheat people out of their money to make them feel guilty for nameless sins they have not committed. As I am sure Mr. Warne will point out on his reexamination of the witness."

Warne did not bother to hide his smile.

Gavinton bit his lip in order to suppress the objection he would like to have made. He was taken by surprise. He had thought Rathbone less brave, possibly even less involved.

Bicknor's shoulders eased and he gripped the railing again, but this time not as if he intended to break it.

"You can think what you like," he said to Gavinton. "It's your job to be on his side." He glanced up at the dock, then back to Gavinton again. "God help you. You've got to live with yourself. My son's got a soft heart, not a guilty one. Maybe a bit of a soft head, to believe that . . . that liar!" This time he only nodded toward the dock.

Gavinton opened his mouth to protest, then glanced at the jury and changed his mind. He sat down and offered the witness back to Warne.

Warne walked over to the witness stand, his limp barely noticeable now. He was smiling, in spite of an apparent effort not to.

"Mr. Bicknor, are you aware of your son having a major issue of conscience at any time in his life, of the sort or degree that Mr. Gavinton has suggested?"

"No, sir, I am not," Bicknor said loudly.

Warne was not finished yet.

"On the other hand, have you known him to be generous to those less fortunate?" he persisted. "To share what he had, for example? To be willing, as a child, to let others play with his toys?"

"Yes," Bicknor agreed immediately. "We taught him in that way. He has sisters, and he was always good to them. Younger, they are. He looked out for them."

"Did they take advantage of him?" Warne went on.

Bicknor smiled. "They're little girls! Course they did! And of me too. Some people think little girls is all weak and soft. I'll tell you, they aren't. Sweet and gentle, all right, but clever as little monkeys, they are. A man who hasn't had little girls has missed out on one of the best things in life. But anyone who thinks they're daft is in for a very big surprise."

Warne's smile was wide and surprisingly sweet. "Thank you, Mr. Bicknor. I really don't think I have to ask you any more. It seems clear to me that your son is a decent man taken advantage of by those he had been brought up to trust."

Gavinton rose to his feet. "My lord, Mr. Warne is making speeches; he is all but directing the jury as to their conclusions."

"You suggested Mr. Bicknor was a guilty man seeking to buy off his conscience with money," Rathbone pointed out. "This seems a fair rebuttal. It is an alternative explanation for a piece of behavior that is crucial to the case." He turned back to Warne. "Please call your next witness, Mr. Warne."

The prosecution continued for the rest of the day. Warne had enough wisdom to choose a variety of people, old and young, men and women, those who had given from wealth and those who had offered almost all they had. In each case they had done so believing it would be used to help those in desperate need. It became very apparent that Cuthbert Bicknor was one of very many.

John Raleigh was also among them. He looked gaunt and worried, a man prematurely old for his years as he mounted the witness stand. He was no more than Rathbone's own age, and yet he looked pale and beaten. It was clear that Warne found it difficult to question him at all, so sensitive was he to the man's deep unhappiness and shame.

And yet Raleigh was exactly who he needed to make the case. He was so obviously an honest man, harrowed by the fact that he was now deeply in debt. Gavinton would have been a fool to attack him. Not only was he sincere, he was articulate.

Warne treated him with respect. He walked out slowly to the center of the floor and looked up. His voice when he spoke was quiet and clear.

"Mr. Raleigh, would you please explain to the court why you went on donating to Mr. Taft's causes when it stretched your means beyond what was wise? Some people may not understand why you did not simply tell him that you could not."

Raleigh looked embarrassed. It was so apparent in his face that even Rathbone, long used to the acute distress of witnesses, found himself uncomfortable, as if he were intruding into some private issue that he should have had the sense and the good taste not to observe in the first place.

"Mr. Taft told us the most pitiful stories of the plight of those he intended to help," Raleigh said, his voice soft but clear. "I was very moved by it," he went on, lifting his chin and facing Warne and the court as if he were walking into battle. "I . . . I gave more than I should have, and then found myself facing the choice of paying one bill, or another. One has certain expenses that one deals with so regularly they become invisible. And then, as always, there's the unexpected thing. I . . ." He took a deep breath.

Rathbone looked at him with concern. "Are you able to continue, Mr. Raleigh?" he said gently. "If you would like a few moments to collect yourself, you may take them."

"No, thank you, my lord," Raleigh answered. "If I am man enough to do it, I must have the honesty to explain myself. I am far from being the only one so . . . embarrassed for means. Mr. Taft asked me how much I had in the bank, and if I would not trust in God to provide for me if I gave all I could to fellow human souls who were perishing for lack of food or shelter. What answer could an honest man give, except that of course I would?"

"And what happened, Mr. Raleigh?" Warne asked, his face filled with pity.

"A slate came off my roof, then several more," Raleigh replied. "I asked the roofer to replace them for me, otherwise the first rains would come in, and the rafters would begin to rot. Before long I should have irreparable damage."

"But you had insufficient means to pay him?" Warne asked.

"I had sufficient funds for the damage I could see. But when he climbed up there, he found other slates were broken and the lead was inadequately laid around the chimney. It cost twice as much as I had anticipated, and I no longer had the funds set aside against such things." There were tears in his eyes, and he blinked them away rapidly. "Perhaps the Lord expects rather more prudence than I exercised."

"Did you consider asking Mr. Taft to return some of your money to you?" Warne asked. "I know the answer, but the court may wish to hear."

"I did." Raleigh's face was scarlet with humiliation, and he stumbled over his words. "He accused me of asking him to rob God. He told me I would forfeit the grace I had obtained, and that I should strengthen my faith if I wanted to be among those in whom God was pleased."

Warne's own face was white now, his voice suddenly rough-edged. "Did you believe that Mr. Taft had the power or the right to tell you whom God would favor, and whom he would not?"

Raleigh looked down at the floor, away from Warne's eyes. "He is an ordained preacher, sir. He was very persuasive. And do I need two coats, when my neighbor has not even a shirt? 'Love thy neighbor as thyself.'"

"Mr. Raleigh, how many coats do you think Mr. Taft possesses?" Warne said softly.

Raleigh sighed. "I have seen him in at least a dozen, at one time or another. I didn't think of that at the time. I admit it, I was gullible, extremely foolish. I really believed that what I was giving would go straight to some poor soul who had not even that night's supper, and I knew I had mine, and to spare."

"And have you now, Mr. Raleigh?"

"No, sir, I have not. I am ashamed to say it, but I am dependent upon my daughter's kindness—and, God knows, she has little enough money to share."

"And has Mr. Taft seen your need and offered to help you?" Warne asked, with an edge to his voice like an open blade.

"No, sir," Raleigh whispered.

Warne thanked Raleigh for his evidence and said nothing more.

Gavinton had the sense not to make his situation even worse. He could see in the jurors' faces, and when he glanced behind him in the gallery also, that if he attacked Raleigh in any way, he would lose even the small hope he had left.

THE FOLLOWING DAY, FRIDAY, Warne called his final witness. Gethen Sawley was a quiet, rather studious young man with horn-rimmed glasses, which kept sliding down his nose. He was bony, as if somehow in the making of him the sculptor had been interrupted before he was finished. Sawley took the oath nervously and faced Warne, appearing as though he had to struggle to hear him.

"Mr. Sawley," Warne began gently, "what is your occupation, sir?"

"I'm a clerk at Wiggins & Martin, but mostly I do the bookkeeping since Mr. Baker left." Sawley pushed his glasses back up his nose.

"Are you a member of Mr. Taft's congregation?"

"I was. I don't go there anymore. I can't take being badgered for more money all the time." He said it apologetically. Clearly he felt as if such a thing should not have bothered him so deeply.

"Is that your only reason, Mr. Sawley?" Warne pressed.

"Er . . . no." Sawley colored. "I . . . er . . ." He stopped again. He fiddled with his glasses, gulped, and then continued. "I was embarrassed because I'd been inquiring into their finances behind their backs, and . . . and I couldn't look them in the eye, for what I thought of them."

The jurors appeared mildly interested.

"We do not want to know your thoughts, Mr. Sawley," Warne said gravely. "Only what you did, and what you discovered that led to your opinions. The gentlemen of the jury will come to their own conclusions. How did you obtain access to these accounts?"

"I know how much I gave to the church," Sawley said carefully, watching Warne all the time. "I had a fair idea how much other people did. Some who gave were not always discreet, if it was a large amount. Not that I believe everything I'm told."

"That is hearsay, Mr. Sawley. What can you tell us that is fact?"

"The name of the main charity that the congregation's money was to go to, sir. Brothers of the Poor. They minister to people in desperate straits, especially in parts of Africa. That is where Mr. Taft said our money was going. Because they are a charity, their accounts are open to inspection, if you know where to go."

Several of the jurors straightened a little in their seats. One rather large man leaned forward.

"And you looked into their affairs?" Warne pressed Sawley. "To what degree? Are you qualified to do this?"

Sawley blinked. "I have no qualifications, sir, but I can do arithmetic. The Brothers of the Poor have sent less to Africa in all their time than our congregation gives them in a month."

"Perhaps they had certain expenses to meet in handling the money?" Warne suggested.

"You weren't listening, sir!" Sawley was becoming agitated, his glasses wobbling down his nose. "In the whole ten years of their existence, the Brothers of the Poor have sent only a few hundred pounds to Africa, or anywhere else. The poverty referred to in their title is their own. They are simple men who labor and pray."

"Are you sure you have the right people?" Warne would not be easily put off. "It seems a simple name. Perhaps theirs is not the only group that uses it?"

Sawley jammed his glasses up his nose again.

"Yes, I am sure. They take some money from Mr. Taft, and they are in regular touch with him."

Warne kept his voice calm. "Then how has this not come to notice before, Mr. Sawley? It would appear rather a gaping hole in Mr. Taft's accounting."

Sawley shifted his weight from one foot to the other. "It isn't there right now so as you can see it. It's all very complicated," he explained.

"Then how is it that you are able to see it, when others haven't?" Warne persisted.

Rathbone wondered why Warne was directing the jury's mind to this. Then he realized it must be because Warne needed to draw out the answer before Gavinton did so, far less gently, when Sawley would not have the chance to tell the court in his own words, or perhaps in Warne's words.

"I didn't," Sawley admitted uncomfortably. "Somebody asked me to look into it, because he was suspicious. And he told me what to look for."

"Who would that someone be?" Warne asked.

No one in the jury box moved.

Sawley avoided meeting his gaze. "I don't know. He did it anonymously. But I was so angry and distressed myself that I took him at his word . . . at least . . ."

"At least what, Mr. Sawley?" Warne was motionless, as gentle as he dared be. "Even if I believe you, and the financial evidence is incontrovertible, my learned friend Mr. Gavinton is going to want to know exactly how you came by it. Who was it that gave it to you? Who started you on the course of your investigations?"

Sawley looked trapped. Everyone in the courtroom listened intently. The jurors were staring at him. Even Rathbone found himself leaning forward slightly as if afraid he might miss a word.

Sawley drew in a deep breath, and his glasses slipped right off and clattered onto the floor of the witness stand. He did not dare bend down to search for them, but stood blinking.

"I didn't really see him. He came to my door one evening, late, well after dusk, and he stood away from the light of the lamp. I just knew that he was at least fifty, to judge from what I could see of his face, and his hair was gray, nearly white. I could see his hair, even though he had a hat on, because it was long. He was clean shaven, hollow cheeked. He was about my height, and thin."

"What did he say to you, Mr. Sawley?" Warne prompted.

Sawley shook his head. "He didn't ask me anything about myself.

As soon as he made sure who I was, he held out a package of papers and said that the information inside was what I was looking for. I didn't know what he meant." He shrugged thin shoulders. "I told him I wasn't looking for anything. He told me that I was. I needed to expose what Mr. Taft was doing, before he ruined me and all my friends. He pushed the packet into my hands then turned around and left."

"On foot?" Warne asked. "Did you see any carriage? Any hansom cab?"

Sawley shrugged again, looking bewildered.

"No. But I live on a short street, and he turned on the first corner. He could have got a hansom within a hundred yards. There's no point asking me who he was, or how he knew what I wanted, because I have no idea."

"And the papers he handed you?" Warne asked.

No one moved in the courtroom; there was not the rustle of fabric or the crack of a whalebone corset, not a sigh.

Rathbone found himself with hands clenched, muscles tight as he sat forward, waiting.

Sawley made a movement to fiddle with his glasses and remembered they were on the floor by his feet. He looked oddly helpless without them.

"Copies of the accounts and certain public charities, of Mr. Taft's Church," he answered. "Lots of figures and calculations. At first it didn't make sense to me, then I looked at them more carefully and cross-checked those with a red pencil mark beside them, and gradually I understood. It was very clear. You'd have to understand fraud to see it, the way the money was all moved around from one place to another. Everything seemed to be paid out honestly, until you followed it all the way, and saw how it came back around again. Hardly any of it really went to the people in Africa it was supposed to help."

"I see. And why would this mysterious stranger bring all this to you, Mr. Sawley?"

Sawley looked totally confused. "I've no idea, sir. I just know that he did."

Warne retired on that note, and Gavinton rose to try to undo some of the damage. He walked out into the middle of the floor without his usual slightly cocky swagger. Then he was obliged to wait to begin while Sawley crouched on the floor of the witness box and retrieved his glasses. When he stood up at last Gavinton spoke.

"Terribly convenient for you, Mr. Sawley," he observed with an acute edge of sarcasm to his voice. "Did anybody else see this . . . this apparition?"

Warne rose to his feet immediately.

"Yes," Rathbone agreed before he could voice his objection. "Mr. Gavinton, if you can prove that this was an apparition and not a real person, then please do so. Otherwise do not present assumptions as if they were facts."

Gavinton's face tightened in irritation, but he obeyed because he had no choice.

"I apologize, my lord. Mr. Sawley, did anyone besides yourself see the extraordinary person?"

Sawley put his glasses back on his nose.

"No, sir, not as far as I know. But the papers are real, and I didn't write them. I'm fairly good with figures, but I'm not anywhere near good enough to have worked out a fraud like this, or to have uncovered one. I had to read it half a dozen times before I saw what'd been done."

"We have only your word for that, sir," Gavinton pointed out.

Sawley shook his head. "If I were that good I'd be bookkeeper to some big company, not just a clerk who fills in for the accountant now and then."

"How do we know you're not good?" Gavinton asked, but there was desperation in his voice, and the jury heard it. His usual confidence was gone. Even in the gallery there was an echo of hollow laughter.

"'Cos if I could make that kind of money, I would," Sawley said simply.

"So you are quite a simple, very average, makeshift bookkeeper," Gavinton responded. "So why on earth did this brilliant stranger who can understand and expose a fraud as complex and cleverly planned as you say this one is—why did he seek out you, and not the police, or some other figure of authority and reputation? How do you explain such an extraordinary and eccentric choice, Mr. Sawley?"

"Maybe 'cos I was one of the congregation, and I know the people who are being cheated, some of them ruined, and I care," Sawley replied. "I'm angry at my friends being made fools of, when they thought they were sacrificing to help the poor, in the name of Christ, and I won't let that drop, however long it takes me, or however much you want to make me look like a fool too. There's nothing wicked about being a fool—there's a lot wicked about making fools of other people."

Rathbone himself, in spite of all his years of courtroom experience, felt a sudden hard tug of emotion. It cost him an effort of will not to voice his fierce agreement. He actually drew in his breath, and then let it out silently. The prosecution had already won.

4

THE NEW WEEK BEGAN with Blair Gavinton rising to present the case for the defense. He looked more confident than Rathbone had expected him to. Rathbone felt a shadow of anxiety that perhaps Gavinton had discovered something over the weekend that threw a different light on events, but he could not think what that might be.

The jurors regarded Gavinton with stony faces. To them he represented a man who abused and then mocked good-hearted, ordinary people who had acted with generosity and were now reaping the bitter harvest of disillusion. They would want Taft to pay an appropriately heavy price.

Surely as he stood and called his first witness, Gavinton had to be aware of that?

The witness's name was Robertson Drew. He walked across the floor and climbed the steps to the witness box with assurance. He was dark-haired, well-dressed, a man who was good-looking and not unaware of it. There was power in his hawk-nosed face and confidence in his voice when he took the oath.

Gavinton began quietly, without drama, as if they were two men whose conversation happened to be overheard by an entire courtroom.

"Mr. Drew, are you a member of Mr. Taft's congregation?"

"I am," Drew acknowledged. "I have been for many years. About ten or eleven, I think. I would like to believe I have been of some help to him in his ministry."

"Are you paid for this, sir?"

Drew looked surprised, even a trifle indignant, although he must have been prepared for all Gavinton's questions.

"Certainly not. It is a privilege that is its own reward."

"Have you had any dealings with the financial side of the ministry?" Gavinton asked, his tone still conversational. "Specifically the collection of donations to be offered to various charities for the poor?"

"I have, a great deal."

Rathbone saw the jurors paying close attention, but their expressions were hostile, ready to disbelieve him. "And did you find anything amiss in the accounting?" Gavinton inquired.

Drew smiled very slightly. "The occasional arithmetical error, usually to the amount of a few pennies. I dare say it would count to shillings, one way or the other, over a year or so. Such errors are always put right when the books are balanced."

"Once a year?" Gavinton inquired.

"Once a quarter, sir," Drew corrected him.

Gavinton nodded. "I see. And what do you make of the claims that there is a profound fraud going on, to the amount of tens of thousands of pounds, all very cleverly disguised in pages and pages of complex figures?"

Drew blinked then looked down at his strong hands on the railing. "Frankly, Mr. Gavinton, when one is trying to minister to a flock, one expects all manner of people. The doors of a Christian church cannot be closed to anyone. Those who come in will do so for many reasons and to fill many kinds of needs." His voice was sonorous with regret.

"We draw the rich and the poor, the strong and the weak, the quarrelsome and the silent." He looked up. "Quite frankly, we also draw the guilty, the troubled, at times the malicious, and also those whose mental balance is questionable, who seek attention and must have it at any cost. Occasionally we even have people who see and hear things that are not there, who imagine voices and labor under the delusion that they speak for God."

Rathbone saw a flash of amusement in Warne's eyes and knew that those words would be brought back to haunt Drew.

Gavinton nodded. "Of course. You do not deny anyone. And I imagine that the most deeply troubled are not always obviously so to the eye?"

"No," Drew agreed. "Some carry their wounds very deep within them. I would say this accusation, which is completely groundless, has come from a badly troubled person who labors under the delusion that he and he alone is vindicated by God to lead people. He possibly sees devils where there are none."

Warne rose to his feet. "My lord, so far as I am aware, the only person in this case who makes any attempt to lead people, and to say that he is privy to the thoughts of God, is the accused."

There were gasps of horror and a surge of nervous laughter from the gallery.

Rathbone had to feign a sneeze in order to cover his own laughter.

Gavinton was red-faced, his hands raised and clenched. From the witness stand Drew glared at him.

Warne stood there looking innocent. It was a feat of acting that earned Rathbone's admiration.

"My lord," he began again, "no witness I have called has claimed to see anything beyond what we can all see, or even suggested the existence of devils. It is Mr. Drew who is indulging in fantasy. Unless, of course, there is some monster here that Mr. Gavinton can see, and I cannot?" He looked around at the jurors, and then the gallery. "I see only human beings, good and bad, all fallible, but only human. Am I alone in that?"

Gavinton's face blushed a deep red, but it was anger, certainly not shame.

"My learned friend does not recognize an allusion when he hears one," he said between his teeth.

"I recognize an illusion when I see one," Warne snapped back.

Several of the jurors laughed then checked themselves immediately, glancing around as if to confirm that no one had noticed their lapse from decorum.

Rathbone smiled. "I think it would be wiser, Mr. Gavinton, if you were to request your witness to stay within the literal. Angels and devils are beyond my jurisdiction."

A juror wiped his eyes with a large handkerchief. In the gallery there was a definite ripple of amusement.

Gavinton looked at Drew with open warning in his expression. "Were you aware of this inquiry into Mr. Taft's financial affairs before you were called as a witness?" he asked.

"Yes, I was," Drew replied.

"Have you any idea where the interest came from that caused the inquiry?"

Drew squared his shoulders. "I took the time and trouble to find out, sir. We are used to having enemies, people whose beliefs are different from ours, or who feel threatened by our calls for charity toward the poor. It is a tragic aspect of human nature that many people who are more than comfortably situated themselves resent others showing the example of Christianity by sharing their substance, and asking that others do so too." His glance wandered to the jury, then back again to Gavinton. "It makes them feel uncomfortable, even guilty. I have begun to think that there is little in the world as painful to the mind as guilt."

A response flashed into Rathbone's mind, but he bit it back.

Warne half rose to his feet, then subsided again without speaking.

"Did you wish to object, sir?" Gavinton asked with mock concern.

"Not at all," Warne replied. "I realize that Mr. Drew may be uniquely qualified to speak on the subject."

It was a second before Gavinton realized Warne's meaning; then the laughter from the gallery enlightened him. He swung back to face Drew.

"Did you find out where this misleading information came from, Mr. Drew?" He raised his voice considerably.

"Yes I did." Drew's answer emerged through gritted teeth. "I am very sad to say that some of our own parishioners at one time or another gave more than they had budgeted for, and then when their expenses increased they were unable to cope. Of course, we knew nothing of it at the time, or we would have done what we could to help, in Christian charity. We could not give back their donations, if they wished us to, because they had already been passed on to the people for whom they were intended."

"Of course," Gavinton nodded. "Please continue."

"Some of these people had enlisted the help, or at least the sympathy, of outside sources who do not understand us or our aims."

"Do you know this for a fact, Mr. Drew? You have seen and spoken to such an outside source?" Gavinton interrupted.

Drew had completely regained his composure. "Yes. After I was aware of the accusations against Mr. Taft, I made it my concern to find out," he said, pursing his lips. "One of them I have no doubt of, having seen this person actually attending one of our services. And if I may say so, asking a number of questions that I ascribed to simple curiosity at the time, but looking back I realize were attempts at learning more of our business, especially our finances."

Gavinton looked skeptical. "Are you quite sure, Mr. Drew? Is it not possible that your own anxieties made you suspicious?"

"I thought so myself to begin with," Drew admitted. He never took his eyes from Gavinton. This time he did not even try to draw in the jury. "But I made a few inquiries out of curiosity, and learned a great deal more of her reputation. She is a childless woman who seems to be prone to finding causes and then crusading for them, not always with fortunate results."

Now he had the jury's attention, if reluctantly.

Warne began to look worried. Rathbone wondered why he had not challenged Gavinton, who was allowing Drew to level charges that lacked specificity. Why had Warne not pointed that out, and required that he name this woman, if he could?

"So you learned a good deal about this woman?" Gavinton glanced at Rathbone, and then back at Drew.

"Yes," Drew agreed. "She has done a degree of good running a free clinic for women of a certain sort, injured or diseased. But her compassion has become undisciplined, and led her into several rash enterprises . . ."

Rathbone froze. Drew had to be speaking of Hester. Did Warne know that, and that was why he had not pressed Drew to be specific?

"You hesitate," Gavinton pointed out to Drew.

"I do not wish to damage the woman's reputation unnecessarily," Drew answered, his voice smooth. "I don't think she intended harm, but at times she has totally misunderstood situations and, like an ill-trained horse, run off with the bit between her teeth."

Gavinton smiled at the expression and shot a dagger-sharp glance at Rathbone. It was only a second's deviation, so slight as to make Rathbone wonder if he had seen it at all or merely imagined it.

Warne stood up. "My lord, this is totally unsubstantiated imagination. A woman came to Mr. Taft's Church and her curiosity was awakened as to its work. Surely only a guilty conscience would see harm or irresponsibility in that? No prudent person gives money to an organization, even one claiming to do the work of God, without making some inquiries."

"Guard your tongue, Mr. Drew," Rathbone warned. "Or perhaps I should suggest, bridle it!"

The nervous tension broke, and there was a wave of stifled laughter around the gallery.

This time Gavinton was not disconcerted. He smiled back at Rathbone, showing his considerable teeth and then inclining his head in a slight bow.

"I shall have my witness be very specific, my lord." He looked up at Drew. "Perhaps, sir, you would oblige his lordship by telling the court

exactly what you know of this woman, and showing us that your information is accurate, provable, and relevant. The jury at least has a right
to this much, if they are to take it into account in their verdict."

"Of course," Drew conceded.

Rathbone grasped at last precisely why Gavinton had looked so
smug when proceedings had opened today, and why he had glanced at
Rathbone with a sly half smile on his face. It chilled him as if someone
had opened a door and allowed in a bitter wind. But there was nothing
he could do. It was a perfectly legitimate tactic. In fact, it was probably
what he himself would have done in Gavinton's place, and they both
knew it. It was going to be a rough few days. He would have to be very
careful not to make any errors or allow his emotions to dictate an action, or even a look or a word. If he did, the damage might be lasting.

No wonder Ingram York was glad not to have the case himself. It
crossed Rathbone's mind that York might also be glad he was the one
who had received it, especially considering how things had gone at the
dinner party. A moment later he dismissed the thought. York didn't
even know him. Why would he care, one way or the other? And what
was one dinner party?

But then, one dinner party had been enough to convince him that
York's wife was one of the loveliest women he had ever seen. There was
a beauty in her face far deeper than feature or coloring; he had seen the
intelligence there, the humor, and a quality of gentleness that seemed
to signify an ability to dream—and to be hurt. He thought of the room
with yellow walls that she desired that would appear as if it were filled
with sunlight. There would be no tension in such a place, he thought.
No seeking to find fault. It would be a place where dreams were safe.

There was a noise of scraping wood.

He was not paying attention. He jerked his mind back. Drew was
speaking.

"The clinic in question is in Portpool Lane," Drew said. "It is run by
a Mrs. Hester Monk. Her husband, William Monk, is commander of
the Thames River Police, and she has been known in the past to have

a considerable involvement in some of his more serious cases, ones of violence and . . . obscenity."

There was a ripple of interest around the gallery and one of the jurors nodded to himself with a little shiver.

"Which is natural enough, I suppose," Drew continued, "because she is in daily contact with much of the lesser criminal elements in the city who might have information that her husband could use in his investigations."

Two more of the jurors nodded.

Gavinton was smiling. Warne was almost expressionless. Had he any idea what was coming?

Drew resumed his explanation. "The establishment Mrs. Monk runs is, of necessity, on the edge of the criminal underworld. Those are the people she is endeavoring to help, and as a woman of compassion, she reaches out to them. The trouble is that her judgment is rather too often swayed by her emotions."

Gavinton held up his hand to stop Drew, and then took a step closer to the stand. His voice was smooth, placating.

"That is a sweeping statement to make, Mr. Drew. I'm afraid you need to be less general, and more specific," he explained. "You cannot expect the court to accept what you say either as factual or as relevant, unless you can show us by an example, the truth of which my learned friend can question and test." He looked up at Rathbone again, and this time there was clear victory in his eyes.

Rathbone would have paid a high price for the chance to retaliate effectively, but he had no weapon, and they both knew it.

Drew was well primed. "Of course." He bowed very slightly, his lips drawn tight in a gesture of distaste, as if he were actually reluctant to answer. "A year or two ago there was a case involving a most unpleasant man by the name of Jericho Phillips." He enunciated each word carefully. "He was accused of using small orphaned children—all boys, so far as I know—in a riverboat he owned. He made obscene photographs of them." His voice trembled with anger. "He even used some of them as child prostitutes, and then blackmailed his wretched clients. The worst of his crimes was the murder of an unknown number of these unfortunate boys when they rebelled, or reached an age when they were no longer to his clients' taste."

He waited a few moments for the horror of what he was describing to sink into the minds of the listeners and take shape, and then he continued, his voice a little lower, as if the horror of it all had crushed him.

"Mrs. Monk's evidence was crucial to his trial." A look of intense regret filled his face. "Unfortunately she was so carried away, so incensed at the brutality of the crime, and so sure in her own mind that Phillips was guilty, that she neglected to be certain of her proof. Her emotion was understandable to anyone, but courts deal in law, as they must, for the protection of both the innocent and the victims, and for those few who are assumed guilty but in fact are not."

It was clever. It was a passionate defense for Taft, while appearing to be about Hester and an entirely different case. Rathbone was seething. The muscles in his body knotted and his jaw was tight, but there was nothing whatever that he could do about it.

From the look of anxiety in his eyes, Warne also knew what was coming next. The case would be familiar to many people. It had been headline news at the time, and what had followed had been even worse.

Drew gave a slight shrug. It looked like regret, almost an apology for so distressing the court. "Because of her ineptitude, her placing of heart before head," he said softly, "Phillips was found not guilty, and set free. As was only to be expected, he continued on his path of repulsive crime. He was, of course, later apprehended and killed, but he did not face the law again, as he certainly should have. Once exonerated, he could never again be tried for that earlier crime."

There was a murmur of distress in the gallery. Several jurors shook their heads sadly. One of them rubbed his hand across his face in a gesture of dismay.

"It was a brilliant lawyer who defended Phillips," Drew went on, his voice now laden with irony. "He tied Mrs. Monk up in knots with the rope of her own making."

He had not looked at Rathbone, but Gavinton did and smiled. He gave a very slight bow, almost too small for one to be sure it had occurred. Those in the gallery might have missed his implication, but most of the jurors would not. If they were curious, it would take only a question or two outside the courtroom and they would have the answer.

"Which, of course, was the lawyer's duty," Gavinton quickly added for good measure. He could not resist the temptation to preach as well. "If the law is not just to all of us, then it is not just to any, and we are all in danger. It would be a license to accuse anyone, and to crucify him for crimes he did not commit. Thank you, Mr. Drew." He moved as if to return to his seat and then swung around to face the witness box again.

"I apologize. In my enthusiasm for the law I forgot to make clear the purpose of raising Mrs. Monk's name. You say she came to your church? To one service?"

"Yes," Drew agreed. "So far as I know she did not return."

"Then what has she to do with this accusation against Mr. Taft? It is not she who is making this charge; it is the police."

Drew smiled. "In Mrs. Monk's clinic for street women she has a bookkeeper who, I hear, is gifted with figures. In the past he indulged in some very . . . creative . . . accounting when he ran the same buildings as one of the most profitable brothels in London. I doubt there is a form of financial fraud with which he does not have at least a passing acquaintance. His physical description answers exactly that of the man who called so mysteriously upon Mr. Sawley and handed him the papers from which he drew his conclusions about the funds of the church. I think the jury may well question Mrs. Monk's reasons for visiting us, and exactly where Mr. Sawley obtained his information."

"Indeed," Gavinton said with gleaming satisfaction. "One might wonder what interested her in Mr. Taft, but unless she wishes to tell us I dare say we shall never know."

"There is not far to look." Drew's smile was now unmistakably a sneer. "She has recently taken on a new young woman to assist her, by the name of Josephine Raleigh. She is the only daughter of the same John Raleigh who chose to give testimony against Mr. Taft last week.

Regrettably he overestimated his finances and is now blaming Mr. Taft for it. We could have given him back some of his money, but we sent it on to the charity for which it was donated as soon as we could. It was no longer in our possession. It is very sad, but it was beyond our power to help."

There was total silence in the room. The air was hot, almost stiflingly so. Rathbone felt as if there were nothing to breathe, and the sweat trickled down his body.

"And you believe this to be Mrs. Monk's reason for asking her somewhat unusual bookkeeper to involve himself in Mr. Taft's affairs?" Gavinton asked with sad understanding.

"I do," Drew answered. "That she did so seems to be unarguable, and I can think of no other reason for it; she has never been to our church before, or since."

"The one occasion you refer to, some eight or nine weeks ago?" Gavinton asked.

"That is so," Drew agreed.

Rathbone waited in vain for Warne to object. It seemed he had been attacked completely on the blind side and had no idea what to challenge, or how. Please heaven that by the time he came to cross-examine Drew he would have some weapon for a counterattack. Gavinton had managed to raise considerable doubt as to the veracity of any of the evidence against Taft. In fact, he had made it look like the fabrication of a rather unbalanced woman, with the help of a frankly semi-criminal former brothel keeper.

There was a bitter irony to it that cut Rathbone deeply. It was exactly what he had done in defense of Jericho Phillips—who had been guilty of far more depravity than Abel Taft. A single look at Gavinton's face showed that he was quite aware of it and that he savored it with relish.

The remaining part of the day Gavinton spent in going through the facts and figures in the accounts that condemned Taft. Drew had explanations for all of it. Gavinton was careful what he chose to ask about, but there was such a mass of information that the jury began to look glassy-eyed. Presumably that was Gavinton's intention. You cannot convict a man if you do not understand the entirety of what he is supposed to have done.

RATHBONE LEFT FOR THE day disturbed by his inability to do anything except watch and listen as Gavinton reversed the whole atmosphere and flavor of the case. He had begun the day backed into a corner from which it looked as if he had no escape; he had ended it having painted Hester as a hysterical and somewhat foolish woman with a habit of meddling in affairs that were really not her concern, at times to tragic results, and that in this case she had accused a good man of a criminal fraud of which he was entirely innocent.

Gavinton would call Taft tomorrow, as soon as Warne had had a chance to question Robertson Drew. Drew was supremely confident; it oozed out of him like sweat on a hot day. Rathbone imagined he could smell it in the air, oily and sickly sweat.

What could Warne attack? Rathbone had no doubt that Drew's account of Hester's involvement was accurate in all its main assumptions. He knew Hester well enough to believe that it was precisely what she would do. He wondered for a moment why she had not mentioned it at least one of the times they had met in the past month. Of course the bookkeeper clever enough and sufficiently well versed in fraud to understand Taft's tricks was Squeaky Robinson. Rathbone had met Squeaky a few times and recognized the description. It was Rathbone who had tricked Squeaky out of the brothel buildings in Portpool Lane, the same buildings Hester had turned into the clinic. Squeaky had had a twisted and reluctant respect for Rathbone ever since. And if he was honest with himself, Rathbone had a certain respect for Squeaky also. That alone might answer why Hester had not burdened him with knowledge of the affair.

How like her!

Perhaps it would be unwise to see her. She might very well be called as a witness.

He thought about it as his hansom wove in and out of the other carriages on the road. He was still turning it over in his mind as he entered his house.

What was there that Warne could rebut? Would it be in his interests or only make matters worse, if he were to delve into the accounts again and try to argue any of the figures? Gavinton had very cleverly seen to it that the jury's threshold for details about numbers was crossed and left far behind.

Rathbone gave his hat and stick to his butler and asked him to bring a whisky and soda.

Were the proceedings Rathbone had watched play out in court, without any interference from himself, evidence of brilliant legal ability on Gavinton's part, or somehow a sleight of hand that he ought to have been able to prevent? Did it even matter, as far as he was concerned, whether Taft was innocent or guilty? His title was "judge," but actually he had no legal or moral right to judge the most important issue they were met to decide. He was there to make sure that the law was observed, to the letter and to the spirit. The verdict was the jury's alone.

But surely there was something he could do?

He chose to sit in his study rather than the withdrawing room. The withdrawing room was beautiful, but it had been so much Margaret's room as well as his that memories of her haunted it. These were not happy thoughts intruding into today's loneliness; they were a sad recognition of things he should have better understood, futile now because he could not go back.

He sipped the whisky and let the flavor and the fire of it roll around in his mouth.

Eventually he put the glass down and went outside to walk through the garden in the twilight and listen to the soft sounds of the oncoming night.

THE FOLLOWING DAY GAVINTON recalled Robertson Drew to the stand. They did not refer to Hester again but instead directed the attack at

Gethen Sawley, the witness who had produced the crucial papers, the only physical evidence of fraud.

Rathbone wondered if Gavinton intended to produce anyone from the charity that supposedly had received the money. Warne had not. Surely, if such a person existed, that would put an end to the matter? Perhaps they did not exist, and Warne would tell the jury so in his summation; that would be the best time to do it. They could not possibly forget!

He returned his attention to the proceedings.

Gavinton was asking Drew about Cuthbert Bicknor.

Drew was very composed today. He shrugged casually. "A pleasant young man, but—I have to be honest—very easily influenced. Desperate to be liked, approved of." He sighed. "It is not a fault. I'm sure we can all understand the need for the regard of our fellows. And if you want friends, where better to look for them than in a church?" He raised his hands in a gesture of inclusion, and smiled toward the jury. "You will meet good people, well spoken, sober, generous, seeking to become even better. But"—he let out his breath in a sigh—"it is possible to mistake a politely friendly manner for something deeper. I think Cuthbert read meaning into people's words that his interlocutors may not have intended. Because of that, he gave away his money too easily and realized afterward that he had overstretched himself, and then he didn't know what to do about it."

"But he was willing for his father to testify on his behalf against Mr. Taft," Gavinton pointed out. "Quite powerfully, in fact. That doesn't sound like the act of a young man so devoted to the church and its congregation that he would bankrupt himself."

Drew waved his hand with a slightly impatient dismissal. "I did not say that he was devoted to the church, sir. I said he was looking for friendship and that approval mattered to him rather out of proportion to . . . I don't want to be unkind, but to an emotional balance. I am sure that if a lawyer as skilled and charming as Mr. Warne were to pay him attention and court his . . . his desire to be important, then he would find some way of obliging him, no matter the request."

This time Warne did rise to his feet. "My lord, Mr. Drew is all but accusing me of suborning perjury, and Mr. Bicknor of being of less than sound mind. Mr. Bicknor is not here to refute that, but I most certainly am. If Mr. Drew believes that I coerced Mr. Bicknor's father's testimony, then I require that he provide proof. And if I were to call him a liar, as I would dearly like to, I still require proof, or I myself will stand condemned."

"Your point is well taken, Mr. Warne," Rathbone said with some relief. "Mr. Drew, you are not free to say whatever you like because you are in the witness stand. If you are suggesting that Mr. Warne has acted inappropriately, or that Mr. Bicknor is emotionally unstable, we require evidence to that end, not just your conjecture. If not, I advise you to be careful, Mr. Drew. I see several journalists in the public gallery, and your parishioners would be less loyal to you, I think, if they fully appreciated the extent, or lack, of your loyalty to them."

Gavinton was furious. His face lost its smooth control. "My lord! Mr. Drew's words may have been a little . . . ill chosen . . . but he is only attempting to tell the court the truth. Cuthbert Bicknor, through his father, has attempted to slander Mr. Taft and accuse him of a most despicable fraud. Mr. Taft has the right to defend himself, and for others to defend him, from this charge. It is not only his livelihood that is at stake—it is also his good name, which is of far more importance to him, as is true of many of us."

"Indeed," Rathbone agreed. "As is Mr. Warne's. Perhaps this problem can be answered by allowing Mr. Warne a certain latitude in questioning this witness, so as to establish what grounds Mr. Drew has for making such an allegation."

Gavinton frowned. He turned to Drew again.

"Let us leave the subject of Mr. Bicknor. The main evidence of a material nature, something more than hearsay and supposition, is this large sheaf of accounting papers Mr. Sawley says he obtained from the man with the long gray hair and apparently without name. Mr. Sawley claimed not to know him, but you have told us that you believe he is a former brothel keeper by the name of Robinson. Mr. Sawley says that he had not met this man before—this Mr. Robinson—that he simply turned up on his doorstep and offered him these papers."

The jury's attention had been captured again by Rathbone's interjection. One rather rotund gentleman took out a handkerchief and wiped his brow. Their eyes moved from Drew to Gavinton and back again.

Warne still looked slightly unhappy.

Gavinton was deliberately, exaggeratedly careful.

"I do not ever imply that Mr. Sawley was telling us less than the exact truth. The story is so extraordinary, how could he have imagined it?" Drew looked up at Rathbone, challenge and loathing in his face, open and unmistakable.

"Indeed." Gavinton swiveled very slightly to face the jury. "Gentlemen, I assume my client to be innocent, as I am sure the court does, unless and until proved otherwise. That is every man's right, is it not? That is the basis of the law. His lordship, you may not know, was the lawyer who so brilliantly defended Jericho Phillips—not because he admired the man, or wished him to escape justice, but because above all other things, he serves the law. He holds it sacred that everyone, no matter who, no matter the crime, is entitled to defend himself."

Warne closed his eyes, his face tight, lips drawn into a grimace. Rathbone realized that Warne had not known it was Rathbone who defended Phillips. And why should he! Why would he study the past cases of a judge, from a time before that judge was on the bench? Surely only his decisions since appointment were relevant?

Or did everything matter?

Rathbone was furious. He felt so cornered that for a moment he lost his temper. "What are you looking for, Mr. Gavinton? A round of applause? Please continue to your point, which I believe had something to do with Mr. Sawley and how he acquired the evidence of fraud—other than by simply opening the door to Mr. Robinson."

"Indeed I can, my lord," Gavinton said, his voice soft, his composure regained. He had pricked Rathbone and he knew it.

In that moment Rathbone felt fear, not of Gavinton, but of failing his own responsibility. He must not allow himself to be provoked again.

It was difficult. Gavinton led Robertson Drew carefully, question after question into destroying Gethen Sawley. It was always to do with the papers, however obliquely. Warne objected that it was irrelevant, and Rathbone was obliged to overrule him. The thread of connection was thin at times, but it existed.

Gavinton asked about the history of Sawley's relationships with members of the congregation, always finding the weak spot, the conversation that could be misinterpreted. He savored the tales of times Sawley took offense where it was not intended and afterward apologized too much, appearing to be emotionally erratic, too eager to please. Drew very subtly held him up to ridicule, questioning his judgment, even his honesty in small things.

Warne objected again.

Rathbone upheld him, but the damage had been done.

"But his religious views were the same as your own, and those of Mr. Taft?" Gavinton persisted.

Warne was on his feet again. "My lord, Mr. Sawley's religious beliefs are his own concern. He is not required to explain them to us, or to anyone."

"They are relevant to his persecution of Mr. Taft, my lord," Gavinton replied with elaborate patience. "If they had been the same as those of Mr. Taft and Mr. Drew, then he would have rejoiced in the opportunity to give to the desperately poor. He would have seen it as Christ's work on earth."

Warne was furious. "My lord, a man has the right to interpret Christ's work on earth in any way he pleases! And he should be free to give help as he pleases—or not! And as his own means allow. To suggest otherwise is preposterous!"

"Of course," Gavinton said with a shrug and that flashing smile with too many teeth. "And Mr. Bicknor was free to give or not. He chose to give, and when he had misjudged his own finances and got himself into debt, he blamed not his own inaccuracies, but Mr. Taft, and set about trying to stir up a wave of accusation against him. I am seeking only to show that Mr. Bicknor—and Mr. Sawley—are unreliable men, motivated by their own embarrassment and inadequacies, not by a love of truth, or a pity for the unfortunate. This whole farrago of lies that this creature Robinson dug up is a pathetic man's revenge, no more than that. In Mr. Taft's defense, I must be allowed to demonstrate that this is the case."

Rathbone was seething, but he could not stop him. Morally and legally Gavinton was right.

Gavinton continued, very carefully, always just within the rules of evidence, always relevant to the accounting proof Squeaky Robinson had given. But piece by piece he also dismantled Bicknor's reputation, creating the impression that Bicknor was weak and indecisive, someone who had acted foolishly and then, when caught out, had descended into spite.

It was an agonizing spectacle to watch and Rathbone longed to intervene, but Gavinton was far too careful to give him grounds to do so.

The case against Taft was slipping away, and Rathbone felt it go. He could see it in the jurors' faces. He looked at Warne, hoping for some retaliation, but nothing came. He looked at Robertson Drew and read the satisfaction in his eyes, his smile, the victory that glowed in his very presence. And as he did so, Rathbone became more and more convinced that it was victory. It was not just defense of a man he was closely associated with, very possibly a long-standing friend, but something more.

A memory flashed across his mind as he watched Drew. He had seen him somewhere else. He tried to recall where it had been. For Drew this was a very personal issue, Rathbone was now sure of it, although he could not have said why he thought so.

But why? Rathbone racked his memory but he still could not recall having met Drew in any other circumstance. Yet, it was clear the man disliked him. What cause could there be for a grudge? He doubted they would've crossed paths socially; perhaps he had encountered him in the courtroom, on a different case?

He looked at Drew on the stand as he continued to tear apart and denigrate one prosecution witness after another. Rathbone could not recall seeing him there before. He tried picturing him differently dressed and couldn't.

His search was drawing his attention from the proceedings, but they were droning on. The heat in the room was oppressive. People in the gallery fidgeted. The jury sat glassy-eyed and uncomfortable. This was Drew's second day on the stand. He was not saying anything different; Gavinton was simply moving to the next witness. The jury believed him. Rathbone could see it in their faces. He could also see that Warne had nothing in reserve. His expression was a mask carefully maintained to conceal his defeat. Rathbone had worn the same expression often enough himself to recognize it in another.

Where had he seen Drew before? It could not be merely that his name was involved with a case in which Rathbone had either prosecuted or defended. He must have been present in court because Rathbone remembered his face. They had been looking at each other. They must have been introduced in some way.

Then all at once it came to him. He had seen Robertson Drew in one of Ballinger's photographs—fornicating with a small boy on Jericho Phillips's boat. That explained where the hatred came from: it had been Rathbone, with Monk's help, and Hester's, who had finally brought about Phillips's death and the end of that particular part of the trade in children. That was why Drew was so pleased to blacken Hester's name, make her appear foolish, overemotional, a meddling woman with more pity than sense.

Of course he had posed for the photograph. That was the piece of wild, unnecessary risk-taking that was the price of admission to the club. Drew must've known that Ballinger had possessed it, especially if he had been one of those Ballinger had blackmailed. But he could not know that Ballinger had bequeathed the photos to Rathbone, or indeed that Rathbone had ever even seen them.

Rathbone looked at Drew again and was certain—almost.

It was not yet half past three in the afternoon. Too early to adjourn. He could think of no excuse to halt the proceedings until tomorrow. Nevertheless, as soon as Drew had finished his long and rather rambling answer to Gavinton's last question, without excuse or giving any reason, Rathbone adjourned the court until the following morning.

Amid whisperings, questions, looks of confusion, the assembly rose and left. Outside in the hallways little groups huddled together earnestly. As he passed one of them, Rathbone was close enough to overhear the urgent questions as to what had happened. What had suddenly changed?

He was not sure that anything had. His mind was in turmoil. He needed time alone in which to think. Did his realization make any difference? Could it?

As HE RODE HOME in a hansom he felt so tense his body ached and his fingernails bit into the flesh of his palms.

The first thing was to be sure. He thought he was right, but he had mistaken people in the street before, thinking he knew them then realizing with embarrassment that he didn't. Once he had even addressed someone, only to have the man turn full face to him, revealing himself a stranger.

As soon as he was in his own house he refused any offer of tea, or whisky, and went into his study, locking the door. No one must ever see him with this horror! He took the photographs from their hiding place.

His hands were trembling, his fingers clumsy as he unlocked the box containing the photographic plates. He opened the lid and it nearly slid out of his grasp. He clutched with the other hand and let the lid fall backward.

The heavy sheets of glass were stacked neatly next to each other but not so close as to prevent them being removed one at a time. The printed paper copies were kept separately in a heavy brown envelope. He had looked at them only once. They held images he would rather not have known about.

He slid the paper out of the envelope onto the table, glancing at the door, needing to reassure himself it was locked. He did not want even the most trusted servant to know of these. How could he explain looking at such things to anyone? Evidence? Yes, they had been, but not in any current case. So why had he kept them? Why not destroy them as soon as they were his and he had the right to? They were obscene and dangerous, the key to blackmailing some of the most important men in the land. There were people he could destroy with these, careers, families he could ruin.

That was not how he had thought of them, though. They were revolting, but they were indelible proof of crimes against children, so repellent and so compulsively woven into the nature of most of those who committed them that they would almost certainly happen again and again.

But what he saw now was the power to humble the men who had had the bravado, the arrogance to be photographed, the power to make them repay some of the debt they owed. They could never make it up to the children themselves—too many were missing or dead—but there were other causes.

Ballinger had begun the whole hideous performance by using the photograph of a senior judge to make him command an industrialist to stop the pollution that had spread disease and death to an entire community. Usurers had been forced to forgive debt caused by exorbitant interest. Other wrongs had been redressed. Then finally the power had become its own end, and all the original passion for justice or mercy was swallowed up—the only thing that had mattered was survival.

Not that Ballinger had survived. His deeds had destroyed him.

But there was a saying that Rathbone could never forget: "All that is necessary for the triumph of evil is that good men do nothing."

Was he going to do nothing while Robertson Drew destroyed Bicknor and Sawley? They might be weak in some ways, but wasn't that true of every single person? And if Squeaky Robinson had said Taft was a fraudster, then Rathbone firmly believed that he was.

But he had sworn to himself that he would never use these pictures again, unless someone's life was in jeopardy, and there was no other way out. This case was only about money.

Or was it? It was also about faith and honor, belief in a church and a God who was both just and merciful . . . a God who loved his people. Taft was not only robbing them of a quality of life, he was robbing them of their faith. Surely that was a sin almost as terrible as stealing their lives?

What does a good, simple man suffer if he is betrayed by the servants of the God he trusted? Who does he turn to then?

The law. And if the law not only allows the injustice to stand but also permits him to be mocked by his peers and ridiculed by those who have robbed him, who then can he turn to?

One by one Rathbone looked through the photographs. Perhaps his memory had led him astray and Drew was not here, only someone who looked a bit like him. Then there was no dilemma.

He was halfway through and the sights in front of him were vile enough to turn his stomach. He could not imagine subjecting an animal to the pain and humiliation these children endured. It was some comfort to know that Jericho Phillips had died hideously, in terror. But that was only revenge; it did not undo what had happened.

If Drew were among these pictures, was that justification for Rathbone to punish him? No, of course it wasn't.

Should he have handed over all the photographs as soon as he had them from Ballinger's estate? No. Too much of society would collapse under the weight, and the horror, of what they revealed. There were pictures of prominent men in this small, heavy box—judges, members of Parliament, of the Church, high society, the army and navy. All were weak men, but perhaps some were guilty of only one drunken excursion into this cesspit of indulgence, a moment they would deeply and painfully regret for the rest of their lives. Did they deserve to be ruined?

Then there it was in his hands, a clear, completely unmistakable photograph of Robertson Drew. It was as he had remembered, Drew staring at the camera, defying it to curb his pleasure.

Rathbone could not look at the child's face.

He separated the photograph from the others, moved it to the front of the pile and put them all away. He closed the lid of the box and locked it again. He replaced it where it had been in the safe, completely concealed. He hid the key, also in a place he believed no one would look, in plain sight, and yet unrecognizable.

He was sweating, and yet he was cold.

He took the brandy decanter and poured himself a stiff drink, then stood by the window with the curtains undrawn and gazed at the evening breeze stirring the branches of the trees. In the last light the leaves fluttered and turned, one moment pale, the next shadowed.

He had never felt more alone.

He finished the brandy and put his glass down again. He had not tasted it; it could have been cold tea.

What was the right thing to do?

Not to act is to condone what is happening, tacitly even to become part of it. He alone had the power to act—he had the photograph.

Later, he lay awake, alone in the big bed, battling with himself. Should he intervene or not? What was the brave thing to do? What was the honorable thing?

Whatever he did it was a decision both he and others would have to live with for the rest of their lives.

By morning, tired, head aching, he had still reached no definite conclusion.

5

WHEN THE TRIAL OF Abel Taft resumed the following morning, Blair Gavinton rose to his feet and straightaway recalled Robertson Drew.

Rathbone sat on his high, carved judge's seat slightly above the body of the court. He felt as if he had sand in his eyes, and his mouth was as dry as wool. The photograph was seared so deeply on his mind it might as well have burned a scorch mark onto his retina.

The jury, to his right, sat in two rows. They looked refreshed. Perhaps they were no longer struggling with decisions. Drew's testimony could have made up their minds for them. Taft was an innocent man, the victim of misfortune and the distress and malice of lesser people, followers who could not keep up the pace of his Christian charity. It was a nice comfortable answer. They would all feel happier with it, sorry for Bicknor and Sawley, especially sorry for John Raleigh, but essentially identifying with Drew—as Gavinton had intended.

Rathbone watched Drew as he climbed the steps and took his place in the witness box again. Was he still the same man inside who had raped that child in front of the camera? Or had he repented of that, perhaps bitterly and with tears of horror and remorse, even secretly paid what penance he could? Was his joining of Abel Taft's Church an act of contrition, a plea for God's mercy as regards his past?

And if it were, or were not, had Rathbone any right to judge the man for it, and exact the terrible punishment that exposure of that photograph would bring? No, of course he hadn't. There was no question about that.

"How long have you known Abel Taft, Mr. Drew?" Gavinton began.

Drew considered for several seconds before replying. "Seven or eight years, as closely as I can recall."

Interesting, Rathbone thought. The photograph had been dated. He had known Taft during the time of his membership in Phillips's club. So his joining the Church was not an act of penance? He must be sure.

He leaned forward and interrupted.

"And have you been a member of his congregation all that time, Mr. Drew?" Rathbone asked.

Drew looked slightly surprised. "Yes, my lord. I met him as I joined. I heard him preach and recognized immediately a voice of conviction rather than the voice of a man merely earning his living by the cloth." He bowed his head a little. "I apologize if that seems critical of the clergy. I don't mean it to be so. I'm sure there are many churchmen who have given their lives to the service of others, and done it with a whole heart. I simply believe that Mr. Taft has given more."

"To charity?" Rathbone questioned mildly. He kept his hands below the level of the ornate bench, where his slightly trembling fist could not be seen.

"Precisely," Drew agreed.

Rathbone let out his breath and leaned back again, indicating to Gavinton that he should continue.

There was little more to add, just a reaffirmation of the amount passed to charity and the denial that any of the papers Hester Monk's bookkeeper had given Mr. Sawley were of any worth or validity at all.

Gavinton excused Drew, with thanks, and called Abel Taft to testify in his own defense.

There was a moment or two of restless silence while Taft was brought from the dock, down the stairs, and back into the courtroom. Previously Rathbone had been able to see only his shoulders and face, and not even that unless he had deliberately turned his head to look up. Now Taft was far more visible. He was a striking man in appearance, of good posture, and with commanding features. His thick, fair hair was streaked with silver at the temples. It was not difficult to see why he commanded attention.

He climbed to the witness stand with confidence. One could not blame the jury if they believed he was an innocent man who trusted that the court, in its honesty, would find him so. Rathbone knew Taft might well leave the courtroom vindicated, more famous than before, and with the sympathy deserved by one who had been falsely accused and had to endure the strain and indignity of a public trial.

He swore to his name and address, and that he was a preacher of the gospel of Christ. Gavinton asked for all of this in a tone of great respect.

He was standing in the middle of the floor, like a gladiator in the arena. Rathbone had stood exactly there himself more times than he could count. He knew the feeling, the rush of excitement, the heart racing—and he knew the effect it had on the jury.

No one coughed or rustled as Gavinton began.

"Mr. Taft, you have been accused of a wretched, devious, and deceitful crime. Many of your erstwhile parishioners have given evidence against you. Loyal friends and colleagues, like Robertson Drew, have defended you with passion, and in detail. Your faithful wife is sitting here day after day, with you in spirit during this ordeal." He made a slight gesture to indicate to the jury where Felicia Taft was sitting white-faced and desperately miserable. At the mention of her name she tried to smile, and the effort only made her distress all the more obvious.

Rathbone considered her. She was a pretty woman, but there was no life in her face, no vitality. Happiness would have made her attractive. All he could feel for her now was a growing pity as he became more and more convinced that, previous to the charges, she had had no idea of any kind of fraud in her husband's ministry. She seemed half numb from the shock. Perhaps for the first time in her married life she was contemplating the possibility that he was not the ideal man she had supposed. What connection had she had with his reality, day by day?

For that matter, how easy is it to dupe anyone who loves and wants to believe? How much had he seen in Margaret that was rooted in his own mind, not in hers? If you truly love someone, should you not bring out the best in them, rather than the worst? And wouldn't you yourself strive to be the best? Was that not a measure of love, rather than need or possessiveness?

Gavinton was asking questions now.

"Mr. Taft, what was the purpose of your ministry, briefly?" he inquired. "I ask so the court can understand your intentions, and the need and use of the funds you receive."

Taft smiled very slightly. "I preach the gospel of Christ to the poor in spirit," he answered. "And by that I mean those who are humble enough to listen, and to help those poor in the world's necessities, the cold, the hungry, and the homeless, sometimes also the sick. Clearly, to do this we must have money." His voice was smooth, well practiced. "We ask those who are true believers, generous of spirit, to give as they can. In doing this, both the giver and the receiver are blessed. It is not complicated. Serve God by loving your neighbor. It is the message Christ himself taught when he was here on earth."

"It sounds very simple," Gavinton said, lowering his voice in respect. "One would wonder how anybody could take issue with it, except perhaps because it requires effort and sacrifice."

Warne rose to his feet. "My lord, if we wish to hear a sermon we will go to Mr. Taft's Church for it. The court requires that he defend himself from charges of fraud, not tell us what Christ taught regarding charity. If my learned friend has no questions for Mr. Taft, I certainly have."

Rathbone looked at Gavinton. "Mr. Gavinton, please phrase what you have to say in the form of questions. We also require that you make them relevant to the case. Be precise. The prosecution has spoken of very exact sums of money given by specific people. That is what you must speak to, if you are to prove Mr. Taft's innocence."

Gavinton stiffened in annoyance, but it was only momentary. He believed he had a winning hand, but he did not take kindly to being told how to play it.

"Of course, my lord," he said a little sharply, then looked up at the witness stand again. His manner altered completely, respectful again. "Mr. Taft, are you aware of the individual sums given by your parishioners?"

"No, sir," Taft said courteously. "I preach, and I ask the congregation to donate when they can in general terms. I am concerned with overall principles. I make it my business to thank people, when I am aware of their gifts, but I leave the details to others."

"Specifically to Mr. Robertson Drew?" Gavinton's eyebrows rose.

"Yes."

"Have you known him a long time?"

"Yes." Taft offered a rueful smile. "More years than I care to remember."

"You trust him?"

"Of course. I would hardly leave something of such importance in the hands of a man I did not trust. That would be not only foolish but morally quite wrong."

Gavinton considered for a moment. Every man in the jury was watching him. He looked up at Taft. "You have heard several men testify in this case saying that they were pressured into giving more money than they could afford and that they therefore fell into financial difficulties themselves, they turned to you for help, and you did not give it. Is that true?"

Taft bit his lip and shook his head very slightly. He gave the impression of confusion and regret. "As Mr. Drew explained, we no longer had the sums in our possession," he said sadly. "We pass over money almost as soon as we have it. The people to whom we give it are in desperate need. Had I known at the time that it was more than the givers could afford I would have declined to take it."

"But you didn't ask if they could afford it?" Gavinton queried.

Taft looked horrified. "Of course not! If a man offers you money to give to the poor, you don't ask him if he can afford it. It is at best patronizing, as if you thought him incapable of managing his own affairs." He gave a little shiver. "At worst it is downright insulting."

"Of course. I wouldn't either," Gavinton agreed. "I dare say no one in this court would. I am going to ask another question that I would not, were this not a trial in which reputations are at stake. Do you trust Mr. Drew absolutely in matters of money?"

"In all matters," Taft said instantly. "I would not have him in the position he is if I didn't."

"Is he responsible for the finances of your Church?"

"He is." Taft straightened even a fraction more. "But if you are implying that any of this misfortune is his fault, then you are mistaken. I placed him in charge. The fault, if there is one, is mine."

"Nobly spoken, sir," Gavinton said warmly.

Rathbone felt a wave of revulsion wash over him, but he saw the respect in the jurors' faces and knew that Gavinton, for all his unctuousness, was striking exactly the right note for them. The disgust in Rathbone, if it were misread in his expression, would reflect badly on him. Whatever it cost him, he must appear to be completely neutral. Above all else, he must not give the defense grounds for appeal because he appeared to be biased.

Warne's frustration was visible not only in his face but also in the angles of his body; yet there was nothing for him to object to in legal terms.

Gavinton continued with Taft, drawing out details of his relationship with the men who had testified against him, first Bicknor, then John Raleigh, and lastly Gethen Sawley. His questioning dragged on until the luncheon adjournment and resumed afterward. Delicately, as if with great reluctance, Taft displayed the weaknesses of each one, exactly as Drew had.

Bicknor was made to sound petulant, emotionally vulnerable, a young man desperate for attention to the point where his judgment was warped. He seemed unable to handle rejection and turned it into blame.

Warne was desperate to refute it. It was plain in his face and in the obvious discomfort with which he shifted position, but there was no legal fault in the line of questioning.

When it came to John Raleigh, Taft was more careful. He spoke of him respectfully; in fact so respectfully it all but overbalanced into sarcasm. Again he echoed the testimony of Robertson Drew.

Rathbone sat watching and listening intently. Had there been the least issue over which he could have challenged Gavinton he would have done so, but the man was clever, well prepared, and meticulously careful. He made no mistakes. He teetered on the edge of irrelevance, even of slander, but he never lost his balance. His only danger was perhaps in drowning the jury in so much information that they became bored. Taft's charm probably compensated for that. Ten years of practice in the pulpit had taught him how to woo an audience.

Gavinton was winning, and he knew it.

Rathbone tried to quash his emotions and think of the facts of the law, but his anger was too great for him to concentrate on the kind of detail that would outwit Gavinton. Innocent, trusting, hopeful people were being picked apart and destroyed as he watched, and there was nothing he could do about it. Taft would walk away not only vindicated but more powerful than before.

It was only as he was looking around the faces in the gallery, not because he expected to see anything of value but simply to calm his mind by momentarily taking it away from Taft's mellifluous denials, that he saw Hester. For a moment he was uncertain if it really was her. Then she moved, lifted her head, and looked straight at him. Even across the space of the open floor and four or five rows of other people, he could see the distress in her eyes. As clearly as if she had spoken, he knew the strength of her wish that he should do something to stop this smooth, choking tide of self-righteous destruction, the painted charade of half lies.

He had not known she was here, but then, it would have been improper for her to approach him. She was not directly a witness, but she was unquestionably involved in the case, having first taken it to Squeaky Robinson. Heaven only knew how Squeaky had found all the evidence he had. Rathbone was happy to remain ignorant of that. It might well have been by moving beyond the law and into criminality. Perhaps that was one of the reasons Hester had not spoken to Rathbone about it. She was protecting the case.

She would not speak now, even if they were to bump into each other in the hall. The appeal was in her eyes. She knew that would be enough. Perhaps she also read the helplessness in his.

It was irrelevant, even inappropriate, but suddenly Beata York's face replaced Hester's in his mind. He remembered her smile, the sudden glance away as something hurt her and she did not want anyone to see, perhaps most of all not her husband.

What would she think of this? Would she be resigned to the law, seeing it as a purpose in itself? Or would she be like Hester, viewing the law as servant to justice, and in this case failing? Would she be disappointed in him that he was not clever enough to find a way of using the law to obtain or create justice? What would her morality require he do?

Why was he even thinking of Beata York? It was ridiculous. She was a woman he had met once. He was not twenty, to allow her face to haunt him like this.

Hester's desires were plain in her face. She wanted John Raleigh saved, Squeaky vindicated, and Abel Taft stopped from ever doing this to other people. She would like to see Robertson Drew shown for the sanctimonious liar he was. And she would probably like to see herself vindicated as well. Drew had given a warped and very partial view of the Jericho Phillips affair. Certainly both Monk and Hester had been shown to be lacking in judgment, especially Hester. Rathbone himself had caused that. It was not an action he was proud of, no matter how legally justified in his defense of Phillips.

Gavinton was recalling Drew's evidence in order to ask Taft his own opinion of the various financial contributions made by different people.

"And you passed all these on to the charities you work with?" Gavinton concluded. .

"Of course," Taft assured him.

"I imagine my learned friend will remind you that Mr. Sawley could find no evidence of these charities ever having received the sort of amounts you were given by your congregation. How do you account for that, Mr. Taft?"

"I can't," Taft said frankly, his face creased in puzzlement. "I have all the receipts, properly in order and countersigned. It is quite necessary that I do, for financial reasons as well as moral ones. If Mr. Sawley had come to me, and given me some valid reason why he should see them, I would have shown them to him. I'm afraid he is . . . not being strictly honest in this."

"He claimed that the charities themselves had received almost nothing from you," Gavinton persisted.

Taft smiled. "Perhaps they misunderstood him. They may have thought that he was asking what they had in hand, rather than what they had received over the years." He lifted his shoulders slightly. "The charity workers are not all fluent in English, and some are elderly, or in poor health. Or, dare I say, Mr. Sawley heard what he wished to hear. Overemotional people, in a state of distress, are prone to do that."

"Indeed they are." Gavinton nodded agreement.

Rathbone glanced at Warne and saw him writing something hurriedly on a piece of paper. Perhaps it was a note to himself for the time when he would have the chance to question Taft.

Gavinton bowed. "Thank you, Mr. Taft. I can think of nothing further to ask you. Perhaps my learned friend has something?"

Warne did not look happy. He had nothing to pursue, unless he

could catch Taft in a lie; everything Taft and Drew had said was so
vague, so much a matter of hint and understanding, implication and
belief, that he was left floundering; it was clear in his face and in the
uncertainty of his gestures.

Rathbone made a decision, knowing that perhaps he would regret
it for the rest of his life. But if he let this go, presiding over a farce and
doing nothing, then his whole purpose was void.

"I think we will adjourn a little early," he said distinctly. "Mr.
Warne, prepare yourself to question Mr. Taft in the morning."

HE WAS OBLIVIOUS OF the streets as he rode home. It was high summer.
Everyone who could be was outside. As usual the traffic was heavy. Possibly someone had lost a load farther ahead, Rathbone thought as he
felt the carriage jolt forward, stop, then move forward again. He moved
his body with the rhythm automatically, trying to ignore the impact of
the thinly upholstered seat on his bones.

The decision was not irrevocable. He had not yet acted. He wished
there were someone he could ask, but he had not the right to. He would
contaminate them with the outcome. If he could have chosen anyone
it would be Monk, but that would be a very particular abuse of friendship. He could imagine the conversation. "I have this photograph of
Drew. Do you think I should use it?"

"How could you use it?"

"Show it to Warne, of course! Allow him to decide whether he will
expose Drew for what he is. Or alternatively blackmail Drew into
changing his evidence."

"Change it to what?"

"To the truth."

He could see the expression on Monk's face.

"Which is? Are you sure you know? Are you sure it isn't exactly
what he testified to?"

"I believe Squeaky Robinson. Don't you?" he would counter.

"Doesn't matter what I believe. Are you sure it matters what you believe? You are there to see fair play, to impose the rules of the law, not to decide yourself what is true and what is not."

"I know."

And he did know. But that was not a sufficient answer, as Monk would tell him. He was dealing with human beings, emotional, erratic, desperately vulnerable. The law was there to punish the offender, but even more than that, to protect the weak, those unable to protect themselves.

That was what the photographs could achieve: give the weak, the helpless in this case, a weapon they could use. Which would he regret the more, the broken promise not to use the photographs again, or the safe cowardice of doing nothing, just watching these people broken, humiliated, losing yet again?

He stood by the window in the withdrawing room and watched the dusk falling. The shadows crept across the grass. The purple asters would be out soon, another month or so. Early this year. No leaves were turning yet, but it would not be long. After that the first plums would be ripe . . .

But he must answer his own question tonight: a broken promise, or the cowardice of not intervening when the power to do so was in his hands? Would he forgive himself for that, when Taft and Drew were found "not guilty," free to walk away, smirking, and begin again?

He had deliberately chosen to stand here rather than in his study. He no longer found pleasure in this room, for all its beauty, and yet in his inner turmoil it seemed the right place to be.

If Ballinger had never been discovered in his violence or obscenity, would Rathbone's marriage to Margaret have grown richer and deeper? Would they even have loved each other with the passion and tenderness, the depth of friendship, that he believed Hester and Monk did? What is love worth if the first cold wind shrivels it up?

Who was he now, with no ties, no considerations to limit him or spur him on? He must decide whether to use the photograph of Drew to condemn him and thus prevent him from destroying the witnesses against Taft; whether to ruin Taft so he could not go on, stronger and

more powerful, richer in his confidence to deceive and defraud others—
to take advantage of their faith and then destroy it. At this moment, as
the light faded from the evening sky, it was that destruction of faith
Rathbone found to be the greatest sin.

Yes, he would use the photograph. He would send it to Warne. It
might bring either good or evil. Warne might use it or he might not.
But if Rathbone did not give him the chance, then Taft would win, and
whatever he did from then on, Rathbone would always know that he
could have prevented it.

He must take it to Warne himself, tonight.

He went into his study and closed and locked the door. Then he got
the key out and opened the safe. His hands trembled as he set the box
on the floor and tried to open it. Twice he missed the keyhole. The
third time the key slid in easily, and he opened the lid.

It did not take him long to slip the picture into an unmarked envelope. It was extraordinary that such important consequences could
spring from such a small action.

He closed the box, locked it, and replaced it in the safe. It was as if
nothing had ever happened. Except—he could feel the envelope acutely,
resting in his inside pocket.

It was a strange journey. He sat in the cab, which rolled smoothly
along the quiet street, as if he were going to visit a friend. The trees
were in full leaf. Flowers filled the gardens, and he could imagine their
perfume. He saw an elderly couple walking together. The man turned
to the woman and laughed. He put an arm around her. Rathbone noticed that she wore a pink dress.

He alighted and paid the driver when he reached the corner of the
street in which Warne lived. He dismissed the cab. He would walk back
to the main road when he was ready.

It was late, and he was quite aware that he would be disturbing
Warne, but having made the decision he would carry it through. Incon-
venience was trivial compared with the issues at stake.

Of course, he would retain Warne's professional services so that the
information was at least privileged, and Warne would not be obliged to

tell anyone where he obtained the photograph. That was an obvious precaution. He had brought money for that purpose.

A startled footman appeared at the door. Rathbone already had his card in his hand.

"My name is Oliver Rathbone. I am the judge presiding in the case Mr. Warne is currently presenting in court. I'm sorry to intrude at this hour, but I am afraid I need to speak to Mr. Warne tonight. Tomorrow will be too late."

The footman took the card and backed away slightly, pulling the door wider open.

"If you will come this way, sir, I shall inform Mr. Warne that you are here."

Rathbone thanked him and waited in the morning room as requested. It was very pleasant, full of bookcases and one or two glazed cupboards with various ornaments, but he was too restless to take any notice of them. He paced the floor, acutely aware that even now he could change his mind. He could apologize to Warne for disturbing him and say that he had reconsidered his action. He would go home again, looking like a fool, but nothing irrevocable would have been done.

Except that that was not true. He would not be able to live with himself if he did nothing. And this was his doing—to say that he was passing the final judgment over to Warne was a coward's lie.

He heard footsteps across the hallway, and the door opened. Warne came in. He looked weary and confused. His dark hair was tousled, as if he had repeatedly run his fingers through it; his face was gaunt. Now he looked anxiously at Rathbone.

"Has something happened?" he asked, closing the door behind him. He searched Rathbone's eyes and clearly found no comfort in them.

Rathbone had tried to decide how to approach the subject, had searched for any way at all to make it less repellent and found none. For a moment his mouth was dry, and he had to swallow and clear his throat.

"I have been struggling with a choice," he said, hearing the awkwardness in his voice. "I had a strong feeling that I had seen Robertson Drew somewhere before. I have now remembered where, and the circumstances. It is not that I saw him in the flesh, but in a photograph." He was speaking too quickly, but he could not help it. "I would prefer not to tell you how I came into possession of the photograph, but I will if you judge it necessary. It was to do with a particularly repulsive case, one that I wish I could forget, but for various reasons I cannot."

Warne looked unhappy and completely at a loss to understand.

They stood facing each other in the quiet room, no sound but a faint whisper of wind in the leaves outside and the ticking of the clock on the mantelpiece.

Rathbone felt ridiculous. He was making this even more unpleasant than it had to be by being less than honest.

"I'm sorry," Rathbone said. "The photograph is for you to do with as you think fit. You may need some time to decide, which is why I felt it necessary to disturb you with it tonight. I'm sorry. I debated whether to come to you at all, or if I should take the decision out of your hands by not showing it to you, but it has a strong bearing on the value of the evidence in the case against Taft, and I believe the decision must be yours."

"I don't understand." Warne looked deeply unhappy. "What decision? What is this photograph? Is it of Taft? Who took it?"

Rathbone was bitterly aware that he was about to increase Warne's unhappiness a hundredfold.

"Before I pass it to you I would like to retain your services as my legal counsel," Rathbone said. How ridiculous the words sounded, in the circumstances, and yet it was critical that he pursue this course of action. "It is to protect you, as well as me," he added.

Warne stared at him, uncomprehending.

Rathbone reached into his pocket and pulled out five guinea coins. "Please?"

Warne nodded, his eyes never leaving Rathbone's face, but he took the coins and set them on the table.

"I now represent you legally."

Rathbone held out the brown envelope.

Warne took it and after a moment's hesitation, opened the flap and picked out the stiff paper of the photograph. He stared at it, blinked, then his face reflected vividly the wave of revulsion that must've welled up inside him. His paramount emotion seemed to be acute distress.

Rathbone wished he had not made this choice. He had done the wrong thing, and it was too late to take it back. Now he was as chilled as if his heart had stopped pumping blood around his body.

Warne looked up at him, his eyes unreadable.

"Where in God's name did you get this? Did someone send it to you?"

There was no possible way out of this. He must plunge through it—with the truth.

"My father-in-law owned these photographs, about fifty of them. He was convicted of murder and sentenced to hang. I defended him, partly because of family obligation, partly because anyone at all is worthy of a defense, as Gavinton has been at pains to remind me. And in the beginning I believed he was innocent. Only too late did I discover that he was not." He drew in a deep breath and let it out slowly. "He always blamed me for not having defended him adequately. As a bitter irony he bequeathed me these damnable pictures."

Warne stared at him, blinking.

Rathbone knew he should not go on, making bad even worse, but he heard his own voice as if it belonged to someone else and he had no control over it.

"He told me that to begin with he used one of them to force a corrupt judge to make an industrialist clean up his factory's waste, which was spreading cholera in a poor area of the city. It saved the lives of hundreds of people. And cholera is a vile way to die."

Warne winced as if he had felt a wave of that pain himself.

"He went on using them," Rathbone continued. "For a while it was always to force justice where it would otherwise be denied. Then he began to do it for less clear-cut reasons. In the end he was thoroughly corrupt. I hesitated whether to give you this or not. You will notice the date on it—after Drew joined Taft's Church. You can see from it that Robertson Drew is very far from being the minister of Christ that he professes to be. He has slandered at least three good men, and probably the finest woman he is ever likely to meet. If the jurors were aware of his nature, I think they would attach a very different weight to his testimony than they do now."

"Indeed," Warne replied, his voice little above a whisper.

"Do whatever you think just," Rathbone told him. "If you believe the man is telling the truth, then the picture is irrelevant. I know Mrs. Monk, and I know Squeaky Robinson. Squeaky is a devious sod and has been on the wrong side of the law most of his life, but I trust him to keep the books of the Portpool Lane clinic. I think he knows fraud when he sees it and knows how to find it—the places where a man who has always been honest would never think to look. If he says Taft is crooked, then I believe he is. And if you are able to take a little time to look more closely at Hester Monk, you will find she has more courage and honor than many a decorated army officer and has done more to help the poor and outcast of society than Taft can have ever imagined."

Warne almost smiled.

"I imagine much of what Gavinton said was aimed at you. He seems to have studied your past cases, and your personal friendships, quite closely."

Rathbone felt his lips curl in a sneer. "A great deal more closely than he has some of the personal friendships of Robertson Drew, from the look of it." Then he looked at Warne's eyes. "But none of that has anything to do with the fact that, in spite of the financial evidence, you have failed to convince the jury that Abel Taft is a fraud and a manipulator of innocent and vulnerable people who trust him because he says he comes in the name of Christ. They believe him because they would not lie about such a thing themselves, and they find it impossible to believe that anyone else would. Perhaps they don't want to. No one wants to acknowledge himself a fool, and maybe a decent man wants even less to admit that the faith he placed in his church was hideously false."

"Most of all in front of his neighbors, and aloud, where they can remind him of it again and again," Warne added. He held the photograph in one hand, by his fingertips, as if touching it soiled him. "Would you use this?"

Rathbone thought for several moments before replying. "I don't know," he admitted at last. "If I did, I would be tormented by it forever. And if I didn't, then everything that Taft gets away with from now on is at my door, whether I want to own it or not. Every innocent man defrauded of his money or his trust is one more victim I could have prevented, had I not placed my own peace of mind first."

"Damn you," Warne said quietly. There was no enmity in his voice, just fear and exhaustion, and a touch of revulsion, for the picture, for the choice he now had.

There was no need for more words. Silently Rathbone took his leave and went out into the night. He walked toward the main road. He had left the photograph behind him, but he felt, if anything, even more heavily weighed down.

CHAPTER

6

THE FOLLOWING DAY THE trial resumed. Rathbone had slept badly, his dreams full of chaos. Now he sat in the high-backed chair and watched the proceedings, feeling as if the air in the room were as thick as that before an electric storm. His chest was tight and his neck so stiff that he could barely turn from side to side.

The gallery was less than full but the atmosphere was heavy. There was going to be no dramatic end. As far as the law was concerned, all was well, but as drama it had failed. Taft was clearly going to be found "not guilty," which meant that everything was going to remain as it had been. It was not worth watching. Those left now were the few with a personal interest in the outcome.

Felicia Taft looked more composed than in earlier days. Perhaps she knew that the worst was past. And yet she did not look happy. If she were exhausted, one could hardly blame her. The pallor of her face, the droop in her expression might be no more than that. She had endured all she was able to. With the end in sight, she had allowed herself to relax.

Gavinton was jubilant. He all but strutted out onto the floor. Abel Taft was on the witness stand again. He was not smiling exactly, but it was as if he felt he no longer had anything to fear, or to apologize for.

Rathbone was so tense his whole body ached. No matter how he moved in the seat, the tension did not let up. He feared he had left it too late. Even with the photograph, there was nothing Warne could do. What was it Rathbone ever imagined he might accomplish anyway? Did he think Warne would show the photograph to the jury and tell them this was the man they were believing rather than the witnesses he had so carefully mocked and belittled?

He could see Gethen Sawley sitting in the gallery, stubborn, white-faced, his body hunched forward as he waited for the ultimate defeat. Why was he here? Why was he punishing himself by watching as Drew and then Taft picked him apart, humiliating him gently, acting as if they were reluctant to say each word.

John Raleigh was still here too, dignified and silent, waiting for his ruin to be complete.

Rathbone could not see Bicknor, but he was probably here somewhere.

What did they expect? Did the desperation of their faith make them think there would be some miracle to make the trial just after all? Rathbone wished that he had the power to produce that miracle for them.

What a horrible irony. Gavinton was asking Taft once again if he believed in Robertson Drew, so the last thing he left in the jurors' minds was the image of Taft as an innocent, trusting man. Nothing was his fault. Because Drew was not charged, in a sense he was invulnerable.

Was Warne going to use the photograph? How would he introduce it? Had he even brought it?

Gavinton was handing over the witness to Warne.

Warne rose to his feet. He looked haggard. There were dark shadows on his face, as if he had not shaved, but as he moved and the light caught him it was clear it was only the hollows of his cheeks. He had probably been up all night pacing the floor, wondering what to do with the terrible picture.

Warne regarded Taft cautiously, but no politeness in his words could mitigate the intense dislike in his face.

"Mr. Taft, it seems you are ill served in your congregation, and indeed by everyone except Mr. Drew," he observed. His voice was gravelly with strain. "Would it be fair to say that that is because your congregation is self-selecting? They come because they have tried other churches, and possibly found them wanting? Your message is the one they wish to hear, for whatever reason or hunger of their own?"

"Yes, you might say that," Taft agreed. There was no visible tension in his body, no strain in his voice. If he were the least afraid he was a master at concealing it.

"Do you ever turn anyone away?" Warne inquired.

"Of course not." Taft made the question sound ridiculous. "The doors of any church are always open. We would ask someone to leave only if he was causing turmoil or distress among the rest of the congregation. I'm pleased to say that hardly ever happens." He gave a slight shrug, and his expression was rueful. "Once or twice someone did take too much to drink. Sober, he would be welcomed back."

"Very commendable," Warne said drily. "It is easy to see how, in these circumstances, you quite often take in the emotionally unstable, and those not to be relied upon. Such people will make errors of judgment, misunderstand, even on occasion do things that are morally, or even legally, wrong."

Taft's expression tightened so slightly it was barely visible. "That is unavoidable," he conceded.

Warne continued to stare at him. "But your friends, your associates in the ministry, and most particularly those who deal with money and the charities you help—you will choose these with great care and diligence, I imagine? You will, with the utmost discretion, of course, find

out all you need to know about their financial honesty, and competence, and their moral character?"

There was a rustle of awakened interest in the gallery, a stiffening
of attention in the jury.

Taft frowned. "Of course," he agreed.

Warne nodded. "Exactly. To do less would be irresponsible."

"Indeed it would," Taft said a little sharply.

"And I assume you take the same care with the charities to which
you give this exceedingly generous amount of money?" Warne went on.

Taft swallowed, hesitated a moment, then answered. "I do the best
I can, Mr. Warne. There is no way in which I can make inquiries regarding their staff. I do not always know them, and they change, but
they are good and honorable people who give of their own time freely."

Warne nodded. "Quite so. But you have never had cause to doubt
either their honesty or their competence?"

"No, never." Taft's voice was losing a little of its smoothness.

Warne gave a slight gesture of denial.

"They are not of the emotionally uncertain nature of your own
well-meaning parishioners—"

He was not allowed to finish. Gavinton shot to his feet.

"My lord, Mr. Taft is not accountable for the morality or errors of
any charity he might donate to. And may I point out that the emotional
fragilities of his own parishioners have extended to false accusation, but
in no case whatever, in any circumstances at all, to the misuse of money."

Rathbone was caught. He could feel his stomach knot and his
breath catch in his throat. Was Warne about to introduce the photograph at last? He had just maneuvered Taft into endorsing Drew once
again, swearing he knew him and all his motives and activities.

Rathbone felt the sweat prickle on his body, and in the heat of the
room, the color flush in his face.

"Mr. Warne . . ." he began, and then had to stop and take a deep
breath and cough. "Mr. Warne, you seem to be stating the obvious. Is
there a question or purpose in what you are saying? Mr. Taft has already
very thoroughly, several times over, sworn to the honesty, diligence,

and general virtue of Mr. Drew. He has also sworn that this is from his personal knowledge, not hearsay or a charitable judgment. What is your purpose in raising this yet again?"

"I wish to give Mr. Taft every opportunity to clear himself of these charges," Warne said demurely. "If in some way the fraud were—"

"There has been no fraud proved, my lord!" Gavinton cut across him. "My learned friend is—"

"Yes, Mr. Gavinton," Rathbone in turn interrupted him. "He is wasting time. You wasted a good deal of it yourself." He turned to Warne. "I think we have established to the jury's satisfaction that Mr. Taft trusted Mr. Drew in all things both moral and financial and that he did so after a long personal acquaintance and with all due care and foresight in making certain that his good opinion was based upon fact, not upon convenience or friendship." He looked at Taft. "Is that a just and true assessment, Mr. Taft?"

"Yes, my lord." Taft could do nothing but agree.

Rathbone studied his face to find even a shadow of reluctance, and saw nothing. If he had any idea of danger, he was a master at concealing it. Or was he so supremely arrogant that the possibility of his own failure never entered his mind?

Rathbone looked at Warne and could not read him either. Warne looked like a man facing impossible odds, preparing for the bitter taste of defeat and yet still seeking some last-minute escape. Perhaps that was exactly what he was. Perhaps he despised Rathbone for having even kept the photograph, let alone descending to its use. Perhaps, Rathbone thought, he had earned Warne's lifelong contempt for no purpose at all, and Warne would rather lose the case than filthy his hands with such a ploy.

"My lord," Warne said gravely, "much of the evidence in this case seems to be believed or discarded based on the reputation for honesty and for soundness of judgment of the person offering it. It does seem, regrettably, as if some of the Crown's witnesses against Mr. Taft are less reliable than I had supposed. My learned friend has been able to expose them as such."

Gavinton smiled and acknowledged the somewhat backhanded compliment.

"If your lordship will allow, one witness who seems to be central to the pursuit of the case and who therefore has had her reputation for judgment, and even for emotional stability, severely questioned has not actually been called to the stand. May it please the court, I would like to call Hester Monk as a witness in rebuttal to the testimony that Mr. Taft has given."

"You have no question for Mr. Taft?" Rathbone said in surprise. What did Warne hope to achieve with Hester? If he called her, then Gavinton would also be able to cross-examine her. The whole miserable episode of her misjudgment in the Phillips case would be exposed in more detail. She would appear to be a highly volatile woman whose compassion had drowned her judgment and allowed a blackmailer, child pornographer, and murderer to escape justice.

Because Rathbone was the man who had defended Phillips and crucified Hester on the stand, he himself would not emerge from it well—in law, yes, but not in the eyes of the jury.

Gavinton was on his feet, smiling.

"I have no objection whatever, my lord. I think it would well serve the cause of justice. I hesitated to subject Mrs. Monk to such an ordeal again. She can barely have forgotten the humiliation of the last time, but I confess it would seem just." He turned his satisfied smile on Warne.

Rathbone felt the control slipping out of his hands, like the wet reins of a carriage when the horses bolt.

They were waiting for his answer. He could not protect Hester. If he ruled against her testifying he would expose himself without helping her. In fact, it might even make it appear as if she had something further to hide.

"Very well," he conceded. "But keep it to the point, Mr. Warne."

"Thank you, my lord." Warne instructed the usher to call Hester Monk.

There was silence as Hester came into the room, except for the rustle of fabric and creak of stays as people in the gallery turned to watch her, fascinated by this woman both Drew and Taft had described so vividly, and in "praise" so worded as to be moving from condescension into blame.

She was slender, almost a little too thin for fashionable taste, and she walked very uprightly across the open floor and climbed the steps to the witness stand. She did not look at Rathbone, at the jury, or up at the dock.

Rathbone watched her with a strange, disturbing mixture of emotions, which were far more powerful than he had expected. He had known her for more than a decade, during which he had fallen in love with her, been angered, exasperated, and confused by her, and had his emotions thoroughly wrung out. At the same time he had admired her more than any other person he knew. She had made him laugh, even when he did not want to, and she had changed his beliefs on a score of things.

Now he wanted to protect her from Gavinton, and Warne had set her in the center of the target—damn him!

She took the oath in a steady voice and stood facing Warne, ready to begin.

Warne, dark, haggard, and clearly nervous, moved forward into the center of the floor. He cleared his throat.

"Mrs. Monk, Mr. Drew has told us that you attended a service at Mr. Taft's Church. Is that correct?"

"Yes."

"Just once?"

"Yes."

He cleared his throat again.

"Why did you go? And why did you not return a second or third time? Was the service not as you had expected? Or did something happen while you were there that offended you to the degree that you did not wish to go again?"

Hester looked puzzled. Clearly Warne had not told her what he planned to say. Perhaps there had been no time.

Rathbone was so tense he had to move his position a little, consciously clench his hands then loosen them. Was Warne going to use her vulnerability to save his case against Taft?

Why not? Rathbone had done it to save Jericho Phillips, of all people! How could he now self-righteously blame Warne?

The jury was tense, staring at Hester, a mixture of sympathy and apprehension in their faces.

Hester answered, her voice even. It was too calm to be natural. "I went because Josephine Raleigh is a friend of mine, and she told me of her father's distress," she said. "I understood her desperation acutely because my father also was cheated out of money and found himself in debt. He took his own life. I wanted to see if there was anything at all I could do to prevent that happening to Mr. Raleigh."

Now there was movement in the court. One of the jurors put up his hand to ease his collar. Another's face was pinched with grief, or perhaps it was pity. Debt was not so uncommon.

In the gallery a few people craned forward, turned to one another, sighed, or spoke a word or two.

"How did you intend to do that, Mrs. Monk?" Warne asked curiously.

Hester moved her shoulders very slightly. "I had no clear plan. I wanted to meet Mr. Taft and listen to him preach."

"To what purpose?"

"To see if there was any chance he would release Mr. Raleigh from his commitment," she replied, choosing her words carefully. "Also to see if Mr. Taft asked me for money, and how he worded it, whether I felt pressured or not, whether he did it in front of others to embarrass me if I refused."

Warne looked curious, but the tension still gripped his body and his hands.

"And did he do any of those things?" he asked.

She smiled bleakly. "I admit I did feel pressured—yes—and it was all carefully wrapped under the preaching of Christian duty: the safe and comfortable should give to the cold, hungry, and homeless. One cannot argue with that and then kneel to pray."

"Did you give, Mrs. Monk?"

"To the ordinary collection, yes. I did not give more than that." There was a faint, bitter smile touching her lips.

"And did anyone make you feel guilty?" Warne pressed.

There was not a sound in the gallery.

"Mr. Drew tried," she answered. "But I told him all the money I could spare already went to my clinic in Portpool Lane. The women there are not only hungry, cold, and homeless, they are also sick."

"Why did you not go back to the church, Mrs. Monk?"

"Because I already understood the pressure Mr. Raleigh, and others, must have felt," she replied. "There is an art to making other people feel as if they should give what they can to those less fortunate. I am not good at it myself. I am far too direct. But I enlist the help of those who are good at it, in order to keep the clinic going. I know very well how it is done. Please heaven, we do not coerce anyone to give more than they can, so putting themselves into debt. We ask small amounts, and only from those who, as far as we can tell, have more than sufficient."

Gavinton stood up, puzzled.

"My lord, I am afraid Mrs. Monk is all very righteous in her work, and in raising funds for it. Different people have their own ways of . . . of doing good." He said it in such a way it sounded like some secret vice. "But what has it to do with whether Mr. Taft is guilty of fraud, or innocent?"

Rathbone turned to Warne. "This is a somewhat circuitous route to wherever you are going. A little more direct, if you please, Mr. Warne."

Warne bowed, his face carefully expressionless; then he turned back to Hester.

"Mrs. Monk, what did you do as a result of your visit to Mr. Taft's Church?"

"I went to see Mr. Robinson, who keeps the accounts for me at the clinic," she answered, her voice low and a little hoarse. "I asked him if he knew of any way of determining if all the money raised by Mr. Taft actually went to the causes he claimed it did. Mr. Robinson told me that he would endeavor to find out, and then later gave me the results of his inquiries."

Gavinton was on his feet again.

"My lord, the court is already aware of all this. Mr. Warne is wasting our time. We know who Mrs. Monk is, and something of her past interference in cases she believed deserving. I am sorry to embarrass her; no doubt she is a well-intentioned woman, but past cases have made it tragically evident that she is also undisciplined." He spread his hands in a gesture of helplessness. "She comes with incomplete evidence, interpreted by her emotions, no doubt out of compassion, but nevertheless, emotions are not evidence. You yourself are only too aware of this. Tactless as it may be of me to remind you, but when you were a prosecutor, my lord, you totally destroyed her on the stand. Your friendship for her did not prevent you from doing your duty, however repugnant to you."

Rathbone waited for Warne to fight back and was met with silence. He felt the heat burn up his own face. What in hell was Warne doing? He had left Rathbone no choice.

"Mr. Gavinton is right, Mr. Warne," he said between his teeth. "This seems to be both repetitive and irrelevant. If you have anything of use to ask Mrs. Monk, please do so. If not, then release her and prepare to present your closing argument." The case was lost. Warne was not going to use the photograph. Perhaps in a way that was a relief. This attempt to humiliate Rathbone was Warne's way of expressing his revulsion at the fact that he had been shown the photograph at all.

"Yes, my lord," Warne said dutifully. "I shall come more immediately to the point. I apologize if I appeared to be . . . meandering." He looked at Hester. "Mrs. Monk, my learned friend has made more than one reference to the unfortunate case of Jericho Phillips, in which you gave evidence that was less than sufficient for the jury to find him guilty. Mr. Gavinton seems to feel that it somehow detracts from the value of your testimony now. Mr. Drew has spoken at length of the moral and emotional"—he hesitated, looking for the right word—

"fragility of the witnesses against Mr. Taft. He has as much as said that they are lightly balanced, prone to misunderstanding and exaggeration, and therefore not to be trusted. He has included you in that category. I feel it is only right that you should have the opportunity to give any testimony that would refute that, and restore your good name—and of course your reliability as a witness."

Rathbone stiffened. What on earth was Warne trying to do? It was too late for this.

Hester said nothing. From her expression she had no idea what she could say or do that would matter now. She had been here a couple of times, but she probably knew from Josephine Raleigh, who had been here every day, that the case had already been lost. Reputations were destroyed beyond rebuilding.

Warne smiled at her, but it was sadly, as if he were apologizing for something.

"Mrs. Monk, I regret having to remind you of what can only be a painful memory for you, but much has been made of your failure to testify against Jericho Phillips with sufficient clarity of thought to secure his conviction. Sir Oliver Rathbone appeared for Phillips at that time and pretty well destroyed you on the stand."

"I remember," Hester said a little huskily. She was very pale.

Rathbone racked his mind for anything he could say to stop this.

Gavinton sat with a slow smile spreading across his face, unctuous and satisfied.

"Why were you so . . . careless in your preparation to testify? Surely you wished Phillips to be found guilty?"

"Of course I did." Her voice was charged with emotion now, and her shoulders were high and awkward.

There was nothing Rathbone could do to help her.

"I was careless," she went on suddenly. "I was so certain he was guilty that—"

"Guilty of what, Mrs. Monk?" Warne interrupted her.

"Guilty of using children," she said sharply. "Boys unwanted by their families, orphans or ones whose parents couldn't look after them, all of them between five years and eleven or twelve years old. He imprisoned them on his riverboat and had the men who frequented the boat pose for pornographic photographs, which he later used to blackmail them—"

Warne held his hand up again to stop her.

"I find it highly unbelievable that anyone would allow themselves to be photographed if they were engaging in such horrible acts, Mrs. Monk. You are stretching the limits of credibility."

"Phillips ran a club for wealthy and influential men," she told him, her voice now sharp with distress. "Men whose ordinary lives no longer gave them the thrill of danger they hungered for. The price of membership in the club was to have the photographs taken. It also ensured that none of the other members would betray the club or one another—they were all in the same situation."

"Very clever," Warne said bitterly. "I can see why the whole matter angered you to the point that you lost your sense of judgment. But in order to obtain a conviction you had to prove that a crime had taken place and that the person accused was responsible. Where did you slip up in this?"

Gavinton stood up again. "My lord, that is irrelevant." He sounded weary, as if his patience had been tried to the utmost. "We all know that Mrs. Monk did indeed fail in that endeavor. I do not contest it. There is nothing to be gained by repeating the miserable affair, and Mrs. Monk herself can only be embarrassed by it. Mr. Warne is wasting our time."

Rathbone felt the sweat trickling down his body. Looking at Gavinton it was clear that he had no idea that Drew was in one of those photographs. Obviously Hester did not either. Was Warne somehow going to bring it in? He could not do so legally without first showing the evidence to the defense.

When Rathbone started to speak his mouth was dry, and he had to clear his throat before he could force his voice to make a sound.

"Mr. Warne? The defense stipulates to Mrs. Monk's distress in the earlier case and the fact that the whole issue was so repugnant to her that she failed to present adequate evidence of Phillips's guilt in the eyes of the law. What is your purpose in raising the subject again? Jericho Phillips is dead, and his crimes have nothing to do with this case."

"I did not raise the subject, my lord," Warne said smoothly, his dark eyes fixed on Rathbone's. "It was my learned friend who brought it up, to discredit Mrs. Monk. He suggested she was overemotional, her judgment warped by her horror at that time, to the degree that her testimony even now is still unreliable. I want to show the court that that is not so. I believe I have that right."

"My lord—" Gavinton began.

Rathbone did not even look at him. "Mr. Warne," he said quietly, "you are trying our patience. If you can show that Mrs. Monk is a reliable witness and we should take what she says more seriously, then do so. But briefly, please."

"Yes, my lord." Warne looked again at Hester. "Mrs. Monk, you spoke of photographs that Mr. Phillips used to blackmail the otherwise respectable gentlemen who were members of the club that indulged in pornography and the sexual abuse of small boys. I think we all find that not only obscene but also, as my learned friend said, highly unbelievable."

Rathbone could hardly breathe. Warne was going to do it. Had he shown the photograph to Gavinton, as the rules of evidence required? If he had not, then Gavinton could ask for a mistrial and Rathbone would have to grant it. Was that what Warne intended to do? Why? It would not ensure a conviction.

"Yes . . ." Hester was saying uncertainly. "It sounds unbelievable. But the photographs do exist."

"Indeed," Warne replied, his voice almost devoid of expression, his face now pale. "I believe I might have one such photograph. Have you ever been on Jericho Phillips's boat yourself?"

Hester was gripping the edge of the rail to the witness box, her knuckles white. "Yes . . ." Her voice was a whisper, but it was perfectly audible in the silence of the courtroom, where it seemed no one else was even breathing.

Gavinton was on his feet, but wearily, no tension or sense of outrage in him, not even of apprehension.

"My lord, the prosecution has not passed over this piece of evidence to the defense. I ask that it be ruled inadmissible—on grounds of irrelevance, if nothing else. I withdraw my remarks as to the unlikeliness of their existence."

Warne was tense, his body awkward as he stared unblinkingly back at Rathbone.

"My lord, the remarks have been heard by the jury, they cannot simply be withdrawn. I have a right to prove my witness's truthfulness."

"You do, Mr. Warne," Rathbone agreed, hating having to meet Warne's eyes. "But the defense also has the right to see the evidence."

With a faint, bleak smile Warne passed the photograph across to Gavinton.

Gavinton took it casually, glanced at it with a look of boredom, then his body jerked and his face went so white Rathbone was afraid he was going to faint.

In the courtroom there was total silence. No one in the gallery moved. The jurors were frozen in their seats, staring at Gavinton.

Gavinton gulped, having difficulty finding his voice. "My . . . my lord . . . this evidence is . . ." He stopped and put his hand up to his throat as if his collar were choking him.

Rathbone's mind raced. He must avoid a mistrial. Warne might even find himself unable to prosecute again. Without this evidence Gavinton would win.

Rathbone leaned forward. "Mr. Gavinton, would you like a brief adjournment to consider this evidence, which appears to have disturbed you intensely?"

Gavinton swallowed, and choked on his own breath.

"If I may intrude, my lord," Warne said politely. "Perhaps we might discuss it in your lordship's chambers?"

Rathbone adjourned the court amid a hum of excitement and confusion, and five minutes later he, Warne, and Gavinton were in his chambers with the door closed; the usher had been told not to disturb them, regardless of the circumstances.

"Mr. Gavinton?" Rathbone asked with as blank a face as he could manage.

Gavinton was still holding the photograph.

"It is obscene, my lord," he said, still speaking with difficulty.

"So I had assumed," Rathbone replied. Trying to remain expressionless, he turned to Warne. "You clearly intended to show it to Mrs. Monk; did you also intend the jury to see it?"

Warne hesitated. He was saved from an immediate answer by Gavinton's interruption.

"You can't! She may be gullible with more goodwill than sense, but she's a decent woman. This picture is vile—it's repulsive."

"Don't be ridiculous!" Warne snapped. "She's an army nurse, you fool! She's seen men dismembered on the battlefield! She saw the original boat with its cargo of imprisoned and tortured children—the real ones, alive, terrified, half starved, and bleeding. What is it you imagine she can see in this photograph that she hasn't already seen? Except perhaps the face of someone she recognizes?"

"Recognizes?" Rathbone said quietly. "Who is in this picture, Mr. Gavinton?"

Gavinton closed his eyes. When he answered his voice was hoarse and no more than a whisper.

"Mr. Drew, my lord."

Rathbone held out his hand. Gavinton gave him the photograph. Rathbone took it and looked at it, not that he needed to; every sordid detail was already imprinted on his brain.

He cleared his throat. "Indeed it is," he agreed. "It is obscene, as you say, and it is quite clearly Mr. Robertson Drew. I imagine, Mr. Gavinton, that you object to this being put into evidence to show Mr. Drew's character as very far indeed from what it seems. However, you repeatedly held him up as an honorable man. Mr. Warne has the right to question that, and rebut it if he can—which, it is now abundantly clear, he is able to do. Upon what grounds do you protest, other than that you apparently did not know that your star witness, who so protected your client's virtue, is somewhat short of virtue himself?"

The air in the room was electric, like that in the half second between lightning and thunder.

"I was given no warning of it!" Gavinton protested.

"I received it only late yesterday evening," Warne told him. "I agree, I should have told you before court this morning. I accept censure for that." He looked at Rathbone, then back at Gavinton. "But I will not accept the suppression of it. You called Mrs. Monk's character into question, on the word of Drew. I call Mrs. Monk to defend herself and at the expense of Drew. Is there something unjust in that?"

"Where the devil did you get this . . . this filthy thing?" Gavinton demanded, the color returning to his face in a wash of scarlet.

"That is privileged information," Warne replied smoothly. "But if you wish to have it authenticated, then of course you must do so."

"It could be . . . some trick!" Gavinton was still struggling.

"I do not believe that," Warne answered. "But I may be able to obtain the original plate, if you feel that is necessary."

"You're bluffing!" Gavinton was all but shouting now.

"No, I am not," Warne snapped, lowering his voice with effort. "But if you wish to take that chance, then do so. However, I think you might be better served by consulting with Mr. Drew on the matter. He will know beyond question that the picture is genuine, and he may wish, quite voluntarily, to be more truthful in his testimony regarding Mrs. Monk's reliability as a witness, and the strength and honesty of her general character. He may also prefer to be more moderate in some of the rather condemnatory remarks he made about the weaknesses or gullibility of the various other witnesses."

Gavinton stared at him as he would at a poisonous snake.

"Were that his choice," Warne continued, "then the photograph would no longer be relevant. You could merely stipulate to its veracity, and to Mrs. Monk's character, and then at the end of the trial I would hand it over to you to destroy."

"And the plate from which it was printed?" Gavinton said huskily.

Warne spread his hands. "I don't have that—but I know where it is. I will see what I can do. That's all I can offer."

"Mr. Gavinton?" Rathbone asked.

"I'll . . . I'll have to consult with my client and with Mr. Drew . . ."

"Of course. You may have thirty minutes."

HALF AN HOUR LATER Hester was told that she would not be needed after all, and Warne called Robertson Drew to the stand.

"My lord, in light of this remarkable turn of events, I should like to ask Mr. Drew if he wishes in any way to reconsider his testimony. He may now prefer to lend more credence to the witnesses he previously condemned. Mrs. Monk, in particular . . . ?" His expression changed almost imperceptibly, and he turned to Gavinton.

Gavinton struggled to find some ground to protest and failed. He sank back into his seat, looking as if he had aged a decade in the last hour.

Several turbulent minutes passed as Robertson Drew made his way back to the stand and climbed the steps, fumbling as if he were partially blind. A bristling silence filled the room, hostile, angry, disturbed.

Rathbone brought the court to order and Warne approached Drew, who clung on to the rails, not as if for support, rather more as if he would exert all the force he had to bend them to his will. He was clearly in the grip of some violent emotion.

Rathbone looked at the jurors. Their faces reflected an intense confusion. They seemed to have been taken entirely by surprise.

Drew was reminded that he was still under oath.

Warne was brief. After what had gone before, anything now would be anticlimactic.

"Mr. Drew, you represented yourself to the court as a man of the utmost propriety, of honor, diligence, and dedication to the work of Christ. In light of the change in circumstances of which Mr. Gavinton has made you aware, you may wish to reconsider some of your condemnation of other witnesses as to their honor and their worth."

In the dock Taft's face was hidden, bent forward almost to his knees.

"Mr. Drew," Warne continued, "was . . . Mr. Taft . . . aware of all your private, very personal . . . tastes? And, by the way, did any of the money paid by the parishioners you appear to despise make its way into your own pocket? That would account for why we find it so difficult to trace it to the charities whose books seem—to put it kindly—chaotic."

"No!" Drew said furiously. "If anyone took it, it was Taft!"

Warne's dark eyebrows rose. "And the little digression into Mrs. Monk's testimony in the Phillips case—which, incidentally, she later solved to the satisfaction of the law, and of society's need for justice—would you agree that was irrelevant, except as a means of trying to invalidate her testimony in this case?"

Drew glared at him. "Yes." The word was barely audible. The jury strained forward to hear him.

"Might the same be said of your attempts to discredit Mr. Gethen, Mr. Bicknor, and Mr. Raleigh?" Warne continued.

"Yes." It was the snarl of the desperate man cornered.

Warne shrugged and turned to Gavinton. "I doubt you will want to pursue it, but the witness is yours, sir."

Gavinton declined. He looked like a beaten man, stunned with shock, reeling from blow after blow.

It remained only for each of them to present their closing arguments. In fairness to Gavinton, to give him an opportunity to collect his thoughts and attempt to recover at least something to say for his client, Rathbone adjourned the court for the day. Warne made no objection. Perhaps he also wanted to collect his thoughts and make certain that between them they had allowed Gavinton no cause for appeal.

Rathbone walked out into the afternoon sun in something of a daze, oblivious of the crowds around him on the footpath.

Warne had used the photograph after all, cleverly—if at some risk to his reputation. He might well be censured for not having given Gavinton the picture at the beginning of the day. He had called Hester, something Rathbone had not foreseen, and then used her courage and dignity, her honesty in admitting her own error with Phillips to his advantage. It was as if Gavinton had pulled the entire edifice of his case down on top of himself.

The crowd was still pouring out of the Old Bailey behind and around him into the late afternoon heat, bumping into one another, jostling for space on the burning pavements. Two well-dressed men were arguing vociferously, voices raised. A fat woman in black struggled with a parasol, muttering to herself in frustration. Another woman's hat was knocked off in the jostling, and several people reached to retrieve it. They would all be back tomorrow for the summations and the verdict. They would not be content to read about it in the newspapers, they would want to hear the words, see the faces, and taste the emotions of it.

Rathbone walked briskly along Ludgate Hill toward St. Paul's, passing in the shadow of the great cathedral and into Cannon Street before hailing a hansom and giving the driver his home address.

He sat back inside, and even before the driver had turned westward he was lost in thought.

Was it justice? If so, what had been the price?

7

RATHBONE DID NOT SLEEP well but was at last resting dreamlessly when his valet woke him. He was startled to see the warm sunlight through the gap in the curtains. He sat up slowly, his head heavy.

"Damn!" he said miserably. "What time is it, Dover? Am I late?"

"No, sir." Dover's face was very grave. "It is still quite early."

Rathbone heard the seriousness in his voice. "What is it?" he asked a little sharply. "You sound as if someone had died." He meant it with sarcasm.

"Yes, sir, I'm very much afraid so," Dover replied.

Rathbone blinked, straightening up. Then suddenly he was ice cold. His father! His chest tightened and he could not breathe. The room seemed to disappear, and all he could see was Dover's white face. He tried to speak and no sound came.

"The case you were presiding over, sir." Dover's voice came from far away. "The man accused . . . a Mr. Abel Taft, I believe . . ." He went on speaking but Rathbone did not hear him.

The room steadied itself, and the warmth flooded back into his body, which was tingling with life. Dover was still talking and Rathbone had not heard a word of it.

"I beg your pardon?" he asked.

Dover swallowed and began again. "Mr. Taft, sir. The police left a message for you. I'm afraid he has taken his own life. Shot himself. But before doing so it appears that he suffocated his wife and his two daughters. I'm very sorry, sir. It is most distressing. I thought you should know immediately. It is bound to be in at least some of the daily newspapers. I do not know what is the correct procedure in court, but no doubt there will have to be an alteration in the arrangements."

Rathbone swung his legs out of bed and stood up slowly, swaying for a moment before regaining his balance. "I shall shave and dress," he said. "And consider what would be best to do. The only part of the trial remaining was the summations. His suicide would make them appear redundant . . . as indeed a verdict would be. Society will make its own judgment now." He took a shaky breath. "But in God's name, why kill his poor family?"

"I have no idea, sir," Dover said quietly. "It seems a very terrible thing to do. I assume the verdict would have been against him?"

"Yes. But it was only for fraud, not murder. He could have faced prison, but that is survivable. Difficult, unpleasant, but far from a death sentence."

"Yes, sir. Would you like kippers for breakfast, sir, or eggs?"

Rathbone felt his stomach clench.

"Just toast, thank you," he replied.

"It may be a difficult day, sir. It is better not to face it on an empty stomach."

Rathbone looked at him and saw the concern in his face. He was doing his job.

"You are quite right. Scrambled eggs, please."

"Yes, sir."

Half an hour later Rathbone sat at the dining-room table. The scrambled eggs had been excellent, the tea was hot and fresh and the toast crisp, the marmalade just as sharp as he liked it. But all he could think of was Abel Taft shooting himself. Why? Was the disgrace really more than he could bear? Could he not face his wife and daughters' disillusionment in him?

Or was it his own disillusion in Robertson Drew? Had he really trusted him and had no idea of the man's secret indulgences? Could he have known of them, and perhaps believed that Drew had repented and changed? Did something of his own value depend on his ability to bring others to redemption?

No, that was a foolish thought. Taft was charged with fraud, with taking money given for a specific purpose and diverting it to his own use. Squeaky Robinson had found ample proof of his guilt. This had nothing to do with Drew's proclivities.

Maybe his death had been an act of momentary despair, perhaps after a heavy night of drinking, an indulgence he might well not be used to. But to kill his wife and children as well!

Had Rathbone driven him to that? Was this his fault?

No! He had driven himself to it, first by fraud, then by believing in a man like Drew, and either using him, or trusting him without any care or responsibility.

It would have to be declared a mistrial. The police would be left to clear up the tragic deaths of his family.

Dover was standing in the dining-room doorway, his face still as grave and shocked as before.

"Yes?" Rathbone asked. Had time slipped by so it was already half past eight and he should be going?

"The police are here, sir. They wish to speak with you," Dover said.

That was a trifle prompt. Of course, they would be here to inform him officially of Taft's death. They would hardly rely on his servants to tell him. Rathbone folded his napkin and stood up.

The police were waiting in the hall. There were two of them, the younger one in uniform. That seemed more than was necessary to pass on a fairly simple message, even a tragic one.

"Oliver Rathbone?" the elder of the two asked grimly.

Rathbone noticed the omission of his title and thought it a trifle rude, but it would be petty and self-important to correct the man.

"Yes. What can I do for you?"

"Inspector Haverstock. I'm afraid I must arrest you, sir, for perverting the course of justice in the case against Abel Taft. I don't want to handcuff you, but if you offer any resistance I will be obliged to. It would be best for us all if you were to make no resistance. I'm sure you don't want to be seen struggling with the police in front of your household staff." His voice was polite but there was no mistaking the threat in his words.

Rathbone froze. This was preposterous. It made no sense at all. Arrest him? They couldn't. It . . .

"Sir!" Haverstock said warningly.

The other man, a constable, came a step closer, his young face flushed with embarrassment.

Rathbone drew a deep breath and let it out slowly, fighting to compose himself.

"I have no intention of making a fuss," he said more tartly than he had intended to. "I have not perverted the course of justice. On the contrary, I have done all I can to see that justice prevails."

Haverstock did not yield an inch.

"Nevertheless, sir, I am arresting you on that charge as I have been instructed, and you will come with us to the police station. You will be formally arraigned later in the day. Is there anyone you would like to inform? Perhaps you would like to give instruction to your own counsel, whoever he is."

"No, thank you," Rathbone snapped. "I think that this will be cleared up and apologized for within a very short while. I am due to preside over the unfortunate end of what will inevitably be a mistrial at the Old Bailey this morning."

"Yes, sir," Haverstock agreed without the slightest change of expression. "I imagine they will call on someone else to do that. Now, if you will come with us, sir . . ." It was a command, and Rathbone had no choice but to obey, one police officer on either side of him, like any other prisoner.

LATER THAT AFTERNOON, SHOCKED and still in a daze, Rathbone rode through the streets toward the magistrate's court, thank heaven in an ordinary cab, but sitting with Haverstock to one side of him and the younger man on the other, all of them squashed together uncomfortably. It was like a bad dream, full of confusion. What exactly had happened? They could only be referring to the photograph. There was nothing else. But how did they know Rathbone had had anything to do with it? At least in theory, it could have come from anywhere.

Warne could not have told anyone where he got it. He had received it under privilege. Rathbone had done that as much to protect Warne as to safeguard himself.

Who else knew Rathbone had them? Only Monk, Hester, and Henry Rathbone. None of them would have told anyone. What had happened? He could hear the rattle of the wheels over the cobbles, the clatter of the horses' hoofs, shouts of other drivers, the general noise of the streets, and none of it seemed real. No one in the cab spoke.

When they reached the building, he was taken in through a back door. There were a few people standing around, even at this hour. A man in ragged clothes leaned against a wall, obviously much the worse for drink. As Rathbone passed close by him he could smell the stench of stale alcohol and human waste.

Inside, in the entrance hall, a woman was sitting in one of the low seats, leaning forward. Her neckline was so deep half her bosom showed. Her occupation was not difficult to guess. A youth with a pinched face was staring at her, but she did not appear to be aware of him. Perhaps she was used to being gawped at by men.

Haverstock guided Rathbone toward a constable on duty beside the

door into the courtroom and spoke to him briefly. The constable nodded, avoiding Rathbone's eyes. He was clearly embarrassed. He listened,
nodded again, and went inside. He was gone several minutes and they
waited in silence for him.

Rathbone felt panic well up inside him. This was real. He was not
going to wake up in his own bed, covered in sweat and gasping with
relief. He had no idea when he was ever going to see his own house
again. Now all the things in it that reminded him of Margaret, of loneliness and failure, seemed infinitely sweet by comparison, with this
bare, stifling corridor filled with the smell of dirt and sweat.

But that was ridiculous! What he had done was within the law. He
had had information relevant to a case and he had handed it to the
prosecution for them to use as they thought fit. He had obtained the
information perfectly legally. It had been bequeathed to him. He would
explain that to the magistrate. The man was probably someone he
knew and would likely dismiss the charge—even apologize.

He wondered if they had arrested Warne for this also. But that
seemed ridiculous; the man had obtained the photograph under privilege, and he had used it. What was he supposed to have done? Ignored
it? Allow Robertson Drew to tear everyone else's reputations apart, by
implication, but preserve his own? The men he had torn down, and the
woman, had done nothing illegal, but Drew had. Sodomy was a crime
punishable by imprisonment, never mind the moral outrage of so using
a child. Even if he was not guilty of fraud—and he may well have
been—he certainly wasn't the upstanding citizen he claimed to be.

There was no more time to think about it. The door opened in
front of him again, and he was led through into the magistrates' court.
It had been years since he had had any occasion to be in one. It was
very small and shabby compared with the Old Bailey. There was no
open space to separate the judge from the people, no tall witness stand
with curved steps up to it. The magistrate sat behind a very ordinary
wooden bench.

"Oliver Rathbone," the clerk said, reading from a piece of paper in
his hand. "Charged with perverting the course of justice."

The magistrate looked at Rathbone, then blinked and looked a good deal harder. He opened his mouth to say something and changed his mind.

Rathbone racked his memory to see if he could place the man. Did he know him? If not as a magistrate, then perhaps he knew him as a lawyer? Nothing came to him. But his mind was in chaos anyway, numb with disbelief.

"How do you plead, Mr. . . . Sir . . . Sir Oliver?" The magistrate was clearly extremely uncomfortable. He was a small man perhaps in his forties, balding early.

"Not guilty," Rathbone replied. His voice sounded a good deal steadier than he had expected it to.

Haverstock moved his weight from one foot to the other. "We request remand in custody."

Rathbone swiveled around to stare at him in disbelief. Custody? Jail!

The magistrate gulped, and stared at the inspector. "Are you sure? This—"

"Yes, sir." He seemed about to add something then thought better of it.

That was it. In two or three minutes it was all over. It was embarrassing, even humiliating, yet if this nightmare went on, far worse would be to come. There was no use in Rathbone protesting his innocence. "Perverting the course of justice" was a catchall sort of charge anyway. It covered all kinds of things. That was absurd! This was just a temporary, rather ridiculous exercise in fear and public shame. It was a revenge, but not by Taft. He was dead.

Again Rathbone wondered why on earth the man had killed himself. A verdict of guilty would have been the end of his ministry, but not of his life. And why in God's name would he harm his wife and children? Had he gone completely insane?

Clearly the answer to that was that yes, he had, tragically so. But was his suicide an admission of guilt? Or was it only defeat, despair, the conviction that there was no justice? Did a man kill himself for that?

Yes, possibly. But to first murder his wife and children? Perhaps he believed he was so vital to them that they would not survive without him and saw it as a favor.

Was he in some way responsible for that? No; most criminals had some innocent person who depended on them. That wasn't reason enough to let them go. And what of those who were dependent upon the victim?

Haverstock cleared his throat, and Rathbone realized it had all been finished, decided. He was ushered outside and walked between the two policemen the short distance along the pavement and into the waiting cab.

THE JAIL WHERE HE was to be held until trial was a continuation of the nightmare, which was growing stronger as the numbing effect of shock wore off. Once inside the doors his manacles were removed and he stood dazed, rubbing his wrists while he was very briefly informed of what would happen to him. He heard only half of it: it amounted to little more than indistinguishable sounds washing around him. He was more aware of the smell, thick and stale, filling his nostrils. It grew so powerful it churned his stomach, closing in on him even more than the walls.

He was searched, and his personal belongings were taken away except for his handkerchief. The items were all recorded carefully by a constable with copperplate handwriting: fountain pen, card case, notebook, small comb, wallet containing money. His money had been meticulously counted and came to a lot: four pounds, eight shillings, and seven pence halfpenny, as much as some people earned in a month. They searched again to make sure that was all he had. Some people carried more things in their pockets, he supposed. He thought better of telling them that gentlemen did not; it spoiled the line of a well-tailored jacket.

Then he was put in a barred cell. Perhaps he should count himself fortunate that he was alone, even though he was clearly visible to the inmates of the cells opposite him. There was no privacy. Perhaps even this much safety might not last if the prison became busy and they had to put someone else in with him.

The other men were staring at him now, curious, interested. He was different from them; everything about him said so, from his carefully barber-cut hair to his white shirt with its starched collar, from his Savile Row suit to his well-polished fine kid boots. Even his hands betrayed him: clean and soft compared to those of a laborer, with no ingrained dirt around his nails.

Even without these features, as soon as he spoke his pronunciation and his choice of words would give him away. He wondered how long it would be before he was recognized as a judge, a natural enemy—in fact the worst one: the man who actually sentenced the convicted to prison or to death.

In truth he had never sentenced a man to death. He had been a judge for only a short time, less than a year. He had been a lawyer all his adult life, both prosecuting and defending. He had won far more of his cases than he had lost. Perhaps he would soon find himself pleading his own defense in front of other prisoners hungry for the only revenge they could see against the relentless machinery of the law, which was usually beyond their reach.

Of course he had been inside prison before. He had visited lots of men, and women, accused of all sorts of crimes. Latterly they had been largely serious crimes: rape, treason, murder. Everyone had known that one did not hire Oliver Rathbone for a mere robbery.

How long would it be before someone knew, and then everyone did? He realized for the first time that he was not only humiliated, he was physically afraid of being alone among the other prisoners. Surely it would not be long before he was able to get help and this ridiculous situation would be over.

But what if the situation was never over and he was here for years? What could he have missed that had landed him here? The photographs were his. Goddamn Ballinger, he had left them to Rathbone in his will, there was proof of that at least. Ballinger had not stolen them from anyone, so his possession of them was also aboveboard, however disgraceful his intentions had been.

Of course they might have been considered seriously pornographic, if sold, or even publicly displayed. But he had not been accused of possessing pornography. Was that yet to come? The thought made his whole body flush with heat, followed by a chill that left the sweat on his skin like ice. He would be more ashamed of that than of an accusation such as theft or even physical violence. It was obscene, unbearably shameful.

Perhaps if it had been Drew who had taken his own life, Rathbone could have understood his actions. Or might Taft be in one of the photographs as well, and Rathbone had simply not remembered it? He had looked at them only once when he first received them. The sight revolted him to nausea. What if that was why Taft had taken his own life? He might've thought that if Warne had the pictures of Drew he might have others. Even so, why kill his wife and daughters? With him dead no one would have reason to expose the picture.

Could someone see his actions as coercion? He had given the picture to Warne without telling him what to do with it. He had left it up to him what to decide. Or had Warne felt the pressure implicit? Rathbone was a judge, and as such, a man of unique power and responsibility. Is that how the police would see it? Could it be Warne who had spoken to them?

Hardly. Warne had received the photograph under privilege, and he had used it. That made him as guilty as Rathbone, morally if not legally.

But it was the law they were concerned with.

Gavinton? It made the most sense—except he could not know that it was Rathbone who had given the picture to Warne. Deduction! From the story Hester had told, it was not a great leap of reasoning. It was no secret that Rathbone had not only been the lawyer to represent Ballinger when he came to trial, he had been his son-in-law. Yes, that made sense.

But what else could he have done once he remembered that he had seen Robertson Drew in the photograph? Silence was unacceptable. Should he have recused himself?

Of course he should've. As soon as he recognized Drew. But that would have taken from him the power to . . . what? The power to make certain that justice was done?

How monstrously arrogant! As if he thought nobody else was capable enough, or honorable enough, to do that. Hundreds of people were! It was terrible, and ridiculous to suggest otherwise.

Legally, he should have recused himself. He was caught—guilty.

"Eh! Mr. Fancypants!" one of the prisoners in a cell opposite yelled out. "Wot are you doin' in 'ere wi' the likes of us, then? Pick someone's pocket, did yer?"

There was laughter from beside the taunter, although Rathbone could not see the other occupants of the cell.

Rathbone smiled bitterly. "Sir Fancypants to you," he corrected with a twisted smile.

There was another guffaw of laughter.

"We got a right comic 'ere!" the prisoner opposite told his fellows. He made an elaborate bow, sweeping his arm up in the air before bending low. "We're goin' ter 'ave some proper entertainment, fellers. Something ter keep us from dyin' o' boredom in the long days. Eh! Fancypants! Can yer dance, then? Or sing, mebbe?"

"No," Rathbone told him. "Can you?"

"We can teach yer," the man replied. "Can't we, fellers? Teach yer ter sing real 'igh. And mebbe dance real fast too, an' light on yer feet, if yer try."

This was met by an even more raucous bellow of laughter.

Rathbone wanted to reply with something witty and brave, but his mouth was suddenly dry as dust. He knew what they meant by "sing" and "dance." He had not realized before how afraid he was of physical pain. Would he even survive this?

But it wouldn't happen. It couldn't. At worst he was guilty of misjudgment, not a crime. He would pay whatever fine was necessary, sell the house. It was no real asset to him now, without Margaret, and there wouldn't be any family to need it.

If he were found guilty of this, his career was finished anyway. That was a new thought. Even if he survived prison and came out alive and whole—no broken arms or legs, no knives in the back or other injuries of prison violence, no disease—his life would be irrevocably different.

"Hey! Fancypants! Gone deaf, 'ave yer? Too good ter speak to the likes of us, then?" The voice was jeering now, on the edge of anger.

"Sorry. Did you speak to me?" Rathbone kept his voice almost steady, his tone neither afraid nor aggressive. It was not easy.

"I said—can yer dance?" came the reply.

"Oh, yes, moderately. But I like a space a little larger than this. Cramped, don't you think?" There was a ring of bravado in his words. Might as well be hanged for a sheep as a lamb.

"Yer know, Fancypants, yer might be worth keepin' alive. I like you."

"Thank you," Rathbone answered, not at all sure if the idea was good or bad.

At that point the jailer came back and walked over to Rathbone's cell, but he did not open the door. Instead he spoke to him through the bars.

"Anyone as we should tell you're 'ere?" he asked. "If yer go missin' I expect it'll take 'em a while ter look for yer, like."

Rathbone had deliberately put off facing that decision. He refused to think what his father would feel when the news reached him. It was too painful to acknowledge. It paralyzed all thought.

Who would he ask? Who would help—or would even try? There could be only one answer—Monk.

"Yes," he said, meeting the guard's eyes. "Mr. William Monk. He is commander of the Thames River Police at Wapping. If you would be good enough to tell him what has happened, and that I am here . . ."

The guard shrugged heavy shoulders. "Yer'd be a lot better off wi' a lawyer, but if that's wot yer want, I'll send a message," he agreed. "See where it gets yer." And he wrote it down carefully on a piece of paper, then disappeared, leaving Rathbone to sit down on the straw-filled mattress and wait.

HESTER WAS TROUBLED AS she worked in the kitchen. It was a beautiful afternoon, warm and bright, but she was unaware even of the sunlight streaming in through the window and making patterns on the floor. Oliver Rathbone had been arrested and charged with obstructing justice. Squeaky Robinson had heard and sent her a message in the middle of the morning. Rathbone was in prison and might be there until he was tried.

It seemed inconceivable. Yesterday he was presiding in court over the end, in all but formality, of the trial of Abel Taft. Now Taft and his whole family were dead and Rathbone was in prison.

She was unaware of Scuff standing in the doorway until she turned and bumped into him. She jumped back and nearly dropped the jug she was carrying.

Usually he would have apologized. Today he stood his ground, his face clouded with worry.

"Is it true?" he asked.

She eased the jug down on the nearest bench awkwardly. She had known this was going to happen and been trying to prepare what she would tell him. Now she must come up with an answer that was honest and yet did not frighten him. He was getting tall, growing out of his clothes every few months, but he was still a child in so many ways. It would be easy to frighten him, on the one hand, by letting him see how fragile his precious world really was, and yet to patronize him with lies he could see through would be worse. It would make it difficult for him to trust her, and with Scuff trust was a delicate matter.

"Yes, it's true Sir Oliver is in prison," she said, walking back toward the stove to pull the kettle onto the hob. This sort of thing was best discussed at the table, over tea. It was not something to talk about when half your mind was on something else.

"What did 'e do?" Scuff asked, following her into the kitchen. There was an edge of fear in his voice.

The kettle was not going to boil for a few minutes; there was no need to reach for cups and the tea caddy yet.

"They are saying that he tried to twist the course of justice," Hester answered.

"But 'e's a judge! Did 'e make a mistake?" Scuff was confused. He stood in the middle of the floor, the sunlight around his feet. He was growing out of those boots again, already!

Should loyalty win out over honesty? That was a balance she must get exactly right. He was watching her intently.

"I don't know," she admitted. "But they are saying he did something on purpose."

"What?"

There it was—the question she could either answer or deliberately evade. He would know if she lied. He had watched her face, listened to her for more than two years now. He had survived on London's dockside by never trusting people he shouldn't, by always getting it right. He was not like a usual child.

She drew in a deep breath. Where to begin in this terrible story? Scuff probably knew more than she did about perversion and the abuse of children along the waterfront. He had once been among Jericho Phillips's prisoners himself. How close he had come to being in one of the terrible photographs she did not know. She had never wanted to, and it was possibly a lot easier for Scuff's dignity if he believed she had no idea. If he did ever want to speak of it, it would likely be to Monk, someone of his own gender. As he grew up there would be parts of his life Hester must be excluded from. It was inevitable.

"What are they saying?" he asked again, more urgently, afraid she was going to close him out. Then his imagination would run to all the darkest and most painful places.

"It's quite a long story," she answered at last. "I'll make the tea and tell you as much as I know. Will you pass the milk jug back to the table, please?"

A few moments later, when the tea had been poured but was too hot to drink, and the cake was on the table, Hester had collected her thoughts to a degree she began.

"You know we gathered quite a lot of information about Mr. Taft and the way he asked people for money?"

"Yeah . . ."

"Well, Mr. Drew—remember him?"

"Yeah, pompous git wi' a face like a burst boot—expensive boot—"

She stifled a smile. "Exactly. Well, Mr. Drew was a witness in Mr. Taft's defense, and he tried very hard to make all the witnesses against him look either stupid or weak, even dishonest, so the jury didn't believe them. It's quite a usual thing to do in court. A lot of testimony is just what one person says, rather than another."

He was losing the thread and she could see it. He was too young even to have been in high court, especially one like the Old Bailey.

"Mr. Drew made them all look like liars," she said more directly. "So the prosecution asked Mr. Taft if he trusted Mr. Drew completely and believed all he said. Mr. Taft said Mr. Drew was an upstanding man, so of course he did. Then the prosecution called me to the witness stand and very clearly asked me about Jericho Phillips." She stopped and watched his face.

The shadow of fear was there in his eyes, sharp and painful. He was watching her, waiting for her to hurt him with it, wondering if she would lie to him because she thought he couldn't take it.

"He made me tell him quite a lot," she continued, "because I was one of the witnesses Drew had made look stupid, so the lawyer was trying to show that I wasn't. That way he made an opening, a legal one, to show me one of Jericho Phillips's disgusting photographs."

He blinked. "Why? Mr. Taft didn't 'ave nothing ter do with that."

"That's just the point, Scuff—Mr. Drew did. The picture he showed me was of Mr. Drew, and a small boy." She stopped, hoping he was not going to ask her for any other details. Several of those boys had been his friends.

He bit his lip, blushing. Suddenly she saw the child he had been then, thin-shouldered, slender-necked, his skin still smooth, unblemished by even the slightest beginning of fuzz. At that moment she could have killed Phillips herself. She might have repented of it—but only long after.

Suddenly Scuff's eyes widened. "Where'd 'e get one o' them pictures?" he said incredulously.

"That is the difficulty," she confessed. "When Mr. Ballinger died he left them in his will to Sir Oliver."

"Oh Gawd!" Scuff covered his mouth. "Sorry . . ." But his eyes were wide with horror and understanding. "Is 'e allowed ter do that?"

"Well, I think that's the whole question. You see how that might change the jury's minds?"

He nodded slowly. "Not 'alf. 'Ow are we going ter 'elp 'im, then?"

"I don't know."

"But we are going ter?" The edge of fear was back in his voice, and in his eyes.

"Yes, we are," she said without hesitation. "But we have to deal with the truth, and we don't know yet what that is." That was something of an understatement.

Scuff stared into his cup.

"What is it?" Hester asked when the silence became too long.

"But Drew is bad, in't 'e? Why is it wrong to show the jury wot 'e is?" Scuff asked seriously.

How on earth could she answer that? What concept did Scuff have of the law, and the role of a judge? He had grown up with the only laws being those of survival and loyalty to your own. What did he understand of impartiality, of playing by certain rules, even if it meant you lost? Why hadn't she even thought of all this before, brought it up earlier somehow, so she wouldn't have to stand here trying to explain it all at once? She was going to sound pedantic, and it would seem as if she were making excuses rather than fighting. Then he would think her a coward. And if he thought that, then when he needed her he would not be able to trust her to come forward and fight for him.

"Well, the whole idea of a trial is so that the police—or whoever has made an accusation—has a lawyer to fight on his side, and the person who has been accused has someone to fight on his. The judge is supposed not to take sides at all, just be there to make sure everyone gets a fair chance to tell their side of it. Sometimes the police get it wrong, and the people they accuse are not guilty. Or there's a reason that makes it not as bad as it looks."

Scuff was thinking about it. He had not even taken a second piece of cake.

"It's like games," she tried again. "You have to obey the rules."

"But what if you're right?" he argued. "What if the other person's going ter win 'cos they're cheating. Can't you break the rules then—if they are? It in't fair!"

"Most people think they're right, even when they aren't," Hester pointed out. "And some people don't care whether they're right or not. They just want to win."

"But Sir Oliver in't like that!" he protested. "We know 'im. 'E really likes you. I seen 'im look at you."

Hester felt the warmth flush up her cheeks. Trust Scuff to have noticed that.

"Even the people we care about make mistakes sometimes," she said, picking her words carefully.

"Does that mean if they get it wrong you don't like 'em anymore?" Deliberately he did not avert his eyes from hers. He was going to take the blow, if it came.

That was the question she had been dreading. What if Rathbone had done something seriously wrong? A mistake, even an error of hubris, was not impossible. She needed to explain to Scuff that however much you loved someone, you still didn't cover for him when he made a grave mistake. Would he understand the morality of a greater good being more important than individual love?

He was waiting for her answer, his eyes grave.

"No, it doesn't mean that at all," she replied. "But you may not always like what they do. You . . . you can't say a thing is right just because it's done by someone you like, and wrong because it's done by someone you don't. It hurts desperately if you have to find fault with someone you love, even worse if it's someone who is part of your life. But right and wrong don't change just because of the way you feel about the people involved."

"Is it always right and wrong? In't there anything in the middle?" he asked hopefully.

"Yes, many times there is," she agreed. "That's when it gets really difficult."

He frowned. "'Ow do yer know if it's right or wrong or something in the middle?"

"You don't always," she admitted. "As you get older you begin to realize sometimes just how difficult it can be and how easy it is to make a mistake, even though you're trying not to. When you've made a few yourself, you get slower to judge other people."

He looked at her very carefully, his eyes wide and clear.

"You've never made mistakes, though, 'ave yer?" There was an innocence in his face, a faith in her. She realized with a jolt how deeply he loved her.

Hester found herself blushing. "I wish I hadn't, except I suppose if that were true maybe I wouldn't understand just how easy it is for mistakes to happen, even when we're really trying to avoid them. That would make me very hard on others. It isn't making mistakes that matters so much as whether you learn from them, whether you admit you were wrong or try to blame somebody else. And I suppose what matters most is that you get up again and try not to keep on making the same mistake."

"'Ow many different ones are there?" he asked.

She gave a twisted little smile. "I don't know. I'm still counting."

"An' yer gotter pay for 'em?" he said carefully. "You 'ave, 'aven't yer?"

"Usually. Sometimes not. Sometimes there's a kind of grace where you get forgiven without paying. You don't really deserve it, so you really truly need to make yourself worthy afterward by being grateful and making an effort to change."

"Is that what yer going to make 'appen for Sir Oliver?" He sounded as if he grasped on to that hope tightly.

"I'll try," she responded. "If he did make a mistake, that is. Maybe he didn't, and we can help him prove that."

Scuff relaxed a little. "That's good. Can I 'elp?"

"Probably. I'll certainly ask you, if I can think of anything."

He gave her a sudden, dazzling smile, and then when he was sure she understood, he drank his tea and reached for the other piece of cake. She always put out two, but it was understood between them that both were for him.

IT WAS EVEN MORE difficult for Hester when it came time that evening to discuss the subject with Monk.

Scuff had already gone to bed when Monk came in, tired and wet after a long day on the river dealing with the discovery of a body and the tedious investigation that had proved the death accidental. Of course, he had heard about Rathbone's arrest very soon after it had happened. The jailer's note had reached him, and he had gone to the prison immediately. He had been permitted to see Rathbone, but only for a matter of minutes.

"How is he?" Hester had asked, almost before Monk was through the door. "Is he all right? What did they say he did?"

"He's all right for the moment," Monk had replied. "The charge is rather complicated. Officially it is perversion of the course of justice—"

"What? But he's the judge!" she had exclaimed.

"Exactly. That makes it all the more serious. It has to do with the use of one of Ballinger's photographs. Technically he should have stepped aside and let someone else take his place."

"As judge?"

"Yes. Which would mean abandoning the whole trial and starting again."

"But they might not even have prosecuted a second time!" she had protested.

"I know. That's probably why Rathbone didn't do it, knowing him."

"What will happen to him?"

"I expect they'll try him. I didn't get the chance to ask much more than that. I asked what he needed—"

"He needs a lawyer! Someone to help . . ."

"He said he wanted a clean shirt and personal linen," Monk then replied grimly.

ONCE HE HAD PUT on dry, clean clothes himself and was seated in the warmth of the sitting room, Monk felt a great deal more comfortable, but only marginally happier. Hester had just told him about her conversation with Scuff.

"What are we going to do?" she asked. "Surely all Oliver did was to nudge justice back into the right path? After all, if Drew was in one of these photographs, then he was hardly the upstanding churchman he pretended. The jury needs to know that!"

She saw the flash of humor across Monk's face, lighting his eyes for a moment out of their somber mood. "I don't think the law sees a difference between perversion and a nudge into the right path . . . as you perceive it," he observed.

She was stung, for all the gentleness in his voice. "You mean you think he's guilty?" she challenged. This was going to be even worse than she expected.

"I don't know. And if you're honest, neither do you." He smiled, but there was pain in it. "I might have done the same thing myself. I don't know. We never do until we're tested. But that doesn't make it right, either morally or legally. I've tripped over my own pride before now."

She ignored the mention of pride. She knew what he meant about Rathbone, and about himself. "But Drew was in that picture!" she protested. "And if Taft isn't guilty, why did he kill himself? Actually, whether he was guilty or not, why kill his family? Do you suppose he's in one of the photographs as well? Was he afraid Warne would produce that one too?"

Monk leaned forward a little, his dark gray eyes steady on hers. "That's a more interesting question—why did they arrest Rathbone at all? How did they even know he had anything to do with it? Rathbone said he retained Warne as his own lawyer, so Warne would be protected by privilege from telling anyone who gave him the photographs."

Hester felt a little chill, as if there were a draft in the room. "Is it possible it was Warne who told them, anyway?" she asked. "But that doesn't make sense. Surely if he were going to do anything it would have to have been before he used the picture, not afterward—wouldn't it? Otherwise, wouldn't he be equally guilty, of violating the privilege?"

"I don't know," Monk confessed. "Perhaps they offered him the chance to escape prosecution if he testified against Rathbone? Or they went for him in the first place, and he gave up Rathbone to save himself?"

"That's vile!" she said with sudden fury. "What kind of a man is he if he would do that? What kind of a lawyer? Lawyers have a duty of confidentiality! They can't just betray anyone and pretend it's all right." She was so angry she could barely get the words out.

"No," he replied, but there was hesitation in his voice. "Apart from anything else, Warne would know such an act would ruin his reputation. No one who had any secrets worth a damn would employ him."

"Everyone facing trial has secrets," she responded. "Even if they're innocent of the particular charge they're facing."

"Exactly. I can't imagine he would risk his entire livelihood to betray Rathbone."

"Then who was it?" she demanded. "If it wasn't Warne, then who could it be?"

He settled a little deeper in his seat, relaxing weary muscles.

"We don't know for certain it wasn't Warne. But Rathbone has enemies, Hester. He's prosecuted some very important people, people who have friends and influence. And he's defended a few people that others would rather see executed. He's stirred up a lot of dirt, one way or another. He's gone where his cases led him and has not been afraid whose toes he trod on. Some of them are going to be only too happy to come out of the woodwork now and kick him while he's down."

Another, darker thought occurred to her. "Worse than that, William, what about the other people in the photographs? We don't know who they are, and maybe Oliver doesn't either, but *they* know. And who is to say Ballinger even had all the photographs. There may be people who think Oliver has their picture, but who don't know for sure—I bet they'd rather see him destroyed and put away so there's not even a chance that he's a risk to them. London could be seething with enemies he doesn't even know he has."

Monk was frowning. "But that would be stupid. Put his back against the wall and he'll come out fighting. He would have nothing to lose. Even if he goes to prison he could have all the pictures published, just to get back at his enemies. That seems even riskier."

She stared at him intensely, her heart racing. She felt as if her throat were so tight she could hardly breathe. "William . . . where are the photographs?"

He caught her fear instantly. "In his house, I suppose. I don't know. Perhaps we'd better ask him and make sure they're put somewhere else. Otherwise someone desperate enough could set fire to it. They could burn the servants alive, and Oliver, too, if they wait till he gets bail and goes back there."

"Yes. They should be in a bank vault or something. Just don't bring them here!"

He said nothing, his expression bleak.

She looked at his face and saw no light in it. "I'm sorry. But, please . . ." She trailed off, more frightened than she wanted to admit. What had begun as a shadow was spreading far wider than she had foreseen. Was the trial of one man guilty of fraud worth all this?

She had thought so at the time when she had listened to Josephine Raleigh and seen herself so clearly in Josephine's distress. It was a chance to put right what she had failed signally to do for her own father.

Taft was vicious, destructive . . . seeing now what he had been capable of, with his actions against his own wife and children, it was clear the extent of his disease of the soul was far greater than she had imagined.

But if she had not meddled, then Taft and his family would still be alive, and Rathbone would be safe at home.

And John Raleigh might be dead like her father.

When do you walk away? How can you know?

"We've got to help Oliver," she said. "For Scuff as well as for himself."

Monk looked puzzled. "For Scuff?"

"For heaven's sake!" She was close to tears. She could feel them prickling in her eyes and the tightness getting worse in her throat. "Oliver is our friend, William! Scuff's watching to see if we're loyal to the people we care for, even if they make mistakes and everyone else turns against them."

He looked startled. "Does he think we'd do that to him?"

"He doesn't know!" she cried out. "He's afraid! He's terrified that love is conditional, that we love people only when they do the right thing, and that that applies to anyone."

Understanding flooded his face. "He's only a child! You don't . . ." He let out his breath in a sigh.

"You were afraid," she pointed out. "When you thought you killed Joscelyn Grey, you were afraid I'd abandon you."

He flushed slightly. "But you didn't think I had!"

"I didn't think so. I didn't know! But if you had, I wouldn't have walked away."

"Were you that much in love with me?" he asked very quietly. "You never said so."

"No I wasn't, you complacent oaf!" she cried in exasperation. "But even if you had killed him, I knew you were a good man, and I couldn't leave you to hang for it. Even good people sometimes do stupid and ugly things. Besides, no one else believed in you. If I hadn't fought for you, who else would have?"

"No one," he said even more quietly. "Sergeant Evan did only because you did. Honestly, even I wouldn't have fought for me. You know, one day you'll have to tell Scuff about that. But not yet. I don't think he's ready for it—and I know I'm not. I need him to think better of me than that, for a while. But if it goes badly with Rathbone, maybe we should tell him. Then at least he'll know you never give up, and never leave." He breathed in and out slowly. "Perhaps we should tell him sooner, after all."

· Hester shook her head briefly, as if to dispel the idea, then started again, even more seriously. "William, do you think Oliver made the wrong decision? I mean morally wrong? How could he sit back and let Taft get away with everything, let Drew slander all those people who were only doing their best to right a wrong? They were so vulnerable and Drew destroyed them with words. And it was him in the picture, unmistakably."

"I know," he agreed, reaching out his hand and catching hers. He held her gently, but with too much strength for her to pull away. "But yes, I think he may have made a mistake in this. He should have destroyed those photos when he first got them."

"But they can be used for good!" she protested. "That would have left him helpless to . . . William, you can't throw away power just because it could be misused, or you might make a mistake, or maybe it'll turn out badly. Because—maybe it won't! Maybe it'll help someone. Can you imagine standing over somebody with a knife in your hand—"

"And using it on him?" he interrupted. "Deciding if he had the right to live or die? No . . ."

"No!" she snapped. "Deciding whether you can really cut out the gangrene or the appendix before it bursts, or open the wound and stitch an artery so he doesn't bleed to death. Deciding if you have the courage to try, or if you'd rather just watch him die and hope you don't get blamed for it. Well, you *are* to blame if you just stand there with the knife instead of using it! If you could have done something and you were too cowardly to try because you were afraid for yourself, then you are responsible. Evil things happen because good people are too scared of what consequences they might bring on themselves. We thought that Oliver was wrong because he intervened. Maybe he was wrong. But what would we think of him if he could have saved someone, and he did nothing?"

"That rather depends on whether he did nothing because he knew it was wrong to do it, or because he was afraid to, for his own safety," Monk answered.

She gave him a withering look. "And we always know the difference there, don't we? I can think of a score of times when I hadn't the faintest idea what was wise or how things would turn out, but acted anyway, because the alternative seemed too terrible. Maybe I wasn't always right—maybe Oliver wasn't. But I'm sure he thought hard about it. He didn't back away because he wanted to be safe. And I would have wagered all I have that you wouldn't either."

She saw his face pale and wondered if she had gone too far. But she meant what she had said, and she would not lower her eyes.

"I have a wife and child to think of now," he replied levelly. "I can't be as rash, or as self-righteous, as I used to be."

"Don't blame me!" she accused him. "And don't you damn well blame Scuff either! He's looking to see if you'll help Rathbone because he needs to know you'll be loyal, come hell or high water."

"He also needs to know I've got a modicum of sense," Monk replied, his body stiff. "And that I love both of you enough not to take stupid risks and leave you defenseless." He gave a twisted smile. "Although looking at you I don't know what makes me imagine you've ever been defenseless."

She took a deep, shaking breath and let it out slowly. "I need you," she said so gently he only just heard her. "Not to defend me, but just because I couldn't bear to be without you. But I need you to be who you are—not hobbled because of me, or Scuff. So what are we going to do to help Oliver?"

"Find out the truth," he replied. "Or as much of it as we can. And not just about who started the prosecution against Rathbone, and why. And why the hell Taft killed his whole family, for that matter. Nothing about this case adds up."

"Good," Hester replied firmly. "And we must get those terrible pictures out of Oliver's house."

"Yes," he agreed. "But not tonight. Let me think . . . and sleep."

She gave him a sudden, radiant smile and saw the relief flood back into his eyes.

8

To begin with Rathbone had been dazed by the speed and the horror of what had happened to him. However, after the first night, when he awoke feeling stiff, his body aching, he knew exactly where he was and nothing of the previous day had been forgotten. Perhaps he had not slept deeply enough for any of it to have left him. All night he had lain on the hard, narrow bunk under a single greasy blanket, which smelled so stale he deliberately kept it low around his chest, away from his face. He refused to think who had been on it before him or when it was last washed.

He was awake when the jailer came with a tin jug and bowl of tepid water so that he could wash and shave and would look at least presentable, if not clean or uncrumpled. They lent him a comb for his hair and took it away again as soon as he had used it. Only then did he wonder if it might have lice in it. He had not even considered that before touching it. The thought was disgusting, and he tried to force it out of his mind. There were immeasurably more terrible things to think about.

Physical discomfort was trivial, and as far as he could see, unalterable. He could adjust his position, sit or stand, but he could not walk more than about five paces before having to turn and walk back. It was good only to uncramp his legs. The sounds of tin or stone, voices, the occasional scrape or clang of a door barely intruded on his thoughts.

If he were convicted, whoever sat as judge would be ordered to give him the harshest sentence the law allowed. This would be partly as an example to all other jurists, that they, above all others, must keep the law, and partly to demonstrate to the public that they had no partiality toward their own. Whatever they felt personally, Rathbone had no doubt that the authorities would make certain there was no misunderstanding in the direction of leniency. They had to, for their own safety.

What could Rathbone do to save himself? Was there a legal defense? He had given the prosecution evidence that called into very serious question the honor and integrity of their chief witness. That was not illegal. Nor could he have given it to the police earlier: he had not realized he had it.

No. The sin was in not having given it to both parties and then recusing himself from the case. It always came back to that. But if he had done so, it would automatically have been declared a mistrial. Both Taft and Drew's reputations would have been unblemished. It was highly unlikely they would ever bring the case again—not unless stronger evidence had emerged.

Somewhere near him two men were shouting strings of inarticulate abuse at each other. More banging of tin mugs against the bars and the sound of footsteps and voices. Was someone coming? Monk again, to see him? Then the footsteps receded and went another way.

Was Rathbone's real crime possessing the photographs in the first place, and not destroying them as soon as Ballinger's lawyer had brought them to him after Ballinger's death? What arrogance had made him imagine he was immune to the temptation to misuse them, as Ballinger had? Why had he thought he was above such human frailty?

He could recall even now the horror with which he had seen them, looking through more than half of them, recognizing faces and realizing the incalculable power he held in his hands. Should he have pushed it away from him then, refused to pick up the weapon, in case it slipped in his keeping and endangered the innocent and gradually corrupted him?

But he had never used those photos for his own gain. In fact, he had barely used them at all! There were men from all walks of life whose faces were in that locked box. Should he destroy what might be the only means to curb their power?

He still was not sure of the answer to that.

He knew one thing for certain: he could not hand over the box of photographs to anyone else. If he had given it to the home secretary it would place on him a burden that would cripple him. There were some things that should not be known, sins that needed redemption in darkness and silence, where their poison could spread no further.

Perhaps, for the sake of those, he should have destroyed them all. But it was too late to wish that now.

When was Monk coming back? Rathbone had been in prison twenty-four hours already, and there had been no one else to see him. Of course Monk was the only person to whom he had sent a message. But it would not be long before everyone knew. He could imagine what the newspapers would make of it.

The jailer came with a breakfast of porridge and tea. The porridge was revolting, thick and lumpy, a bit like tepid glue. But Rathbone could not afford not to eat. He must keep awake, watching and thinking. He must come up with a strategy to defend himself, first from the legal charge, and then later on, if it all came to the worst, from the other inmates.

He was brooding over that with deepening despair when the jailer came back again, this time to fetch him, saying that he had a visitor. He refused to give any more information than that.

Rathbone stood up awkwardly, his muscles almost locked with stiffness after the discomfort of the night. Was it Monk again, at last? Or was it someone else?

"What's the matter, Fancypants?" one of the other prisoners called out jeeringly. He was a scrawny man with matted hair. "Not feelin' so much like dancin' today, are yer? I'll larn yer, after yer bin before the beak!"

"Gracious of you," Rathbone said sarcastically. Perhaps it was not wise, but he could not let them see he was afraid.

The corridors were as dank as before, but he had remembered them as longer, somehow larger. It was only moments until he was in the small room where prisoners were allowed to see their lawyers.

"Fifteen minutes," the jailer warned Rathbone then let him inside, slamming the door. They heard iron on stone; the heavy bolt was locked home the instant he was through the door. A scarred wooden table was screwed to the floor, and two hard-backed wooden chairs sat one on either side.

Monk was waiting for him.

Rathbone's first reaction was overwhelming relief and gratitude. Then, the moment after, he felt an embarrassment almost as acute. Had he been free to change his mind and retreat, he might have. But he was not free—the door had already closed behind him, literally, and in the larger sense of his life and his future.

He walked forward, shook Monk's hand rather as if in a dream, then sat down.

Monk sat opposite him. There was no time to waste in niceties, even a habitual "How are you?"

"You did give Warne the photograph?" Monk said immediately. "Under some sort of privilege, I presume?"

"Yes, of course. I took it to him and told him where I got it and how. I left it up to him whether to use it or not." Did that sound like an excuse? "I didn't know he was going to call Hester."

Monk dismissed that with a slight movement of his hand. "It was the best thing to do," he replied. "And it gave him a chance to show the jury, and anyone else, that she wasn't the emotionally fragile woman Drew had painted her to be. It was the perfect tactic. Calling me might have been practically difficult at short notice and would have looked as if I were defending Hester. Not nearly so effective."

"You make it sound cold-blooded," Rathbone said quietly. He was ashamed that Hester had been used, even though he had not done it himself.

Monk's face darkened with impatience. "For God's sake, Rathbone, you know Hester better than that! She doesn't need protecting, by you or anyone else, and she wouldn't thank you for it. We need to find out who laid the charge against you, and why. Who else even knew about the photographs, and that you have them?"

"I don't know," Rathbone replied, chastened. He was too desperate to be angry. There was no time for emotional self-indulgence. "I've been trying to work that out myself." He smiled bitterly. "I've made a great many enemies in my career, but I didn't realize any of them would stoop to this. Every case is won by someone and necessarily lost by someone else. It's the nature of law, at least in the adversarial system. Sometimes it's the skill of the lawyer; quite often it's simply the evidence."

"Is that how you feel when you lose? That it was the evidence?" Monk asked, amusement flickering for an instant in his eyes then disappearing.

"Not at the time," Rathbone admitted. "But after a day or two, yes, it is." His mind raced; he tried to think of any case he had won that was so bitter his opponent could carry a grudge of this magnitude. Had he ever done anything worthy of such resentment, such patient hunger for revenge?

Monk was not prepared to wait for him. "Why did you give the photograph to Warne?" he asked grimly. "The real reason, not the superficial one. We haven't time for excuses."

Rathbone was startled. "To stop Taft, of course. He was ruining the reputations, and in a way the lives of simple, gullible people who had trusted him—in the name of God—because that was what he asked of them. They weren't doing it for any hope of profit. If it were that sort of confidence trick I'd have less pity for them." He heard his voice grating with anger, his own situation momentarily forgotten. "I know a great deal of the money found its way into Taft's pockets. Very little of it ever went to the charities he named, despite the way he talked his way through the account books. And those who gave so generously ended up cheated and desperate—their faith and their dreams taken from them, and their dignity. And then he mocked them in open court." He leaned forward across the battered wooden table. "Damn it, Monk, Taft and Drew both deserve to be shown up for what they are. I'm sorry Taft killed himself, but surely the fact that he killed his wife and daughters as well says something of what kind of a man he was."

Monk sighed. "The question has passed beyond whether Taft was a cheat, or Drew an abuser of children. It's become whether you, as a judge in our legal system, and therefore in a place of unique trust, used secret knowledge to twist the outcome of a trial over which you presided, and did it for some personal reason of *your own*. They can call it perversion of justice because you should have recused yourself, and you know that, but there's a bigger picture beneath that, and that is what concerns me."

Rathbone heard the words with a surge of anger then, looking into Monk's eyes, a sudden horrifying clarity. Monk was right. He had seen what the legal system was going to see: their desperate need to protect themselves by cutting off the gangrenous limb—himself.

Monk was watching him quietly, as if he could see past all the protective masks into the desperately vulnerable heart inside.

"What motive would they ascribe to me, do you think?" Rathbone said, his voice shaking for the first time.

"Arrogance to think yourself above the law and to retrieve what you lost in the Jericho Phillips trial," Monk answered him. "To give Hester the chance to show people that she has all the courage and judgment that she failed to show then. To turn back the clock."

Rathbone sat silently. Had he wanted to do that? Was exposing Drew only the excuse? He had not thought so at the time. The hot anger in the front of his mind had surfaced on behalf of the same victims Hester had wished to save. But would he have done it if the person involved had been somebody else, somebody he did not know? Or over whom he had not still felt such corrosive guilt?

"I'll find out all I can," Monk was saying. "I think there may be a lot about this that we don't know yet."

Rathbone jerked his attention back to the moment. There was no time to waste—perhaps only minutes left for this meeting. He was a prisoner. He stood up and sat down when other people commanded him to. He ate what he was given, and only at their pleasure. In time perhaps he would wear only their clothes. He would look like any other convict. Would the time come when he would feel like that—seem like that, to others?

His father would never abandon him, no matter how bitterly disappointed he might be.

The thought of his disappointment was so painful it tightened around Rathbone's heart like a closing fist. He could hardly draw in his breath.

Monk was talking again. There was a sudden, intense compassion in his face, burning a moment and then vanishing.

"You must get someone to represent you, as soon as possible."

Rathbone started.

"Don't even imagine you can speak for yourself," Monk said sharply. "You can't do it any more than a surgeon can remove a bullet out of his own back. You must find someone you trust and, more to the point, who trusts you."

Rathbone was shaken. The second of Monk's conditions was something he had not even thought of. Who would trust him? Who would be prepared to jeopardize his own career by speaking up for Rathbone, in these circumstances?

"But I don't even know who to trust because I have no idea who started this prosecution," he said wearily. "I'm as blind as a bat stumbling about at the bottom of a hole."

"I'll do what I can to find out who is behind this," Monk replied without even the flicker of a smile at the absurdity of the picture evoked. "But I think, then, your father is the man to find you a lawyer. With the respect he's earned he'll be able to employ the best person, someone to trust no matter what he thinks of this issue." He smiled now, with both pity and friendly jest. "And whatever he thinks of you in general."

Rathbone wished to protest, but he felt too vulnerable to fight.

Monk must have seen the pain in his face. He leaned forward a little across the scarred and stained table. "You've fought far too many cases for anyone to be impartial about you, and won too many of them. Don't drown in self-pity now. You chose what you wanted to do, and you did it extremely well . . . well enough to have got yourself noticed by the winners, and the losers. It is too late for you to seek solace in anonymity. That door shut a long time ago."

Rathbone had always known Monk had a ruthless streak, but this was the first time he could remember being at the painful end of it. And yet what use to him was a man who flinched at anything or who would step aside from the truth to save a temporary injury?

He had been robbed of a shield, but it was a worthless one, and perhaps he was stronger for the glimpse of reality.

Then the other thing that Monk had said reached him and he was forced to face it.

"I haven't told my father yet. I wanted to have some kind of an answer before I did, so I could soften the blow, tell him what was behind it, and . . ." He stopped. There was no understanding in Monk's face at all, only disgust.

"Rubbish!" Monk said curtly. "You're not protecting him, you're protecting yourself. You're shutting him out from helping you because you don't want to face his pain. Sort out your thoughts right now, and then tell him. To keep him out of this would be both cowardly and selfish. He might forgive you for it because he wouldn't pile his anger on top of what you already have for yourself—but I would damn well be angry! And more to the point to you, so would Hester."

Rathbone winced. Momentarily he wanted to lash back at Monk, hurt him just as much. But it was more than his own vulnerability that stopped him. He remembered Monk's fears in the past. He too had spent time in prison, falsely accused, more falsely than Rathbone was now. He knew what it was like to have all judgment against you. He also knew that the only way out was to fight, to gather your wits and your courage and marshal your thoughts.

And yes, Rathbone must tell his father properly, before Henry heard it from someone else.

"I have nothing with which to write a letter," he said, "and no one to send with it before news of my arrest will be in the newspapers . . ."

"I'll tell him for you," Monk replied. "But it might be better if I ask Hester to. She always got along well with Henry. He'll know that if she's on your side you'll survive it, one way or another."

Before Rathbone could reply the jailer returned and Monk was told that his time was up.

Rathbone was returned to his cell, weary and confused. He had wanted desperately to find some hope before his father found out what had happened. But Monk was right, of course. He would find out soon enough by seeing it in the newspaper, or else some busybody would tell him assuming he already knew, wanting to commiserate with him. The hurt of finding out the details from anyone except Rathbone himself would be the same: the shock, even the humiliation that he had not been told, would add to his father's grief. Telling Henry would be worse for Rathbone than the arrest, the physical discomfort, and the indignity of this wretched prison, but it must be faced. Hester would share only the bare minimum, he knew. Then Henry would come, and by the time he did, Rathbone must be prepared with courage and a plan.

It was almost three hours later when he was called to the interview room again. Henry Rathbone was standing beside the table, tall and lean, though a little stooped now. His face was calm, completely composed, but the grief was unmistakable in his eyes.

The jailer was by the doorway, watching, his expression unreadable. It could have been respect or contempt, a prurient curiosity, or complete indifference.

Rathbone indicated the chair and Henry sat down in it. Rathbone took the other, with the table between them.

"Fifteen minutes," the jailer warned, and went outside, clanging the door behind him and turning the key so the falling of the tumblers was audible.

"Hester told me what happened in court, and that you'd been arrested, but not much else," Henry said immediately. "I assume it *was* you who gave the photograph of Robertson Drew to Warne?"

"Yes."

"Why?" Henry asked. "Why did you give it to Warne? What did you want him to do with it?"

That was the question Rathbone had known he would ask, and he had tried to prepare an answer.

"Because he was losing the case," he said. "I meant him to do exactly what he did. Drew and Taft between them destroyed the credibility of every witness against them, even Hester. Taft was going to be acquitted and set free to do exactly the same thing again, vindicated and with an even wider audience to fleece, even more people whose faith he could destroy."

"An evil man," Henry agreed. "But were you sure that was the only way to deal with him?"

To anyone else Rathbone might have protested that it was, even that Drew deserved nothing but to be disgraced in front of the many people he had tried so thoroughly to destroy. However, he knew that was not the point now, and Henry would not be sidetracked.

"It was the only way I could think of at the time," Rathbone replied. "And it was certain. Just raising a slight doubt wouldn't have achieved anything. He'd been ruthless and the jury believed him." He looked down at his hands on the table. "If you don't lie yourself, you don't have that instinctive feel for other people's weaknesses. You can't manipulate people's faith or gullibility, so you can't see when other people do it because it just doesn't occur to you. Most of the parishioners were like that, and most of the jury." He raised his head again and met Henry's eyes. "For heaven's sake," he said urgently, "we pick our jurors from men of property, men who don't know what it's like to be poor, disadvantaged, ill educated, and on the border of survival. It's supposed to be a jury of your peers, but by definition it isn't."

Memory of the trial was sharp in his mind. He could see Drew on the stand and hear his confident, slightly unctuous voice.

"Drew was very persuasive," he went on. "If I hadn't seen that photograph I might have believed him myself. And if he hadn't savaged Hester, I might not even have looked for the photograph."

Henry smiled very slightly. "And that was the turning point, not the reason?"

Rathbone thought for a moment. It *was* the turning point because without that there would have been no excuse for Warne to raise the picture in evidence at all. But was it also his reason for taking such a monumental risk with his own career? Would he have done exactly the same had Drew not attacked Hester? Had his mind really been totally focused on delivering justice only within this particular case? He had lain awake and thought hard about it before making his decision, but had he thought clearly? Had he been completely honest? With all the disgust, the outrage, did he even know how to be?

Would he have done it at all if he had been with Margaret still, comfortable and happy? Perhaps not.

"I don't know," he answered. "I thought so at the time, but now I don't know anymore. I certainly don't know how to offer any defense."

"Of course you don't," Henry agreed. "But then you aren't going to. I have considered whom to approach to represent you, and in my opinion Rufus Brancaster would be best. However, if you have someone you prefer, please let me know and I shall have him come to you."

Rufus Brancaster. Rathbone tried to place the name and failed. As far as he could think, he had never faced him in court. Certainly in the short time he had been a judge Brancaster had not been before him.

"I don't know him," he said tentatively. The decision was his, everything that mattered in his future rested on it, but he did not want to challenge his father, or sound distrustful of his judgment. Heaven help him, his own had been fatally flawed.

"I know," Henry said with a bleak grimace of humor. "He is from Cambridge . . ."

Rathbone's heart sank. He was probably a friend of his father's, a decent man, elderly, a professor or something of that sort. Either way, a man completely unfit to battle it out in the ruthless courtrooms of London. How could he refuse politely? He looked at his father's face and saw gentleness in it, and beneath that, the fear.

At that moment, Rathbone would've given anything he had to undo his own arrogant stupidity—but it was too late.

He thought about his mother, and what she would think of his betrayal of the family if she were still alive. She had believed in him so intensely as a child, unwaveringly. She had told him he could do anything. She had even sent him away to school, smiling as she hugged him for what she knew would be the last time, and watched him walk away, cheerfully ignorant. She had not clung to him for that extra moment, nor called him back.

What if Henry were doing his best, but Brancaster was useless? How he would blame himself afterward!

"Please ask him to come," Rathbone said, then instantly wondered how big a mistake that was going to be. "He might not be willing to act for me when he knows more of the case. If he can't, then I will have to reconsider . . ."

"I doubt he'll refuse. He's a good man and never gives up a fight. But if he does, then I'll continue to look," Henry answered. There was a shadow of disappointment in his eyes. "Is there anything I can do for you? Do you wish me to see if Margaret is all right?" It was an awkward question, one put only tentatively.

Rathbone smiled, self-mockingly. "No, thank you. There is no help you can offer her, and I would prefer you didn't leave yourself open to her comments."

"Is it finished?" Henry said quietly. There was no way in his face to tell what he felt.

"I think so," Rathbone admitted. "It was more of a mistake than I had realized before. I'm sorry." He was sorry, but the failure of his marriage was only a small part of many other larger and more urgent things he had to grieve over now.

The guard returned and told Henry it was time for him to leave.

Henry stood up slowly, swaying for a moment and then catching his balance by putting his hand on the table.

"I'll come again . . . soon," he said a little huskily. "Keep your heart up." Then without looking back he walked to the door, past the guard, and out. He didn't say anything about his feelings; he never did. But it was not necessary. Of all the things in the world that Rathbone knew, or thought he knew, he had never doubted his father's love. What he felt now was the terrible, choking weight of having let him down.

IT WAS ANOTHER ENDLESS, painful day in the prison, before Rathbone heard that his lawyer had come to see him. He had spent the time grateful to be alone in the cell, although jeered at now and then by the inmates close enough to see through the bars of both their cells and his. He would be no match for them physically. Even the puniest of them would be wiry and quick on his feet, used to fighting for anything he could get. Rathbone had no weapon but his wits.

He had gone over and over what he needed to say in this meeting. Regardless of Monk's warning to not attempt to defend himself, he had still imagined what course Brancaster would take. But each time he did, he felt only more despair—the facts were undeniable, and he was too easy a target. They would make an example out of him, he was certain, no matter what argument Brancaster made.

He had dreaded the guard coming to escort him to the meeting, which was ridiculous because it would be far worse for him if Brancaster did not arrive. Was the man really the fighter that Henry believed him to be? Even if he was . . . not even the best could win without weapons, ammunition.

He did not want to hurt his father. He must accept Brancaster, however futile the battle seemed. He must be courteous, helpful, appear to have trust in him.

The guard marched him along the corridor to the same small, stone-floored cell, and Rathbone found himself face-to-face with a very dark gentleman, no more than forty at the most. He was about Rathbone's height but perhaps a little broader in the shoulder. His features were strong. He was handsome in a mercurial sort of way, and there was a sense of confidence in him almost as if he imagined himself invulnerable.

As soon as the door was closed and locked Brancaster inclined his head in acknowledgment, then indicated the chair for Rathbone.

"We have a reasonable amount of time," he began without preamble, "but there is a great deal to sort through. I imagine you would prefer to discuss the details of the case before deciding whether you wish to retain my services beyond today. I have offered to take your case as a favor to your father, for whom I have the deepest respect—should you agree, of course. When we have discussed the situation, I shall tell you what I believe we may reasonably hope for."

Rathbone found his manner blunt, almost brutal. He would not have spoken to a client that way. But then he had never defended another lawyer, one with more experience and a greater reputation than his own. He looked steadily into Brancaster's slightly hooded, unblinking eyes and had absolutely no idea what he was thinking.

"Agreed," he said simply, not trusting his voice to remain steady for much more.

Brancaster sat back and studied him carefully. His face was unsmiling; yet there was nothing hostile in attitude.

"You are charged with conspiring to pervert the course of justice," he said after a moment or two. "But they are actually blaming you indirectly for Taft's murder of his family and then his own suicide. And you can be certain the prosecution will make sure the court hears all the details. They will most likely have read it in the newspapers, and he will remind them at every opportunity. People hear what they want to hear. But I imagine you know that!"

"Of course I do," Rathbone rejoined. "But it was Drew in the photograph, not Taft. I don't see how the connection between Drew's behavior and Taft's death can be so close-knit that I can be blamed, in a way that will hold up in court, anyway."

Brancaster raised his eyebrows.

"Was Taft in any of the other photographs? There are more, aren't there?"

"Yes, there are. I haven't counted them," Rathbone answered, "but there are at least fifty. I don't remember Taft in any of them, so I assume not, but I could be wrong."

"He's an arrogant man," Brancaster smiled drily. His eyes were fixed directly on Rathbone's; even so it was a second or two before Rathbone saw the flicker of irony in them, not even enough to be called amusement.

Rathbone felt it keenly. If ever a man could be accused of arrogance, it was himself.

"We may be able to win the legal argument, then," Brancaster went on, "or maybe not, depending on if they amend the charge before we get to court. This, as it stands, is enough to hold you, and for now that is all they need. But we must also win the moral argument. I've looked into the case against Taft. From what I read, until the moment Warne produced the picture, Taft was definitely winning. He was a very plausible liar, and Drew even more so. You should have recused yourself. The picture changed the course of justice, whether it perverted it or not. I assume Gavinton was so taken aback that he had not even considered demanding that you prove the authenticity of it?"

Rathbone was beginning to regain a little of his composure. Brancaster was nothing like the dry and rather otherworldly academic he had been expecting. He owed his father an apology for his lack of faith in him. And for a little while it was good to engage his brain in his familiar profession. It was a brief escape back into his own world.

"I doubt Gavinton wanted the jury's mind on the thing any longer than necessary," he said drily. "And he certainly wouldn't want them to have to look at it."

Brancaster smiled for the first time. "I'm sure. Did you think of that at the time?"

"No. I gave it to Warne and let him do with it as he thought right, under legal privilege, of course. I actually began to think he wasn't going to use it at all. Which makes me wonder—who brought the prosecution against me? Why me and not Warne? He is really the one who used the picture, in the end."

"A lot of interesting questions, Sir Oliver," Brancaster agreed. "How did anyone know it was you who gave it to Warne? Who else did you tell?"

"No one but Warne himself," he replied. "And if he thought it was wrong enough to turn me in, why did he use it?"

"As I said, a lot of questions," Brancaster repeated. "What did you tell Warne about where you got the pictures in the first place?"

"The truth!"

"Which is?"

Rathbone felt his throat tighten and a certain sense of shame fill him with unwelcome heat. "They were bequeathed to me by my father-in-law." He saw Brancaster's amazement flash before he masked it, but he did not interrupt.

"He had used them for blackmail," Rathbone went on. He heard his own voice as if it belonged to someone else. "I tried, unsuccessfully, to defend him on a charge of murder. He was to be hanged, from which I could not save him. He threatened to use the photographs to bring down half the establishment if I did not mount an appeal . . ." He found himself breathless, his chest tight.

"How did you prevent him from doing that?" Brancaster asked. "I think I prefer not to know, but I have to ask. This case appears to have some uglier possibilities than I had assumed." It was a thundering understatement, and Rathbone was as aware of that as Brancaster.

"I didn't," Rathbone answered, wondering if Brancaster would believe him—indeed, if anybody would. "He told me the photographs were safe. That they would be in the hands of someone else who could use them. Then he was murdered."

"In prison?" There was a raw edge of incredulity to Brancaster's voice.

"Yes."

"By whom?"

"They never found out."

"And the pictures . . . who had them?"

"His lawyer, I assume. That's who delivered them to me."

Brancaster took a deep breath. "Who else knows this? And please be careful to give me an honest answer. Believe me, you can't afford to protect anyone else at this point."

"I don't know who else Ballinger told. I told Monk, and Hester Monk, and recently my father."

"No one else?"

"No."

"I said don't lie to me, Sir Oliver," Brancaster's eyes were hard, his voice grating. "I should have included 'don't lie by omission.' And, don't be naïve. Did you not mention such an extraordinary event to your wife? She was Ballinger's daughter, after all."

Rathbone noticed the curious use of the past tense, as if Margaret were dead. As far as love was concerned, or loyalty, perhaps she was. That still hurt. Why? Why did he allow it to? He did not know her now.

"She never believed her father guilty." Rathbone said quietly. "I could not shatter what was left of her faith in him by telling her more than she needed to know. And I would not have shown them to her anyway. And without the physical evidence, I know she could have gone on disbelieving me, even if I had told her the truth."

"But you did not feel such a need to protect Mrs. Monk?" Brancaster questioned.

For the first time Rathbone laughed, a hard, jerky sound torn out of him. "Hester saw the live victims," he said witheringly. "She would hardly be thrown into a fit of the vapors by photographs. She was an army nurse. She has seen men blown to bits on the battlefield and gone in to help those who were left alive. For any man I know to protect her from the truth is a laughable idea. Perhaps that's why Warne chose her to identify Drew in court."

"That was rather well done," Brancaster remarked with respect in his voice. "I shall be very sorry if I find it was he who brought you to the attention of the authorities. Have you any connections with Drew or Taft that I should know about?"

Rathbone tried to think of anything. He realized how much he was impressed with Brancaster. It would be a very hard blow indeed if Brancaster declined to take the case.

"Only that Hester—Mrs. Monk—decided to investigate Taft, and it was her inquiries, employing her bookkeeper from the Portpool Lane clinic, that uncovered the main details of Taft's fraud. But I didn't know anything of that at the time."

"And your acquaintance with Mrs. Monk?" Brancaster asked. He did not need to explain his precise meaning; it was perfectly clear from his expression.

"Friends," Rathbone replied, not avoiding his eyes. "At one time I was in love with her. I decided she was not the right sort of wife for me, and she was in love with Monk, whom she married not long after that. We have remained friends."

Brancaster waited for him to add more, perhaps to justify himself, to insist that there was nothing inappropriate in the relationship. Rathbone knew that to do so would be a mistake. Explaining, protesting too much always was. He knew that from his own experience in questioning witnesses.

Brancaster relaxed with a smile. It lit his face and made him look quite different: younger and more vulnerable.

"I cannot promise victory, Sir Oliver, but I can promise an exceedingly good fight." He stood up. "I don't have anything more to ask you at the moment, but I expect I will soon think of things." He walked the short distance to the door and called for the guard. He straightened his suit jacket, and, with the very slight inclining of his head, he went out as the door opened. He did not ask if Rathbone wished to keep his services or not. That was a degree of hubris not unlike his own, Rathbone thought. Perhaps Brancaster was exactly the lawyer he needed.

As he walked back to his cell with the guard at his side, he thought how short a time ago it was that he had sat at Ingram York's dinner table in his magnificent house and celebrated his own handling of another, infinitely different case of fraud.

He had looked at Beata York and thought how beautiful she was, not the superficial loveliness of regular features or delicate coloring, but the deep, inner beauty of humor, gentleness, vulnerability, and the power to understand and forgive.

He was sure she would not understand or forgive this if she could see him now!

9

Assistant commissioner Byrne of the Metropolitan Police stood by the window of his office and regarded Monk unhappily.

"I didn't say abandon him entirely," he said with patience. "Just keep a reasonable distance. Dammit, Monk, the man has let the power of his office go to his head."

Monk wanted to argue, but Byrne was right, at least on the surface of things.

"It's when you are actually in the wrong, or at least in part, that you need your real friends." Monk framed his answer carefully. "That's the time they're probably the only people who'll stand by you."

"He perverted the course of justice," Byrne repeated, his face puckered in distaste. "He has delusions of grandeur we can't permit. If judges don't keep the law, precisely what standard can you hold the rest of us to? You cannot afford to be associated with him."

"And if he's not guilty?" Monk asked. "Wouldn't I then be doing exactly what you say he did—taking the law into my own hands and prejudging a man before he's tried?"

Byrne's eyebrows rose, making his face look oddly imbalanced. "Isn't that what you're doing anyway, deciding he's not guilty before you have the evidence?"

"I'm deciding he's innocent until proven guilty," Monk retorted. He was being argumentative, and he knew he was on thin ice. "Personally I think he's behaved like an idiot—but an idiot who wanted to see an evil man brought to account for his greed and his manipulations of people's gullibility. I think he very possibly used poor judgment in the means he employed. I don't have to debate or weigh and measure whether he's a friend or not. He has been for years, and the fact that that is currently a trifle inconvenient for me has nothing to do with anything."

"I don't know whether you find that easy to say," Byrne observed, "but you may find it harder to live up to. It's inconvenient now; I promise you it is going to get a great deal more so." He shook his head. "Be careful, Monk. I admire your loyalty, but not everyone will. Oliver Rathbone has made a great many enemies, and most of them would be very well pleased to see him brought down."

Monk looked straight at him. "I dare say you and I have also made a few enemies, sir. I would like to believe that my friends would stand by me, were I in his place. In fact, I'd go so far as to say that that decision would define who was a friend and who was not."

Byrne waved his hand in a gesture so small it was barely there at all. "I thought you would say something like that. Don't complain that I didn't warn you."

"No, sir. Is that all?"

Byrne shook his head and turned away, but there was a brief smile on his face, there and then gone again. He had fulfilled his duty.

MONK WENT HOME A little earlier than usual that evening. He knew Hester would be waiting anxiously to learn how Rathbone was and if

Monk had consulted Rathbone's lawyer, or thought of any plan as to how they might be of help.

She was waiting for him in the kitchen. Scuff was there also. They both looked at him as he came in, eyes troubled and expectant. Hester put down the knife she had been using to carve the cold saddle of mutton and came over, kissing him briefly and gently, then stepping back while he touched Scuff casually on the shoulder. Monk felt the boy relax a little. He knew the question they both wanted to ask. Only good manners allowed them to let him sit down first. Hester did not even inquire whether he would like tea.

"The prison's a pretty awful place," Monk said, wondering how much truth he should tell Hester in front of Scuff. "But he looks well enough and he's determined to fight. I'm not sure if he's realized yet just how many enemies he has who'd be delighted to see him topple."

Scuff was regarding him gravely. "Why's 'e got enemies?" he asked. "I thought 'e were a beak now." He turned to Hester.

"A judge," she corrected automatically. "A beak is only a magistrate. A judge is much more important."

Scuff turned to Monk. "So why's 'e got enemies? Did 'e 'ang people as 'e shouldn't 'ave?"

Monk was startled by Scuff's casual attitude coupled with a startlingly clear perception of the ends of the law. He was uncertain how to answer.

Hester did it for him. "Everybody thinks that in their own case they don't deserve to be hanged," she pointed out. "Haven't you realized that people who keep on doing the wrong things nearly always blame somebody else? Perhaps that's a lot of what crime is—losing your sense of fairness."

Scuff frowned. "What did 'e do? I mean, what did 'e really do?"

"He bent the rules," Monk replied.

Scuff turned to Hester. "If yer bend 'em, don't they break?"

She smiled at Monk, laughter flashing for a moment between them before she became serious again. "Yes, they do. Bending the rules is like being a little bit dishonest."

"So 'e done it, then?" Scuff said. His voice was still reasonable, but clearly it was not the answer he had wanted. Rathbone was their friend, so he was Scuff's as well. One never wanted harm to friends. Scuff was fiercely loyal. "What're we going ter do?"

Monk had already decided not to tell Hester about the police commissioner's warning, but it left him with a flavor of deceit. If he went too far over the line, as he might well do, then he would lose his job. He could not afford that. People you loved, who trusted you and whom it was your duty to look after, were one of the greatest joys of life. They were also hostages of fortune and limited your choices to take risks that on your own you might not even have weighed.

"Yer not goin' ter let 'im 'ang, are yer?" Scuff said seriously. His body was tense, his smooth hands knotted together on top of the wooden table.

Monk could only guess what fears were racing through Scuff's mind. This was as much about belonging and loyalty as it was about right and wrong. It was about the kind of safety of the heart that made all other safeties sweet but so small by comparison.

Hester was watching him, waiting for an answer. This time she could not step in. Monk must reply.

"There is no question of his hanging," Monk said clearly.

"The man's dead," Scuff screwed up his face. "An' 'is wife, an' 'is daughters. They wasn't much older'n me."

Monk remembered with a jolt that Scuff had met Taft and his family in church. They were real people to him, not just names. And now that he could read, the newspapers were mines of information, true and false.

"I know, but Sir Oliver didn't have anything to do with that," he tried to explain. "It looks as if Mr. Taft killed them and then killed himself because he knew he was going to be found guilty, and he couldn't face it."

"Would they 'ave 'anged 'im?"

"No. He didn't kill anyone; he just cheated them out of money. They'd have sent him to prison."

Scuff blinked. "And Sir Oliver?"

"If they find him guilty they might well send him to prison too."

Scuff looked deeply unhappy. "'E'll never make it. 'E's a toff. They'd 'ave 'im fer breakfast. Yer gotta 'elp 'im!" It was not a question, it was a demand.

"We will," Monk said rashly. He would never have made such a wild promise to Hester, and it would have mattered less if he had. She would have placed less weight on it, and certainly forgiven him had he done his best and failed. He saw the shadow in her face now, wondering how they would pick up the pieces if they could not save Rathbone.

"What are we going ter do?" Scuff repeated.

"Have supper," Hester replied, turning back to the stove. "We're tired and hungry. Nobody thinks well on an empty stomach. Scuff, go and wash your hands."

He opened his mouth to argue that they were perfectly clean, then changed his mind and went out. He knew a hint now when he heard one.

"I know," Monk said as soon as the door closed behind Scuff and they heard his footsteps along the corridor.

"How is he really?" she asked.

"Scared stiff, I think."

"Good. Then he's facing reality. We've got to save him, William. What he did might legally be a bit questionable—"

"A bit questionable!" he said incredulously.

"But morally it was the right thing, just not the right way," she went on, ignoring his interruption. "Betraying people's faith is a terrible sin."

"I know," he agreed. "But all most people are seeing is that Taft killed himself because of what happened in the courtroom and, far worse than that, killed his wife and his two daughters, who were little more than children. The law is blaming Rathbone for doing something wrong, and they see that as being the cause of three senseless deaths, even if indirectly. Nobody else knows what was actually in the photographs. They might assume it was Taft himself and that the fear of Rathbone revealing him drove him insane."

"If he was in one of them, he could have killed his family because he couldn't bear them knowing, possibly even seeing it. It would be understandable, in a twisted, terrible way."

"If a man would do something he'd rather die over than have people know, or kill his family over rather than have them know about it, how the hell is that the judge's fault?" Monk demanded. "I presume Rathbone's father will get him the best lawyer he can find. Rathbone must be able to afford anyone he wants."

"As long as the best he can find isn't in one of those photographs," she said grimly. "I wonder if he looked at all of them. Has he? Did you ask?"

At that moment Scuff came noisily down the passage and opened the door. Monk caught Hester's twisted smile just as Scuff inquired if it was hot bubble and squeak they were having for dinner with the mutton, and if there were onions in it.

THEY RESUMED THEIR DISCUSSION a couple of hours later when Scuff had gone to bed and they were alone in the sitting room. Monk leaned forward to speak, just as Hester began. She stopped immediately.

He gave a slight shrug. "It is bad, Hester," he said gravely. "We don't know for sure who Rathbone's enemies are, or what power they hold."

"So are we going to have to look at the rest of the pictures and see who we can name?" Her features were puckered with distaste. "William, we have to know who is against him. It's too late to be delicate about it."

He regarded her with the amazement that every now and then washed over him. Seeing her every day, hearing her laughter, and knowing the deep wounds where she was still vulnerable, the things she lay awake and feared, worried about, sometimes made him forget the depth of the strength inside her. He forgot the courage that never backed down or gave in.

She misunderstood. "It's much too late for delicacy," she repeated. "If we don't do something, Oliver could end up on trial before a judge who hates him, or even, without knowing it, have a lawyer who's connected to someone in that wretched collection. I'd hate to look at them, but I will—"

"You won't!" he said before she could finish her sentence.

She smiled for a moment with genuine amusement, almost laughter, and he thought at least in part that it was his leap to protect her that caused it. He felt a very faint warmth creeping up his cheeks, but he refused to acknowledge it.

She changed the subject. "William, someone lodged this complaint against Oliver. It might be Gavinton, because he lost, but I don't think so. Even if Oliver were convicted, that wouldn't win any vindication for Drew, or for Taft. Taft took his own life, maybe because he was sure he was going to be found guilty—but he *was* guilty; nothing that happened to Oliver was going to change that. And whether Taft cheated people or not, he actually killed his wife and daughters. That's a triple murder and suicide. It makes defrauding a handful of parishioners rather pale in comparison."

Monk knew Hester cared about saving Rathbone, possibly even more than he did. Rathbone had been in love with her once and had perhaps never completely gotten over it, in spite of loving Margaret in a safer, gentler way. That was a tragedy that was only going to get worse, since Margaret's love had changed to something close to hatred. Hester felt a desire to protect Rathbone because she had not been able to give him the kind of love he wished from her. The knowledge of that sometimes twisted inside Monk, yet had she been able to remain unmoved, he would not have loved her as completely as he did.

"All right, not Gavinton," he conceded. "Too ambitious to do something so self-destructive. That brings us back to Warne, who we know now hasn't been arrested along with Rathbone."

"I expect he'll be censured, won't he?" she asked.

"Probably. Even if they don't particularly want to, they'll have to, since they are charging Rathbone," he agreed. "But it might be more nominal than actual."

"Do you really think it could be Warne who told them Oliver gave him the photograph?" she persisted. There was a look of intense distaste in her face, and an unhappiness, as if she had liked Warne and this possibility hurt her.

"Rathbone said he'd taken precautions against that," Monk told her. "He retained Warne as his counsel, just for that purpose, whether to protect himself or to protect Warne, I don't know. Maybe both."

She changed the subject, as they were getting nowhere. "Has Oliver seen his father yet?"

"Yes. And so should we."

She winced. "He's so hurt," she said quietly.

"I know, but it'll be worse if we don't," he answered. "Perhaps we should go now."

"It's late," she protested. "We can't leave Scuff alone."

"Hester, he's thirteen. He's lived alone on the dockside, sleeping in crates and under boxes and old newspapers. Nothing's going to happen to him if we're gone for a few hours while he's in his own bed."

She stood up. "I'll go and tell him we'll be back when we've seen Henry Rathbone."

"You'd better add that you'll have his hide if he goes into the pantry!" he called after her.

THEY FOUND HENRY RATHBONE alone and deep in thought. He was delighted to see them and welcomed them in. Of course, he had already seen Hester once, when she told him of the situation and Oliver's arrest.

"You are probably the only people I am actually pleased to see," he said ruefully, after he had taken them into the sitting room. "Would you like tea?" It was an automatic gesture, something one did for any guest. "No doubt you have come about Oliver. I have engaged a lawyer to represent him. Rufus Brancaster. I don't know if you are familiar with his name?"

"No," Monk said. Then he hesitated. "But if you have confidence in him, and he is willing to take the case, then that's a good start."

Hester winced and looked down but could not hide the pain in her face.

"What is it you know and are finding so difficult to say to me? Is Oliver guilty?" Henry asked gently.

"No, that isn't it," Hester said quietly.

"My dear, there are times when it is kinder to avoid the unpleasant truths, or err on the side of more generous judgments. This is not one of them."

He turned to Monk. "If this is not about Oliver, then is it something about Brancaster that troubles you?"

Monk had intended to approach things less abruptly, but looking into Henry Rathbone's clear blue eyes the prevarication died on his tongue.

"I'm—we're—afraid he might be one of the men in the collection of photographs Oliver still has," he admitted. "Or who might fear he is. We have realized that plenty of people may be candidates; they might be unsure if their photograph is actually in Oliver's possession, and be driven mad by the doubt. If Brancaster is among them, then—"

"I see," Henry interrupted him. "I think it is highly unlikely, but I presume that if such men were obvious when one meets them, there would be little secret and little point in blackmail. Perhaps we had better find out for certain. Where are these pictures?"

"I don't know," Monk admitted. "I thought you might."

"Oliver would not have wished to involve me," Henry told him. He gave a very slight shrug. "And I dare say he was not overly proud of possessing them, even though he came to do so by means beyond control. Still, he chose not to destroy them."

"It is hard to lay aside that much power," Monk said ruefully. "It could be used for great good. That is apparently how Ballinger started out."

"I don't know whether I would have destroyed them," Hester surprised them by interrupting. "If I had something with which I could save the lives of an untold number of people, I think I would keep on meaning to get rid of it but always stop short of doing it, just in case the next patient was one I could have saved. I wouldn't be prepared to watch them die, knowing it might've been avoided. It's one of those tasks, the kind you're always going to do tomorrow, until tomorrow comes."

Monk looked at her with surprise. He had expected the opposite from her, the gentle, the conservative perspective. But she had taken the unexpected, braver stand, perhaps the more foolish, definitely the more honest.

Henry was looking at her too, and there was a startling affection in his eyes. Monk realized how much Henry would have preferred that Rathbone marry Hester rather than Margaret. Poor Margaret. Had she ever known that, even if perhaps not putting it so bluntly to herself?

Monk recalled the discussion back to the practical. "One of us has to look at those pictures and see who is in them that might be in the judiciary or in any other position of power regarding this case. Otherwise we are simply moving around blindly and possibly playing right into their hands."

"Agreed," Henry said grimly. "I shall ask Oliver where these damned things are, and then, with your assistance, identify as many people as possible. We must not only find out if Brancaster himself is there—which I profoundly doubt—but also if there is anyone else who might have an influence on him, or on the nature of Oliver's trial." He was looking intently at Monk. "But how do we ascertain that?"

"I'll find out," Monk said rashly. "Perhaps we should also consider who might have influence on Warne, or Gavinton, or anybody else concerned. What a bloody mess." He looked at Hester with a twisted smile. "Still so sure you'd keep them?"

She shrugged. "I didn't say it would be wise, or right, or that I wouldn't regret it. I just said I think I probably would've."

Henry shot her a look of gratitude, then rose to his feet. "I'll fetch you Rufus Brancaster's address. As soon as I have visited Oliver to ask where to find these photographs and if you identify the people in them, perhaps we can begin to understand who is with us, and who against."

Monk drew in his breath to say something then changed his mind. It was Hester who, with brutal honesty, gave words to his thought.

"Even once we look at the photographs, there is the problem, as we said, of photographs that were not in Ballinger's possession. There may be people who were members of the club that we have no way of identifying as such."

"I know," he said quietly, "but there is no value in considering problems we cannot address. You are right, though; we should not allow ourselves a false sense of safety. It is rather sad to think that so many men's lives are so bereft of purpose and their values so diseased as to look for excitement in such places. I'm afraid when it comes to the use of children I have little understanding or mercy for them."

Had he spoken more angrily Monk would have been less moved by his words. He had no memory of his own father and wondered with a rush of nostalgia, even grief, if he had been a man anything like Henry Rathbone. If he had, and Monk could remember it, would he himself be a better man?

Hester was standing also, regarding Henry with the same emotion in her eyes as Monk felt. She was a gift Monk had been given and Oliver Rathbone had not. One makes oneself a better man, in part by the example of those you love, and in part by the act of loving them. He was well aware of how lucky he was.

"We will have no mercy for them at all if they enter into this case," he said. "We have adopted one of those boys, or perhaps it would be more accurate to say he has adopted us. One day, when this is over, I would like to bring him to meet you, if you would agree?"

Henry's face lit with a smile that made him momentarily almost beautiful.

"I should be delighted. Please don't forget to do that."

Monk had not even looked at Hester to see if she approved. He did now, and saw her eyes bright with tears.

THE FOLLOWING EVENING THEY visited Henry Rathbone again. He had the photographs, and they spent a grim hour going through them. It was a sick and wretched exercise, but they were able to identify all the men in them, mostly from the coded notes on the back written in Ballinger's hand.

Henry made a note of the names. They did not include Rufus Brancaster, or anyone who might reasonably be assumed to be connected with him. Monk had made inquiries and now knew the names of most of Brancaster's associates, including, as much as possible, anyone to whom he might owe a favor or who might be related to him.

They celebrated the relief with a bottle of red wine, a plate of oatmeal biscuits, and very fine Brie, following it with plum pie and thick cream.

THE MORNING AFTER THAT they went to see Rufus Brancaster. Because of the importance of the case, and although he was busy, he did not keep them waiting for more than fifteen minutes.

Monk was surprised. He had expected a much older man, and for the first few moments he was worried that Henry's choice was not a good one. But then it was possible that older and more established lawyers might have declined the case. It would take a degree of courage, even recklessness, to defend Rathbone. As this thought was in his mind, Monk realized that although he could understand Rathbone's actions, and might even have done the same thing himself, he most certainly believed Rathbone was at least legally guilty. It settled inside him with an ugly coldness.

Brancaster wasted no time in niceties.

"Tell me about the Jericho Phillips case, and how Ballinger was involved in the whole mess," he said, nodding toward Hester out of courtesy but directing his attention to Monk. "Briefly, but don't leave out anything important."

He did not interrupt while Monk spoke, but he did look at Hester once or twice, and with a new respect.

"And where are these photographs now?" he said finally.

"Henry Rathbone has them. I left them in his keeping. Yesterday we studied them, to see whom we recognized—for obvious reasons."

Brancaster looked anxious. "And you're sure he still has them?"

"Yes. He promised me he would not store them in his home, or any-where else where they could be destroyed. He also swore no one else would have access to them. But I don't know exactly where he put them."

"Good. Did looking at the prints tell you anything of value?"

"Yes," Monk said with a grim smile. "You're not in them."

The pen Brancaster had been holding slid out of his hands. "God in heaven!" he gasped. "Did you bloody well think I was?" He did not even think to apologize to Hester for his language.

It was she who replied to him. "No. But thinking is not enough. And it is not only a question of if you were in them, it's whether you might care about, or owe some favor to, someone who was." She smiled very slightly.

"I was going to tell you how bad it is," Brancaster said bleakly, this time to Hester, "but it seems you know already, maybe even better than I do. We are going to have to dig in for a long battle, and I can't promise that we'll win. We would need a great deal of goodwill for that. Techni-cally Sir Oliver crossed the line. He did go behind the defense's back and give seriously prejudicial information to the defense only, when in fact he should have recused himself. It would be absurd to say that he didn't foresee how Warne would use it, or even that he didn't intend it. Clearly he did. And while most decent men would say he did the right thing morally, legally they could punish him quite severely. And after you've told me what I already feared about the photographs, it's clear a lot of people will be nervous and probably overreact."

"So what are we going to do?" Hester asked him without hesitation.

Although Brancaster's smile was rueful, even twisted, it gave a new life to his face, a vitality and softness that had not been there before.

"I'm glad you didn't ask me if I was looking for a way to back out of the case," he said with a slight gesture of his hands. "I'm going to ask you for a list of the names of those in the photographs, so I also know whom not to trust. Are there any acting judges?"

"Yes," Monk said immediately. "And whether you are prepared to or not, I am perfectly willing to use that information should one of them be called to preside in Rathbone's trial." He smiled bleakly, more of a grimace. "In a legal manner, and well before the trial, of course."

Brancaster bit his lip. "I believe you. But that won't alter the fact that many members of the judiciary will be against Sir Oliver, in spite of the fact that they won't take much to Drew, I'm sure."

He pulled a very slight grimace. "If you turn over a very large, very wet stone, you are going to find a lot of slugs underneath it, plus a few creeping things with too many legs, that you weren't prepared for. Are you ready for that?"

Hester answered him. "Of course not. But if you mean would we prefer to let it go, then, no, we wouldn't. If we try, at least we have a chance of success."

"I dare say they'll attempt to have him imprisoned, simply to seize his property and try to find the original plates of the pictures," Brancaster warned.

"If they're bent on appearing to remain within the law," Monk agreed with a bitter smile. "If not, they'll simply burn the house down. I dare say Rathbone himself thought of that. If not, I'll make sure his father does."

"Would he preserve them?" Brancaster asked dubiously. He knew Henry Rathbone.

"At least for the time being," Monk said wryly. "It's too good a weapon to throw away just yet."

"You'd use it?" Brancaster said curiously. "Even after what you've seen it do to others?"

"I don't know," Monk admitted. Without Hester or Scuff to think of, if he were still the man he had been before, he would not have hesitated. He had often been ruthless, and it was not easy to admit it now. How much of that man was still left in him, if pushed far enough?

Brancaster was thinking. From his face it appeared he was anxious. "It isn't wise for other people to find out that anyone else has access to the photos, or the motive to use them, aside from Oliver," he warned. "He is tucked behind bars, but if they realize you are equally capable of making those images public, it might drive him into a kind of panic, drive him to something dangerous, badly misjudged. Fear has different effects on people. For the moment, be careful to say nothing."

"I will," Monk agreed grimly. "It is ironic that these men resent Rathbone for going outside the bounds of gentlemanly conduct, when they have done things that are far outside human decency. Why the hell do they think Rathbone should guard their secrets, at the price of other people's lives?"

"Because they have no empathy," Brancaster replied. "No conception at all of how other people feel. They don't see any further than their own appetites. As I said, we are in for a long battle."

"We have to face it," Hester said quietly. "We can't let Oliver lose. And"—her whole body tightened—"we can't let them win either. That would be a step into the darkness."

CHAPTER

10

Prison was appalling. Every night Rathbone sank into sleep as an escape from the noise, the discomfort, the stale smell of the blanket, and, in his imagination, the fidgeting, scurrying, and scratching of whatever skittered across the stone floor.

He slept badly, unable to relax, most of the time half awake, drifting in and out of dreams. Often he was finally oblivious of his surroundings only just before the sound of boots on the stone jerked him back into reality. There was a moment when he was still mercifully confused, then opening his eyes brought it all back to him: the physical discomfort, the aching in his body, the scratching on his skin, then the memory that there would be no hot shave, just a scraping of his cheeks with soap and cold water from a bucket. There would be no fresh toast, sharp marmalade, hot fragrant tea. There would be porridge and then tea, dark and stewed, acrid. Still, it was better than hunger or thirst.

Would he have to get used to this? Might it be like this for years? As far ahead as he could see? As a judge he had sentenced men to that. As a lawyer he had pleaded for it, and against it, as he was hired to do, taking whichever side he was offered.

Did that mean he was without conviction, doing anything he was paid for? Or that he believed in the system? And did this adversarial—almost gladiatorial—system produce justice? The system did not look the same from here. It was frightening, offering no certainty of good to come.

He sat in the miserable cell with the noise of other men living around him; he was turning the case over in his mind for the thousandth time to no end, when the chief jailer came. He had the keys in his hands.

"Someone's paid bail for you, Mr. Rathbone," he said, his voice expressionless, except to emphasize the "Mr.," but his eyes were bright and sharp. "I suppose you'll be going home for a while now. Good lawyer you must have. All stick together, I expect. You being a larnt-up man, like, I suppose you'll know your Shakespeare . . ."

" 'First . . . kill all the lawyers,' " Rathbone said for him. He picked up his jacket, which was the only garment he had with him, apart from the clothes he stood in.

The jailer grunted, annoyed at being robbed of his quote.

"Actors, the lot of you," he said irritably. "Strutting around and thinking everyone's listening to yer."

" 'That struts and frets his hour upon the stage' is meant for all of us," Rathbone countered, coming to the door and waiting a step back while the man turned the heavy key.

The jailer glared at him, knowing it was another quote but not able to place it.

"*Macbeth*," Rathbone supplied.

"You tell 'im, Fancypants," a voice called out from the cell opposite and along a bit. "Gonna miss you, I am. Till yer come back again!" He roared with laughter at his own humor.

Rathbone smiled as he walked through the barred door and out into the stone-floored space. He looked across at the cell the voice had come from. Inside there was a gaunt, stringy-haired man; his clothes were filthy, but they had once been good. Rathbone wondered what had happened to him. Maybe the clothes were stolen, or had been thrown out. Or, on the other hand, perhaps the accent and the aggressive manner were borrowed plumage, for self-protection.

Rathbone lifted his hand in a small salute. "Keep it warm for me," he replied. "I regret to say, I might well be needing it."

"Arrogant bastard," the jailer said under his breath.

Rathbone affected not to have heard him.

He had his belongings restored to him and took a hansom back to his home. Only an hour later, as he went in through the front door to the familiar hallway, did he remember that everything else in the world had changed, for him. To the staff he had to be a different person. There would be no more awe, and perhaps even their respectful behavior toward him would now be superficial—merely good manners. He would have no idea what they really thought of him. Did he want to know?

Not yet. There was too much else to think of. For right this moment he could come and go as he pleased. He could wash, have a decent cup of tea, eat what he wanted, and tonight sleep in his own bed, in the softness, enjoying the clean smell and the silence. He could get up when he wanted.

That was reality now: he could stay in bed if he wanted because there was no work to do, no one to talk to, to care for, no challenge except to find something to occupy his mind, to keep himself from sinking into anger and despair.

EARLY IN THE AFTERNOON Henry Rathbone came to visit him.

"Thank you," Rathbone said immediately, choking a little on the words, his voice thick with emotion. He had not meant to lose his grip this way, but his father's familiar face and the sound of his voice overwhelmed him.

Henry turned away and looked for a place to sit while the butler, who had let him in, went away to fetch a fresh pot of tea and some hot, crumbly, buttery scones.

"I paid it as soon as they let me. Would you like to come and stay a few days at Primrose Hill?" Henry asked, regarding Rathbone with extraordinary gentleness. He would say nothing of love, or of anxiety, or fear, certainly not of disappointment, but it was all there in his eyes. He found it embarrassing to speak of such emotions, and unnecessary. A lifetime of companionship, guidance, encouragement, and shared dreams and jokes had made such declarations of feeling redundant.

An immediate refusal rose to Rathbone's lips, then he bit it back. It would seem so callous, like a rejection. What he really felt was that it would add to his own guilt, already weighing him down, if his father were harassed by journalists or prodded with unintentionally cruel questions by his friends. People might hold him in some way responsible, by association. Henry would then be placed in the situation of having to defend Rathbone, to explain.

Friends calling by might find Rathbone's presence awkward. Perhaps they would remain away for that reason. It might place Henry in a position where he would have to refuse invitations, or ask that Rathbone be included. That would be excruciating for his father.

It would be wonderful to be there in the familiar house, to walk down the long lawn in the evening, watch the light fade on the glittering leaves of the elms, smell the honeysuckle, see the flights of starlings swirl against the last of the sunlight. The thought of it suffocated him with emotion, even sitting here in this very formal, very elegant sitting room of Margaret's.

He needed a clear mind if he was to find any way at all out of this mess, which was largely of his own making.

"Not yet," he said gently. "I need to learn a great deal more about this . . ." He saw Henry's face darken. "I'm not going to try to solve it myself," he assured him quickly. "I'm impressed with Brancaster."

A very faint smile crossed Henry's face.

"I know," Rathbone said. "I had the very stupid idea that he was going to be some rather stuffy academic who hadn't seen the inside of a courtroom in years. I apologize for that. But even as good as Brancaster is, he can't work without ammunition, and I haven't given him much."

"Monk will help you," Henry assured him.

"I know," Rathbone agreed. "There has to be a lot more that I haven't considered, especially about Taft. Why in God's name did he kill his wife and daughters? What sort of a man could even think of such a thing? There has to be some major secret that we don't know yet, to make sense of that."

"Why have they not prosecuted Warne?" Henry asked.

"I'm afraid I've made a few enemies who will be only too delighted to ruin me, but who don't necessarily have anything against Warne. Anyway, his error was slight. He should have told Gavinton about the picture straightaway, before the court sitting began. I should have shown the evidence to both of them and recused myself. Those are offences of a very different magnitude."

Henry frowned, a heavy crease forming between his brows. "Oliver, do you know who laid the complaint yet? Was it Drew?"

Rathbone had thought about this again and again. He had decided it could not have been Drew, as much as the man disliked him, unless he was so bent on revenge that self-destruction was a price he was willing to pay.

"I don't know who it was," he said, a little vaguely. He felt as if he were entering a dark room that contained a trap that would hurt him, perhaps very badly, a trap he could not see.

"Oliver, we cannot avoid this," Henry said, his voice quiet but controlled.

Rathbone took a deep breath and let it out slowly. "I know. And I have thought about it. It doesn't make much sense for it to have been any of the men involved in this case, unless one of them has a profound secret. And of course that is a possibility. Perhaps at my age it's ridiculous to have delusions about people, especially considering my profession. But life would be unbearable without hope, and at least a degree of blindness regarding those you love." ·

Henry started to protest, and then changed his mind and remained silent.

"The only other people who knew, apart from you, are Hester and Monk," Rathbone went on. "And about them there isn't even a question."

Henry was thinking. "What about Ballinger's lawyer who brought the photographs to you in the first place? Did he know what they were?"

Rathbone was startled. That idea had not occurred to him. "Possibly. If he were Ballinger's lawyer in any respect apart from in the execution of his will, then I suppose he might well have. He would know they were photographs by the size and weight of the case, even if he didn't know of what nature. But it would be a gross breach of his trust if he were to tell anyone else . . ." He realized even as he said it that the remark was idealistic and, in this present situation, naïve. It was a whole line of inquiry he had not even thought of. The morass of fear and degradation, and the many-tentacled creatures that lived and fed in it, was far more monstrous than he had yet grasped. He longed to be clear from it. And yet he could blame no one but himself. He had tasted its power and been unable to put it down. Now it was too late. Perhaps he was more like Ballinger than he would ever have been willing to acknowledge.

Henry was looking at him, his eyes sad and anxious.

Rathbone forced himself to smother his own fear. He, of all people, had the least justification for self-pity. He had to act with courage.

"I'll speak to Monk," he said, his voice perfectly level. "I know he's not a private agent of inquiry anymore, but he'll know what to do. And I think Brancaster's a good man. Thank you for finding him."

Henry accepted that that was the end of the conversation and deliberately he spoke of other things until it was time to leave. He did not ask again if Rathbone would like to stay at Primrose Hill.

When Henry had gone the house seemed oppressively quiet. The

servants were conspicuously keeping out of his way. Probably they were
embarrassed. What did one say to a master who was out of prison on
bail for a crime you did not understand?

What should he say to them? It was his responsibility to broach the
subject, and at the very least tell them what was happening and what
prospects they had of remaining in his employ. He owed them that.

If he received any jail sentence at all, he would have to sell the
house. What would he need it for, anyway? On his release he would
hardly come back here. It was too big, far too expensive, and he ought
to admit it, he would have no use for a residence in the middle of one
of the best areas of London.

He was alone. If he could afford any servant, then one gentleman's
gentleman could do it all. Perhaps he could hire a woman to come in
and do the laundry and the scrubbing of floors.

Perhaps he wouldn't even be able to manage that, to begin with. He
could very well end up in lodgings, renting one room. Why not? Thousands of people did. That is what Monk had been doing when they first
met. It was a long fall from a house like this, with half a dozen servants,
to being glad to rent one room and share conveniences. But then it was
a long fall from being a judge at the Old Bailey to being an unemployed
ex-convict.

It was different from this side of the picture, very different indeed.
How simple it is when the victim is somebody else. Justice is so easy
from the blind end, nicely cushioned from everything except the knowledge of an uninvolved conscience. *I didn't cause it. This is the law, and I
am not responsible. Now let me go home, forget it, and have a decent dinner
and perhaps a glass of port afterward.*

He forced himself to smile, wry amusement only, no pleasure.

Even if he were found not guilty, much of the result would be the
same. His career on the bench would be over. He realized with a deep
ache that whatever the law, whatever rabbit Brancaster might pull out
of his hat, morally Rathbone had made a very flawed judgment. He was
a good lawyer, even brilliant. He had been called the best in London,

and possibly he was, or had been. But that was fighting for a cause, even crusading, requiring all his passion and will and intelligence to be channeled to one side. No judgment was required.

If he looked back at it now, he knew perfectly well that he had made up his mind from the beginning that Taft was guilty, not only legally but even more so, morally. He had considered Drew a cruel man even before he held the picture, and wasn't going to stand for him destroying other, naïve people from the stand and then walking away without censure.

He was not cool enough to be a good judge, certainly not dispassionate enough. He loved the battle, but did he love the law, above and beyond all else, separated from the human cost and turmoil?

No—perhaps not. And that was what a judge needed to do. A judge should not be partisan, as he was, as it seemed he could not help being.

That would amuse Hester, in a bitter way. She had always thought he was too remote, too controlled. Would she like him better this way?

He would probably never know what she truly thought about any of this because she was too loyal to tell him completely. She would not lie to him, or probably for him, but she would never purposefully hurt him, especially when he was in trouble and alone.

When they all first met she had not known if Monk was guilty of having beaten Joscelyn Grey to death. Reason and evidence said that he was. He even thought he was guilty himself, but the blow to his head in the accident had left him without memory to know the truth. Even now, all these years later, he still knew what happened only from the evidence. Flashes of memory returned, but without connection. There was no narrative of his life.

But Hester had stood by him, even though she did not know, any more than Monk himself did. What would have happened if he had been guilty? It was only a guess, deep-rooted in feeling rather than reason, but he believed she would have stayed loyal to Monk and expected him to pay the price, like a man, and then resume what was left of his life afterward.

Is that what she would expect of Rathbone also? Probably. It had to do with who she was, not with him.

Monk, had he been guilty, would have been guilty of getting rid of a blackmailer who destroyed the families of dead soldiers. Ballinger had dealt in the abuse and pornography of children, in blackmail and ultimately in murder. There was nothing whatever to indicate that he had done it with the slightest regret. He had seen a weakness and exploited it. Rathbone was not sorry the man was gone.

But what about Margaret? He was her father, and she had loved him unconditionally. Where there was doubt, she convinced herself it was because everyone else was wrong. She had turned all her rage and grief against Rathbone, and never once allowed that he had done his best. But Ballinger had been guilty, and no one could have proved otherwise.

And he couldn't blame her. He doubted he would believe anyone on earth if they had accused Henry of something so vile.

He stood at the window again, looking out at the garden. It was only just over a week since he had last studied it like this. Already it seemed changed. The marigolds were fading. The asters were deeper purple. Patches of the Virginia creeper were turning dark crimson. One hard wind and the first of the leaves would begin to fall. Things were dying.

Rathbone wondered whether Beata York would be loyal to Ingram, if he were to find himself in trouble, accused, maligned, perhaps even charged. He did not understand why he kept thinking of her, but he couldn't help it. Almost certainly they would never meet again. Pass on the street, perhaps, but not meet as equals, even less as friends. That was another price to pay.

He was still thinking of that when Ardmore, the butler, came to tell him that Monk and Hester were here to see him.

Suddenly his spirits lifted. Some of the tension eased out of his body, and he realized with surprise and some shame that he had feared they would wish to avoid him. Monk had been to visit him in prison, but what did Hester feel?

One glance at her face answered his anxieties. She might be angry, worried, confused as to what to do, but she had not changed. She was a fixed star in a world turned upside down. Friendship was at the core of every relationship that mattered—allies, parent and child, lovers. On its foundation could be built all the other palaces of the heart.

They sat down and began to weigh the situation and consider what could be done. Rathbone repeated all the points Henry had made, and they spoke of other concerns as well, including the death of Taft.

"There's a great deal we don't know about that," Monk observed. "Even if he had been found guilty, the punishment would have been prison, but not for life. He could even have begun again, changed his name and gone somewhere he wasn't known. For heaven's sake, the whole world was open to him."

"That point aside, how could he kill his wife and daughters?" Hester's face puckered with distress. "It's . . . not sane. I think he was suffering some sort of madness." She looked from Monk to Rathbone and back again. "He just seemed pompous to me, and revoltingly self-satisfied. If he believed anything of what he preached, he wouldn't kill his family, whatever happened to him."

"If he believed what he preached he wouldn't have stolen the money in the first place," Monk said tartly. "But you're right, there is something missing from the facts. I need to know a great deal more about him."

"Do you think it will make any difference to my blame, in the law?" Rathbone asked unhappily. "I can't see how it would, much as I would like to think so."

"I don't know," Monk admitted. "But the reason he killed himself has to be part of the case, and it cannot be coincidence that it was immediately after Drew was exposed. I'll keep looking."

Rathbone nodded, and the conversation moved on to other areas.

Even late in the afternoon, after they had left, some of the warmth Rathbone had felt seemed to linger. Then Ardmore was at the door again, his face as carefully blank as he could make it.

"Lady Rathbone has called, sir. What do you wish me to say?"

How diplomatically phrased. Even while his heart raced and all his muscles knotted up, Rathbone's mind admired Ardmore's grasp of tact, his delicacy of feeling. There was no choice but to see her. It would be childish to refuse.

What did she want? Was it even imaginable she had come out of some kind of loyalty, a remnant of the closeness they had once had? He had thought they had loved each other, but the first real test in their marriage had ripped them apart.

If the tragedy of Ballinger had not happened, would they have lived out the rest of their lives imagining they were happy, never enjoying anything deeper than superficial affection?

Ardmore was still waiting.

"Please ask her to come in," Rathbone replied. "And . . . and ask her what she would like as refreshment."

"Yes, sir." Ardmore bowed, still expressionless, and went out.

A moment later Margaret came in. She was still dressed in black, with only the relief of a pale fichu at the neck and a cameo brooch. He remembered her telling him that it had been a gift from her father for her eighteenth birthday. She looked like a grieving widow. It was irrelevant, but he wondered if she wore black all the time, or if this was to make the point to him that she still felt totally bereaved, of husband as well as father.

She looked as handsome as he had ever seen her. There was fire in her blue eyes and a faint flush to her skin.

"Good evening, Oliver," she said, stopping a good yard and a half away from him. "I suppose it would be foolish to say that I hope you are well, and I think we are long beyond the point where politeness would be anything less than a farce. You can't be well, in the circumstances. Prison is extremely unpleasant, as it is intended to be." She raised her delicate eyebrows slightly. "Not that you have acquired a prison pallor yet. I imagine it will come, when they have found you guilty. From the advice I have received, that seems to be inevitable."

He was surprised by this remark. "You sought advice on the subject? From whom?"

"My lawyer, of course. To whom else would I take such a matter?"

"I don't know why you should take it to anyone." His mind raced, trying to think why she had come at all. There was nothing gentle in her, nothing anxious or concerned. It seemed impossible that they had once made love, lain in each other's arms.

She stood ramrod stiff, her shoulders square, her chin high. He looked at her. At first glance, he thought anger became her. It gave her a vitality, even a passion she did not normally have. Only when he looked more closely did he see a hardness in her, an absence of the warmth he used to see. There was a probing edge to her gaze, a searching for the place most vulnerable to drive the blade home.

He waited for her to explain her purpose.

"It will be a very public trial," she went on. "Just as my father's trial was. Perhaps even more so. It is spectacular, as justice goes, that a judge should answer for himself in court. An irony, don't you think?" She did not wait for his answer. "What you are accused of is despicable because apart from anything else, it is a betrayal of the profession that has given you all you have . . . in fact, all that you are. If we cannot trust judges, then what is the law itself worth? You have damaged anyone who ever trusted you."

He drew in his breath to try to explain, but the fury in her eyes made him realize the futility of that. The hope that she might have come in any manner of kindness faded away. He was foolish to have entertained it in the first place. The whole world had altered for him, erupted and caved in on itself. How he must be an embarrassment to her, even an encumbrance.

When Ballinger had been tried her world had been destroyed. Rathbone's had not. It had hurt, certainly. He had been confused, desperate to find some defense for him, torn between loyalty to Margaret and loyalty to his own duty and beliefs. When it all ended he had been left with a sense of loss, but he was still whole. It was she who had suffered a permanent injury.

Now the tables were turned. This time she would lose very little, actually perhaps nothing at all. He was legally bound to look after her financially, and he would have done it whether the law required it of him or not. But she would not accept anything from him. She would rather live in near poverty with her mother than take his money. If he were sent to prison and therefore had nothing, she would not lose.

Then why had she come? Not to assuage his anxiety for her, but to rejoice in his downfall.

Margaret was regarding him now with contempt, waiting for him to find his tongue.

"Nothing to say, Oliver?" she asked finally. "Did you not know before what it feels like to be accused, unable to prove your innocence and having to depend on someone else to do it for you? Suddenly you're helpless too. Now you know how your clients felt, their fear, and why they trusted you. They did so because they were desperate, terrified, and had nowhere else to turn." She smiled tightly. "To you the law is a way to show off your skills, to win publicly, and of course to make money. To them it's survival or death. It looks a little different from the side you're on now, doesn't it?"

She was being unfair. He had taken every case seriously and given every single one his all, even when in the end he lost, as he had with Ballinger.

"I can give a defense, Margaret," he said with as much self-control as he could. His voice sounded rasping. "Sometimes I can prove a man innocent, sometimes I can mitigate a sentence. I cannot save a guilty man. Are you suggesting that I should? If everyone is to be set free at the end, regardless, why bother with a trial?"

"So that the lawyer can strut around, show off, and earn money, of course!" she snapped. "And the public can have its entertainment." Then she waved her hand sharply, as if she could brush the subject out of the way. "But you are guilty, aren't you? Or are you going to say that it was not you who gave obscene pictures to Warne so that Drew would be destroyed as a witness?" The look of disbelief on her face was savage.

"You think the picture should be suppressed, and the jury have no

idea what kind of a man Drew is"—he put all his incredulity and contempt into his voice—"so he can go on slandering the other members
of the congregation and be believed?"

Her temper snapped. "Don't answer every question with another
question, Oliver! For the love of heaven, be honest for once!"

He felt as if he had been slapped. He knew the color burned up his
face. "That is honest, Margaret. I gave Warne the picture so he had a
choice of defending the ordinary, trusting men and women whom Drew
was slandering and holding up to public mockery. They deserved that."

"You hypocrite!" Her voice was very nearly a shout, her face dark
with fury. "You can introduce that filthy photograph into the courtroom and sit there full of righteous indignation as if you knew nothing
about it. I'm glad they found out that it was you who gave it to Warne.
You can't hide anymore. Everyone will know you for what you are."

The lash of her tongue hurt so sharply that for a moment he could
hardly draw breath to defend himself.

She mistook his silence for weakness. "I wish my father were alive
to see this," she went on, choking a little on her own words. "It would
be perfect. Well, at least I am here. And believe me, I will watch with
pleasure."

"I'm sure your father's appreciation would be the sharpest of all," he
said bitterly. "That is why he had the pictures in the first place, to bring
about justice that could be forced no other way. I understood that in
him—obviously far more than you did, or do even now."

She froze, her face white. "Liar! How dare you suggest such a thing
to me? Is that your defense? To blame a dead man you have made sure
cannot speak for himself? Well, I can speak for him, and I will. The
world will see you for what you are—a man who places pride and op-
portunism before everything else: before family or honor, or even
human decency."

He struggled for something to say that would put them back on
common ground, some shared belief. They had cared for each other
once.

She was not prepared to wait for him.

"I will not discuss my father with you. For you to suggest you are alike in anything is an insult to him, and I won't listen. I came to tell you that I am consulting a lawyer—a friend of my father's, who still has some regard toward the family—because I do not wish to remain connected to you in any way, least of all in the public mind. I don't think it will be difficult, in the circumstances you have created, for me to obtain a divorce. I will revert to my maiden name. I no longer wish to be known as Margaret Rathbone. I imagine you can understand that, but if you don't it really doesn't matter to me. I am informing you simply as a matter of courtesy."

He should have been expecting it. It was the perfect opportunity for her to set herself free. She did not have to accuse him of anything, not that there were many excuses for a woman to divorce her husband. She could not claim infidelity, as a man could against his wife. But society would never blame her if she did not want to be associated with him when he was standing trial for perverting the course of justice.

Perhaps some would have admired her loyalty had she remained with him. He thought of other women he had known who had risked everything they possessed, even their lives, to prove the innocence of the husbands they loved. But then the key to that loyalty was their love.

And those husbands had loved their wives with a matching depth and devotion.

He felt weary, as though his body were bruised from blow after blow. He did not want to go on fighting a battle he could not win. What would winning be, anyway? He could not persuade her to see the truth, still less care for him again. And if he were to tell himself the hard, bare truth, he no longer wanted her to care.

He looked at Margaret. Was there even any point in protesting, saying that it would have been nice had she at least given him the benefit of the doubt first, and got her blow in only after he was found guilty? There was nothing left to salvage: he hoped only to avoid sinking to the lowest in himself. He could force her to reason her way to the truth: that he could have gotten the pictures only from Ballinger, but she did not want to see that.

Anger and bitterness were twisting her face. She had once been so much better than that. She had known gentleness, laughter, purpose. Whether the loss of any of it was his fault or not didn't really matter now.

"Do whatever you think is best," he said quietly. "I shall instruct my solicitor to accommodate you."

For a moment there was victory in her face; then it faded, as if the taste had not been what she expected it to be.

"Thank you," she said in acknowledgment. "Good night."

"Goodbye, Margaret," he replied.

11

"WHERE ARE YOU GOING to begin?" Hester asked Monk over the breakfast table. It was so early in the morning that Scuff was still upstairs getting ready to go to school.

Monk had no need to ask her what she was referring to. The only subject on both their minds was Oliver Rathbone. Monk had lain awake a good deal of the night wondering that same thing himself. He had listened to her even breathing in the dark, not certain if it were actually so even as to indicate that she was deliberately pretending to be asleep; but he had not asked, even in a whisper, because he had no comfort or assurance to offer.

Now she was ignoring her toast and watching him, waiting for his reply, her eyes shadowed and her face tense. He wished he had something positive to say.

"The best thing would be if I could find something to prove that Taft's death had nothing to do with Oliver," he replied.

She bit her lip and pulled her mouth tight. "He still gave Warne the picture. Isn't that what they're going to charge him with?"

"Yes," he agreed. "But he could argue that he only realized it was Drew in the photograph when the case was about to close. But yes, of course he should have stepped down."

"William, he hated what Drew and Taft were doing to those people," she said grimly. "It revolted him as much as it did us. He did it to ruin Drew's testimony because he didn't want those slimy men to get away with it. People are going to know that. But he should have introduced the evidence some other way, so it wasn't sprung on Gavinton."

"That is true, and that is what the prosecution will say," he conceded. "But if Gavinton had had time to prepare a defense, he might have had the picture disallowed, and then its value would have been nothing. As it was, no one else saw it, but they all saw the look of revulsion on Gavinton's face, and they knew damned well that Drew knew what it was."

"But Rathbone was still wrong," Hester concluded.

"Yes." Monk was not yet satisfied. "But if Taft took his own life because he was guilty, it's a hell of a lot more than just suicide. If he'd killed only himself Oliver might be seen as to blame. There's no way anyone could foresee he'd kill his wife and daughters as well. That puts him right outside anybody's understanding, or sympathy."

"So how are you going to find out why he killed them too?"

"Learn everything I can," he replied. "And I'd still like to know what happened to the money. Everyone's forgotten that, in this mess."

Hester reached for the marmalade, then realized she had already put some on the side of her plate. "They spent it," she replied. "That's obvious."

"Is it?"

She pulled a little face, just a twitch of her lips. "William, have you any idea what Mrs. Taft's gowns cost? Or those of her daughters?"

"No." He was puzzled. "I know what yours cost, and it doesn't amount to the sort of money that's missing from the congregation's donations to charity."

She sighed. "I suppose, in a backhanded sort of way, I should be pleased that you didn't notice how beautifully they fitted, or how very up to date they were."

"But that sort of price?" he said with disbelief.

"A good portion of it. Calfskin boots—kid gloves—silk fichus and guipure lace."

"So Mrs. Taft knew about the money too," he deduced.

"Maybe. But not if she simply took delivery of the clothes and never saw the bills. I dare say she never had to manage the household accounts herself and wouldn't have had the faintest idea."

"Could she be so—" He stopped as Scuff came into the kitchen, looking at him, then at Hester. He was scrubbed pink, his skin still damp, his shirt collar crisp and blemishless. He drew in breath to say something, then changed his mind. He looked anxious.

Hester never failed to see an expression, and seldom misread it. "What's wrong?" she asked him.

Scuff cut himself two slices of bread and took the piece of bacon she had left for him on the griddle. He made himself a sandwich and came to sit at the table before answering. He drew in a deep breath, putting off the moment of biting into the fresh bread and the crisp, savory bacon.

"How are we going to help Mr. Rathbone . . . I mean, Sir Oliver?" he asked. "I could do something . . ." He glanced down at his plate then up again quickly.

Hester nearly answered, then left it for Monk.

"We were just talking about it," Monk answered. "I'm going to see if I can find out exactly why Taft killed himself, and why on earth he killed his family. I think there's something important to that that we don't know."

"'E was a thief an' 'e couldn't take it that everybody would know." Scuff said what to him was obvious. "Some people are like that. Truth don't matter; it's what people think that they care about."

"The photograph was of Drew, not Taft," Monk pointed out.

Scuff shrugged and bit into the sandwich. He could no longer resist it. "Maybe there was one of him too," he said with his mouth full.

Hester started to correct him but changed her mind.

Scuff saw it and gulped down the mouthful, then looked at Monk.

"We are pretty certain there wasn't. Though we can't know for sure. It isn't among the ones Sir Oliver had, anyway."

Hester poured tea for Scuff and passed him the mug, but he did not touch it; instead he kept staring at Monk. "Oh. Well, what can I do?" he asked again.

Monk saw the eagerness in his face. Scuff needed to help, for Rathbone's sake, but even more he needed to be part of what they were doing. To shut him out would brand him in his own mind as excluded, and of no use. Perhaps to someone who had always belonged that would be ridiculous, but Monk understood exclusion. His own slow recovery of bits and pieces of his life from before his amnesia had shown him that he had once been a man who did not have a family or a place in other people's emotions. He had been respected, feared, and disliked. The loneliness he remembered from that life, the absence of warmth that comes from being liked for yourself, not for your achievements, had never totally left him. He could so easily recognize the echo of it in Scuff.

He must find something for Scuff to do, something that mattered.

"You ought to be at school," he said slowly, to give himself time to think.

Scuff's face fell. He struggled to hide his hurt and failed.

On the other side of the table Hester stiffened.

"But this is too urgent," Monk went on, scrambling for an idea. "First I'm going to see Warne, the lawyer Sir Oliver gave the photograph to. Hester says that Mrs. Taft probably spent a lot of the missing money on clothes for herself and her daughters. I think that's true, but I need to know for certain. The money doesn't seem to have gone to the charities they named. In fact, we can't find anyone at even the main charity who admits to getting more than a few pounds from them." He kept his expression one of concentration, without the shadow of a smile. "Hester, can you see what is known of the Brothers of the Poor? But be careful. On the slight chance they took the money and put it to their own purpose, they won't welcome inquiries." He turned a little. "Scuff, Taft's daughters were a little older than you are. See if you can learn anything about them, or the family. But you also must be very careful! We can't afford to warn anyone off. Taft is dead, but Drew is very much alive, and he may be dangerous and have some dangerous friends."

Scuff's eyes were bright, his face flushed with excitement. "Yeah," he said with elaborate casualness. " 'Course I can."

WARNE HAD NO HESITATION in seeing Monk; in fact he seemed relieved that he had the opportunity. His office looked chaotic, piles of books and papers on every surface, even one of the chairs. Clearly he had been researching something with a degree of desperation. Monk wondered if Warne, privately, was just as worried as he, Hester, and Rathbone were.

He forced his mind to focus; these piles of law books and references might be related to a completely different case. The law did not stop because Rathbone was in trouble. Hundreds of people were, all over England.

"Sit down, Mr. Monk," Warne said quickly, picking up a pile of papers to make the best chair available. "I am rather taking it for granted that you are here regarding the Taft case."

"Thank you." Monk sat down as Warne took his own seat on the other side of the desk, which was also piled with papers. "Yes. I need to find as much information as I can. There seem to be one or two things that don't entirely make sense."

Warne bit his lip. "I wish it didn't make sense to me. Of course the police have already spoken to me. I couldn't lie to them. They know perfectly well I didn't find the photograph myself, nor could I say it had been sent to me anonymously. If it had, I doubt I would have used it." He sighed. "Added to which, Sir Oliver didn't lie."

"Who reported the issue to the Lord Chancellor?" Monk asked bluntly.

Warne was pale and clearly unhappy. "I don't know. I've wondered that myself. Not that it makes a great deal of difference. Even if we could prove that it was done entirely maliciously, it wouldn't alter the facts. It might make whoever did it look pretty grubby, and spiteful, but it wouldn't help Rathbone."

Monk acknowledged that. He wanted to know out of anger rather than for any practical purpose. However, one never knew what information might turn out to be of value. He smiled bleakly. "I understand that, but I'm desperate. I'll try any avenue."

"Rathbone has been one of the best lawyers in the country," Warne said ruefully. "Kind of the standard we all measure ourselves against. But some people don't take it well when they're beaten, especially if they thought they were definitely going to win. Punctured arrogance hurts pretty badly." He shook his head. "Honestly, it would be hard to find out, and almost certainly a waste of time."

"I don't have time to waste, that's true," Monk admitted. "I need to know the full extent of your case against Taft. I could read through all the court transcripts and try to assess it myself, but it would more efficient if you told me. I'm not asking for confidential information, it's just that I would prefer to have your opinion, the outline of the case."

"Of course . . ." Warne hesitated.

"What is it? Am I asking you to betray anyone else's interest?" Monk asked him. "Or your own?"

"No," Warne's response was instant. "I'd . . . I'd like to help, as I was the one who used the photograph. Rathbone gave it to me openly and honestly. He left it up to me what I did with it. And yet they are not doing anything more to me than giving me a fairly sharp slap on the wrist for not having shown Gavinton the photograph immediately."

"Don't you have to use it, once you've seen it?" Monk asked.

"No, not legally. Morally I believe I did. But morally I'm not impartial," Warne explained. "And really, I'm not even legally impartial, nor am I meant to be. Rathbone is. He should have recused himself, not kept on with the case, even though I'm pretty sure charges wouldn't have been brought again. Taft was nine-tenths of the way to being ac-

quitted. Personally I think he was one of the most despicable criminals
I've ever prosecuted."

There was anger and hurt in Warne's face that made Monk think
of him in a new light. Perhaps in his own way he was as much a crusader
as Rathbone had been. He was now seeing the downfall of a man he
had spent years trying to emulate. Perhaps he also had known people
like the victims of Taft: simple, ordinary people who went to church
every Sunday and gave what they could to the charities that helped
others, people whose faith was central to their lives. It was trust in
those who led them that made the losses and injustices of life bearable.

"It was a just case," Monk agreed. "Was it a good one legally?"

Warne sighed. "I thought it was, to begin with. I had no doubt that
for all his smoothness, Taft was guilty. But as it went on, and Robertson
Drew made my witnesses look pathetic and then ridiculous, I felt it slip
out of my grasp. I think without the photograph Taft would have been
acquitted. Somehow I didn't even consider not using it. The only question in my mind was how to get it in without putting Rathbone in a
place where he had to grant a mistrial. I couldn't risk that; they might
not have brought the case again. It wasn't as if anyone had died, at that
time."

"But now they have," Monk pointed out. "That makes it different,
in the public perception, if not in law."

Warne gritted his teeth. "The jury is drawn from the public," he
pointed out. "And that will play into the hands of whoever tries the
case against Rathbone. There isn't going to be much mercy for him
among their lordships on the bench. He's brought them into public
disrepute. They'll all be watched a good deal closer from now on." He
gave his head a little shake, a sharp jerky movement. "What can I do to
help?"

Monk was surprised at Warne's eagerness. He was beginning to realize how deeply Warne felt, not only because of his past admiration for
Rathbone. Warne's feelings were also fueled by his contempt for Taft
and perhaps a certain conviction that emotion, as much as legal knowledge, was an integral part of prosecution.

"Tell me as much as you can about the evidence," Monk replied. "Including your opinions of the people."

"With pleasure," Warne replied. "Please heaven you can see something in it that will provide a way out. With all the people Rathbone has convicted in his career, I'd be surprised if he lasted more than a few months in prison."

Monk caught his breath. For a moment he was not certain what Warne meant, then he saw the fear in his eyes, and he understood. It was his own worst dread put into words. He did not reply, simply took out his notebook ready to write down anything he might forget. He knew the violence in prison, the accidents, the deaths that no one saw happen. There was never proof, only tragedy.

SCUFF ALSO KNEW VIOLENCE, and how suddenly and easily it could occur. He knew what could happen to Oliver Rathbone, and he had no belief at all that he could be protected if he went to prison. He knew, too, that if they were to help him, they needed to be very careful.

Nevertheless he left Paradise Place with a spring in his step. He did not have to go to school. Not that he didn't like it. It could even be interesting, but it was a bit cramping at times. Do as everybody else does, listen, and remember. We'll question you on it later. You can't just answer. You'll have to write it down, and spell properly. There is only one right way.

Now he was going to do what really mattered: help Monk and Hester—and Sir Oliver, of course. There might be only one right way for that too. He must not make even the smallest mistake. It was not as if he were the only one who would pay.

He had already thought to leave his good jacket at home. His boots were better than many people's, but he could scuff them a bit, get them dusty, and no one would notice. He needed to step back into the person he had been two years ago, cunning, hungry, willing to do most things for a cup of tea and a bun.

Monk had asked him to find out about the Taft family, specifically the wife and daughters. That was what he was going to do. He thought about it hard as he took a ferry across the river and sat in the stern, like a grown-up, and watched the sun bright on the water. As usual, the breeze was a bit chilly. He had known the river smell all his life, and he was used to cold.

How was he going to find out about the Tafts? Obviously he'd ask someone who knew things about them, things the family didn't realize they'd given away. Who would know such things?

He thought about that for quite a long time, even after getting to the other side, paying the ferryman, and walking all the way to the main road and the omnibus stop. The street was busy. There were ped-dlers, men loading brewers' drays, costermongers, shoppers at the vege-table carts, butchers' boys, newspaper sellers. That was the answer: the invisible people saw things because no one noticed them. Delivery boys, scullery maids, postmen, street sweepers, lamplighters, the people you saw every day and didn't remember. You realized they mattered only when they weren't there and you went without something you were used to having.

The omnibus drew up and stopped. Scuff jumped on eagerly. He knew exactly where he was going, and what for. He knew how to be charming, how to ask questions without seeming to and make people think he liked them and wanted to hear what they had to say. He had watched both Hester and Monk do it often. And girls always liked to talk about other girls, and clothes, and romance. He might not find out much about Mrs. Taft, but he would hear all sorts of things about her daughters. He was going to detect. He would learn something valuable first, and then he would tell Monk and Hester how he had done it. He would help them save Sir Oliver.

FROM TIME TO TIME Monk had done certain favors for men from police forces other than those under his own jurisdiction. Perhaps in the dis-tant past, before his accident and resulting amnesia, that might not have been true. Evidence he found suggested he had been grudging to share back then if he could avoid it. Now he thought such an attitude not only mean-spirited but also tactically shortsighted. He saw the wisdom in not only doing favors now and then, but also in being seen to return a favor done for him.

He was grateful to be owed a few that he could now collect. He chose them very carefully. Inspector Courtland was a lean, middle-aged man who had worked his way up the ranks to a position of some power, but he never forgot the great, decent family that had nurtured him. Monk knew that his mother was a churchgoing woman who had raised five children after her husband was killed in an industrial accident. Courtland spoke of her in such a way that Monk had envied him a family childhood, which, if he had had such a thing himself, he could remember nothing of now.

He did not insult Courtland by pretending he was doing anything other than collecting a favor. He would not have appreciated such condescension himself.

"Not my case personally," Courtland explained as they shared a couple of pints of ale and remarkably good pork pies in a public house half a mile from Courtland's police station. "But of course I know about it. What do you need?"

Monk smiled and took another bite of his pork pie. "They do a very good baked apple here."

Courtland nodded. "Good. It'll take that long for me to tell you all I can about Mr. Taft and his unfortunate ending. Mind, you didn't hear it from me."

"Of course not," Monk agreed. "I observed it all myself, or deduced it. I don't know that it's going to be any damned use anyway. But there's something in all this that we don't understand."

"Something?" Courtland raised his eyebrows. "There's everything. Starting with, where is the money? Going on to, where did Rathbone get the picture of Drew? Why did Taft kill himself because Drew was a child abuser and pornographer? And why the devil did he kill his wife and daughters? But the facts say that that is what happened." He took another mouthful of his pie. "And you know as well as I do that if we can prove a thing happened we don't have to find a sane reason for it—or any reason at all."

"Just tell me as much as you know of what are absolute facts," Monk asked. "The sort of thing the best defense in the world couldn't shake."

Courtland stopped halfway through his pie and took another long draft of his ale. He put his tankard down again and met Monk's eyes.

"Taft and his wife came home from court after the revelation about Drew and the photograph," he began. "They got there a little after five o'clock. Both daughters were at home, but there were no servants in the house."

"At five in the afternoon? Why not?" Monk asked, his mouth full.

"Apparently they all gave notice when the scandal broke and Taft was accused of misappropriating the charity money. Mrs. Taft is probably the only one who could confirm that, though, and she's not here to say different, poor woman," Courtland explained.

"But he hadn't been found guilty yet," Monk said with some surprise. "Looks as if they didn't expect him to be acquitted. Why was that? Did they know something more than the prosecution did?"

"A good question," Courtland answered. "But I doubt we'll get a straight answer from them. If they left because they thought he was guilty, they'll want to stay far away from the whole thing."

Monk thought for a moment, drinking more of his ale, and Courtland waited.

Someone slapped the plump barmaid lightly on the behind, and there was a burst of laughter from the next table. She flounced off, giggling.

"Did they go before the trial began, or afterward?" Monk asked. "Because, according to the prosecution, they thought they had a good case against Taft, until Drew started to give evidence. Then he pretty well destroyed it."

"You're giving the servants credit for more foresight than I think they warrant," Courtland told him grimly. "Looks more like they went as soon as they got a decent offer anywhere else. The feeling was much divided in the community. Still is. Servants don't like uncertainty.

Can't blame them. If you've been in a home where there's a scandal it can be hard to find another place."

"Yes, I suppose so," Monk agreed. "So the daughters were home, and Mr. and Mrs. Taft got back at about five o'clock. What then?"

Courtland shook his head. "Their lawyer, Gavinton, called by. He's not sure as to the exact time, but he thinks about half past eight. He said Taft was very upset, but he didn't think he was in the least suicidal."

Monk smiled bleakly. "Well, he would say that. He's hardly likely to admit he found the man looking as if he'd kill his family and then himself. He'd have a lot of explaining to do if he walked out and left them after that."

"True," Courtland conceded. "All the same, it's easy enough to believe that as far as Gavinton was concerned, Taft was distressed at the prospect of conviction, as any other man would've been, and upset to find that the man he had trusted so completely was a child abuser and pornographer. But that isn't the type of distress that drives you to kill your family and then yourself. You really can't blame Gavinton for not noticing that anything seemed out of the ordinary, given what the circumstances were."

"Does he blame himself?" Monk asked curiously.

"Actually, yes, he does. He says he ought to have seen it, but he didn't."

"What about Drew? Did he call?"

"No. Not while Gavinton was there, anyway, and there is nothing to suggest that he came later on. But even if he had, Taft didn't die until a few minutes after five in the morning, by which time Drew was miles away and can prove it. So can Gavinton. Not that anyone suspects him."

"Five in the morning?" Monk was mildly surprised. "That's late to commit suicide. Just about daylight again." Had Taft sat up all night, trying to think of a way out? Or trying to find the courage to end his life?

"Yes, it is," Courtland agreed. "Neighbors heard the shot and sent for the police. They got there from the local station well within half an hour. They found Taft shot through the roof of the mouth. Mrs. Taft had been strangled and both daughters suffocated. The gun was there, the house doors were locked. Drew was at home in his bed, as his servants will testify." He swallowed the last of his pie. "Naturally the police searched the house, but they could find nothing to suggest anything other than the tragically obvious conclusion."

Monk was largely ignoring his food, good as it was. He tried to picture the scene in his mind. It was all too easy. He had tasted despair himself, in the long dark hours of the night. Most people do, at one time or another. Money problems become insurmountable; news comes of a death in the family; there is incurable illness, failure, a consuming love that is not returned; or perhaps there is simply the loss of a friend who to that point had made all other grief bearable.

Some people retreat into silence, some weep, some lose their tempers and break things, very few kill themselves. That is a journey whose end is unknown, except that there is no return from it. Why had Taft, a man who professed an overpowering Christian faith, taken that road?

The obvious answer was that his faith was not real and perhaps never had been—at least not for some considerable time. But Hester had felt that his self-love was real enough; that didn't fit the picture of suicide either.

"Do you believe the police's conclusion?" Monk asked Courtland, looking up to meet his eyes.

"Short of finding some evidence to the contrary, I have to," Courtland replied. "And I can't even think of what that evidence could be."

Monk could think of nothing either. He finished his meal in near silence, then thanked Courtland and left.

MONK SPENT THE REST of the day examining the police evidence in detail, and it stood up to his closest scrutiny. Both Gavinton and Drew's accounts of their whereabouts were unassailable. Gavinton had been at home with his wife and family. His wife was restless and had not slept well. She had told the police, ruefully, that the sight of her husband sleeping, blissfully unaware of her insomnia, had added to her sense of being utterly alone in the house. She had finally given in to temptation, and woken her lady's maid to make her a cup of hot milk. The maid had confirmed this, with sufficient detail to remove doubt.

Monk had not considered Gavinton likely to be guilty of violence anyway. He decided to go to see him only because such an omission would have been incompetent.

He had found Gavinton pale-faced and looking harassed. He agreed to speak to Monk with the air of a man who felt he had little alternative. He was standing behind an unusually tidy desk, no more than one pile of papers on it.

"I'm not sure what I can tell you, Mr. Monk." He waved his hand indicating the chair opposite. "I am as stunned as you must be by Taft's suicide. Even more that he should take the fearful action of killing his family as well. I have no explanation to offer."

"Was there anything he said or did that with hindsight seems relevant to you now?" Monk asked, aware that Gavinton had no obligation to answer him.

Gavinton was profoundly disconcerted. He was not used to a failure he could not deny, or about which he could shift most of the blame on to someone else. He looked down at the all-but-empty desk. "I've thought about that, and in spite of the fact that I defended the man, and therefore I imagined I had come to know him to a degree—I certainly knew where I thought him most vulnerable—the answer is that I cannot think of anything that makes sense of what he's done. Believe me; I want to for my own sake."

Monk smiled bleakly. He had no difficulty in believing that.

"You saw him that evening . . ." he began.

"Yes. He was upset, of course. But he hadn't actually seen the photograph," Gavinton said quickly.

"Did you tell him what it was?" Monk had no intention of letting him escape the issue.

"I had no choice," Gavinton said tartly. "He had to understand why

I couldn't allow it to be seen by the jury. It was . . . repellent. The boy was only five or six years old . . . thin as a rail. If you'd seen his face—" He stopped abruptly, his voice choking off. "I think if the jury'd seen it they'd have wanted to hang Drew. I did myself." He gave a violent shudder, something of a courtroom gesture. Even now he could not entirely stop playing for effect.

"And Taft?" Monk pursued. "Was he disillusioned to the point of despair?" Monk was trying to imagine what might have been going through Taft's mind.

"I described it as factually as I could, without details," Gavinton replied. "Taft was stunned, and angry, but he certainly didn't appear insane or suicidal."

Monk did not reply to that.

"Could there have been a photograph of him also?" he asked instead.

Gavinton looked as if he were cornered, his face tight, eyes moving from one point to another in the room. He considered for a few moments before at last replying, "I thought about that too, but it didn't seem to be on his mind. He was disillusioned with Drew, of course, but his overriding distress seemed to spring from the realization that Drew changing his testimony would mean he himself would almost certainly be convicted. Whatever sentence Rathbone handed down, Taft's career as a preacher was over, and that mattered to him above all else."

"Did you see Mrs. Taft?" Monk asked.

Gavinton looked even paler. "Yes. The poor woman was distraught. I think that up until that time she had believed Taft innocent. Or if not innocent, at least she had convinced herself it was some slight error, a misjudgment, but not more than that. I imagine she wondered how on earth she would survive. His reputation would be ruined. He would be in prison, and I have no idea how she could have provided for herself. I might have wondered if she had taken her own life, but one cannot strangle oneself."

"Many women can make their own way in life," Monk answered, even though a degree of pity stirred within him. "Many widows do, and all women who don't marry. They may have little to spare on luxuries, but they survive. That is the lot of most people in the world. She was still quite young, and very handsome. She could have married again."

"It hardly matters," Gavinton pointed out. "She is dead. Perhaps Taft thought she wouldn't survive without him."

"And his daughters as well?" Monk asked. "What damnable arrogance and stupidity."

"Damnable indeed," Gavinton said quietly. For the first time genuine humility touched him. "I'm sorry. I failed more than I could have imagined in this one." He looked numbed by the magnitude of the disaster.

Monk was uncertain he had learned anything of value, but he thanked Gavinton for his time, rose to his feet, and left.

He also checked Drew's whereabouts at the time of Taft's death, not with Drew himself but with the police. According to their files Drew lived in a modest but very comfortable house two or three miles away from Taft's home. He had two resident servants: a manservant and a woman to do the cleaning and laundry. They both lived on the premises. The door had bolts on the inside, which were not undone during the night.

Drew said he had slept uneasily; that was easy to believe. He had supposedly paced the floor of his study until close to midnight then gone to bed. Within a quarter of an hour of the shots being heard at Taft's house, Drew had woken his manservant when he had accidentally dropped a bottle of whisky in his study and smashed it on the marble hearth.

It was convenient, but it was also unarguable. Were it Drew who was dead, Monk thought wryly, he might have more grounds for suspecting Taft of murder. Even had it been Drew who had committed suicide, it would have been easier to understand. But nothing the police had found involved Drew in Taft's death.

There were at least fifty pictures, aside from Drew's, in Rathbone's possession. But did anyone else have copies of the pictures? Ballinger had run the club, but that didn't necessarily mean he was the only one with photographs. There could be someone else involved, someone who might be protecting his own skin, or cutting himself a piece of the blackmailing profit.

But none of this speculation helped Rathbone. Rathbone needed evidence that proved to the law that he was within the bounds of his judicial behavior, and to the public that he was not responsible for the death of Taft, or his wife and daughters.

Monk had a deep, cold fear that no such thing would exist. Whatever Rathbone's intentions, and he did not doubt them, his actions had been disastrous.

He decided he must find a way to search Taft's house, see where he had killed himself, look at his belongings, and get inside the mind of the man who had done such a thing. And he must do it legally.

FIRST HE RETURNED TO the financial side of the crime, getting all the papers Dillon Warne could give him, but this time looking not for evidence of embezzlement but for an indication of the Taft family's daily life: their tastes, their expenses, their pleasures.

He chose to do it at the Portpool Lane clinic with Squeaky Robinson, because Squeaky could interpret figures into evidence.

Squeaky complained all evening about the time it was taking, and how many better things he had to do, and that this was not what he was paid for. But at the same time there was a deep satisfaction in him that he still might help Rathbone and that Monk had recognized his value and had asked for his assistance. Behind the scrape of his voice there was a distinct pleasure, and he worked with both speed and skill. It was a matter of double-entry bookkeeping; there were payments to companies for shipments that had appeared to take place, but had not done so. Occasionally there were complicated calculations that took very careful repeating to see where the figures had disappeared. Monk found it difficult to follow, but when Squeaky explained it, finally he understood. A little after midnight he leaned back in his chair and looked across at Squeaky.

"I see," he said quietly. "Thank you."

Squeaky inclined his head in acknowledgment. "He was a bad bastard," he said quietly. "He stole thousands, drove some of them poor souls into beggary 'cos they swallowed his lies. Still don't know what he did with it. It's somewhere he can reach it. I'll bet the house on that! Just got to find it. Everything that poor devil Sawley said about him were true, an' they made him look like an idiot. That was wrong."

Monk looked at Squeaky's thin face with its angular features and stringy hair. For all his oddity, his sense of the wrong in humiliating another person gave him a kind of dignity.

"You're right," Monk agreed. "And Robertson Drew deserved to be pilloried for it too. He lied about the money, about people, and probably about everything else. If he were to get blackmailed over his personal indulgences, I would think that a very appropriate fate."

"What are we going to do about all this?" Squeaky said, thinking practically.

Monk noticed that Squeaky still considered himself part of the battle.

"I'm not certain," he replied thoughtfully. "Taft is the only one charged with a crime directly, and he is dead. I imagine Drew will remain very quiet for some time and then probably disappear off to another city and start again—new name, new congregation. Anywhere as large as Manchester or Liverpool and he'd probably never be recognized." He realized as he said it just how much that angered him.

Squeaky regarded him with quiet disgust. "An' you're going to let that happen?"

"First thing is to do something to vindicate Rathbone," Monk answered him. "Once he's in prison we'll not get him out again."

"He won't bloody survive it!" Squeaky agreed, his anger hot again. "Bad bastards he's put away, somebody'll stick a knife in his guts in the first month . . . or sooner. You'd better think sharpish." He stared at Monk as if expecting something immediate in return, a plan of battle.

Monk was stung by the unreasonableness of it, and yet also flattered, which was ridiculous. Why did he care what Squeaky Robinson, of all people, thought of him?

"I can only keep returning to one question: Why did Taft kill himself and his family?" Monk said slowly. "What purpose did it serve?"

"Personally, I'd have wanted to kill Taft. I think he got off easy," Squeaky responded reasonably. "There's something big as we don't know here, if you ask me."

Monk stood up slowly, his back stiff. "I agree. But I don't know how on earth we're supposed to find it." He indicated the papers on the table between them. "All this says to me is that Taft stole a very great deal of money over a long period of time. It would be interesting to know who else got a cut, and in what proportion. But right now I'm too tired to think. I'll start again in the morning. Thank you for your help."

"Ain't finished yet," Squeaky said grimly. "There's something more here. But I s'pose that's enough for tonight."

Monk did not argue. He was so tired his body ached, and he knew that if there was any better answer to Rathbone's guilt, he had not found it.

MONK WAS HOME AND in bed by three in the morning. He slept far later than he had intended to and woke with a start, the room full of sunlight. He sat up sharply, saw the clock, and scrambled out of bed.

Fifteen minutes later he was sitting at the kitchen table sipping hot tea. He was well aware that his hair was untidy and that he was less than perfectly shaved. Many urgent things gnawed at his mind. He was too late to have caught Scuff, who was presumably already off to school, for once perhaps needing no persuasion.

Hester was looking at him expectantly, waiting for him to tell her what he had learned, and he was embarrassed that it was of so little use.

"I've got to find the money," he repeated. "Even Squeaky doesn't have much of an idea where it actually is. Taft lived well, but not well enough to account for all that's missing." He sipped his tea, which was still too hot to drink easily. "If we don't find it, then the court will point out that it could certainly have gone to a different charity, that it just wasn't properly documented."

"If Taft has it somewhere, then it must be where he could have reached it," Hester reasoned.

"Or he gave it to Drew," he added.

She frowned. "Would Taft really have trusted anybody else with it?"

He sat silently for a few moments. "I doubt it," he conceded at last.

"Do you really think it's possible, what you said—that they gave it to another charity and just didn't record it?" she asked skeptically.

This time he did not hesitate. "No. It's somewhere."

"Do you think Drew at least knows where it is?" she asked.

"Yes, probably," he agreed. "I think that when he was testifying it was as much to save himself as to save Taft."

Hester looked at him pensively. "If I had been in Taft's place, I think I'd have wanted to kill Drew, if I killed anyone at all!"

"Of course you would." He bit his lip but still failed to hide a smile. "But then you are about as like Taft as I am like Cleopatra."

She looked him up and down, smiling herself. "I don't see it," she said drily. "Perhaps a slightly better shave?" Then her amusement vanished. "Even if he did want to kill himself . . . his poor family . . ."

"I know that if I were in that kind of trouble I'd want you and Scuff to go and take everything you could with you," Monk admitted. "My one comfort would be that you would survive."

She looked at him witheringly. "And you think either of us would go? I would never leave you, unless it would be to help somehow, and Scuff wouldn't forgive me if I did."

"I would want you to survive," he repeated, refusing to think of it any more vividly. "It would be about the only thing that would salvage some honor—apart from the fact that I love you."

Her smile was so sweet, so gentle that for a moment he felt a warmth rush up inside him and tears prickled his eyes. He felt absurd, overemotional. He was afraid to speak in case his voice betrayed him.

"But then, of course, you wouldn't have gotten yourself into the kind of mess Taft was in," she said, as if continuing her own thought.

He knew she was speaking to fill the silence and save him from the betrayal of his vulnerability.

"There is something we don't know, there just has to be," she continued. She looked a touch desperate suddenly.

"It's not your fault, you know, just because you began the investigation." He said the first thing that sprang to his mind, or perhaps it was there already.

"Yes it is," she responded immediately. "There wouldn't even have been a case if I hadn't listened to Josephine Raleigh and started to look into it. And then I asked Squeaky's help, and it was he who found the financial evidence. Without that, they wouldn't have brought anything to court."

He raised his eyebrows. "So we shouldn't try to catch criminals or prosecute them in case the trial ends badly for some of the people involved? Punishment does slop over the sides sometimes and land on the bystanders as well. Sometimes they deserve it and sometimes they don't. Mrs. Taft certainly didn't deserve to die, but she was quite willing to live very well indeed on the profits of Taft's embezzlement."

Hester stared at him, her brow furrowed in thought. "I wonder how many women bother to consider if the money they spend is honestly earned or not. I know what you do to provide for us, but then I don't have half a dozen hungry children to clothe and feed, teach, nurse, and generally keep clean and happy. Maybe if I did, then I wouldn't have time to wonder about much."

"Mrs. Taft didn't have half a dozen," Monk pointed out. "Added to which, she knew perfectly well what Taft did for a living because he did it in front of her. And she must have seen the clothes of the congregation and been able to have a damn good guess as to their income." He felt the anger rise inside him. "Couldn't you place someone pretty well by their clothes, how many times a collar had been turned, socks darned, children's clothes patched? Don't you know the age of a dress by its cut and color?"

Her eyes flickered for an instant. "Yes," she said gently. "But I care. Perhaps she didn't want to."

"Perhaps?" he said with a sharp edge of sarcasm.

She gave a slight, surprisingly elegant shrug. "It's still not an offense worthy of death."

"Of course it isn't," he agreed. "I'm sorry, that isn't what I meant." He reached forward and touched her hand. "The jury is going to say that this was Oliver's fault, which may not be fair, but we have to deal with the fact. I don't know where further to look for evidence of what really happened, or why. It doesn't seem possible that anyone else killed him."

"Then we need to find the reason why Taft killed himself," she said intently. "Maybe if the trial had gone on, something more would've come out. What if he couldn't face it?" Her voice dropped at the last few words, as if she were not sure if she believed it herself. "He was a very arbitrary, very domineering sort of man."

He was startled. "Why do you think that? You said that in church he was charming, courteous . . ."

She rolled her eyes. "William! People are not always the same at home with their families as they are in public, especially men." Her face softened, her eyes were suddenly very gentle. "If you could remember the past, going to church with your parents, you'd know that better."

The hurt that might have caused was healed before it began by the look in her face. What did the past matter when the present held such sweetness?

He smiled, having no words for what he felt. "So what makes you say that of Taft, then?" he insisted.

"You asked Scuff to find out," she replied. "I know it was mostly to give him something to do, to feel he was helping, but he discovered quite a lot about the family."

Monk stiffened. "Who from? Was he—"

"No, he wasn't in any danger," she answered him with a slight smile. "Actually, he was very astute. You'd be proud of his detective work. He found the scullery maid who was dismissed, and a delivery boy who spent rather more time in the Tafts' kitchen than he should have. Apparently Taft was something of a martinet in his own house. Everything ran to his rules: what they ate and when; family prayers for everybody, like it or not; what they were allowed to read; even what color their dresses should be."

Monk was amazed, and a little doubtful. "And the scullery maid knew all this?"

"Her best friend was the tweeny. They shared a bedroom," Hester explained. "And believe me, between-stairs maids are all over the house and observe a great deal." She bit her lip and for a moment her eyes were bright with tears, pity, memory, and very painful laughter. "If you have a scandal in the house, the last thing you should do is let all your staff leave."

He sat thinking for a moment, absorbing what she had told him. A very different, sad, and frightening picture was emerging of Mr. Taft.

"So he killed himself to save what?" he asked. "Not his family, obviously."

"I don't know!" She clenched her fists on the tabletop.

He hesitated a moment, but honesty compelled him to speak. "Hester, we've got to face it—legally, Oliver was wrong. Morally, I don't know; he meant well, but that doesn't make it right. He shouldn't have kept those pictures in the first place."

"That's like saying you want to have an army to defend us if we're attacked, but for heaven's sake don't give them guns!"

"That's a bit extreme."

"Is it?" she demanded. "Of course power's dangerous. Life is dangerous. I know Oliver's not perfect. But what is 'perfect,' anyway? Most of the people I know who have never made a mistake are that way because they never do anything at all. If people didn't take risks there would be no exploration, no inventions, no great works of art. We certainly won't defend anyone accused of anything, in case they turn out to be guilty. We wouldn't let ourselves fall in love, in case the other person hurt us or let us down or, above all, in case we saw in him some of our own weaknesses."

"Hester . . ."

"What?" She faced him, her eyes blazing and full of tears.

"You're right," he said gently. "Don't ever change . . . please." He stood up. "I've got to get to Wapping. Poor Orme has been covering for me for heaven knows how long."

12

The NEXT DAY, AS soon as he had dealt with the river-connected cases that could not be delegated any longer, Monk went to see Dillon Warne again.

Warne looked wretched. His hair was untidy, and there was a dark uneven shadow on his face and hollows around his eyes. "I have to testify in Rathbone's trial," he said almost as soon as the door closed behind the clerk who had let Monk in. "I hoped I'd get out of it, but they've called me and I have no choice. I've racked my brains to think of anything helpful." He shook his head, the anger evident in his face. "They're not prosecuting me, which makes me feel additionally guilty. I was the one who used the damn photograph!"

"Why?" Monk asked gravely.

Warne did not understand, but he was too tired to be polite. "What?"

"Why did you use that particular piece of evidence?" Monk elaborated.

"Because I was losing the case and I hadn't any other. I already told you that." Warne's voice was weary.

"And was winning a case worth it to you, at any price?" Monk kept his voice level and mild, as if he were merely curious.

Warne blushed and looked at him more intently. "Not usually," he said. "But this case I cared about very much. I'm not sorry that bastard killed himself, though murdering his family was an appalling crime. It just adds cowardice to his list of sins." His voice sharpened. "Why are you asking?"

"Well . . . I imagine Rathbone also felt Taft was pretty low, and perhaps now most of those in the court, including the jury, will agree," Monk replied.

Warne leaned forward a fraction, suddenly eager. "Are you saying somehow we can use the fact Taft was a coward? It'll be the deaths of Taft and his family that the jury reacts to, whatever is said about legal responsibility and details of what evidence should be produced when."

"That's about all I can see to go for, at the moment," Monk agreed. "But I wish we knew how Drew fit into the picture. I mean, he was the one who was so vicious toward Gethen Sawley. He made the man look like a complete fool in front of the jury."

"To defend Taft, of course." Warne replied, and then he drew in his breath sharply. "You think there was some other reason?"

"Could there be?"

"Of course there could be." Warne shrugged. "But nobody's charged Drew with being involved in the fraud. And nobody knows what was in the photograph, except Gavinton, Rathbone, and me. The jury knew it was bad, but not how bad, or of what nature. It might have been Drew with Taft's wife, for all they knew. In fact, because Taft killed his wife, that very possibly will be what they think." His voice was gathering speed. "It would be a fairly natural conclusion. Reprehensible, certainly, but not beyond human understanding. Drew wouldn't be the first man who slept with his best friend's wife." A bitter smile twisted his lips.

"Possibly even a juror or two would find that too close to home to condemn."

"If Taft had lived and gone to prison," Monk said thoughtfully, "it would have been interesting to see what Mrs. Taft would have done—and where the rest of the money went!" Briefly he related the information that Scuff had learned from the Tafts' scullery maid, painting a picture of their home life for Warne.

Warne listened intently, nodding as Monk finished. "I didn't see that," he admitted. "But it fits in with the little I saw or heard. Perhaps I should have had the wits to speak to the scullery maid or the tweeny myself. I never thought of it." Warne was nodding now, his involvement sharp again. "But time's very short. I'll do what I can to help, not only for Rathbone's sake but my own as well. I'm beginning to realize just how much I hate being beaten when I know something doesn't add up."

They discussed the issue for another half hour, precise details that could be pursued, possible avenues to explore. They agreed that Warne should review the evidence and exactly how each fact had emerged, so a new jury would see what little choice Rathbone had. Monk would try to learn more about Taft himself and would keep on searching for the missing money.

THE FIRST PLACE MONK went after leaving Warne's office was the clinic in Portpool Lane. He spoke briefly to Hester, but it was Squeaky Robinson he wanted to see. He found him at his usual desk, bent over the books, a pen in his hand. He looked up as Monk came in.

Monk closed the door behind him and walked across the small floor space to the desk.

"Good morning, Mr. Robinson," he said pleasantly, pulling out the chair opposite the desk and sitting down, crossing his legs comfortably as if he intended to be there for some time.

Squeaky did not reply, but he put his pen back in the holder and blotted his page, resigned to doing no more for a while.

"You've studied the financial papers of the church, and of Taft personally, in great detail," Monk began. "You found the embezzlement for which we are all very grateful . . ."

"Yeah?" Squeaky asked. "Sir Oliver included, no doubt." His voice dripped sarcasm. "He said that, did he?"

Monk ignored the joke.

"I'm being optimistic that if I ask you nicely, you'll help me find even more evidence, which will eventually lead to a more comprehensive picture than the one we have," he answered.

"Really? Like what?" Squeaky raised his wild eyebrows and studied Monk.

"How deeply is Robertson Drew involved in the embezzlement?" Monk said. "In your opinion, did he know the entire extent of it? And if so, what could you prove? There's something we've missed, and it probably lies with the money, and maybe with where it is now. Perhaps Drew's share. What happened to it?"

"I can't tell that from the books!" Squeaky said indignantly. "You think somebody wrote it all down beside one o' the columns o' figures, 'Sent it all to Mr. Smith in Wolver'ampton? First house along the road from the railway station, going north!' What do you think I am? You want one of them old biddies with a crystal ball."

"I want somebody who knows every crooked piece of accounting there is and smells a trick like a dog smells a rat—but whom I can trust. If that's not you, who is it?" Monk kept his face perfectly straight with something of an effort.

Squeaky was quite aware he was being played like a fiddle but he did not mind. Monk meant the compliment and they both understood that. He grunted.

Monk took this for assent. "The police have looked and found nothing in Taft or Drew's affairs. But one thought came to my mind, as I was looking for a reason why Taft would kill his wife as well as himself."

Squeaky pulled his face into an indescribable expression of disgust, but he did not interrupt.

"The facts as we know them don't give him sufficient reason," Monk went on. "What if he discovered not only that Drew was profiting a good deal more than he had thought from their scheme, possibly even more than he himself was, but also that his friendship with Mrs. Taft was closer than any of us had appreciated? That's a guess with nothing whatever to support it, but it would explain a lot. Then Taft would feel beaten and doubly betrayed."

Squeaky shook his head slowly. "But up until Warne sprang that photograph on Drew, Drew was supporting Taft, wasn't he? And didn't you say Taft was set to get away with it?" he asked, his face twisted with disgust. "I mean, why not just let Taft take the blame, let him rot in prison, and get away with his share of the money? All he had to do was act all sad and sorry, like, and pretend he'd been as much took in as anybody else. Would have worked a bit better, and no risk."

"Yes, of course," Monk agreed. "So what if Taft trusted Drew *until* that day, the day of the photograph, when Drew changed his testimony. Maybe it was only at that point he suspected anything, when it all fell to pieces, and then Mrs. Taft somehow let it slip, and that was when Taft killed her and then himself."

"But his daughters?" Squeaky said indignantly. "What were they then, just damage on the side?"

"Yes, probably. Maybe they knew and had to be got rid of," Monk agreed.

"What a real pillar o' the Church." Squeaky shook his head.

"Is it possible? It seems a stretch." Monk pressed.

Squeaky lifted his chin a little. "Maybe. Come back tomorrow—late! I'll see what I can find. Still wish it were Drew guilty of all this, somehow. It would make more sense."

Monk smiled and stood up. "Well, it can't be," he said, hesitating a moment so Squeaky knew that he meant it. "He's accounted for."

ACTUALLY IT TOOK MONK rather longer than he had expected to learn much more about Taft. Scuff's information threw a different light on Taft's nature, and Monk made sure to tell him how vital he had been, which made Scuff puff up with pride. Then Monk spoke with John Raleigh, who was willing to see him and discuss whatever he wished, however personal or painful, out of gratitude to Hester.

"I need to know Mr. Taft better," Monk told him as they sat together in Raleigh's small front parlor. "Something of his character that would explain why he not only took his own life, but that of his family as well.

Raleigh looked surprised.

"The man is dead," he said quietly, shaking his head. "Any judgment of him is in God's hands now. I have no wish to pursue vengeance. It is unbecoming in a Christian, Mr. Monk. Or for that matter a gentleman who considers himself a man of honor, whatever his creed."

Monk found himself with an even greater respect for this quiet, seemingly ordinary man. He marveled at how easy it was to make judgments based on a few outward details, possibly only of worldly success: money, skill, confidence. How wrong those judgments often ended up being.

"It is not vengeance I want, Mr. Raleigh," he said gently. "I need to understand why Taft took his own life, and that of his family. I am hoping to prove that it was in no way linked to Sir Oliver's actions during the trial, his allowing the obscene photograph of Robertson Drew to influence Drew's testimony and thus the outcome. Sir Oliver is a longtime friend of mine, and his defense is important to me and to my wife."

"Ah," Raleigh said quietly. "I see. That is rather different. How can I help you?"

"Tell me something about Taft," Monk replied. "Describe him for me, not his appearance or his dress but his manner. What drew you to him? And please be completely honest."

"I will. I think I owe Sir Oliver, and most certainly Mrs. Monk, the most candid observation I can give." Raleigh thought for several minutes before answering, choosing his words very carefully. "To begin with I thought him a gentleman of great honesty and a remarkable dedication to the Church, and to true Christianity." He measured his words.

"As I came to know him better I found certain mannerisms of his annoying. I considered it a weakness in myself. I am still not certain if it is not so—"

"What mannerisms?" Monk interrupted.

"What seemed to me like a degree more of self-importance than I think to be good taste. A remarkable number of conversations and discussions seemed to center on him. Even stories that held a considerable trace of humor, or of self-criticism, still were always about him. I began to find it somewhat tedious, and was ashamed for doing so. He often spoke of his humility." Raleigh smiled, catching Monk's eye. "So often that I began to wonder why. You understand, humility is not speaking of yourself as humble, it is not speaking of yourself at all."

"A very good distinction," Monk agreed sincerely.

"Thank you." Raleigh colored faintly. "He appeared to be devoted to his wife, frequently praising her virtues. But I noticed he never allowed her to speak for herself. I compared his daughters with my Josephine, at the same age, and they seemed to me in a way crushed, uncertain of themselves, as if they dared not express an opinion of their own. They had not the fervor or the freedom of dreams that the young should have." He stopped for a moment. "I don't know how to express this honestly without sounding as if I am trying to damn a man who cannot speak for himself."

"You cannot help him, Mr. Raleigh," Monk reminded him. "Perhaps you can help Sir Oliver. What were your impressions of Mr. Taft's relationship with Mr. Drew?"

"You are very direct," Raleigh observed. He seemed almost amused.

"Indeed," Monk nodded again but did not say anything further.

"I am less certain about his relationship with Mr. Drew," Raleigh continued. "It is only an impression, but I thought Taft was the leader between the two of them. He was the one gifted with charm and easy words. Drew was more of a man to organize things, to act behind the scenes. He had no apparent hunger for the limelight."

"Hunger for the limelight." Monk repeated the phrase. "That is very well put, Mr. Raleigh."

Raleigh colored. "An unkind observation of a man of the cloth, Mr. Monk. I am not proud of it."

"Many of us do good works with something less than an 'eye single to the glory of God,' sir," Monk said softly. "It does not make the works themselves less good, and it leaves us room for improvement."

Raleigh smiled suddenly. "You make the trait sound almost— likable."

Monk also smiled. "Aside from Drew keeping out of the limelight, did you notice anything else about their relationship?" he prompted.

"I thought they worked very closely together," Raleigh responded. "I saw no friction between them at all. Certainly there was no visible envy or criticism."

Monk was disappointed. "And what was your impression of Mrs. Taft?"

"A very attractive woman, very agreeable. She deferred to her husband, but then perhaps most women do, at least in public. What she said in private I have no idea. Taft seemed deeply fond of her, and of his daughters, for that matter. He might have seemed a little oppressive at times, but he took the greatest care of them. That he should descend into this madness is a terrible tragedy."

"Could his disillusionment in Drew have brought it about?" Monk asked.

Raleigh considered for several moments. "I suppose it is possible," he said at last. "I would swear he trusted Drew. I have no idea what was in the photograph that turned Drew's testimony on its head. It must have been something of extraordinary power. I inferred from the look on Taft's face that he had had no idea. It seemed a terrible betrayal." He shook his head a little. "Yes, yes, betrayal can make a man despair, especially if he is betrayed by someone in whom he had had complete belief, both professionally and on a personal level. Poor man. What a terrible way to end."

Monk could not stop now. "Do you suppose Mrs. Taft was as deeply trusting in Mr. Drew? What was her manner with him?"

Clearly it was a new idea to Raleigh. He stopped for several moments to consider it before replying. "It seemed to me that she followed her husband's lead in that, as in pretty well everything else." He shook his head again, but this time not so much in doubt as apparently trying to clear muddled or displeasing thoughts. "He was a very . . . dominant man. He was always pleasant about it, but he knew exactly how he wished things to be done, and he insisted that they were done that way. But I thought she was a happy woman, despite that. Was I very foolish in my judgment?"

Monk smiled slightly and tried to imagine Hester being so placid, and knew at once he would hate it. Without her occasional dissent, her agreement would be meaningless. He would miss her ideas, her laughter, her occasional mocking and teasing, the whole sense of there being someone else around, a different person, close to him but not always like him. The loneliness would be devastating.

He looked again at Raleigh to try to judge how perceptive he was.

Raleigh smiled bleakly, more out of irony than amusement. "I admit I was deceived by the man and lost a great deal of money because I believed him, so now my opinions may be colored by that. I came to see him as both domineering and manipulative, a little drunk on his own importance. But please take my judgment as that of a man hurt by experience and therefore not impartial."

Monk assured him that he would. However, when he spoke to others over the rest of that day and during the following one, their voices built up a portrait of a man who had such a sense of his own importance at the center of God's great plan as to depart from the reality. Anyone who challenged him was very subtly made to feel as if he or she were inspired by selfishness more than good sense, by greed more than financial responsibility. No gift had ever been enough. Always within a few months, he came back for more. Smooth words of praise concealed the implicit charge of withholding from Christ were they to refuse the next request.

Taft never seemed to doubt himself. No argument was listened to. He did not quarrel. He stated his point of view as if it were fact; he condescended to hear the opposition or the doubts and then branded them as failures of faith, which could be forgiven with repentance. More often than not, the parishioners saw the weakness of their ways and rejoined the fold. Sometimes they even paid more, to cover their sins of dissent.

Monk tried to pity him for his shallowness but found it difficult. In his own way the man both fed others and consumed them, needing their dependence upon him for his own esteem. How would he handle failure, any failure at all? Badly enough to take his own life?

It was not impossible.

It was an emotional world that Monk had never truly looked into before, and it appalled him. The innate fear woven through it was terrible. Pull out one thread and the whole thing unraveled.

Should Rathbone have seen that? Of course not! But that would make no difference to the charge against him. Taft was a prime example of a person who sees exactly what he wishes to see, whose mind distorts the evidence to prove what he needs to believe. A jury might also see what they expected to see—a judge who used evidence to which he alone had access in order to turn a trial the way he wished it to go, condemning a man of the Church.

Monk had gained understanding, but it had not yet helped his cause.

THE DAY AFTER THAT Monk spoke to Rufus Brancaster and told him what he had learned. Brancaster said exactly what he had expected him to.

"It doesn't amount to a defense." He looked tired, as if he were struggling to avoid giving in to defeat. "It does make sense of Taft's actions, but only of the fact that he committed murder and suicide, where any other man would have been devastated but would have survived; perhaps drunk himself senseless, or collapsed with hysteria, but not taken his life. He thought he was necessary to the survival of his family," Brancaster continued. "I've defended a few like that before. Imagine their families cannot live without them, convinced nobody else would protect and provide for their wives. I think it's really a thinly disguised terror that they might not actually be as essential as they suppose. Can't bear to think that anyone could manage without them. Their worst nightmare is to be forgotten."

Monk said nothing. He had spent so much of the life he could remember alone. In the early days after his accident, what he had learned of himself did not encourage him to investigate more deeply. He had not been a necessary part of anyone's life.

Now he was necessary to Hester in that she loved him, but it had never been that she was unable to stand on her own feet, make her own decisions, and, if need be, to earn her own living. She was independent— not a quality liked by all men. She was highly intelligent, articulate, brave, and had a very sharp sense of humor—again not qualities comfortable to all men. She was not beautiful in the traditional sense, but he could see in her a loveliness deeper and more lasting than mere prettiness. He had never deluded himself that she could not find someone else to love her, even if not as deeply or intensely as he did.

Brancaster interrupted his thoughts.

"You and I might see that Taft was self-obsessed, and deluded enough to kill himself rather than face the loss of his fame. But the jury is going to see a man driven—by evidence they have not seen and don't understand—to the point of despair where he took not only his own life but that of his family. They have to blame someone for that." His face was sad, his eyes hollow. "A judge who perverted justice for his own reasons is an easy solution. Nobody cares what those reasons might be. Possibly the prosecution will offer them a few choices."

"Can't we prove . . . ?" Monk began, then saw the exhaustion in Brancaster's face and realized the pointlessness of the question. The law had broken down. A judge had shown his partiality in a way that was extremely visible. If the law could fail, what protection had anyone? The jury would be, by definition, upstanding citizens who did not consider themselves vulnerable to just prosecution, only to injustice. For any argument to work, it must not only be true, it must be something they would have no choice but to believe.

"What can we do?" he asked. "What could help?"

"Something to prove that when Rathbone did this it was in the service of justice and that it was the only course open to him to avoid a severe miscarriage in this case," Brancaster replied. "And believe me, I've been up most nights trying to think of the solution. It's too late now for Taft to tell his side. And it's not Drew on trial."

"The possibility of exposure exists, for every man who posed for one of those photographs, and they must all be aware of that," Monk said. "Not just Drew."

Brancaster chewed his lip thoughtfully. "You have a point there, perhaps one we could use."

Monk was puzzled. "How could we use it?"

"Play on the fear of how deep the corruption is," Brancaster replied, meeting Monk's eyes. "Rathbone has told me that there is a deep cesspit here. We have a very reasonable argument on our hands: if he had gone to any authority with that photo, or any of the photos, they might simply have covered it all up, and possibly destroyed Rathbone in the bargain, just to avoid the monumental scandal."

"But *this* is going to destroy Rathbone," Monk pointed out.

Brancaster smiled a trifle wolfishly. "Precisely."

Slowly a whole new picture opened up in Monk's imagination: full of unguessable risks and pitfalls. It might be necessary to travel down that road to save Rathbone. Was it possibly also justified? It would be a final and terrible end to the whole issue of Ballinger's photographs. Brancaster, Rathbone, and Monk himself could have no idea who they might bring down in the process because they could not know every man's connections.

"Are you prepared to do that? Use the photographs in that way?" he asked, his voice catching in his throat.

Brancaster's face was unreadable. "I'm thinking about it. Perhaps it's time." He gave a very slight shrug. "By the way, I've saved an important piece of information for last. Drew wants to have access to Taft's house to get the papers pertaining to the church."

Monk jerked his mind to attention. "No!" he said simply. "Not yet.

He can have access eventually, but not yet." Even if Drew's request was innocent—which he doubted—he still wanted to go through the house himself before he allowed anything to be removed.

Brancaster nodded. "I thought you'd say that. I already told him so."

Monk felt a very slight, inexplicable ease run through him. "Thank you. I've got to get into that house. And now that you told me this, I'm even more eager. The church papers can't be all that important. There must be something there. And I'm going to look till I find it."

13

OLIVER RATHBONE HAD SPENT some of the most exciting and challenging hours of his adult life in a courtroom. It was where he excelled, where his victories and his defeats occurred. It was the arena for his skills, the battlefield where he fought for his own beliefs and other men's lives.

Today it was utterly different, still as familiar as his own sitting room but as alien as a foreign country where the people had the faces of those you knew, but the hearts of strangers.

Brancaster had spoken to him briefly. It was too late to discuss tactics. It had been simply a word of encouragement. "Don't lose heart. Nothing's won or lost yet." Then a quick smile and he was gone.

Rathbone had never seen the courtroom from the dock before. He was high up, almost as if in a minstrels' gallery, except of course he had jailers on either side of him, and he was manacled. He was acutely aware of these things now as he looked down at the judge's high seat, where he himself used to sit, and at his peers, the jurors, on their almost church-like benches—two rows of them!

The witness box was small, as a pulpit might be, and was reached by climbing a curving stair. He could see it all very clearly. It still looked different from before. But then it was different. Everything was. For the first time in his life he would have nothing to say, nothing to do until he was called by Brancaster. The trial was about his life, and he could do nothing but watch.

He could see Brancaster standing below him, his white lawyer's wig hiding his black hair, his gown over his well-cut suit. They had planned and discussed every possible move, but all that was over now. Rathbone was helpless. He could not object, he could not ask any questions or contradict any lies. He had no way of contacting Brancaster until the luncheon adjournment, and perhaps not even then. He couldn't lean forward and tell him the points he should make, alert him to errors or opportunities. His freedom or imprisonment, his vindication or ruin, hung in the balance, and he could not intervene, let alone take part. It was like something out of his worst nightmare.

Then he saw the prosecution on the other side. It was Herbert Wystan.

Rathbone had known him for years, appeared against him a number of times, and won more often than he had lost. Wystan would no doubt remember that now. It would not make any difference. He was a man who loved and respected the law. He would not care who won or lost. This, of course, was an excellent reason for prosecuting this case with passion. In his eyes, Rathbone had betrayed the very sanctity of the law he was sworn to uphold. For Wystan that would be a crime tantamount to treason.

Had Rathbone done that? He had certainly not intended to. Or at least, he had not intended to betray justice—it was just that justice and the law were not always the same thing. But he knew they were for Wystan. And they ought to have been for him.

Wystan's hair was sandy gray, but now only his beard was visible, his wig hiding the rest of it. He had a long face, very rarely lit by humor.

The judge began with the formalities. For Rathbone, unable to move or to speak, every moment seemed surreal. Had it been like this for the people he had prosecuted? For those he had defended—people who were less familiar with court procedure than he was—had it all seemed like something happening on the other side of a window, almost in another world?

Had they trusted him to defend them? Or did they watch him as he now watched Brancaster, knowing that he was clever, even brilliant, but still only human. Did they sit here trying to keep themselves from being sick? Breathing in and out deeply, swallowing on nothing, throats too tight?

What did Brancaster think as he stood there, looking so elegant and clever? Was it a personal battle for him, a chance to win the unwinnable? Rathbone had always looked as suave and as confident as Brancaster did now; he knew that. But internally his stomach would churn, his mind racing as he balanced one tactic against another, wondering who to call, what to ask, whom to trust.

He breathed in and out again, counting up to four, and then repeating the exercise. His heart steadied.

He should have let Taft get away with it. He had been childish. It was impossible for every case to go the way he thought it should, to be just. His title had been "judge," but his job had been only to see that the law was adhered to.

And that was perhaps the worst thing of all in this whole trial: the judge sitting in the high, carved seat, presiding over the entire proceedings, was Ingram York. How smug he looked, how infinitely satisfied. Was the irony of the situation going through his mind as he listened to the openings of the case? Did he think back to that evening at his own dinner table when he was congratulating Rathbone on the success of his first big fraud trial?

That seemed like years ago, but it was only months. How different the world had been then. In his arrogance Rathbone had thought it would get only better and better. The crumbling of his marriage had seemed his only loss then, the only thing in which he had seriously failed. And he had been coming to terms even with that and understanding that it was not his fault. He had cared deeply for her, or for the person he had believed her to be. And he had learned the bitter lesson, that anyone can love what they imagine another to be; real love accepts a person for what he or she truly is . . .

The formalities were droning on without him, voices echoing, figures moving like puppets.

He did not want to look for familiar faces. He dreaded seeing them, colleagues, men he had fought against across the courtroom. Would they pity him now? Or rejoice in his fall? This was almost beyond bearing, yet he could not sit here with his eyes closed. Everyone would know why.

He recognized an old adversary called Foster. For an instant their eyes met. He could imagine exactly what Foster would say, as clearly as if he could hear his voice. " 'Come a bit of a cropper, haven't you?"

He couldn't see Monk, or Hester. Perhaps they were going to testify.

Was Margaret here now, rejoicing that he was now where her father had once been? Did she really equate them—Rathbone who had made a wild decision, perhaps a moral misjudgment, certainly a legal one—with Ballinger, who had traded in the bodies of children, blackmail, and finally murder?

In the greater sense he realized he did not care if she were here or not, or what she thought. Her opinion was a pinprick, not a fatal wound.

York was looking satisfied. His wig and robes became him well. But then they became most men. The very act of putting them on made one feel taller, more important, set apart from the ordinary run of men. He knew that for himself. What a delusion! One was just as mortal, just as subject to the vicissitudes of the flesh: headache, indigestion, the indignities of bodily functions that would not be controlled, sweating hands, a rasping voice. And one was also capable of all the emotional needs that resulted in errors of the mind: humanity, the longing for love and for forgiveness, for laughter, mercy, and the warmth of touch to steady, to encourage. One could never be truly impartial and still be human.

Did York love Beata? He could still recall her face as exactly as if he had seen her only hours ago. He did not know if she was here. He hoped not. He did not want her to see his humiliation. Anyway, she would hardly come to all the trials over which her husband presided! That would be absurd.

Just in case she was here, Rathbone had to pull his wits and his emotions together and try to show the dignity and the courage he would wish her to see in him.

Hester would be here. They had fought too many battles side by side for her ever to abandon him. She was a woman who might well hate what you had done, but she would go with you to the foot of the gallows, if need be. How badly had he let her down with this arrogance of judgment?

Then he looked at the faces in the courtroom again and saw his father, and his courage bled away as if an artery had been cut. This was the one person he should never have let down, never disappointed. The pain of it left his stomach churning. He would have accepted any failure, any punishment, if only his father had not had to suffer too. This was worse than any other time he had let him down, worse even than when he had failed his exams one time, when, upset about some triviality or other, he had not studied hard enough. Henry had been so angry then, more than Oliver had ever seen him before. This quiet gray was worse. Oliver had been planning to take Henry for a holiday to Europe next year, to see Italy. He had always wanted that. Now it might be too late . . . if he was found guilty . . .

The preliminaries were all finished. The trial was about to begin. Wystan rose to his feet. He was a solid man, not very large, but he looked imposing now as he stood out on the floor alone.

"Gentlemen," he said somberly, looking at the jury. "This may not seem to you a very serious case, compared with some that you might have been called to hear, such as thefts of great sums of money, assault, or murder. But believe me it is. This is a cheating of the process of law to which, as Englishmen, you are entitled. You are subjects of an ancient land that has been ruled by law since the days of the Saxon dooms, before William the Conqueror set foot on our shores eight hundred years ago."

He moved a couple of steps closer to them, his voice carrying clearly.

"When we sit in judgment upon one another, we are following a very tight set of rules, which are there to ensure that, as far as it is possible for human beings, we are fair. We give to each person the chance to defend himself against wrongful conviction, to speak for himself, to answer or refute the evidence against him. Otherwise, how could we refer to it as the justice system?" He hesitated to let the weight of the concept sink into their minds. "If you are not certain of this system, how can you bring anything before the law?" he continued. "How can you hope for peace or safety? How can you sleep at ease in your beds and believe that we strive to be a just and God-fearing people? The answer is simple. You cannot."

He turned very slightly and indicated Rathbone high in the dock.

"This man accepted the position of judge. It is a high and ancient position, perhaps one of the greatest honors in the land, in some ways second only to Her Majesty, and yet a position that intercedes with your lives on a regular basis. It was his task to administer justice to the people—to you. Instead of that, he perverted the law."

Rathbone winced. What could Brancaster say that would undo this damage?

Wystan continued. His voice was quiet, almost without emotion, and yet it penetrated every corner of the room. Rathbone should have remembered this about him. He wondered now how he had ever beaten the man.

"Oliver Rathbone was presiding over a case in which a man was accused of a most repellent manner of fraud, of taking money from those who had little enough, and of then misusing it. Your sympathy may be entirely with the prosecution of such a case. I know that mine is." He shook his head. "But the ugliness of a charge does not mean that the person accused is guilty. He is as deserving of a fair and just trial as is a man accused of stealing a loaf of bread. It is the innocence or guilt that we try; we determine whether or not the crime is as charged, and whether or not we have the right person in the dock."

He smiled very slightly, a mere twitch of the lip. "It is my duty to prove to you beyond any reasonable doubt that Oliver Rathbone abused the trust this nation, this people, placed in him by giving to the prosecution damning evidence as to the character of a witness for the defense, evidence quite unrelated to the charge brought. In so doing he sabotaged the trial of a man who was devastated by these events, by the shattering of his trust, not in the friend who betrayed him but in the law that was sworn to try him justly—so devastated that he took his own life. Upon uncovering the evidence, Oliver Rathbone should have recused himself and stepped aside. You may think this would have caused a mistrial, and you are correct. Nevertheless, that is what he should have done.

"I shall ask you to ignore your own feelings over the guilt or innocence of the man accused in that particular trial, and of anyone else who offered testimony in that trial. You must consider only the greater sin committed by Oliver Rathbone, who perverted the course of justice itself. Force yourselves to think, gentlemen, what refuge, what safety have any of us if the judges who sit in our courts cannot be trusted to be fair, just, and abide by the rules of the law that they are sworn and privileged to administer?"

Rathbone's heart sank. If he were in Brancaster's place now he would be choked, all previous words gone from his mind. He watched as Brancaster rose to his feet. He ached for him, quite literally. His throat was tight, his chest suffocated for breath.

Brancaster walked out into the center of the floor, addressed the judge, then turned to the jury. He did not sound self-important, an orator declaring a great cause. His voice was casual, a man speaking to a group of friends.

"Gentlemen, if this case were easy, we might have disposed of it without taking your time and keeping you from your own business. But it is not simple. That is not to say that it is any whit less important than my learned friend Mr. Wystan has suggested. Issues of justice are at stake—greater even than he has implied to you. The difference between Mr. Wystan and myself is not in our belief as to how this issue lies at the core of justice for all of us, for you, for me,"—he spread his arms in a wide, oddly graceful gesture—"for every man, woman, and child in our country. The difference is that I will not merely tell you what occurred that was so desperately wrong, I will show you, step by step, and in such a way that you cannot mistake the truth."

He smiled so slightly it could almost have been a trick of the light. "I will not ask you to believe anything I cannot demonstrate. Nor will I ask you to reach a verdict other than what sits easily with your conscience, with your sense of the wellbeing of our country, and with the mercy we all wish not only to receive ourselves, but to extend to others. Listen carefully to the evidence." He gestured toward the still empty witness box. "Imagine yourselves in the places of the people concerned, and then give thought to what you would have done, what you would have believed, and what, with wisdom and courage, you would consider to be just." He inclined his head. "Thank you."

Wystan called his first witness. Rathbone was not surprised to see that it was Blair Gavinton. He mounted the stand looking serious and unhappy, which could be interpreted in several ways. The jury would see that the matter was very grave, and Gavinton was sad and disturbed that a man in Rathbone's position had so abused the law. It would not occur to them that he was dubious about the prosecution or that he regretted this turn of events and would rather not be obliged to testify.

He looked at them closely at last, the twelve men who would decide his guilt or innocence. He was used to reading juries. He had spoken to them often enough, watched as they weighed his words. This time it was different. It was he they were judging, and he could say nothing.

Most of them looked to be about his own age. They were in their best clothes, as solemn as if the jury box were a church pew. Only two of them were looking back at him, with curiosity, skin puckered and eyes narrowed, as if trying to focus. A juror farther along had a white beard hiding his expression. Rathbone could judge nothing.

Gavinton swore as to his name and occupation, and to the fact that he had been the lawyer for the defense in the case of Abel Taft. When prompted by Wystan, he also gave a list of the principal witnesses for the prosecution and then for the defense.

It had been a case of moderate public interest. Many in the gallery might have attended, and that would be the reason they were here now. To the jurors the name, at least, would be familiar.

"A considerable number of witnesses for the prosecution," Wystan observed. "What manner of people were they?"

Brancaster stirred, as if to object, and then changed his mind.

Wystan smiled at that and turned back to Gavinton on the stand, waiting for his reply.

"Ordinary, decent people," Gavinton replied. "As far as I know, the only thing they had in common was that they were members of Taft's religious congregation, and they were generous, regardless of their means. Too generous, perhaps. They had all given more than they were subsequently able to afford and were distressed by the consequences."

"Were they good witnesses for the prosecution, Mr. Gavinton?" Wystan pressed. "And I am not looking for a generous opinion of their honesty or goodwill. I need your professional judgment as to their value to the prosecution, their effect on the jury."

Gavinton's lips tightened as if he were suddenly acutely unhappy. "No," he said quietly. "I was able to . . . to expose in each of them a naïveté—a gullibility, if you like—and it made them appear financially incompetent."

"More than that, Mr. Gavinton, were you not able to show in each of them a need to be liked, to be accepted and appear to be more generous, and of greater means than was actually the case?"

Gavinton looked uncomfortable as he moved his weight from one foot to the other. Rathbone saw this as an affectation and had no pity for him at all. He still found him self-regarding.

"I had no pleasure in it, but yes, that is true," Gavinton said.

"Did it profit your case?"

Again Brancaster moved a little, but did not rise to object.

Rathbone felt the sweat break out on his body. Why not? Did Bran-

caster have no idea what to do? Did he not have the heart or the courage to fight at all? He could have objected to that. It was a call for a
personal opinion, not a fact.

Why was he doing nothing? He had said he would fight all the way.

"I believe so," Gavinton replied. "I intended to make them seem
both financially and emotionally incompetent, and I believe I did so."

"How did you accomplish that, Mr. Gavinton?" Wystan pursued.
"Did you cross-question each one and expose his weaknesses to the
court?"

"No. I had one witness who knew them all, and knew both Mr. Taft
himself and also the financial dealings of the church and all the members of the congregation. I was able to draw from him all that I needed."

"And that witness's name?"

Gavinton was clearly uncomfortable now. He moved his head as if
his collar were too tight, even touching it with one hand, and then
changing his mind.

"Robertson Drew," he replied.

"Did you in fact win the case?"

Gavinton made a slight, rueful gesture perhaps intended to be self-
deprecating. "I doubt it, but the verdict was never returned."

"Why not?"

This time Gavinton paused, and the effect, intended or not, was
highly dramatic.

"The defendant, Abel Taft, took his own life."

Rathbone looked at the jury and instantly regretted it. They looked
grim and slightly embarrassed, perhaps at being spectators, albeit un-
willingly, at such a tragedy.

"My sympathy," Wystan said quietly. "That must have been terrible
for you and everyone else concerned. Do you know why he did such a
thing? Did you see him that day, or did he leave a letter?"

"I saw him," Gavinton replied. "He was devastated. He felt totally
betrayed by the fact that Robertson Drew had changed all his testimony under cross-examination. I had no doubt that the verdict the
following day would have been one of guilty."

Wystan looked puzzled. "Do you know why Mr. Drew so radically altered his testimony? Did he give you any warning that he would do such a thing?"

Gavinton's face tightened. Suddenly the charm was gone, and his expression was bleak, even dangerous.

"He gave me no warning. He had no opportunity to. He was on the stand being questioned by Mr. Dillon Warne, counsel for the prosecution, when Mr. Warne produced a photograph and showed it to Mr. Drew. Mr. Drew was clearly profoundly shocked by it. He seemed almost to collapse on the stand. Naturally I demanded to see the photograph myself, and when I did so I requested that we speak to the judge in his chambers, immediately."

"And the judge in question was Sir Oliver Rathbone?"

Gavinton's mouth was a thin line. "Yes."

"Please explain to the gentlemen of the jury why you made such a request."

"Because I had had no warning of the photograph, as the law requires that I should, thence I had no opportunity to verify its authenticity, or to find any indication of what it seemed to purport."

"I assume from the reaction, which you described, in Mr. Drew that it was in some manner damaging to him?" Wystan said innocently.

"Profoundly so," Gavinton agreed grimly.

"Did you manage to prevent it being shown to the jury?"

"Yes, but it might have been shown to them once it had been authenticated, if indeed it could have been," Gavinton pointed out. "However, the damage was done. We returned to the courtroom and thereafter Mr. Drew altered his testimony completely. He went back on everything he had previously said, restoring the reputations of all the witnesses he had previously demolished and ruining Mr. Taft beyond help. Obviously he was terrified the photograph would be used to destroy him."

"And was this photograph subsequently authenticated?" Wystan inquired. He glanced at Brancaster, clearly expecting him to object, but Brancaster sat silent.

"Not to my knowledge," Gavinton answered.

Wystan drew a deep breath and let it out in a sigh. "I will not ask you what was in it, because as you say, it was never authenticated. We may ruin an innocent man's honor and reputation. My point in raising the entire issue—for which I am grateful to Mr. Brancaster"—he looked at him momentarily, then back at Gavinton again—"for refraining from interrupting me with any objections . . ."

His meaning was not lost on the jury, or possibly on the gallery either. Brancaster had already given up the fight. He had lost, and he knew it.

Rathbone felt a panic well up inside him, making it difficult to catch his breath. The room swam around him, disappearing at the edges, closing in. Was this how everyone felt in the dock, imprisoned, helpless, and terrified? He should have taken more care of the people he defended, realized how they felt. He ached to be able to interrupt, to explain. It was all slipping out of control.

Wystan began talking again. His pause for effect had seemed to stretch on and on, but it had been only seconds.

"My point in raising the issue is to find out and prove to this court here today," he explained, "exactly where that photograph came from, who provided it to the court at exactly that moment when it had the most dramatic effect, and why they would do such a thing."

"I cannot comment on the reasons," Gavinton replied. "And as to where it came from, you will have to ask Mr. Warne."

"Oh, I intend to," Wystan said with clear satisfaction. "Believe me, sir, I intend to."

Rathbone had known he would, of course, and yet still his heart sank. He looked at the jury, trying to read their faces, but their expressions could have meant anything. He could not be certain that they even understood. They were clerks, storekeepers, dentists, all kinds of men—the sort he had been happy to trust with other people's lives.

Brancaster rose to his feet. He looked far more confident than he had any right to be. He had started acting, at last! Perhaps a little too late.

Brancaster looked up at Gavinton. "This photograph, Mr. Gavinton. I do not wish you to describe it, to tell me who was in it or what they were doing. It has not been introduced into evidence; indeed, I have not seen it. And because he has not mentioned it to me, I assume Mr. Wystan has not seen it, or does not possess it himself, and has no intention of introducing it as evidence either. However, he has made a good deal of it in testimony." He regarded Gavinton inquiringly. "I imagine it would be fair to say that it is the center of this entire case? Do I understand you correctly that it was at the point he saw this photograph that Mr. Drew changed his testimony to almost the exact opposite of what he had said before?"

"Yes, sir, that is correct," Gavinton agreed. He was grim, but not yet anxious.

"You said that he appeared to be stunned, appalled by it, almost to the point of passing out?" Brancaster pursued.

Gavinton hesitated only a moment. "Yes . . . I suppose that is true."

"You suppose?" Brancaster looked surprised. "Did you not say so, just a few moments ago?"

Gavinton was definitely annoyed now. His voice was sharp. "Yes. He was appalled. It was a very natural reaction, Mr. Brancaster. Any man would have been."

"Really? Quite plainly you have seen this photograph. Perhaps you could explain that to the jury. In what way was it so very dreadful?"

Gavinton's face twisted with disgust.

Rathbone wanted to rise to his feet and protest, but he could not. It was as if he were watching his own execution. What in God's name was Brancaster doing?

"It was obscene," Gavinton replied. "Pornographic in the extreme."

Brancaster looked unmoved. "Really?" His eyebrows rose. "And you believe that Mr. Drew had never seen pornography before? He was sufficiently innocent of the facts of nature that seeing such a thing caused him almost to lose his senses and pass out in public? You amaze me. I might find such a thing in extremely poor taste, even disgusting, but I doubt I would lose consciousness over it."

"You might, sir, if the pictures were of yourself practicing obscene acts with a small boy!" Gavinton's voice was shaking. His knuckles were white where his hands gripped the rail. "I hope you would have the grace to—" He did not finish. The gasps from the jury and the wave of horror from the gallery made him realize what he had said, and his face flamed with embarrassment.

York banged his gavel furiously.

"Order! Order! I will have order. Mr. Brancaster, you are completely out of—" He stopped as Brancaster's eyes opened wide in disbelief. York's face was white. He turned to Gavinton and all but snarled at him. "You forget yourself, sir. One more outburst as utterly inappropriate as that and you will oblige me to declare a mistrial, and then we shall have to send the accused back to prison and await the setting of a date for a new trial." He looked at Brancaster and then back to Gavinton. "And you will not go unscathed either, sir. Remember where you are, and control yourself."

Gavinton closed his eyes, as if by doing so he could block out the room. "Yes, my lord." He did not apologize.

York glared at Brancaster. "And no more parlor tricks from you, sir. This is an extremely serious matter, whether you appreciate it or not. There is more than a man's honor and reputation in the balance, or even his freedom. It is the cause of justice itself."

"I am aware of that, my lord," Brancaster said without a flicker. "I was as much taken by surprise by Mr. Gavinton's outburst as you were. I thought I had made it perfectly clear that I was not seeking such information." It was a blatant lie—of course, it was exactly what he had been seeking—but he told it superbly.

York said nothing.

"Perhaps I had better excuse the witness, my lord," Brancaster suggested. "I would be very loath to provoke another such . . . indiscretion."

There was nothing York could do, but the dull flush of anger still stained his cheeks. Rathbone knew that he would bide his time and rule against Brancaster when he could. Was it Brancaster's tactic to provoke York into doing something that would be grounds for appeal? A very dangerous course indeed, perhaps even lethal.

Rathbone should have burned the whole damnable box and smashed the plates into splinters the day Ballinger's lawyer brought it to him. Too late now. Too late . . . the saddest words in the vocabulary of man.

THEY ADJOURNED LATE FOR luncheon, and resumed again at about three in the afternoon.

Rathbone sat in the dock. He had found it difficult to eat, his stomach rebelling against the clenching of his muscles, his throat so tight that swallowing was almost impossible. He ate the watery stew and soggy potatoes only because he had to, and what he was offered was probably better than the food he would have from sentence onward.

He no longer understood what Brancaster was doing. He feared he was bluffing, playing for time, and that his earlier words of courage to Rathbone were empty. Now he was disturbing people, but possibly to no intended effect. What would it change, beyond lengthening the ordeal?

The next witness was Dillon Warne. He looked wretched. Rathbone knew it was inevitable that he would be called, but it was still painful to see him there and know what he would have to say.

He was sworn in and stood with his hands gripping the rail, his face tense and very clearly unhappy.

Wystan looked at him with grave disfavor.

"You acted for the prosecution in the case against Abel Taft, did you not, Mr. Warne?"

"I did," Warne agreed.

"Did you have personal feelings, Mr. Warne?" Wystan inquired. "I mean, did you grow to feel very strongly about this case in particular?"

"I do find it peculiarly distasteful to see one of the witnesses for the defense mocking and humiliating people I believed to be both honest and unusually vulnerable," Warne answered, looking straight back at Wystan.

"To the degree that you were very upset indeed when you thought you would lose the case?" There was the very slight suggestion of a sneer on Wystan's face.

"A prosecutor who does not care is not worthy of the trust placed in him by the people," Warne answered.

Wystan was annoyed.

At any other time, without his own future in the balance, Rathbone would have enjoyed the exchange. With some detached part of his mind he noticed the jurors' attention sharpen.

"That is not what I asked, Mr. Warne," Wystan said tartly. "As you well know. You are playing to the gallery, sir, and it is most unbecoming. Just because you have escaped prosecution for your part in this miserable and disgraceful affair, does not entitle you to attempt wit at the expense of the proceedings."

Warne's face flushed, and Rathbone was struck with a fear that just as Brancaster had baited Gavinton with indiscretion, Wystan could do the same to Warne. Why was Brancaster not objecting? Rathbone longed to stand up and shout at him.

Brancaster rose to his feet at last.

"My lord, that accusation is unfair and—"

Before he could finish, York cut him off.

"Your objection is overruled, Mr. Brancaster. Please sit down, and do not interrupt again unless you have some point of law to make."

Brancaster sat down as commanded. If he was annoyed he did not show it. Perhaps he had not expected to be upheld. He had succeeded in breaking Wystan's rhythm, and Warne had regained his self-control. That might have been all he had wished for.

"I repeat my question, Mr. Warne," Wystan said.

"It isn't necessary, sir," Warne interrupted him. "I was upset when I thought I would lose the case. I always am if I believe profoundly that the accused is guilty and that if not found so, will almost certainly continue to commit the same crime against more people."

York leaned forward. "You could not know that, Mr. Warne. Please stick with the facts."

Brancaster was on his feet. "My lord, with the greatest respect, Mr. Warne did not say the accused would reoffend, he said such was his belief and the reason he was upset at the prospect of an acquittal."

York drew in his breath, then changed his mind and let it out again. But Rathbone knew from his face that he would not forget. Brancaster might have the jury on his side at the moment, and certainly the gallery, but he had irrevocably alienated the judge. It was a very risky tactic indeed. He must be desperate even to have considered it.

Wystan took up the thread again.

"Up to the point of your showing the photograph to the witness, Mr. Warne, did you believe you were losing?"

"Yes, I did," Warne admitted.

"So this was a last, desperate attempt to win?"

"I would not have chosen the word 'desperate,' but I had no other tactic," Warne conceded.

"And this obscene photograph, why did you not use it before?" Wystan pressed on. "In fact, why did you not show it to the defense, as the law requires? Were you afraid that if they looked into its provenance they would find it far from satisfactory? In fact sufficiently unsatisfactory that it could be excluded from evidence?"

"No, I did not!" Warne said sharply.

"Then why did you not produce it before, as you should have?"

Rathbone had seen the question coming. It was like watching a train crash, but so slowly that you could see the wheels spin and the carriages rear up before they toppled over and the sound of breaking glass reached your ears.

"I did not have it before," Warne replied.

"Indeed?" Wystan affected surprise. "How did you come by it, then, in what appears to have been the middle of the night, Mr. Warne?"

"Sir Oliver Rathbone gave it to me." Warne might have considered lying, or protesting privilege and refusing to answer, but it was clear that the truth was known, and it would add weight to the apparent misdeed if he gave the information only when forced to. Perhaps it was better to do it now, with some dignity.

If the jurors had known or guessed before, they still looked stunned. With Warne's admission it became an irrefutable fact.

"Sir Oliver Rathbone gave it to you," Wystan repeated. "Sir Oliver, the judge presiding in the case."

"I have said so." Warne was grave, the anger barely showing in his eyes and slight stiffness of the shoulders.

"And I assume you asked him where he had obtained this extraordinary piece of . . . of pornography? He is not a man you know to be accustomed to collecting such things, is he?"

There was a loud rustle of movement around the gallery; several people gasped or spoke. The jurors looked as if they were embarrassed and would have preferred to be anywhere else. No one even glanced toward Rathbone.

"He told me it had fallen into his hands, very much against his will, along with a large number of others similar," Warne replied. "He had not yet disposed of them. Only on looking at the face of the witness had he begun to see a resemblance to one of the photographs, and that very night gone to see if he was indeed correct. He had looked at them only once before, at the time of receiving them, and preferred not to look again. But it definitely was the same man who had stood in court and sworn as to his righteousness and honesty of character. To say that he had perjured himself is something of an understatement." He drew in his breath to add something more, but Wystan cut him off.

"So you accepted the photograph, but instead of contacting the counsel for the defense that evening, or even the following morning, you sprang this piece of obscenity on him in open court?" Wystan's contempt was like a breath of freezing air in the room.

Warne blushed. "Yes, I did. I had hoped not to have to use it at all. It was only when the witness went on and on about his own moral and intellectual superiority and I saw the jury accept it that I showed him the photograph. Not the jury. They never saw it. All they saw was the witness ashen pale and shaking, and they realized that he had lost all his arrogance. He then changed his entire testimony."

"You amaze me!" Wystan said with grating sarcasm. "And Sir Oliver, who of course knew exactly what was in the photograph, playacted the innocent and pretended he knew nothing of it. Did he not demand to see it, Mr. Warne?"

"Mr. Gavinton demanded to see it," Warne replied. "I think that might have been the first time he realized just what kind of a man his witness was. Of course he also demanded that we should speak with Sir Oliver in his chambers. We did so, and the picture was never shown to the jury, or referred to again."

"But the damage was done," Wystan said bitterly. "The witness changed all his testimony. It was now damning to the accused, who, while at home that evening and in his dreadful despair at such a monumental betrayal, killed his wife, his two daughters, and himself. Do you consider that you did a good day's work, Mr. Warne?"

Warne's face was white. It was painfully clear that he was ashamed, and yet trapped in a situation where there was nothing he could say either to explain his decision or to escape the conclusion that Wystan was relentlessly guiding the jury toward.

"No, it was not a good day," he said quietly. "It ended in tragedy. But it was not I who betrayed Mr. Taft, nor was it Sir Oliver; it was the witness. And I don't believe even he could have foreseen that Mr. Taft would have murdered his wife and daughters and then shot himself. Perhaps I should have requested that he be held without bail, but I doubt that request would have been granted. He was charged with embezzlement, not violence of any physical kind. He was not yet convicted of anything at all."

Wystan allowed all his scorn to fill his voice. "A sophistry, Mr. Warne. Until lately I had thought better of you. You may be able to escape the truth of this in your own mind, but you will not in the jury's. Sir Oliver gave you the weapon, and God knows, he will answer for that. But you used it!"

He turned away, and Warne drew in his breath to reply. Wystan swung around as if Warne had crept up on him. "And don't tell me you had no choice!" he thundered. "Of course you did! You could have spoken to Gavinton and told him that his witness had a ghastly perversion to his character and that you had proof of it, as you should have done. He would then have asked Rathbone to adjourn the trial until you could prove, or disprove, the validity of the photograph. Or did you know that Rathbone would not do so? Is that the key to your extraordinary actions? Win at all costs? Drag the whole honor of the law into the filth of your one grubby little victory—which in the end slipped out of your hands anyway."

Brancaster stood up, his face dark with anger. "My lord—"

"Sit down, Mr. Brancaster," York said wearily. He turned to Wystan. "We are a little early for speeches, Mr. Wystan. It is just conceivable that the accused has some explanation for his behavior. I cannot imagine what it might be, but we must wait with what patience we can. No doubt Mr. Warne was uncomfortable with this miserable piece of evidence, but he had been given it by the judge in the case. He would hardly be serving the Crown if he allowed it to be ignored." He shrugged almost imperceptibly. "Nor could he reasonably have supposed that Sir Oliver would allow it to be. Are you asking us to believe that Mr. Warne could have persuaded Sir Oliver to rule such evidence inadmissible when he himself had presented it and vouched for its provenance? God alone knows what he was doing with such things, but he had them in his own personal safekeeping and knew exactly where they came from. I think you are expecting miracles from Mr. Warne that are far beyond his skill to achieve."

Wystan's eyes blazed with anger, but he knew better than to argue. He said nothing but walked stiffly back to his seat.

Brancaster stood up and went slowly to the center of the floor. His head was lowered in a moment's contemplation before he looked up at Warne.

"Thank you for your candor, Mr. Warne. I do not imagine you are here willingly. You have no choice but to testify, is that right?"

"None," Warne replied.

"Did you hesitate to use this particular photograph?"

"Yes . . ."

Wystan stood up. "My lord, we have been over this. Mr. Warne may have hesitated all night, for all we know. The fact is, he did use it."

York nodded. "Please move on, Mr. Brancaster. Mr. Warne may well have sat up all night looking at this miserable thing. It may have revolted him until he was ill. The fact remains that he used it, and, more to the point, he does not deny that it was Sir Oliver Rathbone, the judge in the case, there to see that all the rules of the law were obeyed and justice served impartially, who gave it to him. We expect counsels from the prosecution and the defense to be partisan; it is their job! We expect the judge to be utterly without allegiance or loyalty to anything but the law. If he is not, then he has betrayed both the Crown and the people, not to mention his God-given calling. Now if you have anything helpful to say, please say it. Otherwise, we are adjourned for the day."

"I have!" Brancaster said a shade too loudly. Without waiting for York to add anything, he turned again to Warne. "Mr. Warne, did Sir Oliver leave it to you as to whether you used this photograph or not?"

"Absolutely," Warne said firmly.

"Why did you choose to? You must have been aware of the risks."

"I was," Warne agreed gravely. "I chose to use it because if I did not a great injustice would have been done. I believe the guilty should be punished but more importantly that the innocent should be vindicated. The witness in the photograph, a dishonorable man by all rights, had ruined the reputation of several decent men. He had publicly made them appear stupid, weak-minded, and devious when they were the victims of the crime. He had betrayed their goodwill, and been complicit in stealing from them. If he were found not guilty, he would have been free to continue on in the same manner."

"Do you believe that to have been Sir Oliver's motive also, Mr. Warne?"

Wystan stood up.

"Yes, yes," York said brusquely. "Mr. Brancaster, the witness cannot know the accused's motives, good or ill. What he assumed they were is of no value. Had they been despicable, he would hardly have told Mr. Warne so. The jurors must make up their own minds on the subject. Have you anything more to ask? If not, you may go, Mr. Warne, unless Mr. Wystan wishes to pursue anything else in reexamination?"

Brancaster could get no further, and he knew it. He retired with as much grace as he could, and Wystan declined to reexamine.

York adjourned the court until the next day, and Rathbone stood up, his whole body aching, and walked between his guards down the steps and back to the prison to wait for tomorrow. He had never in his life felt so utterly alone and helpless.

CHAPTER

14

SCUFF SAT AT THE breakfast table and ate his two boiled eggs and three slices of toast. He was too worried to be properly hungry, but he did not want Hester to know it. Yesterday, instead of going to school he had gone to the Old Bailey law court and wormed his way into the gallery, standing the whole time, as if he were some kind of messenger. No one had turned him away.

He had gone in part because he actually liked Oliver Rathbone, but mostly because he knew how much both Monk and Hester cared about him. He knew that the trial was not going well. It was horrible seeing Sir Oliver sitting up in the dock between two jailers and unable to say anything, even when people talked about him as if he were not there, and accused him of very bad things. When was he going to get a turn to speak?

Scuff supposed it must be a fair process, but it did not seem like that. Yet maybe he was being really childish in expecting it was going to be fair. Most of the world wasn't. Was he just dreaming of fairness because his own life was so good now?

He would have liked to have ask Hester a few questions about it all, but then she would know that he hadn't been at school, and she would be angry. She and Monk were very worried about Sir Oliver, frightened that he would be sent to prison, but they didn't want Scuff to know that. They didn't even tell him what was going on anymore. It was as if he were a little child who needed protecting from the truth. That was stupid! He was thirteen—probably. Near enough, anyway. He was practically grown up.

He had finished his tea, and Hester poured him some more. He thanked her for it. She got upset about please and thank you if he forgot them.

"I been thinking about Sir Oliver," he said tentatively.

Hester looked up at him, waiting for him to continue.

"I don't understand why everyone's so upset that 'e let them know about the photograph o' Mr. Drew. You said as Sir Oliver's there to see that everyone plays by the rules, so no one gets to win by cheating."

"More or less," Hester agreed cautiously.

"But if you lose the game, they get to 'ang you?"

"Only if you've done something terribly serious, like killing people," she explained. She was looking at him more closely now, listening with attention. "What made you think about this?"

There it was, the question he did not want to answer. Now he either had to lie or plunge straight in. He chose the latter. "I went to the court to listen." He said the words quickly, as if speed might make her miss the meaning of them. "I gotta do something to help," he added. "A different judge were up there, keeping the rules. 'E 'ad a face like one o' them bad-tempered little dogs, all white whiskers an' sharp eyes."

Hester hid a smile almost completely. He saw only the briefest light of it, but he felt the warmth. "So why don't they make different rules?" he hurried on. "Instead o' making it a game so the cleverest one wins, why don't they make it like a treasure hunt—whoever finds the truth wins? Or maybe everybody does. Then as long as it were truth, you wouldn't get in trouble 'cos o' the rules. Sir Oliver wouldn't be in trouble then, would 'e?"

"No, I don't think he would," she agreed. She put out her hand and placed it gently on his cuff, just over his wrist. "It might be a very good idea, but unfortunately we can't get anybody to change the rules fast enough for us."

"But we are going to do something, aren't we?" he asked a little shakily. At what point did you get so bad that people stopped loving you? Even thinking about the word "love" pained him like a knife cut. It was a dangerous word, too big, too precious. He shouldn't even think it. He was asking for trouble.

He was waiting for her to answer. What would she say? Hester never lied.

"We're trying desperately to think of something," she said at last.

"You still like him, don't you?" He ignored the tea. "I mean . . . you're still friends . . . you'll still be friends, even after this?"

"Of course," Hester said fiercely. "We all do wrong things now and then. There aren't any perfect people, and if there were, they probably wouldn't be very nice. It's only by making mistakes yourself and learning how much it hurts, and how sorry you are, that you get to understand other people and really forgive them. And you hope people will offer you the same forgiveness. But that doesn't mean you don't have to pay for your mistakes."

"Does that mean we let Sir Oliver pay?" he asked.

She smiled, a really warm, sweet smile, as if she were laughing at herself inside. "Not if we can help it," she said. "He's already had almost as much of a fright as he can take. And he'll never do anything like this again. Besides, I'm not sure how really wrong it was—though it's not up to me to judge, in court anyway."

He felt a lot better. Perhaps if he did something really wrong, she wouldn't stop loving him either? She might get angry, but she wouldn't send him away. And he would make a mistake one day; he was bound to. "Maybe he didn't mean to do wrong," he said softly.

"You're quite right," she agreed, pushing the butter across the table toward him. "I don't think he did. And to be honest, I'm not sure what I would have done in his place. Taft and Drew had to be stopped."

"Why'd Mr. Taft do that?" Scuff asked. "I mean, why'd he kill 'is wife an' 'is girls too?"

"I don't know," she admitted, frowning at the thought. "Have some more toast. You haven't eaten enough. You won't get anything more until lunchtime."

He buttered his toast and put marmalade on it, but he didn't bite into it yet. "And Mr. Drew's going to get away with it, isn't 'e, even with the photo?" he pressed. "That in't right."

"Maybe," Hester admitted. "But it isn't over yet."

Monk had been standing outside the kitchen door for several moments, not wanting to interrupt the conversation and deny Scuff the chance to say what he clearly needed to. He was taken aback by the weight of Scuff's feelings. He realized that for the last two or three days he had been so absorbed in the desperation of Rathbone's situation that he had succeeded in making Scuff feel excluded. He heard in his questions that continuing, underlying fear that loyalty was subject to keeping up a certain standard, and failure to do that could mean that love ended. He was talking of Rathbone, but, deeper than that, he was thinking of himself.

Monk was consumed by the need to reassure him.

He walked in casually, as if he had caught only the last couple of words of their conversation.

"I am going to go to Mr. Taft's house to take a long and very careful look at all his belongings," he said, to no one in particular.

"When?" Hester asked instantly. "This afternoon? Sooner?"

Monk smiled. "The police have already been there and searched thoroughly. I'm looking for something they missed," he told them both. "It's the scene of three murders and a suicide. They won't have treated it lightly, but it's possible they saw something without realizing its significance. I'll have to get permission first, but I can do that."

"I'll come with you," Hester responded. "I might notice something you don't." She turned to Scuff, who was waiting hopefully. "And you are going to school. If we find anything that matters, we'll tell you. Do you hear me?"

Scuff nodded reluctantly. "Yes." He meant "yes, I hear you," not "yes, I will." He hoped she would appreciate the difference.

"I'll come home and tell you when I have permission," Monk promised Hester.

Scuff looked from Hester to Monk, then back again. "'Ow did they know that Sir Oliver gave the lawyer the photograph?" he asked. "Did somebody tell on 'im?" His expression of contempt showed very clearly his opinion of those who told tales. That was a sin it was almost impossible to forgive. It wasn't a mistake; it was a betrayal.

"Yes, somebody did," Hester replied. "We don't know who."

"Don't you 'ave ter find out?" Scuff asked. "'E's a real enemy, whoever 'e is. It in't safe not to know who 'ates you that much."

"You're quite right," Monk nodded. "But we'll have to do that after we've done all we can to save Sir Oliver from prison. Telling tales is pretty mean-spirited, mostly, but it isn't a crime."

"Isn't it? It ought ter be."

"People have to tell, sometimes," Monk pointed out. "You might need to, to see that justice is done, or even to save someone's life."

"'Who's life did this save?" Scuff's disbelief was sharp in his face.

"Nobody's," Monk conceded. "I promise we'll find out if we can."

Scuff nodded, clearly thinking about it deeply.

Monk would go back and explain it to him in more detail later. He must not forget. Right now there were other things that were much more urgent. He ate his breakfast, excused himself, and went outside to walk down to the ferry to Wapping.

It was a fine day as Monk went down the hill. The panorama of the river was spread before him, but he barely noticed it. Only the sun, bright on the water between the barges going up and down the river, dazzled his eyes for a moment. From this distance he could not see the barges gliding with unconscious grace as they found their way on the incoming tide.

He found a ferry almost immediately and set out into the flow. The air was cooler once they were away from the shore, and the salt and fish smell was keener. He exchanged a few words with the ferryman. He knew nearly all of them. He remembered their names and the few bits of personal information they offered. It was a good habit to cultivate, beyond his own personal interest. Long ago he used to want respect, even if it came with a measure of fear. Now he realized how much more people would do for someone they liked. Stupid that it had taken him so long. He should pass that message on to his men, especially the younger ones, save them the trouble of learning it the hard way.

He reached the north bank, paid and thanked the ferryman, then climbed up the wet stone steps to the dockside and walked across to the Thames River Police Station.

Orme was just inside, his stocky, solid figure blocking the way. He looked grim.

"What is it?" Monk said without preamble. He had learned to trust Orme as he had few other men in his life.

"Assistant Commissioner Byrne's here, sir," Orme replied. "Waiting to see you." He did not need to say more; the warning was in his face and in the fact that he was here at all rather than out on the river, standing in for Monk during his too frequent absences.

"Thank you." Monk walked into his office where Byrne was sitting waiting with ill-concealed impatience. Byrne was good-looking enough. He had strong features and retained a fine head of hair, but he was both shorter and stockier than Monk; he would never have Monk's natural elegance.

"Good morning, Monk," he said, rising to his feet. "I've been waiting for you."

"Good morning, sir," Monk replied. He knew an apology was expected. It riled him, but he imagined it would be an unwise start to evade it. "I'm sorry to have kept you."

The commissioner did not acknowledge it. "This business with Oliver Rathbone," he said instead. "We cannot afford to be seen as partial, Monk. We talked about this before, but it's only getting worse. I know you consider him a friend, but you cannot be seen to stand by him now; it looks bad for the entire force. If you are called to testify, be discreet. Do you understand me?"

Monk hesitated. He wanted to say that he heard and understood, but he would not obey an order he considered to be contemptible. He took several deep breaths to give himself time to think. It was a time to be clever, not bold.

"I believe so, sir," he answered carefully. "You do not wish me to speak in any way that suggests that the police force has any interest in the matter other than to uphold the law and see justice served. I had not intended to do so, sir. And so far, I have not been called to testify, but of course that could change."

The commissioner looked at him with a degree of disfavor. They stood perhaps a couple of yards apart, the sun shining through the window, casting rainbows on the wall as it passed through the glass paperweight on Monk's desk.

The commissioner chewed his lip. "I don't know whether to believe you, Monk. Your history suggests that loyalty to a friend runs deeper than obedience to orders. How can I make this crystal clear? Rathbone has made a mockery of the law by giving the prosecution this obscene photograph, while keeping it from the defense. It is inexcusable. Give me your word as an officer of the Crown that *you* did not give him the damn thing in the first place. You were on both the Phillips case and the Ballinger one."

Monk felt a wave of relief, and then the next instant warned himself that he was far from in the clear yet.

"I give you my word, sir, I have never had the photographs in my possession to give to anyone."

"And if you did, you'd have damned well given it to the prosecution too, wouldn't you?" the commissioner said drily. "It was your wife who got that disreputable bookkeeper of hers on to the Taft case in the first place, wasn't it?"

"Yes, sir. He was robbing his congregation."

The commissioner sighed. "I know. None of that excuses Rathbone abusing his position as a judge to get the verdict he wanted."

"No, sir," Monk agreed, knowing as he said it that he could not—would not—let Rathbone suffer if there were any way he could prevent it.

The commissioner glared at Monk. "Keep your distance from Rathbone, do you hear me?" he ordered.

"Yes, sir, I hear you." And he did. But he knew he would not listen. One did not abandon friends because they made mistakes. That was what he had promised Scuff, and obliquely, Hester as well.

If he lost his job in the police over this, that would be a blow. He had no idea where he would find another, or how he would support himself and his family. He loved the work. It was the only job he had ever done, as far as he knew. But Hester was certainly the only woman he had ever loved, the only person, really, apart from Scuff. To lose them was a price he was not prepared to pay, not for any job on earth.

If Monk had to abandon Rathbone, his friend would understand why, but Hester and Scuff wouldn't. And he wouldn't be able to live with that.

He watched Byrne leave. Then he found Orme and told him that he had to go and investigate the scene of a murder.

"Need my help, sir?" Orme said without a flicker in his smooth, windburned face.

"Only in that you look after everything here," Monk answered, also not betraying the slightest emotion. They understood each other too well for an explanation to be necessary.

"Right, sir," Orme agreed.

Monk hesitated. "Thank you," he said with more feeling than perhaps Orme appreciated. "Thank you very much."

SCUFF LEFT HOME AND waited until he saw Monk take the ferry across to the Wapping Police Station; then he found another ferry and paid the extra fare to be taken to Gun Wharf, two stops along, so there was no chance of his being seen by Monk, should he still be standing on the dock, or possibly by Mr. Orme, who also would recognize him.

Next he took a public omnibus, changed, and took another, until more than half an hour later, passing as an errand boy with an urgent message, he found his way into the Old Bailey and seized his chance to follow a rather self-important-looking journalist into the courtroom where the trial of Oliver Rathbone had just resumed.

Scuff was uncomfortable, but he continued to stand where he could still look like a messenger waiting for someone. He hoped nobody would actually give him any notes to carry. He knew the riverbank as if it were his own backyard, but this part of the city was a foreign land to him. He would just have to find a way to refuse to accept any errands without getting thrown out. He hoped he had not lost any of the quickness in the invention of lies that he used to have before he met Monk. All the reading and history and school-learning of facts might have pushed it out of his head.

The prosecutor, who was called Wystan, was just getting into his stride. He was a fuzzy, pepper-and-salt-looking man with a self-satisfied face. Scuff did not like him.

The present witness was an old woman. The stand was some height above the floor, up its own curling set of narrow little steps, and Scuff watched her climb up with some awkwardness. Or perhaps she wasn't so old, just a bit too heavy, and sort of faded-looking, as though it were a long time since she had been happy.

Wystan addressed her as Mrs. Ballinger, and after a moment or two Scuff realized who she must be. It was her husband who had been accused of murdering the prostitute Monk had promised to keep safe. Monk had been terribly upset about that; he had given his word and her death had really hurt him.

Ballinger had been murdered himself, in prison, when he was waiting to be hanged. No wonder this woman looked so miserable. She had an awful lot to be miserable about.

And another thing he was sure of, she would be no friend to Sir Oliver. That would be why Wystan had gotten her here, to say what she could that would make him look even worse.

But if she was Mrs. Ballinger, that meant that she was Sir Oliver's wife's mother. Was she here too, his wife? Had she come to be a friend to him, the one face he would look at that would make him feel he wasn't alone?

Scuff was standing against the wall, to the side of the court, so he could see only the backs of people's heads for the most part. If Sir Oliver's wife was here, she would be nearer the front of the gallery than he was, wouldn't she?

Scuff was still not all that tall. He hoped he would grow a lot more, maybe as tall as Monk, one day. He was a lot less skinny than he used to be, but he was thin enough to squeeze between people if he tried. Maybe if he was careful and didn't tread on anyone's feet, didn't push too much, he could work his way around nearer the front so he could see people's faces.

When he was another ten feet farther forward, it still took him several minutes of searching before he saw her. He had been to the clinic with Hester a few times, and had met Lady Rathbone. He remembered because she was the first "lady" he had ever seen, and he had expected her to look different. She had looked different from Hester, but then everybody did. As far as Scuff could see she was much like anyone else that you might see in the street, clean and well dressed. But he remembered her. She had had a nice face.

Except that right now she looked angry, sort of pinched and bitter. But then, she must feel awful, with Sir Oliver sitting up there in the dock.

Wystan was asking Mrs. Ballinger about Sir Oliver. He was being very gentle with her.

"I know this must be difficult for you, Mrs. Ballinger," he said quietly. "The whole court will sympathize with you, being placed in a situation where you have to testify as to the character—as you have witnessed it—of a man who is married to your daughter. However, it is necessary, in the service of justice. I'm sorry."

"I will do my duty," she said without change of expression. "But thank you for your courtesy."

"I will keep it as brief as I can," Wystan promised. He began slowly.

Scuff thought he was pompous. "Did you come to know the accused well when he was courting your daughter?" Wystan asked. "I mean by that, did you entertain him at your home, for example? Did he dine with you? Did you learn his tastes and opinions? Did you become aware of his education, his income, his prospects, his ambitions?"

"Of course." There was still very little compassion in her face. Whatever memory she had of those times, it brought no light to her eyes, no flashes of past pleasure remembered. He couldn't even detect any sorrow for broken dreams. It was as if all feeling had been crushed out of her.

Scuff was sorry for her, but he found such coldness oddly frightening.

"We would hardly have allowed our daughter to marry a man we knew nothing about," she said stiffly, as if Wystan had insulted her. "Love can so . . ." Now at least there was grief. "Love can so easily be mistaken."

"Indeed." Wystan acknowledged the truth of that with an inclination of his head. "And your opinion at that time?"

Her face was tight, as though she were barely keeping control.

"That he was a gentleman, a brilliant lawyer of excellent means, and that great success lay ahead of him," she replied. "He seemed to care for Margaret, and she certainly cared for him. We thought it a most fortunate match."

There was a slight murmur around the gallery. Next to Scuff a man shook his head and sighed. A rather large woman in black, sitting on the end of the row, looked at the man beside her and said, "I told you so." The man ignored her, his eyes never leaving Mrs. Ballinger on the witness stand.

"I am sorry to raise this, Mrs. Ballinger," Wystan went on, "but when your late husband fell into difficulty, you had sufficient trust in your son-in-law to ask him to represent your husband? That is to say, you trusted both his professional ability and his personal loyalty?"

Her mouth flattened into a thin line. "We did," she agreed hoarsely. "To our great grief."

"Why was that?"

Her voice wobbled a bit as she tried to control it. "That was when we learned the extent of his personal ambition, his . . . his ruthlessness." She stopped and gulped for air. Her face lost its bitterness and merely looked wounded, vulnerable.

"I am so sorry, Mrs. Ballinger," Wystan said, with apparent sincerity. "I deeply regret the necessity for obliging you to relive such tragedy. I assure you it is necessary for justice to be done. Oliver Rathbone stands accused of misusing his position as judge, for personal reasons, for power, causing the ruin of another man for purposes of his own—"

Brancaster rose to his feet. "My lord, nowhere is such a wild statement set out in the charge."

York pursed his lips. "I think you are splitting hairs, Mr. Brancaster. Nonetheless, Mr. Wystan, perhaps you would be wiser to allow the jury to draw their own conclusions as to the motives of the accused. People pervert the course of justice for many reasons, some of them more understandable than others. Please proceed."

Brancaster's face flushed with anger. "Sir Oliver has been accused, my lord. He has not yet been found guilty of anything at all. I would remind the jury of that."

"You may remind the jury of what you please, in your summation," York said tartly. "Until then you will refrain from interrupting unless you have some point of law to make."

"Innocence is a point of law," Brancaster retorted instantly. "Until proven otherwise, beyond reasonable doubt, it is the whole point of the law."

"Are you presuming to direct me in the law, Mr. Brancaster?" York said with dangerous calm.

Brancaster controlled his temper with an effort so obvious even Scuff could see it from the side of the court where he stood squashed against the wall.

"No, my lord," Brancaster said, his voice choking.

York smiled bleakly. "Good. I would not like the jury to be in doubt as to who is the judge here. Please continue, Mr. Wystan."

Wystan inclined his head. "Thank you, my lord. Mrs. Ballinger, just to remind you, you said Oliver Rathbone was profoundly ambitious, far more than you had previously realized. What did he do, or fail to do, that brought you to this unhappy conclusion?"

Mrs. Ballinger had regained her composure. She was now quite eager to answer.

Scuff looked to where Margaret was sitting and saw the expectancy in her also. Her shoulders were stiff. She sat so upright he could imagine the ache in his own back simply from looking at her. But it was the expression now filling her face that he did not understand. She seemed to be both afraid and excited at the same time.

"Mrs. Ballinger?" Wystan prompted.

"When he was defending my husband, we believed at first that he was doing everything he could to prove his innocence. But gradually he became less devoted to it, less . . . positive," she answered.

"Really? Did he give you a reason for this?" Wystan looked puzzled.

The bitterness returned to her face, anger overtaking grief again.

"The tide of feeling turned against my husband, and Oliver went with it. It seemed he did not wish to become unpopular, or even worse, appear in a case he might lose. He had no loyalty at all, except to his own career." She took a deep breath. "It broke my daughter's heart. She admired her father and was convinced of his innocence. She could hardly believe that her own husband would not use every skill at his command—and his skills were great—to defend one of his own family. It made me realize that his ambition was everything to him. Nothing else mattered."

Again Brancaster rose to his feet.

"Is this a matter of law, Mr. Brancaster?" York snapped.

Brancaster must have known that he was not going to win. Scuff saw his face tighten, and he would have told him not to bother, but of course he was much too far away, and the lawyer wouldn't have listened to him anyway.

"Yes, my lord. Most of what the witness says is hearsay, not fact."

Wystan smiled. "If my learned friend prefers, and your lordship feels that we have time, I can take Mrs. Ballinger through each step of the trial to see what the accused did and did not do. I am trying to spare a bereaved woman the extra grief and humiliation of having to go into detail. But should you so direct me, my lord, reluctantly, then of course I will."

"I do not so direct you," York replied. "If you wish to pursue it further, perhaps you will be a little more specific. It would allow the jury to make up their own minds."

It was the worst possible answer for Brancaster. He sat down, beaten.

Wystan turned to Mrs. Ballinger and began again, picking specific points in the trial of Arthur Ballinger but never reaching the verdict, as if his guilt were still a matter to be decided.

Scuff stopped watching Mrs. Ballinger and turned to look at Margaret again. He couldn't really see Sir Oliver very well from where he was, and he didn't want to look at him anyway. In a situation like this, where someone had to be suffering horribly and feeling as if everybody hated him, it felt like a terrible intrusion to look at him, a bit like bursting into the bathroom when somebody was in there privately.

He knew as soon as he saw Margaret that he was not intruding by looking at her. She wasn't really suffering at all; in fact her face was bright as if she were enjoying herself. There was something almost like a smile on her lips. She looked up once to the place where Sir Oliver was sitting, and hesitated several moments. Then she looked away again, back at her mother, who was still talking about Sir Oliver. She was saying how cold and selfish he was. Even at family gatherings his mind always seemed to be on his work. She recalled two occasions when he had simply walked out, almost without explanation.

Scuff was angry now. Sir Oliver wouldn't be here at all or accused of anything if somebody hadn't told on him. It seemed he had given the prosecution that horrible photograph of one of the main defense witnesses, and as far as Scuff was concerned that was fair enough. It showed what kind of a man he was. Apparently it wasn't the photograph that

was the problem; it was that he had given it to the prosecution and not
the defense. It was the way he did it that was wrong; it was seen as not
being fair to both sides.

And then apparently he should have told them that he couldn't be
the judge anymore. The whole trial had to stop, and then maybe start
all over again with someone else. Or on the other hand, maybe they
wouldn't bother, and the man who had stolen all that money from the
congregation would get away with it, and just go on stealing. That really, really wasn't fair!

Telltales didn't usually have to even prove their information because for a start they usually go to a person who wants to get someone
else into trouble and who will take their word and run with it. Any fool
knows that! There are always snitches, and everybody hates them.

So who knew that Sir Oliver had the photographs, and wanted to
get him into trouble? Mr. Ballinger, but he was dead. He couldn't tell
anybody anything. Monk and Hester, of course, because Sir Oliver had
told them. But they would rather have their throats cut than be snitches.

So who else knew about the photographs? The person who brought
them after Mr. Ballinger died? Did he know what was in the box?
Maybe. More likely he didn't.

But Mrs. Ballinger might have known about them, and Margaret—
Lady Rathbone. Scuff would be prepared to make a bet with anyone
that she had worked it out—if not before, then after the photograph
turned up in court.

He watched Margaret as the testimony went on getting worse and
worse for Sir Oliver. She was smiling now. She wasn't upset for him at
all. The conviction settled on Scuff that it was she who had snitched.

He watched and waited until the lunchtime adjournment, then,
before the general crowd rose to their feet and made their way out, he
wriggled from the spot he was in and put his head down to force his way
between people, as if he were on a really urgent message, pushing forward toward the hall.

When he was there, he stood to one side, looking at every person who came out. He was angry and trembling, but at least he was too full of fury for there to be any room for fear.

Several people passed him, fat people and thin, ones in fancy clothes, ones in old clothes worn nearly to rags. Some were talking to one another; some were silent.

Then he saw her. She had that shadow of a smile around her mouth, as if she had eaten something really good and she could still taste it.

Scuff stepped out in front of her and she stopped abruptly. She had no idea who he was, but she was mildly annoyed that he was obviously not looking where he was going. Then she saw the fury in his face, and the words she had been starting to say died on her lips.

"You told on 'im, didn't yer!" Scuff accused. "It was you as went an' told on 'im that 'e were the one what gave the lawyer that photograph, weren't yer?"

She drew in her breath sharply, but the color that flushed her cheeks gave her away.

"Who is it?" her mother demanded from just behind her. "What's the matter? For heaven's sake, give him a penny and let us leave this place."

"It's . . . it's that little urchin that belongs to Monk," Margaret replied. Then she turned to Scuff again. "Move out of the way, or I shall call an usher to have you put out. In fact, I will . . ."

Scuff smiled at her. "Yer done it. I can see it in yer face. For all yer 'igh and mighty airs, yer just a bleedin' snitch."

She pushed past him and went as quickly as she could toward the wide-open doors at the far end of the hall.

Scuff stood staring after her, not sure now what to do with the piece of information he had. It would hurt Sir Oliver if he knew that, yet how safe were you if you didn't even know who your enemies were, especially if they weren't who you expected?

And if he told Monk or Hester, he would also have to tell them how he knew. Well, that was a bitter medicine he would just have to swallow.

He made his way to where Margaret had gone out through the big
doors onto the steps, then down into the busy street. He had enough
money to get an omnibus. He would probably have the best part of an
hour in which to make up his mind how he was going to explain himself when he got home.

Mㅐonk was back in his home just before midday, sitting at the kitchen table with Hester, a pot of tea between them and a crusty loaf of bread with butter and crumbly Wensleydale cheese, and of course homemade chutney. Hester had discovered, to her surprise, that she was rather good at making it.

Monk had told Hester about the commissioner's warning. He would much rather not have, but if she did not know, it was much more likely that she might make some slip that would eventually get back to the commissioner. Then Monk might be dismissed, or at the very least, severely reprimanded. Possibly Byrne's warning had not so much meant "don't do it" as "do it discreetly enough that I can pretend I don't know about it."

"We've got to find out something," she said urgently. "Oliver doesn't have a chance without it."

Monk looked bleak. "I'm not sure he has a chance, even if we do," he warned her, his face filled with unhappiness.

She knew he was trying to help soften the blow of defeat, if it came, but she did not want to hear that. She was being childish, and Monk was allowing her to be.

"I know," she said. "I'm sorry. It's time I grew up, isn't it? You don't have to think how to protect me. I know Oliver was wrong, even if he did it for the right reasons."

He reached across the table and put his hand over hers gently.

"I still think there's got to be something we can do. Have you been able to get permission to enter Taft's house?" she went on quickly, in case he got the idea that she was giving up gracefully.

"I'm trying, but I have to be pretty devious about it." He smiled slightly in spite of himself. "We don't even know who our enemies are in this, Hester. There are some very important people looking to convict Rathbone because they need to show that you can't expose people the way he's done with the photograph of Drew. And it's not only that, it's what else Rathbone could do. If you go out hunting something really dangerous, you either kill it with your first blow or you run like hell without firing, because you know that if you give it the chance to fight back, it would finish you. They see Oliver as that dangerous animal, and they just want to feel safe again."

She felt the cold ripple through her as if no heat could ever quite get rid of it. "So what are we going to do?" Her voice wavered a little. "Sit here paralyzed? Isn't that just what they want?"

He pulled a face of disgust, but it vanished after an instant. "Yes, but we don't know who else is drawn into this." He lifted his shoulders a fraction; it was barely a movement at all. "Not Byrne, I don't think, but what if he has a brother in one of the photos? Or his favorite sister's husband? Or his father, or son . . . people do terrible things when they're afraid."

"Or they do nothing at all," Hester said very quietly. "And they let innocent people go to the wall."

"Oliver *isn't* innocent," he said gently, watching her face to see how deeply he had cut into her emotions, her intense and at times unreasoning loyalty.

She knew that.

"He is guilty of being stupid! I've done lots of stupid things, and I didn't have to pay for all of them like this. It shouldn't be so easy to punish people when you know you've deserved worse yourself."

He took her hand gently. "I love you."

She smiled at him.

"That doesn't make you right about this," he added.

In spite of herself, in spite of the twisting sense of fear inside her, she laughed. "I know."

He stood up. "I'm going back to the local police station nearest Taft's house. It's time I stopped asking nicely for favors and started demanding them."

"I'm coming too." She rose to her feet also. "I'll wait outside while you talk to them."

It took some considerable argument, and Monk did not tell Hester what threat or favor he had used, but after a heated forty-five minutes he emerged from the police station and found Hester on a bench in the sun, where she had been sitting waiting for him. He had been told not to touch anything. The police had already thoroughly searched the whole house at the time the deaths were discovered and found nothing of interest.

Monk and Hester quickly walked the short distance to Taft's house.

"What are we looking for?" Hester asked as they lengthened their stride for the slight gradient in the road.

"I don't know," Monk admitted. "The only thing that gives me hope is that I'm told Drew still wants to get in—so he hasn't found what he wants." He was walking a little faster than she was, and she had to hurry to keep up with him. She was a little breathless and really had no useful reply to offer, so she said nothing.

The house was attractive, solidly built of brick, and in its own very well-tended garden. They walked up the driveway and Monk produced the key to the front door.

Hester was surprised almost as soon as they entered the hallway. Just inside the door was a vestibule with exactly the sort of things she would have expected: an umbrella stand; pegs for outdoor clothes of the heavier, winter sort and for casual hats; a long mirror, possibly to make last-minute adjustments as one was leaving. But farther inside, the room opened out into a wood-paneled hall of some size. From it rose a very gracious staircase with a large, heavily ornamental newel post and then a curved stair, which was wide at the bottom and swung around against the wall, up to a gallery with passages running off in both directions.

"My goodness!" she said in surprise. "Looks as if this is where at least some of the money went. Unless Mrs. Taft was an heiress?" She looked at Monk questioningly.

He was standing still on the polished parquet floor looking at the red-carpeted steps and then up to the various paintings on the wall, hung at different levels to complement both the upward climb and the different levels of the paneling.

She watched him with growing interest as he regarded the pictures more and more closely. They were all landscapes. One was of sloping parkland billowing with trees, another of a churchyard with soaring skies behind it, a third of a headland with a pale beach and open sea.

She waited for him to speak.

"If they are originals, not copies, then there's a very great deal of money here," he said at last. "Not to mention some excellent taste in art. If he sold this lot, he'd have enough to buy a new house. I wonder if there are more in the other rooms."

"Are you sure?" she asked with surprise and a new eagerness. She moved forward to take a better look herself.

"If they're not copies, yes," he answered, standing in front of one of them. He stared at it for so long she grew impatient.

"What is it?" she asked. "Is it real or not?"

"I don't know," he answered thoughtfully. "It took me a moment or two to realize what's wrong with it. It's the proportion. The bottom three quarters of an inch or so has been cut off by the frame."

"So?" she said, puzzled as to why he was bothering with so minute an issue. "Maybe they are only copies, and not as good as you thought. I never understood why, if a thing is beautiful—and I think that is—it should matter so much who painted it."

Monk shook his head. "I don't understand why, if he is clever enough to paint something so lovely, he would cut it short like this. But more to the point, why he didn't sign it."

Then she understood. "You mean he did, and the framer has deliberately excluded it?"

He turned to her and smiled. "Exactly. Maybe Taft wanted the pleasure of looking at it, even showing it off a bit, without letting anyone know exactly how valuable it is. He probably told people it was a good copy, to explain his having it. No signature, so it's not pretending to be real."

"Couldn't that be the actual explanation, though?"

"Of course it could. But I'll wager it isn't!" He stepped back. "Let's see what else we can find."

They separated, to save time. It was a large house and to search thoroughly enough to see anything the police had missed they would have to look very closely. Monk went upstairs, leaving the downstairs for Hester.

She started in the kitchen, not expecting it to be different from the one in the house where she had grown up. She found it was well appointed. The pots and pans were copper and had been carefully polished.

She searched the kitchen, scullery, pantry, and the larder cupboards and found nothing. All the food had been removed; only the various pieces of equipment remained. It was interesting only in that everything was of such high quality. The laundry was the same.

Next she moved to the dining room and again found excellent silverware and porcelain, crystal glasses, fine linen, most of it embroidered. She wondered what would happen to it, with no one left in the family. Had there been siblings who would inherit? It seemed no one was in a hurry to move all these beautiful things. Had grief frozen everyone? Or were there inheritances to debate and perhaps argue over?

The withdrawing room also was filled with beautiful carpets and furniture as well as ornaments, which Hester was not experienced enough to place a value on, though she suspected that some, at least, were collectors' items and could be sold for very good sums.

She studied the pictures at greater length. One in particular was quite breathtaking: a wild seascape, with the waves so well depicted she felt as if she could have put out her finger to touch it, and it would come away wet. She imagined doing it and could almost taste the salt. She hoped that when it came to be sold—or inherited, if there were anyone to claim it—that it would end up in the hands of someone who loved it.

Had it been loved here? Or was it simply an investment? She had met Mrs. Taft, and yet she struggled to recall anything of her beyond the smooth face and fashionable clothes. What kind of a woman had she been? Had she loved her husband, or was it a marriage of suitability? They had daughters of sixteen or seventeen, so presumably they had been married close to twenty years. How much had they changed in that time? Had their feelings deepened, or faded?

She thought about herself and Monk. When they had first met they had irritated each other enormously. She had thought him cold and arrogant. He had thought her abrasive, unfeminine, and far too opinionated. They had both been right, to a degree. They had certainly brought out the least attractive qualities in each other. With a smile she remembered how angry he had made her back then. Was that because she had realized, deep down, he was a match for her, and the thought had frightened her?

Why was she questioning that now? Of course she had been afraid; she had known that he could hurt her, that it was all too likely she would care for him far more than he could possibly care for her.

Was that why he had been so sharp with her in return? Fear as well? She smiled even more. She knew the answer to that also. He was so very much more vulnerable than he was willing to admit. She could not have loved him were he not.

Did she love him more now than then? Yes, of course. Shared time and experiences, and the way he responded to them, had deepened everything: not only love but understanding, her own patience, the things they found beautiful or funny or sad. She was a far wiser, gentler woman because of him. He had gone from bringing out the worst in her to magnifying the best—and she would like to think she had done the same for him. Is that not what love is—an enlargement of the best and a healing over of the worst?

Had Felicia Taft loved her husband? If so, was she then completely unaware of his abuse of the parishioners who trusted him? Surely the realization of that would have wounded her almost beyond bearing.

She was still in the withdrawing room looking at the bookcase when she heard Monk's footsteps in the hall and his voice, sharp and excited, calling out to her.

She closed the glass-paned door of the bookcase and went out immediately.

"I've found something!" he said urgently. "One of the bedrooms upstairs has been turned into a study, and I've found a safe behind a large painting. Come and see." Without waiting for her acknowledgment he turned and led the way, going up the wide, curved stairs two at a time.

She picked up her skirts to avoid tripping and ran after him. He strode across the landing and in through the door of a middle bedroom, now turned into a workroom, which contained two tables covered with papers and pamphlets, at a glance all apparently of a religious nature.

Monk stopped in front of a full-length portrait of a middle-aged clergyman, the portrait being little short of life-sized. He pressed his hand on the right side of the ornate frame, which seemed to release a catch, and then pulled the same edge of the frame forward. The whole picture swung outward on a hinge, revealing a flat wooden board. Very gently Monk leaned his back against it, balancing his weight one way, then another. At last he found exactly the right adjustment of pressure, and the whole panel moved inward. The cavity beyond it was about three feet deep and four feet wide. There was nothing in it whatever.

Hester felt a rush of disappointment.

Monk stopped also. He too had clearly been expecting much more. He looked to one side, then the other. Then he glanced upward inside the cupboard and drew in his breath sharply.

"What is it?" Hester stepped forward to stand almost at his shoulder. "What's there?" she said more urgently.

"A ladder," he replied, his voice husky. "It goes up into . . ." He stopped and raised his arm to grasp the bottom rung and pull it down. It came easily, all the way to the floor.

"We'll need a light," Hester said frantically. "I've seen an oil lamp somewhere. I'll go and fetch it. There must be matches still. Wait for me!" She turned back to him as she said the last, to be certain he would not go without her. "William!"

"I'll wait," he promised. "Not much point if I can't see, although it doesn't look pitch-dark up there."

"Wait for me!" she said fiercely, then turned on her heel and hurried to look for a lamp.

When she returned more than five minutes later, carrying a lit oil lamp, he was still at the bottom of the ladder. She gave him a dazzling smile, then passed him the lamp.

He took it and began to climb very carefully, testing each rung before he put his weight on it and carrying the lamp in his left hand. When he got to the top he set the lamp down and reached out his hand to help her.

She went up rather more cautiously. Not for the first time in her life she found her skirts awkward: the fuller they were, the more they got in the way. No wonder men did not encumber themselves thusly.

She kept hold of Monk's hand until she straightened up at the top and stepped away from the ladder. They were in a large attic that stretched at least twenty feet in length to a doorway at the far end; the roof sloped down on two sides. Various boxes were piled up along the edges of the room, presumably from when the Tafts had first moved into the house. Near the hatch and the ladder down were a couple of very old cabin trunks, which, to judge from the dust on them, had not been used in a decade or more. There seemed to be nothing of interest, let alone of relevance to Taft's death or the murder of his family.

With a slight shrug, Monk carried the lantern to the far end and tried the door. It swung open easily, shedding a little light, as if the new room had led toward daylight.

Hester went after him. There was nothing on the floor to trip over.

Monk stood in the middle of the room, the lantern untended on the floor. He was motionless, as if transfixed by what he saw.

Hester reached him and understood. The room was entirely empty except for a small table on which rested an extraordinary contraption. And yet as soon as she saw it she understood exactly what it was. A gun was wedged between two weights on the table, and above it, joined by a wire around the trigger, was a tin can with a hole in the bottom. Underneath the can was a container, now dry, but with a very slight rime around the edges, as if the hard, local water had left its imprint.

Her eye followed the path a bullet would have taken, but she saw no mark on the wall.

Monk looked toward the window. It was open several inches.

She turned to meet his eyes, waiting, puzzled.

"For the noise," he said quietly. "It was rigged up to go off at about five in the morning. With the silence of the night and that window open, the sound would carry so the neighbors would be bound to hear it. It fixes the time of death. The bodies downstairs would still be warm, even if they died a bit earlier. When the police came, they found a triple murder and a suicide—a woman, her children, and her husband. They wouldn't be looking for hidden doors into attics. Why would they?"

"They wouldn't," she agreed. She looked toward the gun and its extraordinary mechanism. "It would have taken quite a lot of trouble to rig this up, and whoever did it hasn't been able to come back to get rid of it. That must mean it's Drew, mustn't it? This is what he wanted to come for—to get rid of it before anyone found it."

"Yes," he said. "But we can't prove it. He could affect to be just as surprised as we are. All he has to do is say that he wanted the rest of the church papers, in order to pay the bills outstanding, and carry on. And he can," he added bitterly.

"No. All London must know about the embezzlement now," Hester argued. "And if they didn't with Taft's trial and then his death, they will with Oliver's."

"Then Drew can go to Manchester, or Liverpool, or Newcastle," he pointed out. "There are plenty of other cities." He bent to look at the contraption again. "So simple," he said, tightening his lips into a thin line. "I wonder why no one heard the real shot. Pillow, I suppose. It explains why the daughters and the wife were killed as well. They must have known who else was in the house. He couldn't afford to leave them alive."

Hester shuddered. She tried to block out of her imagination the scene as it must have been, the fear and the tragedy. Had Drew shot Taft first, and then gotten rid of the witnesses? Or had he killed them first, separately, keeping them all silent? How loud would you have to scream in the silence of the night to be heard by the neighbors? Someone tired and sound asleep might not hear even a stranger in the room, let alone a woman fighting for her life in the house next door, across fifty feet of garden with trees and bushes. The thought of it chilled her through.

Monk had finished searching. He had found the bullet, lower down in the wall than he had expected. The recoil must have jerked the gun out of alignment. He left it where it was. It would be evidence. He was standing back at the trapdoor again, waiting for her.

She pulled her attention back to the present, glad to be taken away from her imaginings. She walked over to him. "What are we going to do now?" she asked.

"See what else we can find," he replied, holding her hand while she moved across to grasp the rungs and climb down.

They searched the rest of the house for anything else of significance and found nothing beyond a few goose feathers under one of the chairs in the morning room, which was where Taft had been found. It might indicate that a pillow had been used to muffle the sound of the shot, but it certainly did not prove it.

"I wonder what time Taft was actually shot," Monk said, chewing his lip a little. "It can't have been all that long before he was found, or the body would have been too cold."

"About three," Hester suggested. "Drew was back home at five, we know, because he woke his valet. But he could well have been here at three."

"It doesn't have to have been Drew," Monk argued.

She looked at him witheringly. "Who else? It wasn't a burglar. This was prepared very carefully by someone who was here often enough to know about the ladder into the attic and who could set up that contraption feeling confident that he would be able to come back here, without raising suspicion, to take it down again."

Monk went on playing devil's advocate. She understood what he was doing.

"Why?" he asked. "Murdering four people is pretty extreme."

"Maybe in his mind it was only one," she reasoned. "Just Taft himself, because he knew how deeply Drew was implicated. He couldn't be trusted, especially once the case turned against him. Mrs. Taft and the daughters were just necessary tidying up."

He thought for a moment. "But wasn't there always the risk that Taft would turn against him to free himself?"

"It seemed that he trusted not," she replied. "But then he was exposed in the photograph and was forced to change his evidence entirely. So if Taft really didn't know about Drew's perversions, that might well have been the end of any loyalty Taft felt toward Drew, and certainly the end of any belief that Drew could, or would, help him stay out of prison." She knew she was right even before his face broke into a smile and he straightened up.

"Right, I believe you," he said with conviction in his voice. "Now let's find out how he got in. He wouldn't have had a key, and he certainly wouldn't have rung the doorbell at three in the morning."

"How do you know he wouldn't have a key?" she said, then saw the look in his eyes. "Oh—of course. If he had a key he wouldn't be asking the police for permission to get in. He'd have been back ages ago to dismantle that contraption. In that case, why hasn't he just broken in?"

"He'd be seen in the daytime," Monk answered. "This place has some very curious neighbors now, whatever they were before. I saw one of them watching us when we came in. If we'd picked the lock instead of having a key, I'll wager either they'd have been around here finding out who we were or they'd have sent for the police. At this time of the day it wouldn't have taken them long to get here."

"At night?" she persisted, smiling herself now.

"I can't think of anything but the risk of getting caught. A silly chance to take, if he can come in here openly with a perfectly believable excuse."

"What if the police had sent somebody with him?" Hester wasn't going to give up so easily. "He couldn't go up to the gun, or they'd have seen him."

"He could have come into the study and gone up without anyone knowing. I doubt someone would've escorted him the whole way."

She raised her eyebrows. "And carried down the gun and that contraption off the table?"

"No need. Just hide them in one of the boxes up in the attic," he replied. "It would take only moments. Actually, even if anyone knew he had gone up to the attic, so long as they didn't go up before he'd hidden it, it still wouldn't matter."

"Right, I believe you," she mimicked his line exactly, with a wide smile.

"So—back to the question of how he got in that night when he killed Taft and his family," he went on.

"A window?" she suggested. "One of the side or back doors, maybe?"

Together they went around every door and window in the house.

The doors were all fast and showed no signs of having been picked or otherwise tampered with, but one larder window had scratches that indicated a very carefully and quite skillfully picked catch, probably with a long narrow-bladed knife.

"I'll find you a hansom," he told her as they closed the door and walked out onto the sunlit street. "I need to talk to the police surgeon again, then I'll go to speak to Dillon Warne. I don't know when I'll be home, but if I'm late, you and Scuff have supper without me. I can't afford to wait with this."

"I know," she agreed. "And I'll find my own cab."

"No. I'll take you . . ."

"William! I can find a hansom cab for myself! Go and see the police surgeon."

He touched her cheek with a quick gesture, smiled back at her, then turned and walked away rapidly.

She walked in the sun toward the main road and hailed the first passing hansom cab, then settled down for the long ride home.

MONK DID NOT HAVE to wait long for the police surgeon. The man came in, glad to be interrupted in his paperwork. He looked interested as soon as Monk told him which case he was referring to.

"What did you find?" the surgeon asked, waving at a hard-backed leather-seated chair as an invitation for Monk to sit down. He leaned against the table piled with papers and cocked his head slightly to one side, his eyes sharp.

"When you found the bodies of the Taft family, what was your estimate as to time of Abel's death?" Monk inquired.

The surgeon pursed his lips. "Not a great deal of skill needed. The shot was heard and reported by neighbors, on both sides, actually. Just after five in the morning."

Monk nodded. "I read that. But could it have been earlier, medically speaking?"

The surgeon frowned. "What are you getting at? He killed himself with the gun that was found at the scene, and the shot was heard at just after five."

"Yes, but is there anything to prove that the gun at the scene was the same one that fired the shot that the neighbors heard?" Monk asked.

The surgeon narrowed his eyes and his body stiffened. "I presume you have more to do with your time than play silly games. What the devil are you driving at?"

"From the medical evidence," Monk said patiently. "Could he actually have died as early as . . . say, three o'clock—never mind the shot?"

"Yes," the surgeon agreed cautiously. "In fact, it would suit the medical evidence rather better. Now would you please explain yourself?"

Monk told him about the attic, the open window, and the contraption designed to fire a gun at a considerable delay. He saw the surgeon's attention, saw his face light up with perception, and finally saw a smile, as the man nodded slowly several times.

"Clever," he said appreciatively. "Very clever. Yes, that fits perfectly. He was a little cool for having shot himself at five. Not beyond possibility, but enough to make me notice it. I didn't think to question it, though, with the neighbors hearing the gun and all." He shook his head. "What a hell of a thing to do. Do you know who did it?"

"An idea," Monk replied. "Can't prove it yet. But your evidence will help."

"Get the man," the surgeon said simply. "It was a vile thing to do. If you'd seen those girls, and the woman, you'd not stop till you hanged the bastard."

"I don't intend to stop," Monk promised him, rising to his feet. "I've more against him than just this, and this is bad enough. Thank you."

NEXT HE WENT BACK farther into the city and caught Dillon Warne just as he was about to leave his chambers and go home.

"Sorry," Monk apologized. "I can't wait until tomorrow. I need an hour or so of your time."

A flash of hope lit Warne's dark face. "Something happened?"

"Yes. And I'll tell you after you've answered a question that is still outstanding," Monk promised. "I'm still trying to fit the final pieces together."

Warne told his clerks they could go and went back into his office. He closed the door and stood facing Monk. "I still don't know where the missing money went, if that's what your question is," Warne said unhappily. "I've had people go over it again and again. I would dearly like to have proved it in court, but it was done extremely cleverly."

"That isn't what I need," Monk told him. "I think I can account for a good deal of it, actually. The paintings on the walls of Taft's house—they're framed slightly off-center, not from side to side, but up and down. The artists' names are blocked out, and a new, slight scrawl is on them, mostly half hidden by grass blades, or fence posts, that kind of thing." He saw Warne's puzzled look. "I think they're pretty valuable works of art, disguised as pleasant copies," he explained.

"Good God!" Warne breathed out. "We saw no papers on them. But how does it help now? What is it you want from me?"

"I need to know—is there a way to see whether they were registered as owned by Taft? Are they in his will, for example?"

Warne straightened up. "I don't know. I've got a copy of it, but I hadn't looked over it very carefully. Let me find it." He went over to the safe in the corner and came back holding papers in his hands. His eyes were bright, and there was excitement in his voice. "This is a copy, as I said—but it appears the paintings are owned by Drew—lent to the Tafts and to the Church. They're marked as of no particular value, but definitely they belong to Robertson Drew. Do you think Taft was taking the blame for both of them, then?"

"A sort of great sacrifice for the good of the Church?" Monk said with a twist of irony. "No, I don't. I think Drew was the prime mover. I think he gave most of the orders and took most of the stolen money. Taft was the man with the golden voice, and Drew used him."

"And poor Taft killed himself when he was thrown away . . ." Warne's voice was full of a sudden dark pity.

"Actually—no," Monk replied. "Drew betrayed him more terribly than just giving him up in court when Rathbone left him no choice." He told Warne what he and Hester had found in the attic of Taft's house.

Warne sank back and slumped into the big chair a couple of steps behind him. "What a totally evil man. God, what a mess!" He looked at Monk with intense emotion in his face. "What are we going to do about it?"

"I'm going to give all the evidence to the police," Monk replied. "And we've got to save Oliver Rathbone, if possible. He in no way is to blame for these deaths. I'm going to see Brancaster right away."

Warne hauled himself to his feet, his face pale. "And do what? Ask for an adjournment? Believe me, York won't give it to you."

16

In the courtroom at the Old Bailey Rathbone sat in the dock feeling utterly powerless. At the lunchtime adjournment he had found it difficult to swallow anything. Even the tea, too strong and not hot enough, had tasted sour, but at least it had eased the cramp in his stomach. Now he was back, forced to listen to his own condemnation without being able to speak. No matter what was said, he could not defend himself. Perhaps he had deluded himself that he even could. He would be wiser to face reality now, to plan how he could deal with the inevitable verdict. Should he sell the house? He would have no income. How long could he maintain it? It was of no real use to him now, anyway. The servants would find other positions. A recommendation from him would hardly help! He regretted that. It was unfair. They had been loyal over many years.

How he would fare in prison was another matter. The thought of it knotted his stomach again. How would he live on that food? Uglier and

far more painful, how would he ever defend himself? Who would care
for him if he became ill? Or if he were injured? He thrust the thought
away—it was too much to bear at this moment.

Wystan began the afternoon session by calling a police officer who
had arrested a man Rathbone had defended. The man was wealthy and
had been accused of systematic fraud. Rathbone had not known
whether he was guilty or not, only that the prosecution had not proved
him so, beyond a reasonable doubt, as the law required.

Wystan questioned the man, always slanting the words to make
Rathbone sound unreasonable and vindictive, a lawyer who had to win
at any cost, the fight for justice being his vehicle to wealth and fame.
Other men's reputations, even their lives, were there solely to serve his
purpose.

The bare facts were correct. There was nothing Brancaster could
disprove. The condemnation was there in the language used.

"And. was Mr. Rathbone determined to win this case?" Wystan
asked, his eyes innocently wide. "By that I mean did he use every ounce
of steel at his command, work tirelessly, pursue every possibility and
cross-examine every witness over and over again until he obtained the
answer he wished for?"

Brancaster rose to his feet. "My lord, every lawyer is supposed to do
that for every defendant. My learned friend is trying to make it sound
as if it is an extraordinary and unusual effort."

York's heavy eyebrows rose. "Are you objecting to Mr. Wystan trying to persuade the jury that the accused was an energetic and diligent
lawyer, Mr. Brancaster?"

Brancaster's face tightened. "No, my lord, I am objecting to his
making it sound as if Sir Rathbone treated this case differently from the
way every defense lawyer should treat every case."

"That is not an issue of law, Mr. Brancaster," York said tartly. "Please
do not keep interrupting pointlessly. You are wasting the court's time."

Rathbone could see from where he was that Brancaster's face was
pale with anger. He sat down slowly, reluctantly.

Rathbone looked at the jury. It was a different thing to read their mood when you were the accused; fear colored his ability to assess them objectively. And yet once he had allowed himself to look, he could not tear his eyes away. The man farthest to the left on the upper row looked worried, as if something in the evidence or the proceedings troubled him. The man next to him appeared to be bored, as though his attention were on something else. Had he already made up his mind? But the defense had not even begun!

What defense could there be? Rathbone had given the photograph to Warne. That was not arguable. He had weighed the right and wrong of it and made his decision. It was not unreasonable that he should have to pay the price for that. The personal accusation of pride and ambition was unnecessary—and irrelevant. Why did Brancaster not object on those grounds? Perhaps Brancaster thought Rathbone was guilty, exactly as everyone else seemed to. And they were right. He had made a selfish and stupid misjudgment.

He looked away from the jury, unwilling to meet their eyes. He looked instead at the front rows of the gallery. No one was looking back at him; everyone's attention was on Wystan's next witness, a young lawyer Rathbone had defeated when he was prosecuting a case a few years ago. He had disliked making a fool of the lawyer, but the man had not prepared his case well. He had been slipshod, and it had showed. Now he was complaining about Rathbone's underhanded tactics and suggesting mysterious undue influence.

Rathbone looked away and suddenly saw Beata York, the light catching her pale hair. He froze. There was nobody he wanted to look at more. She idealized the gentleness, the strength, and the humor that he understood now was what he hungered for. There was a beauty in her that he thought he had seen in Margaret, a courage, a generosity of heart and mind.

He had run away from Hester because she would always have challenged him. She might also have made him happy.

Was that what he saw in Beata—another chance at least to know and care for a woman uniquely beautiful in such a way? It could never be more than friendship, but even that would have been precious.

Then as if she had felt his gaze on her, she turned her head and looked up at him. She gave a sad little smile, not cold, not condescending, but as if she felt for his distress. She hesitated only a moment, long enough for their eyes to meet, then she turned back to the witness, as if she did not want to draw attention and prompt others to stare.

He felt his face burning, a rage of conflicting emotions inside him. What had she meant? How much was his imagination making her expression into what he had wished it to be? Maybe he was replacing regret with something gentler that he would find easier to bear: sympathy for a man in pain, rather than pity for someone who had been given so much and wasted it.

Wystan was rambling on and on. The afternoon seemed endless.

Rathbone did not look at Beata York again. Nor did he look to find Henry Rathbone. To see his distress was more than he could handle. He needed to keep some composure.

At last Wystan closed the case for the prosecution, eloquent and satisfied. York adjourned the court until the next day.

Rathbone waited in the hope that Brancaster would visit him, at least to discuss the progress of the case and tell him what he planned to do next; but the silence dragged on, and there was nothing but the briefest message from Brancaster telling him to keep hope.

The long prison night seemed like the worst in his life.

THE NEXT DAY RATHBONE was led back to the dock, still without having seen Brancaster. He felt numb, as if his body belonged to someone else. He stumbled and banged his elbow sharply against the wall. Even the pain of it barely registered. He was like a pig on a roasting spit, stripped of all moral and emotional dignity, stared at, talked about, and unable to do anything but listen.

The fight over his future, his reputation, his life, went on anyway, with or without him.

If ever he were able to practice law again, he vowed never to do what Brancaster was doing to him; from now on he would talk to his clients, tell them what he planned and why, what he hoped to achieve. At the very least he would make them feel part of the proceedings and let them know that he cared, that he understood what they were experiencing and how they felt.

But it was too late for that now. He wouldn't practice law again. It was all pointless and too late.

Rufus Brancaster rose to begin his defense. The jury watched him, but their faces suggested good manners rather than interest.

Brancaster called Josiah Taylor.

Rathbone struggled to remember who he was and what on earth he might have to do with the Taft case. Was he one of the parishioners Rathbone had forgotten?

Taylor was sworn in. His occupation was apparently as an accountant in a small business. His face looked vaguely familiar, but Rathbone struggled in vain to think from where or when.

Brancaster seemed to ramble on, asking questions that appeared pointless, but Wystan sat smiling, never raising any objection. York looked more and more irritated.

Then Rathbone recalled how he knew Taylor. He had been an expert witness in a case of embezzlement some three or four years ago. What on earth did Brancaster hope to get from him? All he could offer was that Rathbone had won that particular case, and done it with some skill, according to Taylor, and with an unusual degree of consideration for the witnesses, and for the victim of the crime. In Taylor's view, Rathbone's courtesy and honor were exemplary. He was a character witness, no more.

Rathbone had studied juries all his professional life. He knew that most of this jury had lost interest now.

York was becoming quite openly restive when Brancaster drew to a close.

Rathbone knew that this was the moment when Brancaster gave up. After all the hope, absurd as it was, and the brave promises, he had nothing.

Wystan rose to his feet. He looked infinitely satisfied. Not that he must have ever doubted that in the end he would win.

"No questions, my lord," he said simply, and sat down again. Apparently he did not feel he needed to add anything more. Victory was in his hands. He could afford to be casual.

"I call Richard Athlone," Brancaster said loudly.

A couple of the jurors stirred to attention. Several of the others looked embarrassed, as if decency required that the end be swifter than this.

York sighed.

The usher repeated the call, and after a few more seconds a tall, lean man with receding hair emerged from the doors into the hall, walked across the floor, and climbed to the witness stand. He was duly sworn, and he faced Brancaster.

The man had a thin, intelligent face, deeply lined but good humored. Rathbone tried to place him, and failed.

Brancaster walked out onto the floor and looked up at Athlone with a slight smile.

"You are a professor of law, is that correct?"

"Yes, sir," Athlone agreed.

"And as well as the law itself, you have made a speciality of studying most of the more famous cases that are recent—shall we say, within the last thirty years?"

"Yes, sir," Athlone replied.

York shifted his position and glanced at Wystan.

Wystan rose to his feet. "My lord, the prosecution is happy to stipulate that Sir Oliver has been an outstanding lawyer and won remarkably many cases. Indeed, we would state it positively. It is part of our own case that his extraordinary success has led to his arrogance, and is at the very least a witness to his supreme ambition. He must win at all costs, even the cost of loyalty to his wife and her family and, beyond that, to honor and to the principles of the law. That is the heart of the case against him."

"If you believe the law is as important as you say," Brancaster retorted instantly, "then you will allow that the accused is entitled to the best defense he is able to find."

Wystan rolled his eyes, unusually expressively for him. "If this is the best defense you can find, then by all means, make it, sir!"

Brancaster bowed. "Thank you." He turned back to Athlone.

"Professor, perhaps we might pick two or three of Sir Oliver's most remarkable cases and mention, very briefly indeed, some of the truths that he uncovered in court, so that justice was done where it had previously appeared that the truth was the exact opposite of what had actually transpired. Shall we say one for the defense, one for the prosecution? And so that we do not exhaust the patience of the court, let us keep it to not more than five minutes each?"

"By all means," Athlone agreed. Then he proceeded to tell the story of how Rathbone had defended a man who appeared to be unquestionably guilty but, by brilliant questioning, Rathbone had left no doubt at all, either with the jury or with the public in general, that another completely different person was in fact to blame.

Athlone recounted it with wit and a considerable flair for drama. Not a single member of the jury moved his eyes from him while he spoke. The people in the gallery sat motionless, silently staring at the witness box.

Athlone started with the second account, this time a case where Rathbone had appeared for the prosecution. The crime was particularly unpleasant and the proof slight. The defense was brilliant, and it seemed inevitable that, at least legally, there was reasonable doubt. This time Rathbone had found a witness who was able to discredit the accused totally, and within the space of minutes the entire trial turned the other way. The man was convicted.

At the end of his account several people in the gallery actually cheered. Even the jury looked impressed.

"That is an excellent example, Professor Athlone, but I rather expected you to cite the case of Mr. Wilton Jones."

Athlone looked slightly puzzled. "Wilton Jones? Remind me, sir."

"A man of great skill, and villainy," Brancaster replied. "But his violence was always well concealed. Frequently he corrupted others to do his worst work. He presented himself as a gentleman, but he was greedy, cruel, and totally ruthless. That case was one of Sir Oliver's greatest victories."

"Ah. Yes." Athlone smiled. "I believe I recall the case now. Was that not the one where another gentleman of excellent family, and rather a lot of influence, swore to Wilton Jones's innocence, how he was misunderstood, misrepresented by lesser men envious of him . . . ?"

Brancaster nodded and smiled.

"Yes, indeed," Athlone picked up the thread. "Sir Oliver turned this witness against Wilton Jones. As I recall, he tripped him on a statement as to where he was at a particular time, and suddenly the witness changed his entire testimony. Instead of defending the accused, he condemned him. I believe Jones was found guilty and must still be in prison." Athlone smiled, as though he were pleased to have been of use. "A brilliant piece of work," he added.

"Justice was served." Brancaster apparently could not resist adding the point. Then he turned to offer the witness to Wystan.

Wystan rose to his feet and all but swaggered out onto the floor before looking up at Athlone.

"I don't recall the case myself, Professor, but you have described it particularly well—with a little prompting from my learned friend. You say that this witness—rather like Mr. Drew, come to think of it—suddenly changed his testimony. Was there any reason for it that you are aware of?"

Athlone looked slightly puzzled.

Rathbone could see what was coming. His mind was completely numbed. He couldn't remember the case. Even the name Wilton Jones meant nothing to him. It seemed as if his mind was paralyzed.

"Professor?" Wystan prompted.

"He did change his mind absolutely, as I recall," Athlone agreed.

"Because Rathbone caught him out during his testimony. If I have the right case, of course?" He made it a question.

"Oh, I expect you do," Wystan said, his tone lofty. To Rathbone, it seemed as if satisfaction oozed out of him. "You see, Sir Oliver did exactly the same thing recently, as a judge presiding over a case—he managed to change the sworn testimony of a witness, turning the verdict toward the side he personally had concluded to be right." Wystan swung away from the witness stand, took a few steps, and then spun around again. "Professor, as the law is the subject upon which you are an expert—is it a judge's task to decide whether the accused is guilty or innocent?"

"Of course not," Athlone replied with just the slightest edge to his voice. "That is the duty of the gentlemen of the jury. The judge's task is to preside over the proceedings and make certain that all is conducted fairly and according to the law."

"Thank you, Professor. Now, if you please, tell us, how would counsel, or anyone else, make a witness suddenly recant his entire testimony—given under oath and therefore making him liable to charges of perjury—and then swear to the exact opposite?"

Athlone shrugged. "Catching him in a lie, making him see an error, making him fear reprisal, bribery . . . there are several possibilities."

"Threat of ruin?" Wystan asked.

Athlone sighed. "Of course."

Wystan smiled for the first time, so widely that he showed a flash of white teeth. "Thank you, Professor. You have been a perfect witness yourself." He swiveled a little to Brancaster on a gesture of invitation.

Oddly enough, in that moment Rathbone felt most deeply for his father, who had chosen Brancaster with such faith. The pain of it was almost unbearable; it was like a stone weighing hard and heavy inside him.

Brancaster rose to his feet and looked up at Athlone. He took only a couple of steps out into the wide space of the floor. His body was rigid with tension.

"Professor, you agree that threat of ruin is a possible motive for changing testimony, even if it might result in charges of perjury, am I correct?"

"Yes," Athlone agreed. "I imagine if the threat is serious enough, most of us would risk perjury."

"As, for example, if an outwardly respectable man, possibly a man with power, feared the exposure of his proclivity for performing obscene and criminal sexual acts with small children?"

Athlone winced. "Of course. That would be extremely effective. And the more power the man in question possessed, the more effective such a threat of exposure would be."

"He would be likely to testify however you wished him to?" Brancaster pursued.

Rathbone felt as if he were facing a firing squad. Whose pay was Brancaster in that he was doing this?

"Certainly," Athlone agreed.

York looked satisfied, even pleased.

Wystan resembled the cat who had eaten the canary.

Brancaster shook his head. "What a terrifying thought. And of course the man who is the subject of such a photograph, who can be twisted this way and that, could be anyone, couldn't he? What I mean is we do not know such people by sight; they would look exactly like any other respected and powerful man on the surface, wouldn't they?"

"Of course," Athlone agreed. "Your banker, your lawyer, your physician, your member of Parliament, for that matter. Even your judge in court, your minister in government, the senior officers of the police whose word might well be taken ahead of your own. Your bishop. Anyone at all." He looked pale as he said it, and his voice was now hoarse with emotion. "The thought is a nightmare. A living hell of corruption."

"I think you are frightening us, Professor," Brancaster said grimly.

"I am frightening myself," Athlone agreed. "It presents a terrifying image. I wish I could say it is a hideous dream and we shall awaken from it. But Mr. Wystan has made it clear that it is all too real."

Suddenly Wystan looked puzzled. A shadow of uncertainty crossed his face.

Brancaster was still rigid.

"I think perhaps, Professor, we need to know what you mean. Of what specifically are you afraid, sir?"

Athlone was very grave. "I gather from what I have overheard while in the hall waiting to come in, and from the questions that both you and Mr. Wystan have asked me, that there is a serious question as to whether photographs of both obscenity and crime have been used to sway the testimony of witnesses in criminal trials. Mr. Wystan said that such a photograph is what Sir Oliver Rathbone is accused of having used and that it is a very reasonable suggestion, far too serious to be ignored, that another such photograph may have been used in another trial, again to oblige someone to change their testimony. It could not have been done unless he, or someone extremely close to him, was the subject of the photograph." He looked harassed with anxiety.

There was not a whisper of breath in the court. Every juror stared at Athlone as if he had risen out of the ground like an apparition.

Brancaster was as motionless as a statue.

"Which forces us," Athlone continued, "to ask how many of these photographs there are, and of whom? Perhaps the most terrifying thing of all is that, if we do not know, then we must suspect and fear everyone. And yet if we are not even aware of this horror, then it will continue unseen among us. Justice, the government, the police, the Church, medicine, every aspect of our lives may be poisoned by it, and we shall not know or understand why things go terribly wrong, or who is to blame."

Wystan shot to his feet like a jack-in-the-box.

"My lord! This is preposterous. Mr. Brancaster is blowing this completely out of proportion. He is attempting to frighten us out of all sense and judgment. It is perfectly reasonable to draw the conclusion that Rathbone used one of these vile photographs to cause Robertson Drew to change his testimony and thus condemn Abel Taft." His face was ashen white. "Which, we may draw the unspeakable conclusion, caused the poor man to take not only his own life but also the lives of his wife and daughters . . ." He shook his head. "And though unproven, it is possible he has done this one other time in the past, judging from the facts Professor Athlone brought up. But implying this . . . this further web of terror is unnecessary and unfounded."

"I agree," York said a little hoarsely. He too was pale. "Mr. Brancaster, please restrict yourself to the matter in hand."

Brancaster smiled, but there was no humility in it.

"My lord, Mr. Wystan opened the door by suggesting to Professor Athlone that Sir Oliver may have used obscene photographs in more than one trial. That necessarily implies that there are other photographs. How are we to know how many more?" His dark eyes were wide. "Or who possesses them? Is it a subject we can leave hanging in the air? The jury knows of them. The gallery knows of them." He waved his hand airily in the direction of the gallery. "And no doubt when the newspapers are printed tomorrow morning, all London will know of them. Can we possibly put a lid on such a matter and hope it will stay closed? Indeed, the question is—should we?"

There was a terrible silence. Suspense crackled in the room like the air before a great storm. Not a juror moved.

Rathbone looked at York, whose face was pale, eyes like hollows and so dark as to seem lightless.

Then Rathbone looked at Wystan, and for the first time saw a shadow of unmistakable doubt in his face.

Was this the edge of the final disaster, or was it the beginning of hope? His heart pounded; the weight inside his chest was painful.

Very slowly Wystan rose to his feet. "My lord, I withdraw my objection. Mr. Brancaster is quite right. This prospect is too appalling to leave it in the air, unresolved. It would cause a public panic."

York looked at Brancaster with loathing.

"You have raised a demon, sir. You will now deal with it."

Brancaster inclined his head in acknowledgment. "I cannot do it alone, my lord, but I will seek such help as I need. Tomorrow morning I will call the accused to the stand."

Rathbone felt the sweat break out on his body. It was a terrible gamble Brancaster was taking, but he was playing for the highest stakes of all—the complete exposure of the photographs with all the ruin they would bring. Was it a defense? It was certainly an attack. Could they win? Or was he prepared to sacrifice Rathbone if he had to, to end it once and for all?

If he were honest, Rathbone had to admit that, unwittingly, he had sacrificed himself.

It was the longest night Rathbone could recall. He tossed from one side of the wretched mattress to the other, hot one minute, cold the next. Did soldiers feel like this waiting to go into battle the next day? Victory and honor—or death? He had no escape. He was locked in, as he might be for years. However unrealistic it was, this was the last night he could cling to hope. He was torn between wanting to savor every minute of it and wishing it were over.

The morning began as the one before had, a breakfast of bread he could barely swallow and tea that was revolting. He took it all, to steady himself. He could not allow his nerves to betray him now.

Even so, he was sure his legs were shaking as he walked across the open floor to climb up the steps to the witness stand. Certainly he had to grip the railing to keep his balance. How ridiculous he would look if he fell down the stairway. Worse than that, he might injure himself, break an ankle. He would be vulnerable enough in prison without having broken bones.

But the humiliation of being carried off, unable even to testify, would be the worst. Was Beata York here today? He did not want to know. Would he look for Henry Rathbone's face in the gallery? He was not even certain about that.

He had reached the top of the steps and held onto the rail, taking the Bible in his other hand and swearing on it to tell the truth.

What was the point of that? Didn't accused men usually lie? Wasn't that somewhat taken for granted? He could tell the truth as exactly and

honorably as he wished, and most of the people here would still think
him a liar.

He must look at Brancaster and concentrate. This was his only
chance. The rest of his life depended on what he said now.

Brancaster was standing in front of him, looking up, his face intensely serious.

"Sir Oliver," Brancaster began. "You have heard Mr. Wystan suggest that there might be a number of obscene photographs similar to
the one of a witness in the trial of Abel Taft, a trial over which you
presided. Do you know if indeed there are other such photographs?"

Rathbone cleared his throat. It was so tight he gulped before he
could find his voice.

"Yes. There are nearly three score that I know of."

"Really? So many. How do you know of them?"

"I . . . I have them." How bold and ugly that sounded.

There was a rustle of movement in the gallery, gusts of breath let
out, murmurs of disgust.

"I see," Brancaster pursed his lips. "Do you know who is in them?"

"Not all of them. Of course, the one I gave Mr. Warne in the Taft
trial, and one or two others."

"How is it that you don't know who is in all of them, if you own
them?" Brancaster tried to look curious and succeeded only in looking
wretched.

No one objected or interrupted, though York was drumming his
fingers on the bench.

"I looked at them once," Rathbone replied, remembering the inci-
dent with revulsion. "I should have destroyed them then, but I did not."

"Why not?" Brancaster asked.

Rathbone thought back. "I recognized some of the faces. I was . . .
stunned, horrified. As Mr. Wystan suggested, there are among the abus-
ers men of great power and privilege. The man who possessed them
before I did used them—at first to force those men into doing the right
thing, saving lives rather than destroying them. I thought I might do
the same. That was a mistake. Such power corrupts more than I real-

ized. And—" He stopped abruptly. Was he telling the whole truth? Did he really wish he had destroyed them all? After all, he had done some good with them. Exactly as Arthur Ballinger had done, in the beginning. It was Ballinger's final revenge: to make Rathbone into what he himself had become. Exquisite. If he were somewhere in a hell of his own and could see this, he would be savoring it. There was a perfect irony to it.

"You were going to say . . . ?" Brancaster pressed him.

"And I am not immune," Rathbone said bitterly.

"You spoke of a previous owner," Brancaster observed. "Who was it? And how did you come to own them?"

York looked sharply at Wystan, but Wystan did not move.

Rathbone realized with a flood of amazement that Wystan intended Brancaster to uncover this story. He had perceived a greater purpose than merely convicting Rathbone of having transgressed the law in the trial of Taft. There was a greater issue at stake. Had that been Brancaster's game all along? If so, it was dangerous, but perhaps brilliant.

"Sir Oliver?" Brancaster prompted. "However unpleasant the truth, and whoever it implicates, this matter is too grave to remain secret any longer. It is not your own innocence you are protecting, or that of any other individual. The honor and integrity of all our institutions is at stake. Perhaps it would not be too extreme to say it is the core of justice itself, for which you have fought all your professional life, at no matter what cost to yourself. Over and over again you have risked your reputation to defend those whom others had condemned or abandoned."

Wystan stirred in his seat.

Brancaster knew he would be allowed no more latitude.

Rathbone knew it also.

"I don't know how much detail you wish me to tell," he began, then had to stop and clear his throat.

"All that is necessary for the court to understand is the nature of the photographs, and how it is that you possess them," Brancaster instructed.

There was no escape. The truth must be told publicly. Rathbone could see Margaret in the gallery, well toward the front. She was here to watch his humiliation, the end of the career she thought he had placed before honor or loyalty. He could not protect her from the facts anymore.

When he began, his voice was surprisingly steady.

"There was a club created by a man of very comfortable means," he said. "So far as I know he did not indulge in obscene pastimes himself, but he understood the excitement some men feel when they deliberately expose themselves to intense danger. The photographs I have mentioned were the initiation rite to this particular club. It was in a way a safeguard to each member; a way to ensure no one spoke about the obscenities being practiced by all of them."

No one moved. No one even attempted to interrupt him.

He took a deep breath and swallowed hard. His mouth was dry. Then he continued. "They were also a perfect tool for blackmail. The man who created the club told me that the photographs were never used merely to extort money, and I believed him. It was always about power. He said that the first time he used one, it was to oblige a senior judge to rule on a case in such a way that a factory owner would be forced to stop the effluent from his works polluting the drinking water of a large number of poor people who were becoming diseased, even dying, as a result." Again he took a deep breath. He felt as if his pounding heart was shaking his whole body. "At first I was repulsed by the idea of such blackmail, no matter the ultimate outcome. Then I thought of the children dying of the poison in the water, and the factory owner's refusal to sacrifice some of his profit to clean it up." His voice was growing stronger, the pain inside him easing. "I wondered—if I had the same power, would I refuse to use it and let the children die? Would it be better to cost many innocent people their health, merely to keep my hands clean of such methods?"

There seemed to be not even a breath drawn in the room.

"He chose to use the weapon he had," Rathbone said. "I do not blame him for that."

There were murmurs now, voices in the gallery.

"That was the only specific example he gave me, but he said there were others like it," Rathbone continued. "I did look up that case, and the judgment. He was speaking the truth. The industrialist he mentioned had steadily refused to yield until the judgment went against him. I also know the photograph existed because I have seen it."

"That is very frightening indeed," Brancaster said grimly. "But it does not explain how you come to have these photographs now."

"I was still horrified," Rathbone went on. He knew there was no escape now. It was far too late. "I participated in the closure of the two different clubs involved. The whole situation included the murder of a man who ran one of them, a man named Mickey Parfitt. It was investigated by the police. The man was of the dregs of humanity, but murder is still a crime, no matter who the victim or who the offender."

He looked at last at Margaret, and saw her staring back at him. Her face was twisted in anger and so white she seemed bloodless. There was no going back now.

"Sir Oliver . . ." Brancaster prompted him again.

"The man accused of the murder was prosecuted," Rathbone resumed. He was finding it difficult to speak. His mouth was so dry it was blurring his words. "I was asked to defend him, and to begin with I believed him innocent. Then another person was also murdered, a young woman who was no more than a witness. It soon became clear that her death was planned by this man, in order to keep her from testifying. But I still did all I could to defend him, because that was my duty before the law, no matter what my own feelings. I tried everything I could think of, but I failed. He was found guilty, and sentenced to be hanged."

Brancaster did not move or speak. No one in the entire court seemed to do more than breathe.

"He asked me after the sentence was handed down to visit him," Rathbone went on. His voice suddenly sounded loud in his own ears. "I did so. That was when he told me of the existence of scores more photographs. He said that if I did not find a way to save him from the rope they would fall into the hands of someone he trusted, and the blackmail would go on. I would have no power to stop it, and the foundations of everything we value would be undermined. He told me there were judges; government ministers; bishops; leaders of industry, science, and the army and navy; even distant members of the royal family involved, if not captured in the pictures themselves."

Rathbone felt again the desperation with which he, Hester, and Monk had searched everywhere they could think of for those damned photographs.

"And you found them?" Brancaster asked in the total silence that followed.

"No," Rathbone replied. "I went back to plead with him, and . . . and I found him murdered in prison." The horror of that scene crept over his skin again like an infestation of lice. "It . . . it made me realize just how wide and how deep this circle of corruption went. The police never found out who killed him."

"But you did not find the photographs?" Brancaster's voice cracked as he spoke.

"No," Rathbone answered. "That was the bitter irony. They found me. The man had left them with his solicitor, left them to me in his will, to be delivered to me as a final punishment for not having saved him."

Brancaster smiled bitterly. "And this man you refer to—that would be your father-in-law, Arthur Ballinger?"

"Yes," Rathbone said huskily. "It would."

In her seat in the second row, Margaret sat like stone, as if she would never move again.

Rathbone would have spared her that. But there was nothing he could do. The reality was there in the courtroom like something alive, unstoppable.

"Thank you, Sir Oliver," Brancaster said with a sigh. He turned to Wystan.

Wystan rose to his feet stiffly.

"It paints a very clear picture, my lord. I imagine Mr. Brancaster will be calling other witnesses to verify your story. For the sake of many people who may be implicated, I would like to reserve my questions until that has been done."

York, his face full of anger, adjourned the court.

17

THE NEXT PERSON TO testify was Monk. He walked across the floor and climbed up the steps, trying to look grave but unconcerned. He certainly did not feel that way. Brancaster was taking an extraordinary gamble, but it was perhaps the only move they had. He had a strong idea of what Brancaster was going to do, but Brancaster had deliberately not prepared him. He said he wanted it to sound unrehearsed, almost as if Monk, too, had been taken by surprise.

The one thing he hoped would not come out in any way was the fact that they suspected Margaret had been the one to turn Rathbone in. Scuff had told him what had happened the second time he snuck into the courtroom. Monk, for better or worse, had decided that it was not relevant to the murder of Taft. Margaret had been blighted by what had happened with her father; she had sought revenge, and she had been in the right place at the right time to get what she had wanted. Rathbone, already so hurt, would be wounded even more deeply to learn how she had betrayed him. Maybe there would be a time to tell him, but it wasn't now.

Monk swore as to his name, occupation, and rank in the Thames River Police, and of course to tell the truth. Then he faced Brancaster.

"Commander Monk," Brancaster began, "were you in charge of the investigation into the murder of Mickey Parfitt, whose body was found in the Thames?"

"Yes, I was."

Brancaster nodded.

"I will be as brief as possible in establishing your connection with this present case, so forgive me if I appear to leap over great areas of your earlier involvement. What was Mr. Parfitt's occupation, Commander?"

"He ran a club for wealthy men with a taste for child prostitution and pornography," Monk replied. "He based it on a barge moored on the river, which is how it fell under my jurisdiction. He also blackmailed several of his clients, vulnerable because exposure would ruin them."

"How did he do that? What evidence did he have of their involvement?" Brancaster managed to sound as if he did not already know.

"Photographs," Monk replied.

"Why would a vulnerable man allow himself to be photographed in such a situation? Forgive me, but does a photograph not require you to maintain a motionless position for some time while the photographer performs his art?" Brancaster looked puzzled.

"Yes, it does," Monk agreed. "But having a compromising photograph taken was part of the initiation into the club. You could not be a member without agreeing to it."

"I see. And did Mr. Parfitt own this . . . club?"

"No, he just managed it."

"Did you discover who owned it?" Brancaster inquired.

Again the court was breathless; every member of the jury was staring at Monk.

"Yes—Arthur Ballinger," Monk answered.

Brancaster also looked only at Monk. "The same Arthur Ballinger who was father-in-law to Oliver Rathbone?" he inquired.

"Yes."

"Is there any doubt about this whatever?" Brancaster persisted.

Monk shook his head. "No. Quite apart from the detailed proof he provided, in the end, when he was facing the hangman's noose, he did not bother to deny it. In fact, he deliberately bequeathed the collection of pictures to Oliver Rathbone."

"I see. And what was Rathbone's reaction to this . . . bequest?"

York finally lost his composure. "Mr. Wystan! Do you not wish to object to this? Are you asleep, sir? Mr. Brancaster is asking for the witness to give an opinion, to state facts he cannot possibly know."

Wystan rose to his feet. He looked very pale.

"I apologize, my lord, if I seemed inattentive. I assumed that Mr. Brancaster was asking Commander Monk if he observed any reaction in Sir Oliver, not what he imagined Sir Oliver's feelings to be."

A dull flush spread up York's face, but the answer was perfectly reasonable.

Monk noted that Wystan had made an enemy for himself, but he felt a certain respect for the man. He was following his own judgment, regardless of the favor or disfavor it earned him. As it was a complete about-face from his previous position, it must have been hard to do.

Brancaster acknowledged it with the slightest inclination of his head.

Monk glanced at the jury. Every single one of them was watching Brancaster, waiting.

"Do you know of anything Sir Oliver said or did as a result of having inherited this terrible legacy?" Brancaster clarified his question to Monk.

"He told me about it. He was horrified," Monk replied. "I am also aware that he used a photo to force someone to act honorably in circumstances where they refused to do it of their own volition. It is one of the worst choices a person can have, when no matter what course you take, it is going to cause pain to someone." He knew this was not an answer to the question, but he guessed it was what Brancaster was giving him the opportunity to say. "If it were my friend or my brother

who had joined such a club, I would want to protect him, let him keep
his hideous mistake private. If he continued to practice such abuse of
children, I might feel less like protecting him."

There was a murmur around the room, a rumble to which it was
difficult to put a meaning, but it sounded more like agreement than
anger.

"But I have no doubt," he went on, "that if it were my wife or my
friends who needed help, and some man in one of these photographs
refused to give it though he was quite able, I would wish that whoever
had the power to force him to act would use it, no matter how high the
price. Wouldn't any man?"

"Yes, I think so," Brancaster agreed. "I certainly would. I could not
see anyone I loved punished, tortured, perhaps killed if I could exert a
pressure that would save him. Tell me, did Sir Oliver expose the man in
the photograph that you speak of, and ruin him?"

"No. Of course not. He kept his word."

Brancaster gave a slight shrug, still frowning a little. "Did he ever
say anything that led you to understand why he wished to keep this
power in his hands? Or for that matter, why did you, as a policeman, not
expose the men in the photographs anyway? The acts depicted are not
only revolting—they are criminal. It was within your right."

The air in the room crackled. No one moved even a cramped limb.

Monk gave a small, tight smile. "Because as I think we have already
established, the men involved are in all walks of life, almost all highly
placed. There was no purpose in seducing or photographing men without money or influence or a great deal to lose if the pictures were made
public. To expose them all would, at the very least, rock the foundations
of our government, possibly the Church, the army, and the navy. I have
no wish to do that. Apart from anything else, it would expose the nation to ridicule and contempt. Which of our ministers would be able to
sit at the international tables of negotiation without embarrassment?"

Brancaster bit his lip. "Perhaps I had not appreciated just how wide
and how deep this is. It . . . it is very frightening." He took a deep breath.
"I begin to grasp just what Sir Oliver was struggling with, and so per-

haps why he took the irrevocable step of bringing it into the open in this particular way—we do not know who is involved, and yet we cannot possibly legally or morally turn our backs on the problem and pretend it is not real, dangerous, and terrible."

York leaned forward. "Mr. Brancaster, before you elevate the accused to sainthood, perhaps you should remind the jury that Abel Taft, a man who was yet to be convicted of anything at all and was charged with fraud, not violence, not obscenity, is dead! As are his poor wife and his two young daughters—as a direct result of this act of Rathbone's that you are attempting to paint so nobly!"

"Thank you, my lord," Brancaster said with a sudden appearance of humility. Then he turned back to Monk. "Commander Monk, I believe you have been reinvestigating that tragic event, to which his lordship refers, specifically the issue of where the large amount of money that was embezzled—still unaccounted for—went. Is that correct?"

Wystan looked puzzled. He made as if to rise, then eased back into his seat again but paid even closer attention.

"Yes, that is correct," Monk answered quickly, before York could intervene, or Wystan changed his mind. "I went back to Taft's house. The matter is now being looked at by experts called in by the local police—"

"How is this your concern?" York interrupted angrily. "Are you not Thames River Police? Since when did your jurisdiction run to an embezzlement investigation, miles from the river, over a case that was already closed?"

That was the question Monk had been hoping to avoid.

"It does not, my lord," he said as deferentially as he could force himself to. "Which is why, when I found the evidence, I turned it over to the local police. I went in there with their permission," he added, before York could challenge him on that also. He did not want to get the officer who had granted the help into trouble. "We cooperate with each other, my lord," he added, seeing the irritation in York's face. He already disliked York, for Rathbone's sake, but he knew the man had a point.

York hesitated.

Brancaster quickly broke in. "Evidence, Commander? Evidence of what?"

"Murder," Monk replied. He was leaping far ahead of the way he had intended to tell the story, but he dared not risk being blocked now.

There were gasps around the court. In the gallery there was a buzz of amazement. In the jury box every man stared at Monk as if he had only this moment appeared there by magic.

York was furious.

"If you are deliberately trying to create a sensation, Commander," he snapped, "in the hope of making us forget why we are here, then you are making a profound mistake. This is the trial of Oliver Rathbone for perverting the course of justice and abusing his office as judge."

Monk hesitated. Dare he defy York, or might it only bring down further disaster, on all their heads? Suddenly the issue of the photographs had been obscured and the defense was losing clarity. He must think of an answer to York.

He took a bold risk. It was all he had left.

"I think Sir Oliver may unintentionally have caused the murder to happen," he said, his breath almost choking him.

There was utter silence.

"I beg your pardon?" York said at last. Then, as Monk drew in his breath to repeat his words, York held up his hand. "No—no, that is not necessary. I heard you. I just failed for a moment to believe my ears. If this is some elaborate trick, Mr. Monk"—he dropped the courtesy of using his rank—"then I shall hold you in contempt of court."

At last Brancaster stepped in. "Perhaps, my lord, it would be best if Commander Monk were to tell us, as briefly as possible, exactly what the evidence was, so the jurors may interpret it for themselves?"

York had no possible course but to agree. He did so reluctantly.

"Proceed. But if you stray off the point I shall stop you and rule you out of order. Do you understand?"

"Yes, my lord," Monk swallowed his dislike and turned back to face Brancaster. He must recount this in exactly the right sequence, or York would stop him before he reached the end. He considered for a moment leaving Hester out of the account, because he could not give any good reason why she should have been there, but being caught in any kind of evasion would be dangerous.

"I took my wife with me when I went to Abel Taft's home," he said straightaway. "I knew the search would be faster with two people, and her medical skill might prove useful if we discovered anything unusual. Also a woman can read the meaning in certain domestic arrangements that a man might miss."

"And did you discover such things?" Brancaster said swiftly, to forestall any interruption from York, or even Wystan, although Wystan seemed as interested as the jurors, who were grasping every word.

"Very little," Monk replied. "What we did find dismissed everything else from thought."

"Money?" Brancaster asked innocently.

"Paintings," Monk answered. "Framed so as to conceal the artists' signatures. Experts are examining them now, but there seems to be a very considerable collection of good paintings disguised as copies. Their value, if authentic, would be enough to live on, more than comfortably, for thirty or forty years if sold judiciously over time."

"Does the value about equal the money that has not been accounted for?" Brancaster questioned.

Wystan stood up. "While this theft was well detected on Commander Monk's part, my lord, it is a long way short of murder. Unless he is somehow suggesting that Taft killed his wife over the paintings? I don't see any evidence whatsoever to indicate such a thing."

"Your point is well taken," York replied. "If that were so, it might relieve Rathbone of the moral guilt of causing the Taft family's deaths, although even that seems to be questionable. You are not advancing your case, Mr. Brancaster." He smiled thinly, a faint, bitter satisfaction.

Brancaster's cheeks colored with anger. "My lord," he said between his teeth. "If we might allow Commander Monk to complete the account of what he found . . ."

"Then get on with it!" York snapped. "You are trying the court's patience."

Without replying to him Brancaster made a small gesture with his hands, inviting Monk to continue.

"One of the larger paintings, an almost life-size portrait of a man, swung away from the wall in the upstairs study," he said a trifle too quickly. "Behind it was a panel that, when pushed in, revealed a space containing a ladder up into the attic . . ."

The gallery rustled. Every juror leaned forward. Even Wystan turned in his seat to stare at Monk more intently.

Monk bit his lip to stop himself from smiling. "Naturally I went up, and my wife came with me. We found ourselves in a large space with a few of the things we would expect to see—empty boxes, a trunk or two. It was the second, smaller room that mattered. There was a door into it, and as soon as we opened that, we saw the contraption."

There was not a sound in the entire courtroom.

"Contraption?" Brancaster asked huskily.

"A pistol on a table held steady by two weights. Tied to its trigger was a wire, which passed through a ring in the ceiling, and was attached at the other end to a tin can with a very small hole in the bottom," Monk explained. "It is difficult to describe it so as to make its purpose clear, but the moment we saw it we understood. It was a device created so that as the water dripped out of the can, the can became lighter, slowly rising to the point where the cord went slack, thus releasing the trigger and firing the gun. The can was empty when we arrived, and we found the bullet in the far wall. The water that had dripped out had been caught by a container beneath the can, and had evaporated. And the window was wedged open."

Brancaster affected confusion. He shook his head fractionally.

"Are you saying that Taft arranged this extraordinary piece of machinery to shoot himself?"

"No, sir. As the medical examiner would testify, it seems Mr. Taft and his entire family were already dead, possibly for a couple of hours, when this gun went off. Because the window was open the sound of it could be heard by the neighbors, whose houses were approximately fifty feet away. The purpose of the shot was to establish the time of Mr. Taft's death—wrongly."

"I see!" Brancaster's face lit up. "So it was to mislead the police as to the time of Taft's death, presumably so whoever killed him could prove that he was elsewhere at that precise moment?"

"Exactly," Monk agreed. "The police are now considering it to be murder of all four members of the family, Taft himself included."

There were gasps from almost everyone in the court, even several of the jurors.

Brancaster cleared his throat.

"And whom do they suspect, Commander Monk?"

Monk spoke quietly. "It all comes back to the missing money. The paintings are actually registered as owned by Robertson Drew. They have already arrested him, and I imagine they will charge him with all four murders, if they are not already doing so as we speak."

"Ah!" Brancaster let out his breath in a sigh, as if it were now all perfectly clear. "So it is possible that Robertson Drew strangled Mrs. Taft and her daughters, shot Taft himself, and then rigged up this contraption in the attic to make it seem as if Taft's death happened at five in the morning—a time at which Drew can fully account for his whereabouts, I imagine—when the neighbors heard the shot, rather than a couple of hours earlier?"

"Yes," Monk agreed. "It is quite possible."

"Just one other thing, Mr. Monk: If Drew went through all that trouble, why did he not remove the machine from the attic? If you had not found it, we would have known nothing about it at all. It seems extraordinarily dangerous, a careless piece of arrogance."

"He tried to," Monk said with a bleak smile. "He had to be careful not to seem too eager to get into the house, or he might have aroused suspicion, but he did ask the police several times. In fact, it was his eagerness to gain access to the house that made us decide to look there as well."

"I see. But there is still one piece that puzzles me." Brancaster knew that every man and woman in the courtroom was listening to him, and he made the most of it. It was a superb performance. "If he had to ask for police permission to get into the house to remove this contraption, how did he get in, in the middle of the night, to murder the entire family?"

Monk had been waiting for that. "On the night he killed them all, we suspect he entered through a loosely fitted larder window, at the back of the house where in the dark no one would have seen him climb in. After the deaths were discovered, and the police knew it was the scene of a crime, even if they did not understand the full nature of it, they secured all the windows and locked the inside doors. The house was then their responsibility, and there was a great deal that was of value still inside—silver, crystal, paintings, and such. So they kept a careful eye on it, as, I might add, did the neighbors, which prevented Drew from breaking in again."

"I see." Brancaster nodded. "Yes, that makes excellent sense. A very terrible crime. Thank you for your diligence, Commander Monk. Without it, poor Taft would have gone down in history as a murderer and a suicide, when in truth he was no more than a thief and an exploiter of the humble and the generous. In the end he was a victim himself. Justice owes you a great deal." He bowed to Monk, then before anyone could intervene, bowed very slightly to the jury also.

"But of course your task, gentlemen, is to weigh the justice of a far less violent but more evil and dangerous crime, one that has already eaten deeply into the fabric of our nation—that of the torture and abuse of children for the obscene entertainment of men without honor or decency. It has been exposed, at great risk to himself, by Oliver Rathbone. Do we ignore it, and thus allow it to go on corrupting the soul of our nation? Indeed, do we punish the man who has forced us to face this terrible truth? Or do we thank him—and begin to root its poison out of our society?"

"Mr. Brancaster!" snapped York. "If you have finished questioning this witness, then allow counsel for the prosecution the right to do so. I will tell the jury when it is time to consider their verdict—not you! I will also correct your somewhat loose interpretation of the law!"

Wystan stood up. "Thank you, my lord. I don't believe I have any questions for Commander Monk. The issue seems tragically clear to me. I wish there had been some other way to expose this mighty evil, but I fear if there had been, then we did not avail ourselves of it."

Brancaster stood as if afraid to move, staring at Wystan. Wystan swallowed. Monk could see the movement of his throat even from the height of the witness stand.

When Wystan spoke again, his voice was hoarse. "My lord, the prosecution is aware that Sir Oliver made grave judicial errors. He took the law into his own hands, and that cannot be permitted. However, we do not ask for a custodial sentence in this instance. We trust that the professional discipline the Lords Justice wish to exercise will be adequate for the offense relating to how the evidence of Robertson Drew's character was presented to the court."

York stared at him.

"Thank you," Brancaster said breathlessly. "Thank you, Mr. Wystan." He turned slowly to Monk. "Thank you, Commander. It seems you are excused."

"Silence! I will have silence in the court," York yelled as the noise of the astonished onlookers rose to a pitch.

Slowly the buzz ebbed away. Every eye was on York.

"Gentlemen of the jury, the accused has presented excuses for his behavior, but he has not attempted to deny it, therefore it is not open to you to bring in a verdict of not guilty. The court thanks you for your service."

The foreman of the jury glanced at his fellows then rose slowly to his feet.

"My lord?"

York looked at him grimly. "Have I not made myself clear, sir?"

The foreman swallowed. "Yes, my lord. We wish to know if it is open to us to agree with the prosecution, and ask that Sir Oliver just serve the time he already has done in prison, and then the Lords Justice discipline him whatever way they have to? Can we do that?"

York's face was pale. "You may recommend whatever you wish," he said somewhat ungraciously. "Thank you for your consideration."

The foreman sat down again, apparently satisfied.

In the dock Rathbone was so weak with relief he felt dizzy. He was guilty. Perhaps that verdict had been inevitable. It was almost a relief to acknowledge it to himself. If you break the law, for whatever reason, then you must pay the price for it. If it had been anyone else he would have said as much. But the price was not prison. Certainly his resignation from the bench would be required, probably even his right to practice law, at least for a while. But he would be a free man, living in his own home, able to choose his path. He was overcome with gratitude for a price less than he deserved to pay. The room swam around him, wavering in his vision. He saw Monk go down the steps and across the floor to where Hester and Scuff were waiting for him. Hester abandoned decorum and hugged him, and he put his arms around her, then around the boy also. Henry Rathbone joined them, tears of gratitude gleaming for an instant on his cheeks.

Brancaster was shaking hands with Wystan. The jurors were turning to one another, smiling, happy, relieved that they had served justice well, but had also acted with honor.

In the third row from the front of the gallery seats, Margaret sat motionless, her face white and stricken, as if she were mourning a death all over again.

Rathbone felt a wave of pity for her. He had no joy at all in seeing her so bitterly forced to stare into the reality of her father's corruption. It was a tragedy, not a victory. Ballinger had yielded to the same power that Rathbone had. The only difference was that it was Ballinger who had created that particular monster, and he had had no friends with the courage, the skill, and the loyalty to rescue him, such as had rescued Rathbone.

Rathbone could never go back to her. That door was closed forever, for both of them. But he could wish her well, wish her healing and one day even happiness. And he found he did.

They were ushering him out of the dock. It was all over. At least as far as this trial was concerned, he was free. He would have tonight's supper in his own home. He would walk around and touch things, gaze at them, treasure them—before one day soon selling the house and getting rooms elsewhere. Not too far—his friends were here; but he needed a new start.

He walked a little shakily down the steps toward the ground floor. He would have to find something else to do for as long as he was banned from practicing law, however long that was. But he had learned something about law that few other lawyers would ever know. He might not have any greater legal skills than they, but now he would have other gifts, gifts of empathy, of humanity. He had paid dearly for them. A chance to use them again, in the future, was a grace far greater than he had once dreamed was possible.

A WEEK LATER THE INITIAL relief had passed and Rathbone faced a different kind of reality. The verdict and sentence of the judiciary had been passed on him. His resignation from the bench, and the crown of his career he had so long worked for, was a thing of the past. He was also banned from the practice of law for an indefinite period. He could appeal to be reinstated in a year. That might, or might not, be granted.

He considered what else he had lost, what of himself, and the inner things he valued more dearly than position or career. Monk's friendship he did not question. Monk himself had traveled some of the darkest halls of guilt and self-doubt. Rathbone appreciated that now with a sharper and far keener edge than he had before. Much of his own certainty in all manner of things had eroded away in these last months. Some of the old safeties were shown to be far more fragile than he had believed. Now he was aware of his own deep flaws of judgment, and the fact that he too could face the censure of his fellows and fall short in the eyes of those he loved. Forgiveness was suddenly a far sweeter, more tender thing than he had ever known it to be.

It was past time he stopped telling himself that one day he would take his father to Italy, spend time with him, listen a great deal more. He could do it now, this autumn, as soon as he could sell the house and would have the funds to do it. He would make it the trip of a lifetime, to be savored in all the years ahead. It was one thing that would hold no regrets. In time it would crowd out all the sorrows and perhaps leave behind only the lessons learned.

THE NEXT MORNING DAWN rose over the Thames, spilling light across the water, as Rathbone sat with Monk in a police boat. They were on a lonely, deep stretch, where the bottom mud was thick. Nothing lost here would ever be found again.

Monk shipped the oars and rested them. He was here as a witness, but even more as a friend.

Rathbone picked up the heavy box of photographic plates that Arthur Ballinger had bequeathed him. Inside it was everything that was left of them. He stood up, balancing carefully, and dropped it over the side. It went down like a stone, leaving barely a ripple on the water.

"Thank you," Rathbone said quietly, tears stinging his eyes in the cool morning breeze.

Monk smiled, his face serene in the widening light.

About the Author

Anne Perry is the bestselling author of two acclaimed series set in Victorian England: the William Monk novels, including *Blind Justice* and *A Sunless Sea*, and the Charlotte and Thomas Pitt novels, including *Midnight at Marble Arch* and *Dorchester Terrace*. She is also the author of five World War I novels, as well as eleven Christmas novels, including the upcoming *A Christmas Hope*. She lives in Scotland.

WWW.ANNEPERRY.CO.UK

ABOUT THE TYPE

This book was set in Goudy Old Style, a typeface designed by Frederic William Goudy (1865–1947). Goudy began his career as a bookkeeper, but devoted the rest of his life in pursuit of "recognized quality" in a printing type.

Goudy Old Style was produced in 1914 and was an instant bestseller for the foundry. It has generous curves and smooth, even color. It is regarded as one of Goudy's finest achievements.

About the Type